THE IMMORTAL TRANSCRIPTS I

QUIVER

LISA BORNE GRAVES

AUTHORS 4 AUTHORS PUBLISHING
Marysville, WA, USA

Published by Authors 4 Authors Publishing
1214 6th St
Marysville, WA 98270
www.authors4authorspublishing.com

Library of Congress Control Number: 2020930098

E-book ISBN: 978-1-64477-108-2
Paperback ISBN: 978-1-64477-109-9
Audiobook ISBN: 978-1-64477-046-7

Edited by Rebecca Mikkelson and Brandi Spencer

Cover design ©2021 Brandi Spencer. All rights reserved.
Statue from cover image:
Cupid Triumphant by Bertel Thorvaldsen
Thorvaldsen Museum
Copenhagen, Denmark

Cover and interior design by Brandi Spencer.

Authors 4 Authors Publishing branding is set in Bavire. Titles and headings are set in Goudy Trajan and Mr Darcy. Text messages are set in Source Sans Pro Semibold. Journal entries are set in UglyQua. Handwriting is set in Reey for Lucien, Architect's Daughter for Callie, Allura for Archer, and Freebooter Script for Aroha. All other text is set in Garamond.

THE IMMORTAL TRANSCRIPTS I

QUIVER

LISA BORNE GRAVES

Authors 4 Authors Content Rating

This title has been rated 17+, appropriate for older teens and adults, and contains:

- Frequent intense kissing
- Intense implied sex
- Graphic violence
- Moderate language
- Moderate alcohol use
- Mild positive fantasy drug use
- Mild negative illicit drug use
- Discussions of incest

Please, keep the following in mind when using our rating system:

1. A content rating is not a measure of quality.

Great stories can be found for every audience. One book with many content warnings and another with none at all may be of equal depth and sophistication. Our ratings can work both ways: to avoid content or to find it.

2. Ratings are merely a tool.

For our young adult (YA) and children's titles, age ratings are generalized suggestions. For parents, our descriptive ratings can help you make informed decisions, but at the end of the day, only you know what kinds of content are appropriate for your individual child. This is why we provide details in addition to the general age rating.

For more information on our rating system, please, visit our Content Guide at: www.authors4authorspublishing.com/books/ratings

DEDICATION

For Ann Reed, who got me interested in my Greek
ancestry; Katie Grant for reading six pages and insisting I
had to be an author; and Cameron Scott Wright for all his
editing work. Cameron, I wish you got to see this in
print. RIP, my friend.

WORKS BY LISA BORNE GRAVES

Celestial Spheres

Fyr
Draca
Bladesung

Wundor (June 2023)

The Immortal Transcripts

Quiver
Fever
Shudder
Glimmer (February 2024)

Stand-alone Titles

Apidae
"Dare"

TABLE OF CONTENTS

NOTE TO READER

The following is a faithful transcript for the use of the newly formed International Republic of Immortality (IRI) in its inquiry behind the altercations involved in the Olympian sector. As far as the signed witnesses state, everything was recorded with complete honesty, arranged chronologically, and written separately so as to not influence one another's accounts. ~~The IRI reserves the rights to this manuscript, and it is by no means to be reproduced nor shown to any creature mortal. Mortals who read may be subject to permanent silence.~~

In case we are executed for our "crimes," I pass this on to you, mortal, in hopes to continue our memories into the future. Welcome to our world.

CHAPTER 1

I found myself adrift in a sea of fog, so I knew it was one of my repetitive dreams. Trouble for me always starts with dreams—and women—but women in dreams is the worst combination. As soon as I saw those gates appear out of nowhere, I recognized that this was a compounded problem involving both. They were gilded wrought iron gates that reached from the ground full up into the sky, far beyond where the eyes could see, where they disappeared in a delicate layer of bright clouds. On both sides of the gates were ancient stone walls that appeared to be meticulously built by hand and extended so high that one wondered how on Mother Gaia they could stand without toppling over. The gates, on squealing hinges, creaked open enough for my body to slip through. I wasted no time but entered quickly as I always did in these dreams, finding myself in a field of barley that rippled beautifully in the wind. The sun shone brightly, the fog not penetrating this oasis. In the distance, I could see specks on the horizon of what appeared to be poplars and an appealing grove of shade. On the wind, I could hear a trickling of a stream in the distance.

I felt at peace until the apparition appeared in front of me, only a few yards away. She was as beautiful as ever with her hair in thin chestnut braids hanging down her back and her dark eyes glistening in the bright sun. She was full-bodied, perfect in the supple areas of a woman with round breasts and thicker hips, but by no means overweight. She had that classical beauty of antiquity and the bronze tan to match. Every time, I had an insatiable desire to take her in my arms and kiss her, but I refrained because in the past dreams, she'd run from me if I tried. Each dream, I got closer, though. "Patience," I told myself.

She greedily ate away at a pomegranate—seeds and all—which reinforced the idea of where I really was. But I was not dead, and no one could answer what Elysium looked like; those who arrived there never returned. Yet, here I was in my sleep, a place I often found myself. Something I've never told anyone. Ever.

She spotted me and eyed me demurely.

"You again." She smirked. "Don't you ever learn?"

"Learn? It is you who brings me here, my oracle."

"Oh." She gasped. She was clearly frightened. This was different. Usually, she just flirted and teased me.

I took full advantage of her sudden hesitation and crossed to her and took her into my arms.

"Yours?" She gave me a smug smile that told me I was being foolish.

"Ah." I realized my folly. If she wasn't my oracle, then... "Before my time?"

"Shh," she hissed, pushing me away and scanning the horizon in anticipation. "I am not supposed to speak to you." She spun around wildly. The wind changed course suddenly, whipping at us, and I heard the baying of dogs in the distance. The barley rippled eerily around us like the wind was going in every direction.

"Show me," I insisted, searching for the oncoming threat. "You brought me here for a prophecy; now, do it!" My heart beat with anxiety as I heard the dogs getting closer.

She gazed at me, her eyes ablaze with something that wasn't exactly passion or fear, but a combination of both. She pulled me to her again and then kissed me deeply. Images were thrust into me with a jarring pain, robbing me of the pleasure I should get from such a kiss. I tried to focus, but it was futile. The images would be embedded into my brain and would drive me mad until I puzzled them out. Certain images swirled around slow enough to discern them: my father cowering, lightning striking, my friend Archer screaming, fire, and a girl—a beautiful girl I had never seen before—war, death, chaos. The rest I couldn't discern.

The oracle thrust me away and shouted, "Run, foolish boy, run!"

I sprinted for the entrance—desperately attempting to find the fiends that were barking—but all I saw were black shadows zipping and curling through the barley. They were ghosts made of nothingness, just thick black air, like smoke in the breeze. She called after me loudly as I ran, but I could hardly make out the words over the barking and growling.

I raced toward the gates, afraid to turn around, although I heard the creatures on my heels. I wasn't going to make it. The shadow dogs went in for the kill.

I shot awake in bed in my room, sheets tangled and soaked with sweat. The phone was ringing, scaring my already rapidly beating heart, and I instantly picked it up. "Hello?"

A familiar female voice began to speak; it was the current oracle, an alive one, her voice raspy with old age. "Everything as we know it will change forever."

"How?" I could think of nothing else to ask, my mind muddled between the fright of my dream and the grogginess from just waking.

"Love."

Then the line went dead.

CHAPTER 2

Callie

I was in complete hell, emotionally and psychologically speaking. I, Callista Syches, had just moved to a new city at seventeen to start my senior year in a new school, and to make things worse, the school year had already started weeks ago. It wasn't just any old city, but New York City; it wasn't just any old school, but the prestigious Royal Prescot Academy, which Dad had said I was lucky to get into.

To bitch about the big move wasn't an option. It was ridiculous and selfish to complain. Dad was terminally ill with a disease that had a really long and difficult-to-say name and no cure, but the big-wig physicians in NYC promised him time through a complicated plan involving therapy, diuretics, and some miracle trial drug. I would've put my foot down and refused to move until I graduated, but that was as bad as wanting my father dead. I wished he could live forever, but as Dad liked to remind me, *memento mori*—remember that we all die one day. We're mortal, and to dream of such things as immortality here on earth is a child's game. And I had to act like an adult, forced to be more mature than any other seventeen-year-old I knew because I had to stare into death's face every day.

Like today, when Dad shuffled out of his room, moving like a man twice his age, most likely drawn out by the smell of the bacon I was frying up. I had cooked us a full breakfast to stave off my first-day jitters. I had hardly slept, dreading the first day of school.

"My, my, Callista darling, I think you have settled in already. Raphael will be pleased to see he has nothing to do," Dad said, a smile on his face and a pep in his voice. He looked better than he had in days, and his optimism was showing. Raphael was his personal assistant who acted as servant, editor, driver, and nurse to my father, since Dad was limited these days. His face was flushed again, though, and he missed picking up his fork twice, so his vision must have been blurred. He was only acting better, not feeling better, and the symptoms were all still apparent.

"Trying my best." I matched his brightness. It felt tiresome to pretend I was fine, to act like he was fine, but it made him happy to think I was well adjusted.

"I know this move was hard on you, Callista—" he began gravely.

"No Dad, we've gone over this a million times. It's for the best. It's what you need and what I want. I'd go through worse to have more time with you."

He met my gaze, his eyes watering, patted my hand, and focused on his breakfast. He could say no more, and I didn't want him to. Talking about the future with Dad was too painful. He wanted me to talk about my dreams and aspirations, but I didn't want to think about a world that excluded him. I had no idea what I would do when he was gone.

I cleaned up the dishes while Dad got ready.

"I've got the car coming back for you after Raphael drops me off."

"Dad," I whined. "I don't want to show up in a Rolls Royce with my chauffeur on the first day. What would the other kids think?"

"That you're like them? Callista, this is not like Somerset. You live and go to school in the Upper East Side now. Kids at this school have much more money than you are used to. They will all show up in the same."

Dad referred to the small town where I grew up in Minnesota. There, we were considered the rich oddballs because most people there were middle-class. Oh yeah, my father definitely had money, which was how we found ourselves in a penthouse apartment in the Upper East Side. My dad was a historian and an archeologist, among other things. He'd discovered many different artifacts, but he was best known for finding the Aegis, the legendary shield that the Greek goddess Athena used. Of course, no one believed a goddess actually used it (except Dad), but the fact it was made of pure gold, with golden threaded tassels, had an engraving of Medusa's head, and dated back to the Bronze Age made it almost priceless. Dad had sold it to the British Museum. That is where a lot of the money came from.

"Great," I sighed in disbelief. Now I was even more nervous. I was used to hiding the fact we had money, but what would these kids be like? Hell. This would be like hell, like one of those movies where the popular girls end up being psychos and bully someone to death: me. Stop it. I took a deep breath to hide my anxiety from my father. He didn't need to worry about me, just his health.

After Dad left for the doctor's office, I showered, wrapped myself up in my fluffy purple bathrobe, and dug through my boxes of clothes in search of the perfect first-day outfit. Everything I owned was wrong. One outfit would have them judge me as a broke charity project; another would show off too much, like I was challenging their worth. I almost regretted telling my father my only stipulation about my new school was sans uniform (*almost* being the key word). I decided on a simple outfit: jeans and a fitted T-shirt, but of designer labels. It seemed safe, average but still spoke money. I grabbed a light jacket, just in case, although the weather was actually pleasant.

One last satisfied look in the mirror, and I was as ready as I'd ever be to face the political arena one calls high school. A glance at the clock told me I'd better hurry.

I hustled out the door and down the hall, when I came across a guy waiting by the elevator. I slowed down, not wanting to draw attention to myself, not wanting to socialize. There'd be enough strangers to make small talk with at school today.

His back was to me, so all I could see was a tall frame, leaning toward the lanky side but not without definition. His hair was blond, cropped short, the tips sun-kissed. If he grew it out, I imagined it'd be curly. Yes, I was totally staring and obsessively observing him, but he didn't know that. And now, without even seeing his face, I was keen on socializing.

He turned, and our gazes met, his eyes piercingly blue, poignant, and wise-looking—like he must be mature beyond his years. Maybe he was losing someone he loved too. Doubtful, as that was just my unfortunate lot.

His face was beautiful—there was no other word for it—with slender, chiseled, and astonishingly perfect features, like Michelangelo had sculpted him from marble. He had a little upturn to his nose, a cute little pug to it—not snobbish, but refined like those noble guys from period pieces I wished were real. Prince Charming came to mind.

Besides his Prince-Charmingness, he had a strong and defined jawline, a muted cleft in his chin, and adorably kissable lips. His skin was slightly pale yet with a soft glow and rosy cheeks, as if he'd just walked in from the sunshine. In short, he was ridiculously gorgeous and not at all your run-of-the-mill all-American boy—he had a foreign air to him, one I couldn't quite place. Wherever he was from might be where I would move next (it was only a fleeting, pathetic thought).

"Going down?" he asked in a mild, friendly tone. His voice was like a complicated and beautiful Beethoven symphony, full of every emotion possible but restrained. If so, I wondered if I could even stand hearing it at full throttle. I felt his pain, his sorrow, his happiness, his hope—I shut out the thoughts. I had to stop reading too much into people.

"Yes, please," I answered. My voice, sadly, sounded quite mousy. I cleared my throat in hopes of sounding better the next time I spoke.

The elevator doors opened, and he motioned with his hand for me to enter first. I walked in, noticing for the first time the angled mirrors and how they multiplied my reflection throughout the elevator, a million of me down a long tunnel. I was unexpectedly self-conscious, wishing I had worn that sexy new low-cut shirt I had that contrasted well with my olive skin tone, the one my dad insisted I wear a tank top under.

When the marble statue walked in, he was multiplied next to me as well. I liked the look of him next to me; I liked it too much. I risked another glance at the beautiful specter on the elevator doors after they closed to find him already staring at me through the mirror. His pink cheeks flared up to a brighter hue, his lips suppressed a smile, and his gaze dropped to the floor. Was my ogling that bad? Or did I just witness him checking me out as well? The latter would be preferable, obviously, but I really didn't have time for boys. I had to spend as much time as possible with my father since there was so little of it left.

The elevator ride seemed endless. The silence felt stiflingly awkward.

He cleared his throat and said, "Did you recently move here? I don't think I've seen you before." He spoke in a polite cadence without any hint of an accent, just like a movie star. (He was cute enough to be one.) Usually, my intuition was dead on, but I was wrong for once—he wasn't foreign as I had first supposed.

I judged people very well off first appearances. It was a trait I'd picked up from my dad, knowing people from merely glancing at them. Dad called it a "telepathic anomaly." I called it good intuition. Him and his harebrained ideas.

"Yeah. Just arrived last night," I told this adonis, trying to overcome the timidity that squeezed out in my voice. I sounded like a childish dork, which was not like me. Something about his nobleman–movie-star face numbed my brains.

"I'm Archer. Apartment 3004."

"Callie, 3001." I swallowed my insecurities and, with more nerve, said, "Archer? First or last name?"

"First." He laughed. "Unique, I know. Last name is Ambrose."

"Callista Syches, officially," I explained, pronouncing it correctly as in "Sikes." Most people butchered our name when they said it.

"Syches," he echoed.

"Yep. I get teased about it all the time."

"Teased?"

"Yeah, sounds close enough to psycho. I got Psycho Syches a lot growing up," I blurted out.

"Oh," he said with his complex tone full of sorrow, surprise, and remorse; I had an inkling there was much more behind it. Then again, I was probably imagining it all. My father always said I was too perceptive for my own good. I agreed...the few times my guesses were wrong, that is, which was rare. That was another reason they thought I was psycho. I could figure out what people were thinking sometimes, just off a whim.

To my surprise, Archer didn't laugh. "That's not very nice of them."

"A lot of people aren't."

"There are good ones out there."

"Sorry, I'm a pessimist," I said, enjoying the flirty banter.

"You shouldn't be. There's a lot to...*love*," he said the word with a deep multifaceted feeling, "in this world." Hmm, he was like an onion I wanted to peel.

I pressed my lips firmly together to suppress my next comment, partly wanting to explain my crappy lot in life, but this guy was just some stranger who didn't need my sob story. I wanted to make a good impression. He didn't need my baggage.

I was saved from any embarrassing outbursts by the elevator door opening. He let me walk out first and followed me outside. The Rolls Royce was parked by the curb, ready for me. I paused to zip up my jacket, and when I reached for the door of the car, I saw Archer Ambrose grab it first. We both stopped, laughing.

"Is this yours or mine?" He smiled broadly, exposing a perfect set of straight, ultra-white teeth. He was too gorgeous to be real. I subtly pinched my own arm to make sure this wasn't a dream. Yep, he was real.

"Uh...I don't know."

"Archer, hel-lo!" a bubbly voice called from an identical car two spots ahead.

The beautiful face of a blonde-haired, blue-eyed girl peeked out the window. Of course, he had a girlfriend. Typical.

"Sorry, my mistake," he said, walking to the other car. He loped with a graceful swagger that was confident yet oddly cautious and then turned to me, hands in pockets, and said with a nod of the head toward the blonde, "My sister." Then he fluidly turned away, but I could see his cheek rounded like he was smiling, and I felt myself smile as well.

I peered again at the beautiful girl in a new light. From afar, she appeared to be a female version of Archer: blonde, blue-eyed, beautiful smile, and a little pug nose. The only difference was, where he was more chiseled and angular, she was sleeker and softer. How had I missed their resemblance at first?

As I climbed in the car, I decided New York definitely had at least one perk, and that came from suite 3004 of my new apartment building.

CHAPTER 3

Archer

I knew things were going to be different that day from the start. I woke to the smell of meat and thyme seducing my senses. My stomach growled. Someone cooking in our house when we didn't have a servant was unheard of—unless I was at the stove. Aroha—my sister, to the mortal world, for all intents and purposes—was capable of throwing together a great meal, but this didn't mean she would break a nail doing so if she could help it.

It meant one thing. She wanted something from me.

Sure enough, she was at the stove, cooking. The table was spread with bread, *kopanisti* cheese, and a box of my favorite sweets, *loukoúmia*. Bribery food.

"Who are you, and where is Aroha?"

"Ha, ha, Archer." She glanced up. "Can't a terrible mother compensate by making her little boy some breakfast every now and then?" she asked sweetly. Too sweetly.

"What do you want?" I demanded.

"Nothing," she said with poorly feigned innocence. She could fake being mortal well, but she could never pretend to care about others more than herself. "I'm trying to be nice."

She was obviously beating around the bush, but I'd let it go for now and let it play out. "Then what's going on? What are you cooking? It smells divine."

"*Paidákia*, with a pinch of thyme, your favorite." She batted her eyes at me. "Can't I cook for you without sixty questions?"

"No," I said, sounding like a pert child, while trying to grab a cutlet from the pan. She smacked my hand with the wooden spoon, preventing me. My hand hit the sizzling skillet, and I yanked it away but too late. There were burns across my fingers. Aroha gave me a serves-you-right glare. I watched my hand curiously as the welt disappeared within seconds. Immortality meant I would always heal and do so fast. It always fascinated me, much to my mother's dismay, particularly when I had gone through an injure-myself-for-fun phase as a youth.

"It's almost done," she scolded. Frowning, she added, "I resent your saying that."

"Just cut to the chase, *Mána*," I taunted her by using the Greek word for mother.

"I hate it when you call me that."

"Because it makes you feel old. What is it?" I pressed, tiring of her avoiding the issue.

"Well..." she began, "The messenger has been by with a message from *him*. Wants *me* to try to talk sense...threatened to force me back with... I shouldn't be threatened like that, really." She said in heated jumbles.

"I'm not going to talk to Dad," I insisted, knowing where she was going. My grandfather was meddling—as always—and was pitting my parents against each other. "You married the warmonger; you deal with him."

"That's not a nice way to talk about your father, even though it is true." She paused, taking the food off the stove and dividing the lamb chops onto two plates. "Can't you make him fall in love with someone?"

"For the millionth time, no. It's impossible. He loves war. He loves world domination. He has no time for anyone but himself," I insisted.

"Have you even tried?"

"Yes. You don't know how many arrows I've wasted in vain. And don't tell me you haven't tried a thousand times. He is obsessed with the sport of it."

"Always was after the chase and never wanted to settle. I suppose I must talk to your grandfather about it. Don't see what *I* can do," she murmured the last bit as we sat down to the table to eat.

"Distract him. You're the only one who can."

"That's what your grandfather will say, I suppose, but he can't control his own son, for crying out loud."

Her comment made me stop loading my plate with cheese and bread. Why couldn't he pull rank on my dad? My grandfather could control all of us.

"By the way, darling, could you do me a little favor..."

"I knew it." I put my fork down. "What now?"

"Todd is getting so tiresome. Make him fall for someone else. Oh, I don't know, that Mary Beth would be sweet with him, no?"

I sighed, annoyed, wanting to just eat, but it was such a little favor, considering I wouldn't perform the other, much more difficult, task of sorting out my dad. "Fine."

13

THE IMMORTAL TRANSCRIPTS: QUIVER

I closed my eyes, searching within the confines of my own mind, mentally gliding through the streets over the gridlock of the city. Each human registered like a beacon on a huge internal mental map, where I could zoom in and out to find whom I wanted, traveling at a nearly infinite speed across the entire world if I pleased.

But this morning, my prey was in Manhattan and was easily found walking along Seventy-second Street and Madison, headed in the direction of Fifth Avenue. In my mind, I drew back the imaginary poisoned arrow, filled with an elixir more potent than anything known to man and unique with an essence of Mary Beth, and fired it into Todd's heart. Vicious-sounding but physically painless. Emotionally? It can be rough. I'd misfired into myself once long ago and wasn't eager to ever fall in love again.

Why arrows? It was simply a way for me to understand how to direct my powers since I developed them at a young age. It was rare, but I had to learn to control them, as to not destroy mortal lives.

I took myself across a few blocks to find Mary Beth and shot her with my invisible arrow to make her fall in love with Todd. Ma hadn't asked me to meddle with Mary Beth, but I always felt better when matters were fair. When it came to love, I believed things should always be equal. There were others who saw to those situations where love was thwarted or unrequited.

I opened my eyes, picked up my fork, and jammed a large piece of lamb in my mouth. It was even more delicious than it smelled.

"That was quick. Are you sure it worked?"

I gave her a glare, trying to swallow my food. Once I could speak, I said, "He'll be in love with her, and she with him."

"Fantastic. Thanks, my *ligí agápi*." She began to eat, humming happily to herself.

I glowered deeply at her for using one of the many pet names—little love—she'd used for me when I was a small child. She gave me a wicked grin and continued humming.

Aroha took forever to get ready, so I lay back down for a nap before we had to head to school. When she barged into my room, saying we'd be late while brushing her still wet hair, I got up again, hopped in the shower, and got dressed. She still wasn't ready, so I nagged her back, and then we were out the door by the elevator.

Damn it! I'd forgotten my gym clothes.

The elevator pinged open, and Aroha went in.

"I'll be a minute. Just get the car pulled around."

Aroha rolled her eyes to insinuate I was the one who made us late on a daily basis, despite her atrocious track record. I trekked back to the apartment, grabbed my gym bag, and stuffed clothes in. Then I was back waiting for the elevator, when I heard hurried footsteps on the carpet behind me. I forced myself not to turn, since mortals wouldn't hear someone who was so far away. Everything in my life had to be measured and carefully planned, even the way I moved, to fit in with mortals. When the person's steps slowed, I turned to see a beautiful young woman. Dark eyes and hair, olive skin, just your average attributes, but on her, they were utterly breathtaking and...perfect.

At first, I thought she was one of us. No human could have such beauty. As we waited for the elevator, I thought she might confront me in the typical way our kind does, the classic greeting used over centuries: "How is he?" in reference to the god of the gods whom I called Grandpa. But nothing otherworldly escaped her lips. She was apparently mortal. For some reason, that disappointed me. I rarely took a second glance at a pretty girl, but she pulled me in—no, more like yanked me. It was that strong and uncontrollable. Like a moth to a flame, I told myself in warning, and yet it was futile to deny my attraction.

I wanted her, and I was the kind of being who always got what he wanted.

When I slipped into the car with Aroha, she gave me that maternal side-eye that chided me for some unknown offense.

"You kept me waiting."

"I forgot my gym clothes."

She scoffed—to her, me being chastised by a mortal gym teacher was beneath us. My mother never wanted to stop being worshiped, and the fact that our bodies didn't decay and froze us at eighteen forever added to her overabundant ego.

"Who was that pretty little girl?"

"Who?"

She gave me a leveled glower. So she'd picked up on my feelings, great. I'd have to hide things from her. She could be a domineering bitch at times, and she could pull rank. I literally had a hard time disobeying her, not a terrible drawback to living forever young, I supposed.

"A girl named Callie who lives on our floor. Apparently just moved in."

"How old is she?"

I shrugged.

"Far too much beauty for a mortal. I'll need to have a chat with the retinue." And with that, she took out her phone, leaving me to my own reveries while she most likely sent texts in lieu of a "chat." A chat from my mother was berating you for your ineptitude. I felt bad for those receiving her digital wrath.

"At least that girl will age." Aroha sighed happily.

Callie aging. The thought chilled me. I pushed her from my mind and was pretty successful...

Until she showed up at our school.

CHAPTER 4

Callie

I got a lot of stares at school, being the new girl and all, but people were friendly enough. Homeroom consisted of the teacher giving me my schedule and me sitting there trying to blend in with the furniture for fifteen minutes. First period went without any hitches, except that it was history, which was my least favorite subject because I learned much more, and in a more interesting way, from my dad than memorizing boring dates. It also always came to me so easily that I lost interest in the lesson. After seeing and touching real ancient artifacts, a textbook picture lost its luster. The class dragged on forever. I was not at all used to this block scheduling where classes were an hour and a half long. The only thing that held my interest was the girl I sat next to who never seemed to stop talking. She introduced herself as Emily and involved me in gossip that I hardly understood. Her friend was a little more aloof but eventually warmed up to me when she realized I lived on the same block as her, and she introduced herself as Linda. Emily had an elegant, classic beauty; she reminded me greatly of a young Sharon Stone (the movie icon Dad was madly in love with), whereas Linda was more of a young Lucy Liu (another favorite actress of his). She was thin, with beautiful, clear skin and dainty features.

They walked me to second period, where unfortunately, I had to begin again, but they promised to save me a seat at lunch, which dismissed my greatest fear. No one wants to eat alone. It was social suicide, making one a leper for life.

I walked into second period for AP Chemistry, and my stomach took a spin. There were lab tables instead of desks, and I surveyed them, hoping to find one completely empty so I wouldn't have to force myself on any already established cliques. In my search, my eyes glided over and stopped instantly on Archer Ambrose. My stomach immediately settled, the anxiety of not knowing anyone having left me.

Archer had a pencil resting between his fingers, the eraser loosely balanced between his lips, as if he were deep in thought. Then he glanced at me. His first expression was shock, but then a small smile of recognition spread across his face as he motioned me over. I sat down next to him with a sigh.

"You don't know how happy I am to see you!" I blurted out.

His cheeks went red, and he stared down at his hands. He let out a nervous laugh. I felt at ease enough around him to be my free-flowing self—saying what was on my mind, regardless of how stupid it sounded. In hindsight, this wasn't one of those moments where I wanted to be that outlandish. I clearly embarrassed him with my enthusiasm. Was he really that shy?

"Sorry. I mean, new kid, not knowing anyone...first-day jitters," I explained.

"I'm glad to be of service." His stare lingered on me, and I didn't want to break my gaze from his.

"And who is this?" A deep male voice cut through what had seemed to be a moment between Archer and me. I wanted to shoot the guy a death stare...until I saw him.

Another gorgeous specimen of perfection sat down next to Archer. Where Archer was light, this boy was dark. He was tan, a Mediterranean bronze that was darker than my complexion. He was made of sinewy muscles, with untidy thick black hair and beautiful sparkling, dark emerald eyes. He had to be wearing contacts; no one had eyes that green. And his skin, even more than Archer's, was warm and glowing, as if the sun were always shining on him, despite being indoors. I almost wanted to reach out and touch this boy's arm to see if it was actually warm (I refrained).

Was every person at this school so unbelievably attractive? Or had my self-inflicted vow to not date this year driven me to insanity?

"Lucien, Callie. Callie, Lucien," Archer explained, the annoyance in his tone badly masked.

"Nice to meet you," I said.

"Callie lives in my building," Archer said.

"Poor thing." Lucien smiled at me with a wink. They had some inside joke or understanding that I couldn't comprehend.

"I'll tell Aroha you're publicly slurring her again."

"I was referring to you," Lucien responded through clenched teeth. He quieted down with the jokes and grew sullen. Apparently, Aroha was not a girl to cross. I'd be sure not to upset her.

Class began, and thankfully, the teacher forgot to introduce me, but unfortunately, the conversation with the ridiculously gorgeous boys ceased.

I could tell I'd enjoy being partners with these two—one thing was for sure: they would make class interesting.

After the bell rang, I gathered my books up slowly. The two adorable boys were talking and laughing in hushed tones and sneaking peeks at me.

"Wanna sit with us at lunch?" Lucien asked.

"Oh...um...thank you, but I already told Emily and Linda I'd sit with them." I half regretted how easily I'd agreed to sit with them earlier. Besides the fact these boys were freakin' hot, I felt irresistibly drawn to them. I wanted to spend as much time as I could with them, Archer especially. And that was utterly illogical. Formerly, I had been the type of girl who was well-grounded in all that made sense.

"That's okay." Archer's tone was glum.

"No, it's not. We'll steal you away. They always sit next to us anyhow," Lucien said, rolling his eyes. He didn't like the girls.

We began to walk toward the cafeteria. The energy they gave off made me feel like I could be more outgoing; I could be myself.

"You don't like Emily and Linda?" I prompted.

"I didn't say that," Lucien said. Then he mischievously continued, "but you're observant."

"They're nice." I frowned.

"It's just...they're typical girls," Lucien said.

"And?" I challenged. "I'm typical."

"You're *not* typical." Lucien scoffed.

I stared at him oddly, waiting for more, but he just kept laughing and shaking his head as if to tell me I could neither pry any more out of him nor would I understand what he meant. I wondered if he was complimenting or picking on me. He was too mysterious to understand.

"What Lucien is unsuccessfully attempting to explain is that you seem...down to earth." Archer chose his words carefully. "And exceptionally pretty."

This last part made him blush, and he peered down at his feet as he walked. He couldn't look at me when he made the compliment. Was he not used to flirting with girls? I couldn't believe that. My face flared up warm as well, and my heart was thumping wildly in my chest.

Lucien coughed and choked down a mocking laugh, but I didn't care. Being called exceptionally pretty by the most gorgeous boy I had ever seen could not be ruined.

We entered the cafeteria, and I joined the line with the boys. I had to admit, the food in this school actually appeared by all counts to be edible. I piled on a ton of food, even though I wouldn't eat it all because I was still nervous. The first day could make or break your entire year; it was a lot of pressure—cool, attractive, and most likely popular table, or the "typical" table. A lot was on the line here.

I tried to hand the lunch lady my debit card, but she looked at me as if I were stupid and said, "Your boyfriend already paid for you." She then glanced at Archer, who was waiting for me, holding his tray and suppressing an uncomfortable but satisfied grin. I had to turn away, too embarrassed to hold his gaze. The lunch lady assumed we were together, and it thrilled me. Who else might make that assumption from his innocently kind gesture? And they said chivalry was dead.

"You didn't have to do that." We walked together, following Lucien.

"Yes, I did. First days are always atrocious. I'd know. We move a lot. I've had a lot of first days." He smiled at me. "You?"

"Not really. I've moved twice in my life. Well, and traveled a bit."

"Lucky. I can't remember how many times I've moved. If I had to guess...well, you wouldn't believe me if I told you," he said with a smirk.

"Military parents?"

Archer let out a loud, dry laugh. "You could say that. My dad's in the military. My mother can't stand staying settled. Divorced, you see, moves around all the time." Then he stopped as we approached the table.

The table was almost full, and mostly of boys. Only three girls sat there, one of whom was Archer's gorgeous sister, surrounded on all sides by boys vying for her attention. The other two girls were sitting comfortably close to two boys, most likely their boyfriends. There were only two chairs left, but Lucien was sliding one over from the next table.

"What about you? Why'd you move here? Six weeks into your senior year and everything?" Archer asked, highly interested.

"Hey, we're saving that for..." Emily began but, on seeing me, stopped.

"Would it be awful of us to steal Callie today for lunch?" Lucien said in a sweet, adorable voice, leaning slightly toward Emily with a sincere grin and batting his eyes. He was freakin' batting his eyes. But it was eerily charming, so much so that I thought Emily might literally swoon in her seat.

"Um...yeah...okay..." Emily stammered with a huge grin. She giggled loudly, blushing. "Anything for you guys." Then she was a hot mess of giggles, squeals, and whispers. When I was seated, I peeked over to Emily to give her an apologetic look, but she was ogling the boys on either side of me. Now I understood what Archer had meant by down to earth and why Lucien had called them typical girls. They'd meant I was acting like ridiculously hot guys like them were normal, that I wasn't a boy-obsessed, slobbering, giggling girl. And yet if they could read my thoughts...

Archer still awaited an answer.

"Oh, sorry. Yeah, my senior year. I wasn't happy." I hesitated, wondering how much I should tell him. I felt like I could tell him everything, but something in me hesitated, reminding me that I hardly knew him, and unloading the truth on strangers was a pretty crummy icebreaker.

"Not happy is an understatement. You seem sad." Lucien scrutinized me, and his green eyes felt freakishly probing. Archer quickly gave Lucien a reprimanding glare and a small shake of his head before he focused his attention back on me.

I swallowed hard. How could he see that? Was it so plain on my face? "Is it that obvious?"

"No. Lucien is very observant." Why did Archer give Lucien another reprimanding glare? What was with their nonverbal communication, and how did they know I was depressed? I felt like I was imposing on some exclusive club they were in, surrounded by secrets and completely lost.

"Well, I might as well be upfront about it. We came here because my dad is dying. NYU is including him in experimental treatments that might give him more time. He has...a fatal heart condition."

"Which one?" Lucien asked.

I was a bit confused. "That's weird. Most people jump on the sympathy wagon instead of wanting a detailed diagnosis."

"I'm going to major in pre-med," Lucien said, but somehow, it rang false. Why would he lie, though?

"Oh," I replied, still finding it strange. "He has Loeffler endocarditis. It's a form of hypereosinophilic syndrome—if you've ever heard of that."

Lucien sighed sympathetically. "I actually have."

Archer studied Lucien's expression.

Lucien huffed out an uncomfortable breath, and I knew what was coming. "It's um...a fatal muscular heart disease where the tissue of his heart, like, slowly thickens, which kind of weakens him and deprives his body of oxygen." Lucien's gaze met mine. Those rich green eyes held too much sympathy for me to handle, so I turned away and blinked in case tears wanted to come. "I'm really sorry," Lucien broke a silence that had been forming.

THE IMMORTAL TRANSCRIPTS: QUIVER

Then I said the same thing I had said for many years, for what felt like a million times. "Why are you sorry? It's not your fault."

"What about your mom? She didn't mind the move?" Lucien asked. I figured he was trying to change the topic, and little did he know, it was worse territory.

"I dunno. She died in a car accident when I was little. Seriously, I wouldn't ask any more questions, or you'll feel sorry for me, and I hate it when people feel sorry," I said quietly and uncomfortably. I had an inkling my first day was about to go to shambles. If they apologized one more time, I might scream (that would definitely ruin my first day).

"We'd never feel sorry for you," Archer said. I could feel him move slightly closer to me, a shift in weight, his presence and warmth a little closer. My heart leaped to my throat, and my stomach did a somersault. It felt like ages since I had been interested in a boy. Most boys back home would ask me questions and hardly listen to the answers. They were always after something else, and I wasn't the type of girl to give in to anything of the sort. I wanted to fall in love, and I hadn't yet met a boy I loved, so things always tended to end before they began. This pleased the parental unit since no one was "worthy of me."

"Who is this?" the bubbly, high pitched, and beautiful voice of the blonde from this morning cut off my thoughts. She was scrutinizing me, judging me—harshly, if the calculated look in her eyes was any indicator. Her beautiful blue eyes narrowed at me. They were different than Archer's when closer up, not as intense in gaze or hue, but a paler, softer blue than his. The butterflies her brother produced in my belly died out, and an anxious sour queasiness overtook me.

"Callie, this is my twin sister, Aroha," Archer said, his voice hesitant. "Sis, this is Callie."

Aroha gave me a plastic smile. "Wow, you are really pretty, Callie," she said in a tone that made me feel she wasn't complimenting me at all. I wasn't sure how to take it as an insult, but her voice betrayed a vicious undertone.

I put on my game face. "Um...thank you. You are too."

"It's a pleasure to meet you. You must sit with us every day. I insist."

"Sure, thanks," I told her awkwardly.

It was clear that my fears of not fitting in were well grounded. She was the queen bee of this school, and she was rejecting me. I scrutinized her back, trying to use my innate intuition to read her twisted, hidden motives.

Was it because I was possible competition? At least, that's how I thought she viewed me. By asking me to sit with them, she was keeping her enemies close.

But there was more than her thinly veiled rejection that bothered me. There was something about her, odd and out of place. She seemed older, mature, like a middle-aged woman who resides in the Hamptons and travels abroad often. Her air was pompous, her voice aristocratically tight-lipped. The bubble-gum ditzy voice sounded forced. There was nothing real about her character. Her looks, however, were natural under the make-up. She had a regal beauty, like a princess in a Renaissance painting, majestic and ethereal. Aroha was literally the prettiest person I had ever seen, just like her brother was the handsomest.

"Sorry, she's a little full of herself," Archer whispered to me. His breath felt warm and stirred my hair, tickling my ear. I randomly thought of picking honeysuckles with my mother when I was really small. Something reminded me of that, but was it a real memory? I didn't remember my mother.

"As she rightfully should be. She's gorgeous." I smiled, hiding from him how much she truly bothered me. Aroha, my first enemy in the new school, was related to my new crush—I could never win.

For the rest of lunch period, I had study hall. It was divided up alphabetically, so I was split off from everyone, except Lucien, whose last name was Veras. It felt nice to get away from Aroha's penetrating gaze, but I had to admit that I wouldn't complain about more time with Archer. The study hall monitor nipped any hope of conversation in the bud right away, so I set to work trying to start the mountain of work I had missed in only two subjects so far. This was going to be a rough few weeks of homework.

Third period was awful. Number one, no one I had met in my other two classes was in it. Number two, it was Greek, which I only took to please my father. And third, there were only ten other kids, all the nerdy type who, I'm sure, were nice, but they took one glimpse of me and silently rejected me, telling me I didn't belong. An outcast among outcasts made me feel the lowest of the low. I wasn't extraordinarily smart like these kids, and I cared more about fitting in than they did. They probably could smell the Ambrose popularity wagon scooping me up already. I tried to concentrate on the material, regretting taking a new language right away.

It seemed like the class would never end, but when it finally did, most of the Greek I had learned as a child had come back to me. I was going to have to spend a lot of time reviewing, since my old school never offered the language. There, I had learned French and hadn't bothered with Greek since I was ten.

Fourth period, I suited up in the locker room for gym. Chatty Emily was there without Linda, so she sucked right up to me and offered to let me share her locker. I hadn't realized we had to lock our school things up, but Emily explained through various long-winded examples that theft still occurred in the school every now and then, despite the school's prestige. I think she was just obsessively possessive of her new phone. Either that, or she didn't have as much money as most of the students, which would be why she clung to her material possessions so tightly. I think it bothered her that her family's wealth wasn't enough for her. Again, I needed to stop my wild speculations.

"So, what are we doing right now in class?" I asked.

"Archery." She rolled her eyes. "But it's not so bad because we're not separated from the boys." She shimmied into her tight T-shirt and super-short track shorts. She definitely dressed to show off for the boys. I was hopelessly dull in my graphic-T and the appropriate three-inches-above-the-knee shorts. Apparently, dress code rules did not apply to gym class. Either that, or Emily ignored them.

We trekked outside. It was warm, almost hot if it hadn't been for the chill in the wind. I hoped for a long Indian summer. As we made it down to the stadium, I noticed Emily staring longingly toward a throng of boys who were goofing around with one another. On seeing us girls, they began to get rowdier, showing off in their idiotic ways, thinking we liked it when they acted like a bunch of apes. Emily did like it, apparently. Well, to each her own.

Archer was on the periphery of the boys. I couldn't tell if he saw us or not.

"Here goes Ar-cher! Ready to show off, as usual." One boy I hadn't met yet grabbed him around the neck roughly.

Archer shoved him off, laughing. "You're just jealous."

He laughed back.

"I am," another guy protested. "He's like a freakin' chick magnet." He followed up with buzzing noises as if Archer were some sort of magnetron.

"Yeah right. He reels them li'l fishies in, but he never closes the deal," a third boy said smartly, making the rest of them burst out in expressions of disbelief at the third boy's nerve.

According to them, Archer wasn't as experienced as most hot and popular guys tend to be. I wondered if that were true (I really hoped it was).

"Lay off it!" Archer barked at them and turned to peek over at us. He smiled at me and waved. I waved back.

"Who is that?" One boy studied me.

"Callie Syches," Archer enunciated clearly, his eyes never leaving mine as he said it, and he smirked smugly afterward.

"Introduce me, man!" the same boy pleaded. He wasn't bad looking, just a little short and stocky but with a bright smile. He was no Archer Ambrose, though.

"Fat chance. Introduce yourself," Archer said, drifting toward Emily and me.

"Oh my God, he's coming this way," Emily squeaked, squeezing my arm so hard, I thought it might bruise.

"Hey," Archer said, slightly less confident than he was among the boys. "Two classes, lunch, and we live in the same building. That's beyond luck."

"Who's the lucky one, me or you?" I countered. This made him smile.

"Well, *I'm* the lucky one, but that lot has been giving me hell." He pointed over his shoulder to the wild apes who were catcalling us. "Please, Callie, I beg you, help me save face?" His eyes really did plead sadly, as did his melodic voice, but his lips curled into a smile. He held out his arm, as a gentleman would for a lady in an old novel. I slipped my arm in his, and he led me down the hill.

I peered at him out of the corner of my eyes, ignoring the jeers from the boys.

"What?" He acted all innocent.

"Like you need saving." I gave him a fake glare.

"Everyone does now and then," he said matter-of-factly.

I glanced behind for Emily and caught her glowering at me. Her gaze darted quickly away but too late. It was obvious she liked Archer, and he didn't notice she existed at all. I wasn't in a position to make enemies, but I wasn't sure how to remedy the situation.

Once down on the field, the teacher handed out bows and arrows and told us to partner up. Apparently, they had been working on archery for days now.

"Know what you're doing, partner?" Archer subtly asked me to be his partner.

I had never attempted to shoot an arrow in my life. "No clue," I responded. I warily examined the weapon in my hand. Weapon, key word, meaning it could kill, especially in my hands.

"Don't worry, Callista, is it? Archer will take care of you. State champ last year," Mrs. Cooper, the gym teacher, informed me proudly. She patted his shoulder, then moved on to the next pair.

I raised my eyebrows at Archer. "In archery?"

"Yeah," he said modestly, shuffling his feet.

I burst out laughing. Emily defiantly glowered at us, envious of what was going on. I tried to ignore her.

"What?" he asked, confused. I felt awful for laughing at him (only a little bit, though).

"How appropriate. Archer, archery."

"Think that was the idea. Runs in the family," he said quietly, smiling.

"I'm sorry." I suppressed my laughter.

"All right, Syches, you give it a try!" he taunted me, pointing to the target. His face lost its humor, and he paled. Then a second later, he swallowed hard, and the smile was back on, and he was happy again. What the heck just happened to him?

"I'll kill someone."

"Injure, maybe. Kill? No. These are pretty dull arrowheads, and the fletching is absolutely dreadful. Cheap crap." He took the arrow, placed it in the bow, pulled back quickly and naturally as if he shot bows every day, and released. He didn't even take time to aim, but the arrow hit the direct center of the target.

"Show off," I growled, glaring at him.

My feigned hate made him smile. "Here, try." He handed it to me.

Now, I felt embarrassed. I had never attempted to shoot a weapon of any sort in my life, not even in gym class in my old school. "After that?" I asked, astounded that I was supposed to follow after the best archer in all of New York. It's a huge state with a lot of people.

"I'll show you," he told me, coming closer. Just as during lunch, I could feel his warmth, his presence, near me. The butterflies returned, and my heart raced in anticipation. He put the bow in my left hand, "Right-handed?" he asked.

I nodded.

He put the arrow in my right. I placed what he told me was the nock in the bowstring, and aimed toward the target. Archer took my hands in his, leaning his body against mine, his head hovering over my shoulder so he could get a better perspective from my angle. I felt his breath curling on my ear and my neck, which made my pulse quicken. I wanted to turn to face him, to kiss him. Underneath the scent of soap, detergent, and cologne, there was this strange earthy, sweet smell emanating from him that was addicting, like honeysuckles. I couldn't recall a time in my seventeen years of being so drawn, so attracted, to someone.

Archer gave me some pointers I could hardly comprehend because I was so distracted by how close he was to me. I felt his soft but nimble fingers part my own, placing one above the fletching, one below. He then raised my left hand, aimed me, and let go of me, stepping back.

"Now, pull back until you feel the strain build, and then release. Keep your left hand steady the entire time," I heard him instruct. His voice was barely audible over the frantic beating of my heart.

I wanted him close again, to feel him almost against me. My mind whirled into dizzy thoughts involving him and kissing on a white sandy beach with clear waves crashing behind us...

I squinted to rid myself of the silly fantasies going on. I wanted to impress him. I wanted to do well. I concentrated on the target, zeroing in on the center, where his arrow remained, and then released.

To my luck, it actually hit the target in the red ring, which wasn't too bad. It wasn't far from the dead center of the target for a first attempt. It could have been much worse.

"Not bad." He smiled at me. I couldn't get enough of that smile, and he wanted to keep flashing it at me. I tried to give him the bow, but he simply retorted, "I've shot enough arrows for a lifetime." Something in his voice again betrayed a dozen emotions, and I wondered if he meant something more than his boredom at being the best archer in the state.

Unfortunately, gym class was over much too quickly. After a reluctant goodbye to Archer, I went back inside. I tried to appease Emily's blatant jealousy, and she acted nicer, but I wondered if it was because I was her ticket to the cool clique. Still, Linda was genuine, so I'd deal with Emily since they were a package deal. Dad would be excited to hear I'd made a couple friends on the first day.

Overall, it ended up being the perfect first day. Well, as perfect as a first day could be. Most of it had to do with a beautiful blond boy who seemed to be as interested in me as I was in him. Best of all, he lived in the same building on the same floor... New York would be much better than I had anticipated. To think I had been dreading the move for over two months, and all it took was one day to set it right. It was like Archer was a gift from God (or the gods as my harebrained father would say).

CHAPTER 5

Archer

I was a goner. I was sucked in by this mortal, powerless against the very feelings I instilled in others. When she showed up to school, I was intrigued, but by the time gym class was over, I was addicted. I needed to keep her close. I didn't want to part ways. On impulse, I stopped her by the gymnasium doors. Even in her gym clothes, she was perfection itself: neither short nor tall, but up to my shoulder and slender in build yet with an athletic definition. She made me have trouble channeling my thoughts into sentences.

"Callie, could I ask you...that is...what are you doing after school? You see, a few of us are headed to the pool hall. We go every Monday. Do you want to come with us?" I tried to sound noncommittal, test the waters by asking her out in a group. Mother Gaia and all that is godly, I was having trouble forming my words for many reasons, the most prominent one being her rendering me speechless.

"I...uh...I want to, but I can't." She stressed the words, giving them a different meaning. There was so much to her, so complex for a human. Damn it. I needed to learn more.

She folded her arms, chilled by the wind. The act accented her chest, and the human part of me rekindled. It had been ages since I'd felt mortal urges. Callie was definitely supple in the right areas, but by far her best attributes were her eyes. They were large, almond shaped, and dark mahogany, with a glimmering, internal shine that had tricked me into believing she was more than human.

"I understand," I told her, although I really didn't. I had the impression she was rejecting me, which was a new and different feeling for me.

"No, I have to take care of my dad. Cook him dinner, unpack the house," she explained. Her tone sounded genuine. She nervously twisted a ringlet in her finger. She had her dark curly hair, not those tight ringlets but loose cascading curls, pulled up off her shoulders, exposing a strong jawline and an elegant, slender neck, which I hadn't seen until gym class. I felt the urge to kiss that part of her, where her jaw met her neck right under her ear.

"You're seventeen. You need to have fun," I insisted.

"On the outside. Inside, I'm extremely old."

"I know exactly how you feel," I told her. Somehow, she truly understood me. "Maybe another time. This weekend or something like that."

"Yeah, that'd be great." She smiled, parting her full lips to reveal a perfectly aligned white smile. Then, like that, she turned away and slipped inside. A cloud went over the sun, blocking out the light, giving what poets like Lucien claimed was a metaphor for my mood once she was gone.

Even after school, I couldn't get Callie out of my mind, which wasn't at all like me. Hoping for a distraction, I met up with Aroha, Lucien, and a few of the mortals who followed Aroha around like a pack of hungry wolves. She kept them all to feed her pride. It was kind of weird, but centuries of seeing my mother date mortals and immortals—pretty much consistently—desensitized me to it. She wasn't promiscuous or anything, but I'd wager a lot of guys called her a tease.

Mondays, we shot pool. The rest of the week always consisted of different activities. Homework didn't need to be done since I'd gone through school scores of times. I had accumulated enough knowledge over the years to get through high school, college, and beyond. I'd probably done every job or career possible, so when I repeated them, the information and skills came back easily. Because of how young I looked and how mortals did less at eighteen than prior centuries had done, I was stuck in the crappy high school and college routes.

Lucien appeared relieved to see me. He was beginning to be frustrated with Aroha. It would be only a couple years before he left us again. He was my best friend, but even best friends get on each other's nerves every hundred years or so. And parents were completely unbearable after a decade or two. I might leave with Lucien when the time came. I longed for an island in the Caribbean: somewhere warm, paradisiacal, and different than the States.

Lucien nodded me toward a pool table, breaking me from my reveries. "What's the score? 1,142 to 1,140?"

"This century so far," I countered. "I had you last century. Beat you by over 50 matches."

"I keep getting better, though," he answered with a smile.

"Rack 'em then." I gave him a wry grin. Our competitions were fun now, but they hadn't always been.

"You fancy that new girl, don't you?" Lucien asked.

I hesitated in answering, trying to gauge if I was walking into a conversation with an uncle who would lecture me or if I was simply chatting about a hot girl to my best friend. Lucien was my dad's half-brother and was probably one of the most gifted of us: he could control the sun, heal mortals, and tell prophecies, and he'd invented music, poetry, and medicine, among other things. And he was rarely modest about his talents.

"As far as I remember, so do you." I decided to try to push him toward the friend role by teasing him.

"Can't say I don't, but it's not like you to...*try* so hard." With all his talents, he had a weakness. He was also the god of truth, so he knew when mortals were lying, but in turn, he couldn't lie to immortals. He literally had to tell me he fancied her. Normally, I'd laugh at him for admitting something like this, but this strange feeling of resentment started rising up in me, making me want to punch him and tell him he couldn't touch Callie.

I subdued the anger and said, "Didn't realize I was trying."

"Come on, Archer. You were pathetic. I could practically see the drool dripping from your mouth while you ogled her," he teased.

"You're just jealous."

"I am," he muttered, his gaze darting away, most likely annoyed at his inability to hide his feelings from me.

"I asked her to come here, but her dad and all."

"You didn't!" Lucien stopped playing pool and stared me down in shock. Great, what else would Lucien say to put a damper on my day?

"I did. So what?"

"Be careful. Those binding words could get you in trouble," he warned.

"I didn't ask her *out* out. I asked her to meet up with all of us. Besides, what's the harm in a little innocuous flirting? I've done it a million times before."

"It's different—" he resumed the game "—when you actually mean it. The Fates can tell when you mean it." Lucien purposely brought up the Moirae to unnerve me. We all feared them—in a way, they were more powerful than any god, more omniscient, and able to create life, mold destiny, and end life. They were the oldest immortals, and their powers were never fully understood. We gods willed things, and they ensured it happened. "Tell me exactly what you said."

I told him every detail of how I "asked" her out.

Lucien listened patiently. "That's it?"

I nodded.

"You're okay for now." His laugh told me I was doomed later.

I mulled it over for a moment, trying to remember the details of the rules dealing with mortals, the laws for our kind once we went underground when monotheism relieved us of the limelight. I hadn't really paid attention since I was never in danger of breaking them, at least, not in the last two millennia.

"Refresh my memory. The whole binding thing, how does that happen?" I asked.

"By the beard of Zeus," he said, huffing in exasperation. He added a dramatic eye roll for effect, making me want to punch him. "Archer, you're hopeless. You're already a goner."

I studied the pool table to avoid his gaze, which would confirm I already was. He was winning this game, distracting me with his mockery.

"Whatever happened to your last slip up?" I shot back to wound him. He'd broken the rules many times over his long life, so he couldn't chastise me. Hypocrite.

"Mila? She thinks I died. Still pining, though. You think you could make her love someone else for me? I'm beginning to feel bad about it," Lucien blurted out, annoyed at his loose tongue. It pained him to be so blatantly honest sometimes, but I had to point out his hypocrisy for mocking my ignorance about binding when he was the king of binding and breaking human hearts.

"What will you do for me in return?" I bartered.

"I'll think of something. Even you get in a scrape every now and then."

"Liar." I laughed.

"You will be if you pursue that girl." Here came the lecture. His gaze darted toward Aroha. Yes, my mother was always a problem when it came to my business. Somehow, I wished he or I had that rare godly gift of foresight. Sure, he had his prophecies, but they were always vague and far into the future, useless.

"Fair enough. I'll help you if you help me. Binding?"

Lucien sighed and stared me down. "You can't ask her out, to be yours, to get married, etcetera, etcetera... Stay away from words like 'I love you.' The Man always keeps an eye out for that slipup. You can't make the first move; remember, she must ask you out first, kiss you first, and never,

ever tell her who you really are. The Man will strike her down with lightning if you do. Exposure is Zeus's biggest fear."

"And once I let her make all the first moves, I'm okay to ask or do what she has initiated right? She kisses me, then I can kiss her whenever I want?"

"Yeah, but if you slip up and make a move first—"

"She'll love me for the rest of her life, right?" I interrupted to verify the rules of mortal relations that were hazily coming back to me. This is what Lucien had done. When caught up in the moment with his Mila, he'd bound her to loving only him for the rest of her life. However, Aroha or I could remedy it by breaking the bond and poisoning her heart for someone else. Unfortunately, we were ordered to do this often. Gods and goddesses were damn awful when it came to settling down, to put it nicely. Aside from Zeus, Lucien needed our help the most frequently.

"It's not as nice as it sounds."

"I dunno. Eighty years with someone like Callie seems extremely bearable," I thought aloud. Lucien was falling behind in the pool game. His scolding responses to my questions began to distract him.

"Ten years max, Archer. She might just notice you don't age. It's better to stay away, and you know it."

"But I don't want to. I don't think I can."

"Let her make the moves, then. Just watch what you say," he said, shaking his head. "Bad idea if you ask me."

"Good thing I didn't ask," I mumbled sourly as I potted the eight ball. "1,141. I'm only one down."

"Rematch?" He raised his eyebrows, smiling.

Aroha and I didn't get home till well after nine, and Lucien and I were tied yet again. I grabbed my bookbag and headed toward my room. I wasn't going to do any homework, but I wanted to be alone to think about things away from my mother's prying gaze, one that could read men like a book.

"You off to bed so early?" Aroha asked as she began to load the dishwasher without bothering to rinse caked-on food off the plates.

"Do it right, Aroha, or get a maid again. Rinse them first."

"I think I will, and have her cook for us as well. You didn't answer me. Off to bed?" She was studying me, trying to see what I was up to.

"Off to work, really. The world won't fall in love by itself."

"Oh, why bother with those mortals?" she scoffed, rinsing the dishes now.

"We'd be bored without them, no?" I pointed out, not waiting for her answer. She'd be lost without her male worshipers. I, however, cared about them. I had been given a job, and I would do right by them through it.

I went to my room and lay down on the bed in the dark. I closed my eyes, clearing my mind, listening, and surveying the city first. There was a mortal in distress in Queens, Margot Hampton; I hadn't a clue who she was, but she was crying out in prayers.

"Please, God, I'll do anything. I love him. Please don't let him leave us, please," she cried. I zoomed in over her, figuratively in her room. She was a fairly pretty woman, on her knees, her hands clutched together so tightly that her knuckles were white. Her head was cast down, streaming with tears, her hands resting on the bed. Her stomach was swollen with a child destined to be born very soon. "Please, don't let him leave us. Make him love us again."

Poor Margot was going to be forsaken and with a baby on the way. But who was the man? I couldn't help unless I found out who he was. I edged myself closer to Margot until I broke into her mind, found the information I needed, and left as quickly as I could. As I left, she shivered, and her frightened eyes wildly inspected the room.

There was no way not to have mortals feel my presence when I entered their minds, but usually, they just caught a chill, felt for a moment they weren't alone, and shook the feeling off. I knew how it felt for them, for it felt the same for me, but it was part of the job. I had retrieved what I needed: the man's name was Brad Riley.

I found Brad Riley shooting up heroin under an overpass. Now, this wouldn't do for poor Margot. Even I couldn't make him love her. Breaking a mortal off his drug was harder than tearing Ares himself from a battlefront. I'd tried once—to cure a mortal of addiction through love—and it killed her. Love can kill, after all.

But who would do for Margot? I scanned the city, trying to remember past cases that I had left unresolved. Then it dawned on me: the young widower doctor who'd lost his wife, how long ago, three or four years? It was a perfect match, not just in circumstances, but also in character, feeling, and temperament. You see, I don't usually just throw people together, because those loves, like Todd and Mary Beth's, don't last. Normally, I make sure everything matches up perfectly. One of my talents is the ability to see how a person's mind works the moment I enter it.

The widower, Gary Curtis, was finally contemplating moving on but needed that nudge. I'd help him and Margot in the only way I could, by making them love each other.

After I left Gary's house, I was sure he'd fall in love with poor Margot. I saw then, too, that Margot would love him. All that awaited was their meeting, but that was up to the Fates. They usually work well with me, foreseeing what I'm up to, ensuring my work follows through. Or perhaps I alter what destinies the Moirae make. I'm not quite sure how it works, but somehow it pans out.

I zoomed out of the city, helping those most desperate cases all over the world. Each case usually takes me only a moment or two to accomplish. I prevented a dozen break-ups, let several dozen people move on, made thousands of adolescents grow crushes. It was enough for a night's work, and the unseen cases would be visited tomorrow. Then I remembered Lucien's ex, Mila, who still pined over him, despite believing him to be dead. He had bound her to him, so it would take a little more concentration and two arrows: one arrow to break the bond and one to make her love another.

When I left Mila's home in Nuremberg, she was sleeping peacefully, thinking of Henrik, a shy but kind young man who had been devotedly attached to her for some time now. I mentally transported back to Manhattan, thinking perhaps I could make one more mortal happy tonight, when I heard a word that unconsciously attracted my attention.

"Callie," a male voice murmured endearingly. I centered in on the voice coming from the Upper East Side and beelined there. Daniel Eagen, the guy from my school who had been so eager to be introduced to Callie during gym class, was sleeping in his bed, groaning and mumbling her name in his sleep. Dan was dreaming about her. In most cases, I would shoot the object of his affections to make her love him back. Technically, he was a friend—as much as a mortal could be to me—and I should've helped him out.

No. Something in me wouldn't budge. I wouldn't let him have Callie. He could try without my help, but I would never pierce Callie with an arrow for him. In fact, I wanted to make him love someone else, but who? Angie Berman? Jenny Phife? Aroha? It was wrong, obviously, but Aroha asked me to meddle all the time.

I was torn. Rarely had I ever felt so against allowing people to fall in love. I needed to find out how Callie felt. If she liked him at all, I'd do it. After all, my life had been full of sacrifice. I could give her up now before it would be harder later on. In eighty years or less, she'd be gone from this earth, and she'd fade from my memory as so many other mortals had. At least, I tried to convince myself that. It wasn't working.

I found myself in Callie's bedroom before I even envisioned going. My stomach churned with guilt, feeling I shouldn't be there invading her privacy, despite the fact that I did it all the time to others. She wasn't in bed, even though the nightstand clock read two o'clock in the morning. I had been working longer than I had anticipated. I pulled back a little to survey the entire apartment. She was in the master bathroom with her father, so I entered.

Her father was being sick over the toilet. Callie, clad in her bathrobe, held a cold compress on his neck.

"Oh, Callista, just leave me. It's just the medicine."

"I'm staying right here, Dad, until I get you back in bed," Callie told him, trying to hide the fear in her voice.

"Go to bed, Callista."

"Is there anyone I can call? The doctor? Raphael?" she pleaded.

He was sick again. Her frown deepened.

"It's part of the side effects. It should only last a couple of days."

"A couple days! You need more fluids." She stood up and padded out into the kitchen in her slippers and a fluffy purple bathrobe. I followed her, entranced. I had to know more about her.

She took a glass out of the cabinet and filled it with water. Instead of returning immediately to her father, Callie put the glass down, pressed her hands on the counter for support, and stared into the sink.

Her frame shook violently with silent sobs, her eyes squeezing shut to prevent the tears from coming. But Callie couldn't stop them, and the tears rolled down her cheeks anyway.

I tried to empathize with what she must be feeling. What was it like to live in fear and pain that you may lose the person you loved? I couldn't fully fathom it. My family and my friends were all immortal. I'd had loved ones die, and I understand the human emotion of grief too damn well, but each instance had been so sudden. It was the fear before the loss that I couldn't quite fathom, seeing someone slowly dying, where there was nothing one could do to stop it. We don't fear Death because we know him personally. But this fear, actually knowing a loved one is leaving the world soon, intrigued me.

Before I realized it, my curiosity took me further than I wished to go, and I invaded Callie's mind. What I felt made me dizzy. Callie was envisioning her father's pain, his upcoming death. She felt alone, helpless. His pain was her pain. She wished she were a normal, carefree teenager and then regretted the thought. She loved her father. She'd give him every ounce of energy she had until he was gone. *Forget friends*—Emily and Linda popped up in her mind. *Forget boys*—and I saw myself.

Then I was somehow ejected from her mind. I saw all that in a millisecond. If only I could have stayed in her thoughts a moment longer to see what she was really thinking about in reference to me. But there were more important concerns than me.

I didn't understand it. How was I pushed out? What force propelled me from her mind? I had never had a mortal push me out before. Callie searched the room, staring right through me. She rubbed her arms, quivering to rid herself of the chill I had given her, then wiped her tears away with conviction, took up the glass, and marched back toward her father's room.

She was so strong, handling something so heavy at such a young age, at the precipice of adulthood. I admired that fortitude.

I opened my eyes, finding myself in the dark of my own bedroom, feeling alone, desperate, and in pain. I took on everything Callie was feeling and now felt what I had been curious about—the pain and fear of losing a loved one—and regretted facilitating my abilities to see more than I wished for.

I had made a deal with myself. Dan was the furthest thing from her mind, so I wouldn't make her love him. But it didn't seem fair to force him to love someone else just because I had a little crush on his object of desire. And part of me wanted to see where Callie's heart naturally would lead her without help or hindrance. I was unfairly testing her, but if I were ever to take the plunge again, was it wrong for me to be positive first?

I decided to do nothing but get some sleep, wondering what tomorrow would hold.

The next morning, I woke feeling rejuvenated and actually hopeful. I walked out into the kitchen, slipping my shirt on over my head. Aroha was talking to someone. There was an elderly lady in the kitchen, clad in an apron, writing down instructions as Aroha dictated them. Another maid.

I gave the woman a nod, gathering my things for school. Breakfast was now a nuisance with a mortal lingering about. I rushed into the bathroom, hearing the woman ask about our parents. I wonder what lies Aroha fed her: a workaholic father, a mother who was in Paris with her new boyfriend, or perhaps both.

I washed my face, brushed my teeth, and ran some leave-in conditioner through my hair. Gods forbid that I embarrass Ma if I wasn't the image of perfection; no really, she was murder, so it was easier to obey. I didn't feel like waiting for Ma, who was going to be late for school again, so I went down to tell Rupert, our driver, to wait for her. I could drive my car, but then again, why not use a cab? I hated being the driver in a standstill of traffic.

When I made it downstairs and out onto the street, I told the doorman Thomas I needed a cab. He walked out to the street to hail me one. I zipped up my jacket. It was the first cold morning in the last couple of weeks. Perhaps next I'd move to somewhere incredibly warm, like Ecuador or Hawaii, somewhere like that.

I saw Callie exit, her face haggard. There were black rings under her eyes from lack of sleep, but she was still utterly beautiful. She was helping her father into the car. He looked on the verge of death. I surveyed the area, but I did not see Thanatos—the god of death—nearby. Callie's father would live for now.

"I should come with you," she protested.

"Raphael is going to the hospital with me. He'll take care of me. You need to go to school, Callista." Her father endearingly touched her cheek. "Go to school." He shut the door, and the car drove off.

She stood there motionless, watching after the car even after it was lost in the traffic.

"Mr. Ambrose, your cab," Thomas announced. Callie turned on hearing my name, and her almond-shaped eyes met mine.

I offered her a ride, nodding toward the cab without uttering a word. I was afraid to ask her anything, afraid of the bind, because I felt so much. She nodded and came over toward the cab. I opened the door for her and offered my hand, but she climbed in without it. I kept forgetting how modern girls don't expect chivalry. I slipped in behind her.

Callie was quiet for a few moments but finally noted in a small voice, "Where's your car?"

"Aroha's running late. I don't feel like driving. Felt like a cab ride," I mused.

"Thank you for letting me tag along."

I shrugged. She said nothing more to me the entire way. Her thoughts were with her father, and it would've been terrible of me to take her from them. There were so many things I wanted to say to her and so many things I wished I could do to alleviate her pain, but it was futile. It was odd how I felt so drawn to her, how her emotions had become my own. After the epiphany of my feelings surfaced, I no longer felt at ease around her, and I became tongue-tied. She had become so important to me almost instantly, and the part of me that knew how to relate to women was long gone, dried up, frozen. Sure, I'd had my fair share of innocuous flirting, but when it came to true feelings, I was at a loss. It had been so long—thousands of years—since I had felt that wonderful human emotion: love.

CHAPTER 6

Mankind proclaims men are straightforward beings, and we ladies are the ones who use arts and manipulation to get what we want. Well, I tell it straight. I could sum this whole problem up with one word: Callie. Yet others will be much more diplomatic, I am sure.

Did I know Callista Syches would send a ripple through my life when I first saw her? No. She was nothing. Inconsequential. Mortal. But she was pretty—in an unconventional way, of course—and I didn't like that. I mean, she was nothing in comparison to me. I was beauty incarnate, the most beautiful being in existence. This fact, and being forever young, tends to fluff one's ego. At the same time, since we do not age, some of us tend to mature slowly over time. Perhaps this is the reason the myths gave us all a flaw: pride, adultery, or greed, for instance. Archer was led too much by the heart; Lucien was overly obsessed with truth; Ares loved conflict and war, and not much else; Zeus loved women, too many of them—flaws everywhere. However, not all of us fell victim. I had no shortcomings whatsoever.

I tried to be nice to this *Callie*, especially because it seemed my son liked attending to her. I didn't wonder where he spent his time nor how he got to school. We lived together, but our lives had become completely disjointed. I could hardly understand him. He, despite how he would disagree, was his father's son, or at least nothing like me. Perhaps there was something flawed in his makeup. Some said he was a spoiled brat, but I didn't agree with that. He had always been such a peculiar child: a dear, loving child when he wasn't being naughty or disobedient, but peculiar in that he was always serious about his duties concerning the mortals and their affairs. It was true he had an important job, but those simple beings would fall in love without his help...eventually, and with the wrong people as they do anyway with their fickle, fragile hearts.

There were too many concerns crowding my mind these days. I longed for the simple times to return, when love didn't have to be managed, beauty distributed correctly; before the ex-husbands, one of whom had the baggage of wars to deal with, another who obsessed over me still; oh, bigger, more powerful gods breathing down my neck for me to get things done. My life was far from simple, and now things were much more complicated and irritating with the emergence of that awful mortal girl wedging herself between my son and me. Something had to be done about her. It wasn't natural for a mortal to be so beautiful. Even some goddesses weren't as pretty as she. There had been some mistake. I hadn't given this mortal beauty, for that is part of my job, and if I had, I would not have given her enough beauty to make her my rival—not that she could rival me—but still, where had it come from?

I could barely stomach my lunch, with Dan paying attention to her instead of me and the traitors, Lucien and my own son, being highly civil. I had decided only yesterday that Dan probably was the most attractive mortal in the school. It had been Todd until he got too clingy.

"We're all going to the coffee house. You should come," Dan told the hideous usurper of my attention.

"Oh, I don't know," Callie said simply. She wasn't flirting back. Ugh. I wanted more of a reason to hate her.

"No, do come," Archer insisted. He was in a weird somber mood, the same with Callie. If neither of them cheered up, it would be a drag at the coffeehouse. What on Mother Gaia was wrong with my son? He isn't exactly victim to bouts of melancholy—not like Lucien was. I did not like the way he salivated over the little mortal. He was almost genuinely lovestruck, which is something that does not happen to him or me. We give love much more than feel it ourselves, a defense mechanism or something, an inverse of the power we exude.

"Bunch of college kids hang out there. Archer and I like to put the pretentious NYU students in their places. Pedantic sycophants," Lucien muttered the last part.

"Yeah, it's a good laugh," Dan interceded. Dan leaned in closer to Callie to say quietly, "Those two are like wicked smart."

"So, what happens when you become NYU students?" Callie shot Lucien a reprimanding side-eye. The clever, coy little girl was able to get under his skin. She was a bit more interesting than I'd first supposed, but I refused to entertain the idea of liking her.

"I'm not going to NYU," Lucien said. Wasn't he? Archer, Lucien, and I had said we would give Manhattan eight years, the high school and college circuit. And that little booger can't lie. He was changing his plans. We had hit NY before, a hundred years ago, and even though NYU did admit women back then, we ladies couldn't earn degrees. It had bothered me—like

41

a crush that slipped away—so I decided it was time for me to get a degree from the first place I'd ever attended. Now he dared to change our plans? He was the one who'd wanted to leave Germany a couple years early to come to the US. Some stupid prophecy told him to. It was always weird that he listened to them.

Archer and I exchanged a look, him catching the same thing as I had. Then my son refused to hold my gaze. He was planning to forsake me as well. Just great. The eight-year plan was drawing to a close after four, it seemed.

But what had I expected? Son or not, he needed his space every century or so. A mother always needed to know when to let go. I've had to several times throughout my existence, but it wasn't so bad when I was sure I'd be reunited with him again one day.

"I still don't know," Callie whined.

Give it a rest already, sweetheart. I took the "interesting" compliment back.

"Why don't you check in at home, and if everything's all right, then meet up with us?" Lucien offered. Oh yes, I'd forgotten the little mortal lived in our building, and her father was ill. Thomas had babbled on about it this morning outside. I had hardly listened to what the peon said. After all, the doorman was always full of useless mortal gossip, like I cared about them. Ha!

Dan gave Lucien a glare, but why? Was Dan so wrapped around Callie's finger in the three days she had been here that he was jealous? He should've been wrapped around *my* finger, like he had been before the little trollop reared her wretched head. I did not like Callie Syches, not at all.

"I'll take you, if you ask me to," my Archer said quite charmingly, showing off the perfect smile he had inherited from moi. What was my conniving little brat up to, though? He was careful with his words, being sure not to directly ask the wench questions, which meant he actually was afraid they may bind him, and that meant the asinine child was falling for this girl. I thought he had learned his lesson much earlier in life not to fall in love with a mortal. That was an utter disaster. Little witch Psyche got between my boy and me. Then, after all was said and done, his grandfather gave her to him, which I found unbelievable. Spoiled him really, gave his love immortality, and what had she given my son in return? Six hundred years, if that? Then she went off with that mortal man, taking my dear granddaughter with her. Oh, she came back, of course, but Archer had learned his lesson and divorced her. I never got to see Hedone again after her mother stormed out for good that one evening in what, the six hundreds? Five hundreds BC? It was hard to keep time straight. Then, after her first mortal died, she picked another and then another, always choosing mortals instead of immortals. Stupid, fickle Psyche. And then I had to nurse my broken-hearted boy for years. Archer had never been the same since he lost his daughter. Hedone didn't make it halfway through her third millennium, which is still fairly young for us. I had been celebrating my first millennium for millennia, but a goddess never reveals her true age.

"I can drive you in my new Cayman," Dan blurted out desperately. When Callie didn't respond, he added quite pathetically, "It's a Porsche."

"Oh, Dan, have you completely forgotten about me?" I called out, using my charm and wiles to gain his attention back. "It's a two-seater, and you promised to take me for a spin."

The goddess thing came in handy. I had to hold back my extraordinary powers among mortals. It wasn't hard to do, almost as easy and involuntary as breathing. Just to reel Dan in, I slipped out about one percent of my charm, which snapped his little mortal neck in my direction, and those of a few other boys nearby as well. I have the power to attract everyone to me. If my charm were let out full throttle, then I'd have to run for my life from thousands of mortals, men and women alike, who would want to literally and figuratively love me to death. Whenever I used it, most male gods called it cheating the system.

Lucien gave me a look of contempt. He had noticed.

But it worked. Dan's gaze flew to Callie, then to me, and he smiled sheepishly. "I forgot." Then he came back over, smiling, and sat down next to me. He slipped his arm around me.

Ha, I still had an edge over that silly mortal girl.

"Which gives me a car," Archer said to Callie, "and you in need of a ride." He was crafty. He had learned that from his father, who was extremely gifted at telling people what to do in such a way that they didn't realize they were being cornered into an agreement. That was how he'd cajoled me into leaving poor Heph—my first husband. When that didn't work for Ares, he'd unleash his temper. I couldn't live with Ares, but I couldn't imagine a world without him in it.

"Do you mind stopping at my house first?" Callie asked. Point to Archer—he had forced Callie unknowingly into asking him.

"Not at all," he said triumphantly. I hated when he acted so much like his father. That self-satisfied, smug smile—ugh! Ares always claimed I was overly confident, and Archer inherited it from me, but I beg to differ.

THE IMMORTAL TRANSCRIPTS: QUIVER

Callie and Archer showed up at the café a half hour after we arrived. They both looked happy. Too happy. And they weren't the only ones. Dan sat up excitedly in his seat when Callie entered, like a puppy whose owner had just returned. His eyes narrowed at Archer again. This had to end. I couldn't endure losing my prized pet's affection and attention for the likes of a measly mortal. I would ask Archer for another favor tonight. He'd do it as well. Archer is very obedient. He has to be. I couldn't leave this week to go to Zeus and come back and find my little Danny-boy gone.

Callie sat in the only open seat, sandwiching Dan between us in the cozy booth. This would be the true test of Dan's love for me. Archer pulled a chair up to the table next to Callie. She gave him a shy smile that gave no real feelings away, and he gave her the same. Like playing poker, they didn't want to reveal how high the stakes had gotten.

Dan began speaking to Callie right away. "So how are you liking Manhattan?"

"It's different," Callie said diplomatically.

Before I could interject myself in the conversation, Lucien, who was sandwiched between me and the newly and happily matched couple of Todd and Mary Beth, began speaking about the homecoming dance. Mary Beth was on the committee and was speaking of possible themes. I perked up. I never missed an opportunity to dress up and show off my assets.

"Well, we've been tossing around a dozen things, but I'll tell you guys what's going on the ballots because...well...we're among friends, and you'll find out Friday anyway." She squeezed Todd's hand lovingly. Good old Archer went all out for Todd, making Mary Beth love him back. She might have anyway, without love's poison. I gave Archer a look, and he smiled in full understanding of my thoughts. He was adorable when he wanted to be. Bratty as he was at times, I loved him only as a mother could: unconditionally.

"Well some of them are ridiculous. My idea was lovers in literature. You know, *Wuthering Heights*, *Romeo and Juliet*, and such. That's on the ballot."

"That's a great idea," Todd said, with eyes only for her. What a relief he didn't annoy me anymore. To him, I no longer existed, when only days ago, he was a slobbering, obsessed mess. Mary Beth was unfazed by his clinginess.

"You have themed homecomings?" Callie interjected. "I thought that was only in the movies."

"Oh no, we do this every year. Prom's normal, of course," Mary Beth told her. "Another one on the ballot is red-carpet couples, but everyone will dress up the same—Hollywood glamorous—and it'll be just like prom."

"The others?" Lucien asked, half-interested. He was bored. That's why he wanted to leave. Boredom was dangerous for our kind. When one lives forever, boredom can lead to depression. Every now and then, we had to go home. To Zeus and the others, I mean. Living among the mortals forced us to hide every part of our nature. It was like constantly acting, playing a role 24-7. Every few decades, I had to go somewhere where I could be myself.

"Oh, mobsters and vixens, like the 1920s and 30s; Classic icons, like Elvis and Marilyn Monroe, which will be a disaster. Oh yeah, and gods and goddesses," Mary Beth rambled on. Her last three words were highly intriguing.

Lucien choked on his latte and almost spit it out on the table. I gave him a thwack on the back, and he coughed to clear his throat.

"What was that last one?" I asked.

"Gods and goddesses. You know, everyone wearing togas and fig leaves," Mary Beth babbled.

Archer laughed loudly, too loudly, but I admit, it was quite funny. Fig leaves? What a foolish girl. They were laurel leaves, first of all, and were very renowned back then. Like the diamonds and platinum of today.

"There's more to it than togas," Callie countered.

We all regarded Callie in a new light. What could she possibly know about the gods? This could be a really hilarious conversation to joke about with the boys later and to bring Callie down in Archer's esteem. I couldn't wait for her to make a fool of herself in front of them.

Callie blushed. "Well, I think it's an interesting idea. Were they thinking along the lines of Greek or Roman?"

"I dunno. I don't know much about it." Mary Beth said.

"Well, Greek would be better. The Roman gods were counterfeit copies of the originals," Callie mused. "They were the same peop—I mean, icons. You see, Rome became the center of civilization, so all things Greek were adopted by the Romans."

This all seemed surreal, as if Callie was onto us. She almost said "people," like she was aware the gods actually existed. But how could she possibly know we all moved to Rome and changed our names? That was impossible. Any leak of our existence into the mortal world would have been immediately dealt with. Lightning would strike, and a mortal would die.

Lucien, Archer, and I all exchanged quick glances, questioning one another. Did this mortal mean more than what she was saying? Or was this a simple coincidence? Was she just intelligent? All of our eyes revealed to one another these questions. Archer imperceptibly shook his head to tell us it was not his doing.

I wondered how to figure out the extent of her knowledge without prying. I could just read her mind, but that took concentration, and it would be a little odd if I spaced out on all of them.

"Would you come to the homecoming committee meeting after school tomorrow and give them ideas, like all the gods and such?" Mary Beth asked Callie. "It was Amber's idea, but she didn't know much about it."

"Oh, uh...I dunno." She suddenly got bashful. I thought she had been a bit too cheeky for her own good, but here she was with this contrasting timidity. Either she was a hypocrite or complex for a human. I couldn't quite get her yet.

"Please? Sounds like you're practically an expert on it."

"I suppose I could just for one meeting, but I can't come all the time," she said noncommittally.

"That's great!" Mary Beth smiled happily.

"Greek gods, how interesting," I said innocently. All of us remaining silent would be a bit suspicious.

"Every girl will want to be Aphrodite, I suppose, which proves no theme is perfect," Callie said.

"Oh, really?" I raised my eyebrows, loving the compliment.

Lucien rolled his eyes at me. I wanted to smack the sardonic grin off his lips. I deserved to be worshipped.

"I'd be Hades," Archer said, suppressing a smile and enjoying the inside joke the mortals were ignorant of. Hades wasn't a bad guy if you stayed on his good side.

"Oh, you're wicked, Archer!" I laughed back.

"Was that the drunk one?" Todd began. "I'd be him. God of alcohol."

"No, that was Dionysus, Todd." Callie frowned. "I feel bad for Hades."

"Why's that?" Dan asked her.

"Well, he's just doing his job, isn't he? Someone has to do it. Like a lawyer defending a guilty client."

"Hold up here, are you defending the Devil?" Dan asked, astonished.

"No, Hades isn't the *Devil*. Oh really, if you don't know anything about mythology, then never mind." Callie sighed, frustrated.

Dan was crestfallen from her reproach.

"You do seem like an expert on the subject, Callie," Lucien pried. I was hoping the purveyor of truth could lead us to answers.

"I guess I do. I've been bred to know all of ancient Greek history. If you only knew." Callie laughed, drinking her latte. Archer gave her a quizzical look, but she shrugged. "Long story. I'll tell you later."

I wanted to press, but Archer anticipated my thoughts and gave me a quick glance that said, *Let it go. I'll find out later.* This was unnerving. Her comment sounded coded like one we gods would make to each other in front of mortals.

"Anyway, you pick a character for me, and we'll go together," Dan said to Callie.

I froze. Archer froze, his hands tightening dangerously on the table. I hoped he wouldn't dent it and raise suspicions. Callie almost knocked over her coffee.

"That's kind of you, but I can't make any future plans. I don't know what life will be like in a month. Actually, I shouldn't even be here..." Callie gathered up her purse and went to stand up. Archer pulled her hand to urge her to sit down again. Callie was clearly puzzled but neither removed his hand from hers nor attempted to stand again. She awaited an explanation from him.

Archer's beautiful face contorted into a grimace, most likely suppressing what he wanted to say. I was ready to interrupt if he was about to say something irrevocable. His eyes pleaded with her to stay. If she left, he'd feel physical pain. Archer's greatest physical flaw was his easily exposed emotions. You could *see* how he felt in his eyes and hear how he felt in his voice. But these were things mortals never perceived.

"Don't go," he told her. The simple statement was filled with complex subtexts, so much so that I marveled at his ability to say so much with so few words.

Callie took her hand out of his and picked up her coffee but appeared to obey him.

"I don't get it. Why can't you go to homecoming?" Dan asked stupidly.

"Oh, Dan, you really are thick sometimes," I said to him, playfully scolding.

Dan turned toward me, his cute brow furrowing. I winked at him and put my fingers to his lips for him to be quiet. He crossed his arms like an angry child.

"Thought we were going together?" I said quietly.

Dan didn't answer me but, instead, stared at Archer bitterly. This had to stop and very soon. The little witch had him spellbound. Both of them. Come to think of it, Lucien watched her a lot too. What was going on? Who was this mortal, and how was she doing this?

"So, Callie, you a god expert or something?" Todd spoke up, trying to restore the light mood we had lost. It was the last thing we wanted to talk about in light of Callie's possible knowledge. However, if Callie was onto our existence, then she would be dealt with, and I would no longer be aggravated by her existence. The thought of Zeus smiting her made me smile.

"Oh, no." She forced a weak smile. "My father..." her voice cracked. She took a deep breath. "My father sort of is."

Dan watched her like a sad puppy that had been reprimanded. It made my blood boil.

"He's a mythologist," Callie said.

"Is that a real occupation?" Lucien asked, abashed.

"Well, that's what they call him. Call it what you will: historian, archaeologist, expert on antiquated literature, anthropologist. He's got a lot of degrees," she babbled on, almost teary.

Oh, really! Little strumpet, get over it. Every mortal dies.

"Dan, you ready to go?" I pushed, tired of the whimpering creature enrapturing her male audience.

"Yeah, fine," he said stubbornly, glaring at Archer again.

Once we were outside, I stopped, tugging roughly on Dan's hand. I must have pulled much too hard, for Dan gaped at me, stunned. Gods are much stronger than mortals, part of our genetically superior makeup. He noticed I was too strong, so I spoke to distract him. "How could you embarrass me like that?"

"What?" He stared at me as if I were insane.

"Asking Callie to homecoming when you've been insinuating the entire time that you and I were going together."

"Funny how you kept leading me on until another girl came along. You've been treating me like crap, acting like you're too busy to hang out, like you're too good for me, and you were all about Todd. And now you suddenly care?" He scoffed, opening the car door for me.

I stood there, staring him down. "Are we going together or not?" I laced the question with an ultimatum.

"Well, she said no, didn't she?" He glared at me. "So, I guess so."

"What?" I flared out with a temper that would impress Ares himself. "I'm your second choice? Forget you, Dan! I can do much better than you!" And I stormed off, not knowing where I was walking except away from him. I had to use all my willpower to remain at human speed—another genetic advantage is that we're fast, really fast.

"Aroha," he pleaded. "I'm sorry."

"Why?" I glared at him, choking on angry tears. I wanted to throttle him, but it would most likely kill him. I reigned in my temper.

"Why what?"

"Why do you like *her* more than me?"

"Aroha," he pleaded.

"Answer me!"

He sighed and then said, "Callie's sweet and nice and beautiful—"

"More beautiful than me?"

"No, not at all! She's just...different. Nicer. Much nicer to people than you are. I mean, Aroha, you order me around, yell at me, treat me like a doormat. You strung me along while you were with Todd. There's only so much a guy can take." He turned away with a frustrated sigh. When he turned back to meet my gaze, he appeared torn. He rubbed my shoulder gently. "I'm sorry."

"I won't be second best."

"Then we shouldn't talk anymore."

"Fine!" I glared at him and walked off, ignoring his entreaties to at least get a ride home from him. He sped off like all mortal teenage boys, recklessly trying to show off—this time, he was showing me his anger.

I turned around after a moment and went back into the café, where Archer and the little usurper were both lost in each other's eyes without speaking. They were content just gazing at one another, something only pathetically-in-love couples do. Was my boy so far gone already? I definitely had to sit him down and talk some sense into him. He barely knew the girl!

I surveyed past the lovebirds to see Todd and Mary Beth kissing in public, oblivious to the people around them. Lucien, downcast and lonely, was the only one who noticed me enter. He cleared his throat to warn Archer of my approach, but it was too late.

"Archer!" I said with my maternal voice of command. He almost jumped out of his skin, breaking his gaze from the strumpet. He glared at me a bit petulantly, as he had when he was a child on the brink of throwing a fit.

"I want to go home," I ordered. Archer scanned me with probing eyes but decided not to ask about Dan.

"You ready?" he asked Callie.

Callie's gaze darted from him to her unfinished coffee.

"I'll see she gets home." Lucien stepped in. He gave Archer a warm smile, too warm. He was trying to get Archer jealous. I swear, the games these boys play.

I could see Archer struggle with the decision, which wasn't right. I was his flesh and blood. I bore him, bred him, gave him every advantage possible, and here I was, about to be cast aside.

"I'll see you tomorrow?" Archer asked her, trying to hide his disappointment.

She nodded, smiling shyly. "I'm sure we're bound to run into each other."

Archer smiled at that and left with me. I couldn't help but notice that he touched her shoulder gently as he walked away. He better not have kissed her first.

"You're quite pathetic," I scoffed as we headed to the car. "Didn't we learn our lesson last time?"

"Shut it," he growled at me defiantly. "Just because your mortal prefers her—"

"You know nothing!" I punctuated my words with a slap.

Mortals passing by gaped at us, shocked. I'd hit him with inhuman strength. Archer's jaw tightened, and he used his hand to realign it, which made a grotesque clicking sound. I had broken his jaw, which was good because he wouldn't be able to speak for a second. I didn't need to feel guilty; he'd heal in a split second, which was yet another fabulous immortal trait. Instead of speaking, he gave me a glare, his eyes literally lighting up with indignation as he climbed into the car. I followed. The ride home was in complete silence; so was the elevator ride up the thirty stories. The entire time, I could feel his fuming anger. Once we were inside, and I dismissed Miss Whittle for the evening—assuring her our "mother" would be pleased with the place—I turned to him.

Archer glowered at me as I locked the door.

"You will do me a favor," I said.

"I will do you *no* favors!" he spat back, his face reddening from anger. His eyes shone with that eerie power he'd inherited from his deadbeat father.

"You really look like your father when you're angry, and it's not becoming," I said, taking dinner out of the oven, where Miss Whittle had left it warming. I was trying to stay busy enough to avoid his glare.

"No wonder he doesn't want to be with you. You're an evil, spiteful, angry, jealous woman!"

"Jealous?"

"Yes," he said, calming down, sitting at the table smugly. "You're angry because Dan is in love with Callie. To think I almost united them just the other night. Hadn't a clue you were choosing Dan. Or did you choose Dan after you found out he was in love with her? Do you have to have everyone love you?"

"Dan is not in love with Callie. She's just the shiny new toy the little boys will discard when she loses her luster."

"No, he loves her. I saw it."

"He can't." I couldn't help my voice from quivering. Then again, why would he lie to me? "Make her fall in love with someone else," I added.

"Don't worry, she doesn't love him."

"Who's she love, you?" I raised my eyebrows.

"No one. Her dad's dying. She doesn't think of love. But I could change that. I could make her love me," Archer said with a smile. The thought made him too happy.

"I think that's too dangerous for you. You're already falling for her. Shoot yourself again?" I scoffed.

"No, I haven't." He rolled his eyes.

"I want you to make her fall in love with the vilest creature we know. Ooh, Vinnie Petreck."

His face contorted. "Not this again. That's hardly fair, to punish a beautiful, innocent girl because one of your boy toys fancies her. Punish Dan."

"It will be good for you as well. Self-discipline, Archer. Wait a minute. Did you call her beautiful? Surely, she isn't more beautiful than me. She's a mortal."

He shrugged.

"Archer?" I pressed.

"You're my mother. I can't look at you like that. But Ma, she's the most beautiful being I have ever—"

"That's it!" I'd had enough. "I leave tomorrow to deal with our dysfunctional family. When I get back, I expect that vile little creature to be in love with Vinnie."

THE IMMORTAL TRANSCRIPTS: QUIVER

I put his dinner in front of him and stormed into my room, so he couldn't protest. The thought of Callie and Vinnie made me smile. I brushed my hair a hundred strokes like I did every night, thinking the entire time of beautiful Callie with pompous, pimple-faced, pedantic, halitosis Vinnie. He was one of the boys who should've been humble about his awkward face, bony weak frame, horrific skin and breath—one would cringe to gaze upon him. However, he thought of himself as a lady-killer, thought he was Zeus's gift to mankind. The thought of him and little "innocent" Callie gave me shivers of pleasure.

CHAPTER 7

I hadn't seen such drama as that created by Callie, since the Middle Ages. Back then, it had been Aroha who—per usual—kicked up all the fuss, creating commotion where, before, all had been calm. Perhaps I lingered all these years with her and Archer because it was entertaining. Something always happened with Aroha around. This year had great promise of turmoil concerning, of course, the drama queen herself but Archer as well. The god of love in love? It was too ironic. But I had to admit, there was something about Callie, an uncanny attraction that drew me in inexplicably. I wasn't quite infatuated, but highly intrigued. Her character demanded that attention. Callie was as beautiful as a goddess yet, being mortal, was modest, humble, shy, and the terrible situation with her father gave her a grave, mature air of solemnity that improved her appeal. What really added to her character was her innate confidence. She could look the gods in the eye as an equal and did not turn into a giggling mess or swoon when we spoke to her like most mortal girls. Yes, her beauty turned my head, but her personality made me stare. It was easy to see why Archer was falling victim to her natural charms. It was as if his own weapons had been turned against him. Everything about us gods was molded to attract women, and now things were reversed for him. For both of us. I couldn't remember the last mortal woman who interested me the way Callie did. Mila, my latest mortal conquest, had quickly become a distant memory.

Lunch was relaxing without Aroha's now blatant jealousy of Callie. Aroha had gone to speak to Zeus about Ares, and I desperately hoped they'd reunite, and Aroha would stay away from New York. Frankly, the immature games she played to gather her mortal worshippers was plain sad. But Archer had much more reason to fear her return than I had. How deep and complex that fear ran, I didn't know, but I noticed a jumpy edge to him. My curiosity grew, along with concern for one of my oldest and best friends.

"What's up, Archer?" I asked. We were on the way to fourth period.

"What do you mean?"

"You're jumpy, nervous, worried. You were practically wringing off that poor girl's hand at lunch," I told him.

"Was I?" he asked, his mind elsewhere. He ran his hand through his hair with a sigh, making it stick up. "Lucien, I can't tell you what I've done because you won't be able to hide it from her. I'm not listening to Aroha anymore."

I stopped walking. The prophecy came slamming back at me, and my mind recalled the images. I saw Archer again, screaming, fire, and Callie. I hadn't recognized her when I'd dreamt it, not knowing her in person yet, but it was unlike me not to realize it had been her once I met her. But how? But why? I couldn't fathom how one mortal girl would change the immortal world forever. "Love," the oracle had told me. I thought she had meant figurative, that through love the world would change, but what if the coded message had meant Love personified, as in Archer? Now figuring out who in Hades this girl was had become paramount.

I masked my concern but was freaking out inside. He had to listen to Aroha. It should be impossible for him to ignore her demands.

I lowered my voice and spoke too quickly and quietly for mortal ears to register. "You mean you stopped obeying her? How...I mean, how is that possible?"

Archer was supposed to follow Aroha's orders. When one of our superiors—superior as in a parent or an elder—makes a command of us, we cannot easily ignore them. Yes, there are some small loopholes, but most of the time, Archer had to obey us previous generations of gods. The older we become, the stronger our blood becomes, and the harder we are to disobey. None of us, even the oldest blooded, including the surviving Titans, could defy a direct order from Zeus. He held a power over all of us that we could not fully understand. The god of gods answered to no one.

"I don't know exactly. Sometimes I can disobey if her choices are selfish," he explained.

Well, that was pretty often, but I held my tongue on that. "I see where this might be going." I put my hand up to stop him. Once he told me the truth, I'd be unable to hide it; assumptions were safe from Aroha's probing questions, and when Aroha got to cross-examining, she was relentless as Socrates crossed with Poirot.

What Archer was cryptically telling me was that Aroha most likely wanted Callie to be in love with someone else, and knowing Aroha, she'd chosen someone awful. Plus, it was obvious from Dan's pathetic lamentations over Aroha's absence that Archer had made him in love with her. It was a killing-two-birds-with-one-stone situation: Dan would forget about Callie, and him liking Aroha would appease her forever-ravenous ego. It wouldn't work, but I didn't have the heart to tell Archer. Aroha's fury was not something I wanted to witness.

"Hell hath no fury like a woman scorned," I warned Archer about his mother.

"I swear she is descended from a fury." Furies, or Erinyes, which was what we originally called them, are awful beings from Tartarus, which is not a part of the Underworld any god wants to enter. Not at all something he should liken to his mother.

"Stop insulting your mother." I commanded him, testing him to see how much he could disobey.

He opened his mouth but then closed it, his eyes full of anger. "I hate it when you do that."

"What?" I played dumb. But I was relieved. He couldn't disobey me. All was still right with the world. I'd try to forget the prophecy for now. It was insane to think some mortal girl could change the world, our world, which had been the same for thousands of years.

"Pull the seniority card on me." Then he sighed and gave me a hopeful grin. "I need you to go to the movies with me and Callie tonight."

"No, I'm not playing the third wheel." I'd sell my soul to Hades rather than be alone with them, but I also couldn't tell him all my reservations about Callie. He never understood the prophecies—it freaked him out that I relied on them when I was unsure where they came from. At least, that was what I told the others. They'd be unnerved if I told them of my dreams. Ghosts from the Elysian fields haunting me in my sleep was not something I wanted to share, even with my best friend. Somehow, the Fates always allowed me this one lie. I never had to divulge where the prophecies came from; it seemed dreams weren't part of truth's domain.

"No, I mean say you're going and then cancel. I can't ask her to go alone with me, can I?" He was fidgeting.

"I can't lie," I reminded him.

"You can to a mortal."

"I don't want to. Don't get angry with me. I need to know the truth if I am going to support you with this. Did you make Callie love you? Have you—"

"Did I shoot her? No!" According to the expression on his face, I was mentally unhinged for the mere suggestion.

"I had to check. Seriously, do you really like this one?"

"Yes," he said with such conviction that I had no choice but to believe him.

"Then forget the binding nonsense. Be with her. Bind her to you. You can give her around ten years."

"Then what?" Archer gave me a look of horror at the mere thought of only a decade. It was beyond anything I understood. He was so pathetic and intense when in love, so sickening to me, that I could hardly stand him. At least, he had been with Psyche in the beginning. I really hadn't seen him in love since. Aroha would claim Archer was a true lover and that I was a chauvinist afraid of commitment. What did she know? She was more in love with herself than with anyone else. She whined all the time about Ares loving war more than her, when all she had to do was take a glimpse in the mirror to see she was the same. If I let myself ponder too long on my fellow immortals, I would get depressed again. This was a long existence. Sometimes bitterly long.

"Then you'll have to leave her," I told him. "That's the way it works. I forget how you never fall in love."

"And what if I don't leave?" His jaw set defiantly.

I gave his shoulder a squeeze. "Archer, you'll have to. She'll find out something is up if you don't age, and you can't tell her the truth. Remember Semele?" I tried to warn him that this might go horribly wrong on him. The prophecy showed me as much.

"Dionysus's mom? I don't remember her personally, no." He was younger than Dionysus, so the thick sarcasm was not lost on me.

"Quit being a smartass. You remember the legend?"

"Hera tricked the mortal woman into asking Zeus to reveal his true identity after he had sworn on the Styx, and he was forced to destroy her." Archer mumbled. He sensed a big lecture was coming.

One does not swear on the Styx lightly. Archer summed up a serious affair in one sentence, but it was much more complicated than that. Zeus was forced to destroy Semele, even though he loved her more than anything. She beheld him in "all his glory," which killed her. No human can withstand the full brunt of our powers. The mortal mind is unable to handle it, and sometimes their hearts cease to beat, but it all depends on what kind of powers we are predisposed with. I most likely would blind someone, like staring directly into the sun during a partial solar eclipse. We constantly hold back our powers to protect mortals.

"I'm not going to be stupid enough to swear on the Styx." Archer rolled his eyes. He had no trouble acting like a mortal teen, being spoiled and pampered his entire life. He was Zeus's favorite grandchild, or at least, that's how it looked to all of us.

"You don't have to mess up that drastically to get her destroyed. No one can know about us. The rules are there for a reason. Just be careful, be guarded, and see how things pan out. You met her a week ago. Stop getting so ahead of yourself." I should have told him about the prophecy, but how could I if I couldn't fully decode it?

He gave me a bitter smile. "Yeah."

"And watch the father. The mythologist who has bred her to know all of ancient Greek history? Do not let them figure out anything." Of course, he picked the worst human possible to be with, who knew all about us, possibly even that we were real. I began to wonder if that was the answer. If Callie found out who we were, Zeus would smite her, and if Archer were truly in love, would he dare to avenge her? But how could he? Zeus was more powerful than five of us put together. Just ask the Titans in the Underworld.

No, there was more. There had to be. Sometimes Zeus let a mortal or two into our world as long as they told no one else. It was a way to get new blood into our family tree by making the demigod from such a union immortal. Some of us—degradingly so—referred to them as "hybreeds," a crossbreed of human and god. This was where Dionysus, Athena, and various others came from, including the rest of Aphrodite's love retinue, who had been left behind with Zeus. Archer scoffed. "How could a mortal ever find out about us?"

"Dr. Syches. The name sounds familiar. I don't know why," I mused. I'd have to Google him later. "Be careful, Archer. Zeus could kill her if she or her dad finds out." I could do no more without telling him about the prophecy.

After school, I searched the parking lot for Archer. He was sitting on the hood of his BMW, driving today, which was unlike him. Bet he did to show off for Callie. I met up with him to find him all smiles, completely untroubled, unlike earlier.

"What's with the mood swing?"

"It's just a beautiful day." He said simply. He smiled, shifting his gaze to the school.

I turned to see Callie enter the sunlight, scanning the parking lot and shading her eyes. Beautiful was an understatement. She spotted Archer and came over to us, only having eyes for him. Did I dare ask him again if he shot her with an arrow last period? Could he be that selfish?

"Hey, can I have a ride again?" she asked Archer.

"Sure, but I'm headed to the movies," he said slyly.

"What are you seeing?"

"Dunno yet," he shot back with a grin.

I shifted my weight to my other foot uncomfortably.

"You going?" She turned her attention to me.

"Uh...wasn't planning on it." I decided not to play into Archer's game of lying to her, then standing them up.

"So, who's all going?" she asked, beginning to get confused.

"You, if you come with me," he said.

"Are you asking me to go to the movies with you?" she asked shyly, biting her lower lip. She was utterly adorable. I was beginning to see why he was having so much trouble leaving her alone. There was this mysterious magnetism.

"I'm inviting Lucien as well but fully intend to tell him the wrong place and time," he said to her, winking.

"Ha, ha. I don't want to go." I could kill him sometimes. Normally, I wouldn't care if he'd make himself look better at my expense, but with Callie, it felt different. I was actually embarrassed. I cared how this mortal viewed me. I could see it already. The way Aroha, Archer, and I were responding to her was already changing us, our dynamic, and how we related to one another. I didn't understand why, but I had to figure out who she was, and by doing so, I could solve this mystery.

"So just me and you then?" she asked, not understanding how difficult she was making it for Archer.

I suppressed a smile, gloating over his struggle.

"Where did I say I was going?" Archer played dumb.

"The movies." Callie's brow wrinkled, not understanding why he was behaving so oddly.

"So, you're asking me to go to the movies then?" he asked, following it up by giving her the smoldering look mortals swooned over, while trying to suppress a smile. It was creepy how it drew them in. But she didn't crumble into the blubbering mess most girls did when we gazed upon them. I found this interesting and unnerving, but Archer didn't notice.

"I thought you were asking me, but if it helps, I'll ask you," she toyed back in a flirtatious banter, finally catching onto his game.

"It helps tremendously." He grinned.

"Can I go to the movies with you then?" she said, blushing, embarrassed. She was playing his game without understanding why.

"Thought you'd never ask." He put his arm around her shoulder, pulling her closer.

Archer then glanced at me, eyes questioning, wanting to see if he was safe. He was being careful. She had asked him out first. Now he could ask her anything—well, almost anything—without binding her to him.

I gave him the nod. "Well, I'll see you later then." I excused myself.

As I walked away, I heard Archer ask her, "What do you want to see?"

I didn't listen for the answer but walked on. I couldn't help but feel alone now. Archer's sudden discovery of happiness made me yearn for my own. This did nothing to improve my depressed and troubled spirit.

My mood sank lower, as it always does when night approaches. Obviously, I adore the light. The sunlight promotes truth; under the cover of dark, metaphorically and physically, lies breed. I was stronger in the sun. Like a plant, it was food to my flesh. But it wasn't just darkness that made my mood sink. I had nothing to do. No Archer. No Aroha. I never realized how much I had depended on them during the last century, and only days ago, I had thought of leaving them. Worst of all, I had no one to share this mystery with.

I settled down to my duty much earlier than I normally would. I sat at my desk, took out my laptop, and scoured news headlines from today, from all around the world and in multiple languages. I searched for infamous court cases. Not much new caught my attention as I speed-read through over a hundred websites, just a few small cases and crimes the humans could deal with themselves. I took out my list, added a few cases that needed watching over—guilty people where everyone knew it. Usually, the evidence was so overwhelming against the accused, the mortals could manage justice without immortal influence, but as seen in the past, this assumption was wrong often enough.

The top of my list needed attending to. A child's murder in France where the man might be let off because his wife was going to testify as his alibi. Without her, the evidence was more than enough to convict him, but she was ready to perjure herself to protect him. I couldn't take the chance. Truth would prevail as long as I existed.

I was surprised Athena hadn't stepped in yet on this case. Our line of work brought us constantly together, figuratively that is. I would expose the truth, she would force justice, and one didn't work without the other: *veritas est aequitas*—truth is justice—meaning that truth exposed brings justice to the people. It was the motto I adopted when we lived in Rome. Athena and I had a brief courtship during the Roman Empire, if I could even call it that. It never progressed. Athena was a lover of the mind and soul, not the body, but she had taught me to view women differently. Back then, men barely regarded women as people, and Athena proved them all wrong. I was a man, though, and I still needed the body. A brilliant mind is a brilliant mind, while a brilliant body is...well...enough said. Basically, Athena might still be a virgin, and as much as I should respect that—over thousands of years of celibacy? Yeah, not me, no way. That's crazy. I'm lucky if I leave mortal girls alone for a year.

I focused back on my work. In France, I found Madame Pinchet at home, restlessly attempting to sleep. I pictured myself in her mind and was there. "You will tell the truth tomorrow," I commanded her.

She sat up in bed, shocked, searching for the source of the unseen voice.

"This is your conscience speaking. You will tell the truth or suffer the consequences. Think of that child. Your husband is guilty."

"He's guilty," she repeated in a trance.

I left her mind.

"He deserves to die. I'm not going to jail for him," she murmured as she turned over in her bed. Madame Pinchet was quickly fast asleep, the arms of truth soothing her into a peaceful slumber. It had set her free, and she would do the right thing tomorrow. It always worked, mortals' minds being so malleable.

Back in New York, I continued to promote truth where needed. I kept an eye on criminals, helped the police find leads, and exposed cheaters, thieves, and liars; basically, I did all I could to make the mortals honest people and expose those who were incapable of telling the truth. There were so many lies and injustices breeding around the city that Athena must not have visited the US in a while. I wondered what she was up to and where she was in the world.

It was late when I gave up for the night. I went to bed, but despite being tired, I didn't fall asleep. My mind wondered about Archer and how his date with Callie had gone. I couldn't help my curiosity as it strayed toward truth-seeking, and I found myself in Callie's room, mentally that is. She was fast asleep, a small smile playing on her face. Satisfied, I returned to my own room—admittedly, after I watched her sleep for a while. I fell asleep thinking of her.

I woke up the next day with two problems: first, the realization that I had developed a full-fledged crush on Callie, and second, an awful stomachache of guilt. How could I be so weak to let myself fall victim to a mortal, especially one my best friend was hopelessly falling in love with? Another thought crossed my mind as I lay in bed feeling terrible: perhaps there was something special about Callie we were seeing, something otherworldly that drew us in? Because I'm the god of truth, because I was irrevocably drawn in, I needed answers. There had to be a reason we felt this way about her, and I bet it had everything to do with the prophecy.

I decided to call out sick from school, pretending to be my overworked absentee dad, so I could find some answers and, more importantly, not to face Archer. I was afraid he'd see through me and get angry. Our friendship had gone through a lot in the last couple thousand years, but we'd never had issues over a girl before. He'd been as cold-blooded as Athena when it came to passion for ages now, and I would never have called us good friends during his first millenium when he had been in love.

After I called out sick, I wasted no time. I flipped open my laptop and went online. I set to my first task: finding out who Callie's dad was. I Googled "Sikes" and then "Sykes," searching for that old-fashioned Anglo-Saxon name, but nothing pertaining to Callie or her father cropped up. I tried to remember how she spelled her name, but over the short duration she had been here, I'd never watched her write it. I hacked into the school's database quickly and pulled up the school rosters. That's when I found it and saw it was spelled strangely: S-y-c-h-e-s. I felt a chill go down my spine for some reason, and my mind made a connection to a long-dead goddess. Surely, I was making leaps here in logic, no?

I let it go and Googled her father with the proper spelling and first found internet companies, and then a yellow page site for Syches Incorporated. I clicked on it. The company was a restoration service involved in the buying and selling of antiquities, which was owned by a David N. Syches. I got wrapped up in reading his biography and achievements. He had published dozens of articles and a few scholarly-sounding books. Just as Callie had said, they were all based on Ancient Greece and mythology from different lands. The bio said he was currently expanding an article, "Mythology or History? What Artifacts Are Really Telling Us about Greek Gods" into a full-length book. Was he really implying the gods existed? How much did he know or assume? This did not bode well for Archer. He would have to hide everything from this man. And mortal men are extremely observant when it comes to evaluating their daughters' boyfriends. I know from experience.

The site also mentioned Callie as the sole survivor of Dr. Syches's family. No other directly related Syches were alive, which might make tracing Callie's ancestors pretty straightforward. It also mentioned his illness. Even I, as a god of healing and father of medicine, could not cure him. The illness had all the tell-tale signs of godly influence—most likely, Zeus was trying to silence him. I would not doubt it from the amount of information Dr. Syches could have if he surmised our existence. The only reason, perhaps, that he was still alive was the fact there wasn't proof out there. We gods cleaned up after ourselves these days. We avoided photos when possible—an ever-increasing problem in the digital age—avoided any careers dealing with fame, and had to use aliases and avatars if we made online accounts of any sort.

I saved Dr. Syches's website to my favorites and planned to use his full name instead of Callie's for my genealogy search. I went to the Mormon website I found most useful in researching genealogy—you have to hand it to the Mormons, they keep some of the best records in the world. It was a website I always used to keep track of my little mistakes. I'm not that bad, not like Zeus; in fact, I'm very careful about things, but one does tend to fall for women several times over all of eternity, and with that comes marriages and children. I only had one living mortal child left, if you could call him that since he was middle aged now, but all my past children had had children, and so on and so on. I had a few immortal children as well, but that is an entirely different story.

Aroha hardly ever had to keep track of these things because immortal women were not as fecund as mortal ones, but when in a scrape, she gave her children away. I was more responsible and always kept a guardian's eye out for my descendants. Archer, on the other hand, somehow had no living offspring with mortals or goddesses, which I found irritatingly moral.

On the genealogy website, I was successful in finding Callista Ellen Syches, daughter of David Nelson Syches and Ellen Thea Corbitt Syches. I traced Dr. Syches's lineage and was surprised at how far back the records went. Records began, or shall I say ended, with his ancestor Marshal's death in Massachusetts Bay Colony. The only other record I could find was Marshal's marriage to an Émilie Jacques in France. But everyone must be born. Although birth certificates weren't issued back then, churches kept punctilious accounts of baptisms. An hour search yielded nothing, so I tried alternate spellings. What I found made my skin crawl: in 1571, a Marshal Psyches had been baptized at a Grâce de Dieu orphanage.

I shut the computer down, feeling even more ill. The earliest Syches, who actually was born as Psyches, was left in 1571 in a French orphanage. The spelling of Psyches, and how it was pronounced in French, as a nod to the goddess Psyche could not be pure coincidence. Had Psyche herself given birth to the child and bestowed upon him that name in hopes one of us would one day find him? If so, the child, Marshal, was not fully a deity, or we would have known of his existence, and he wouldn't have died decades later as the records stated. Callie's ancestor could possibly be Psyche's child with a mortal man. His changing his name's spelling before his marriage was highly suspicious. I tried to remember that far back into the past. Psyche was killed in the witch hunts, along with Hedone, her and Archer's only child. After their deaths, I returned to Archer's side, but he hadn't been with Psyche in the end. They had separated roughly two thousand years prior to her death.

One thing was clear: Callie was possibly Psyche's descendant. The thing that wasn't clear at all was whether to tell Archer about it. How would it help him to open old wounds? But was it right to hide the fact he might be falling for perhaps the last fragment on earth of his once-beloved Psyche? Was it this and this alone that made him love Callie? If so, was that fair to Callie?

I needed tangible facts. I'd go to France. I'd find out everything I possibly could before I told anyone anything. Absolute truth was necessary.

CHAPTER 8

Callie

The messages from my Somerset friends began to dwindle. It was less their fault than mine because everything in New York was new and exciting or equally stressful and depressing, and they were always talking about stuff I had already done or didn't care much about. I didn't want to lose them but was at a loss of how to keep the connection going. If I lost old friends, I would need to make new ones, so I invited Linda and Emily over after school a couple days that first week, even though I wanted to hang out with Archer and his clique. I didn't want to become one of those girls in my old high school who obsessed over a guy and ignored her friends completely. If I dated him (like I desperately wished to), I didn't want to lose my friends. If it ended badly (ugh, I would die), then I'd have no friends left.

So here I was with the two of them after turning down poor Archer, who had tried to get me to go shoot pool with them all before. Emily filled me in on gossip about everyone at school. Linda filled me in on the who's who in family circuits in the Upper East Side. I never realized there were such politics and schmoozing in high school society. I could tell Linda was a socialite, and I thought the Ambroses would be as well, but Linda said they kept to themselves. Apparently, it was all about parental connections, and Archer's parents were consistently MIA.

It was fun hanging out with them that first week, but then something profound happened. Archer asked me out, for real, to the movies. Only, he didn't actually do the asking. He spun circles around me and made me ask him (weird, but it got the job done).

And here I was, in a darkened theater with the most attractive boy I had ever seen, feeling a little guilty about not spending time with my dad. My father had insisted I go, and I was glad because there was no way I wanted to cancel on Archer. Dad wanted me to have as normal a life as possible. I should have been in complete bliss, but I felt rotten. I could hardly pay attention to the cheesy love story's plot. They're all the same, though: boy and girl meet; they fall in love; some kind of crisis or deception occurs; they forgive each other and live happily ever after. None of that ever seems to happen in real life. In life, there are no endings—you can't just stop life at the happiest moment. Sometimes, I wish you could, but the only true ending in the story of life is death...

A soft fingertip touching the back of my hand broke me from my morbid thoughts, and I glanced over to Archer. He peeked at me slyly from the corner of his eye, not paying any attention to the movie either. His perfectly sculpted lips curled up in a mischievous grin, dimples exposed briefly (how had I missed those puppies?).

I peered down to see his index finger brushing the back of my hand. I didn't want him to stop, so I flipped my hand over to force him to touch my palm. He intertwined his fingers in mine, holding my hand gently. I met his gaze, and his hand tightened on mine. His eyes flickered to and danced across my face, and his other hand reached across and gently touched my cheek. I thought he might kiss me then and there, but his smile faded, his hand smoothed my hair back, and he tore his gaze back to the screen. The tension was excruciating, at least for me. He, on the other hand, was a mystery to me. I just couldn't read him as well as other people, not yet, at least.

I thought he liked me: the way he looked at me, lighting up with a smile (as I did) when we saw each other, the flirting, compliments he gave me, handholding, an occasional touch of my hair, my face, a half hug. Yet with all these flirtations, nothing seemed to progress between us. It was like he was awaiting something or hesitating for some reason. Don't get me wrong; it wasn't as if I wanted to tap that right away. Well, that's a lie. I should rephrase—I *wouldn't* do that. All I wanted was a kiss, to know how he felt, to have him ask me to be exclusive. Was that too much to ask? After all, it had only been a week, but it felt like much longer. Archer understood me instantly, better than anyone I had ever known. It sounded peculiar, but we had a strong connection, that if he would just let me in a little more, then I could read him like a book with my uncanny intuition. However, I had no idea what made him act the way he did: so distant yet so drawn to me, fighting off the very urges that were natural for two people who are falling in love to feel.

I heard him sigh deeply with a hint of frustration in his breath. He flipped up the armrest that separated us, put his arm around my waist, and pulled me snug against his side. I felt his oddly sweet-scented breath curl around my ear; he was that close. If I turned...he'd have to kiss me. My heart skipped a beat, and I froze. I couldn't move an inch. My stomach fluttered, full of butterflies. I willed myself to turn, but my body didn't respond to the command.

"Callie?" his voice broke in its whisper.

"Hmm?" was all I could get out.

"I'm not sure how much more I can endure," he said quietly, his hands gripping me tightly, one around my waist, the other on my hand. Archer's hands were clammy and warm. He was nervous as well.

"Endure?" was all I could ask, still insecurely hesitant. Did he mean the movie? Or did he feel (as I did) that he might burst at any moment unless he could kiss me? I was powerless to control the turmoil of feelings and urges echoing through my frame.

"Can you?" he asked cryptically. His nose burrowed under my jawline where it met my ear. Goosebumps spread down that side of my body.

"No," I breathed so quietly, I wasn't sure if he heard me at all.

"Neither can I," he whispered in my neck, his lips against me, but he applied no pressure. I couldn't qualify it as a real kiss (oh, but I wanted to).

I turned my body slightly to him, which made his hands grip tighter, almost painfully on me. Archer backed away, his eyes ablaze with what seemed like an intense I-want-to-kiss-you-damn-it look. I swore his eyes were aglow, but it must have been a trick of the light, a reflection from the screen. He let go of me, grabbed my face in his hands, and brought his lips closer with a struggling pant. His breath was sweet like honeysuckles. My mother popped into my mind (freakin' inappropriate and weird), but I banished her, focusing on the adorable boy who was about to kiss me. I closed my eyes, awaiting our first kiss, but instead, his hands tightened and pushed me away gently.

My eyes shot open. What had I done wrong? Did my breath smell? It couldn't. I still had gum in my mouth. Archer had his face in his hands, his body tense. What had happened to make him go from wanting to kiss me to bugging out like he was?

"Archer?"

"I'm sorry. I really am," he murmured. Then he stood up, took my hand, and pulled me up with ease. "Let's go." It wasn't a question or a suggestion, but a command.

Shocked and confused, I allowed him to lead me out of the theater, even though the movie wasn't over. Once we were outside, I stopped, which pulled Archer off balance and against me.

His hands gripped my waist for balance, and he stared down at me with a torn expression. I couldn't deny the oddity of his eyes now that we were outside. They shone as if the sunlight was in them, brighter than usual, and I couldn't blame it on the lighting or the movie screen this time.

I dared to reach out and touch his cheek. He pressed his cheek against my hand, closing his eyes with a ragged sigh. Then he pulled me into a tight hug, his warm body pressing against mine. So many sensations and images flittered through my mind. I had to focus before I forgot what I was about to say. Being a head taller than me, he rested his chin on my head.

"Archer," I murmured in his chest.

"I can't." His voice choked. What was he trying to tell me? He couldn't...what? It was obvious he wanted to kiss me, and that wasn't some dreamed-up fabrication of an overactive mind. He was fighting so hard not to give in, it was now obvious what he truly wanted.

He let go of me, took up my hand, and led me toward the parking lot. The moment was leaving us. He had denied what he wanted to do, what I wanted him to do, and I refused to leave without some answers as to why.

"Can't what?" I tried to hide how terrified I was of what he meant, unable to conquer the growing insecurities in my mind. Can't like me? Can't date me? Can't be with me?

"Kiss you," he said simply, not looking at me, but staring straight ahead. "I want to," he said wryly. "Trust me, I *really* want to, but..." Shock spread across his face as if he realized he said too much.

"But what?" I asked.

He opened the passenger door of his car for me and left me standing there as he headed to his side and climbed in without a word. He was buying time.

"But what?" I pressed, being firm after I climbed in.

He started the car and pulled out quickly. "You wouldn't understand," he muttered. It was obvious he was hiding something from me.

I wasn't about to let this go. It was a wall between us, one I couldn't see through to truly understand him. "Try me. After *that*, what happened in there, I deserve some kind of explanation. Do you have a girlfriend already or something?"

"No," he said firmly. His eyes flickered to me, probing, searching for something on my face before his gaze darted back to the road. As soon as he pulled out onto a main road, we were stuck in traffic, hardly moving.

"Then..." I tried to urge him.

"Callie, you can't possibly understand what I'm thinking."

"Try me," I challenged.

Archer was taken aback by my tenacity. This time, his stare rested on mine. I met his gaze steadily, trying to appear firm but understanding. He gripped the wheel tightly, taking his frustration out on the steering wheel, and sighed deeply. His eyes were dimming, the light beginning to fade from them.

"It's against the rules, kissing you." His face reddened, his eyes focused on the slow-moving traffic. After such a weird statement, he didn't dare look at me.

"The rules?" I asked skeptically. A strange Kool-Aid-drinking cult came to mind.

"Yes. You have to kiss me first. I can't make the first move."

Now I was confused. He hadn't fully answered my question. "Whose rules are these?" I decided to play along with his explanation to get the details before I judged him.

Archer's face screwed up in indecision: he was choosing what to tell me, what to hide. He was serious about these silly rules, but I was lost as to why there was such a high need for secrecy.

"Call them self-imposed if you must," he growled, beginning to get frustrated.

"Any other *rules* I should know about?" I countered mockingly.

"I won't ask you out either. That's up to you."

This was ridiculous. "You're right. I don't understand you. You appear all old-fashioned and chivalrous—"

"Old-fashioned." He laughed dryly.

"And then you want some ultra-modern woman who has to make all the moves?"

"You understand me much better than you think," he said quietly.

"It doesn't fit."

The car was stiflingly silent for a moment.

"I'll take you home then," he said, defeated. I could tell he wouldn't explain any further. His voice and eyes were extremely sad and solemn. I could tell I would have to let it go for now, or he'd never talk to me again. The thought of that frightened me; he had become the only light in my dark world right now. Moronically, I'd allowed myself to depend on him. It wasn't like me, but here I was (stupid girl).

"I didn't say that," I told him, crossing my arms. I was a little upset and very confused, but I still wanted to be with him.

Archer looked over at me, surprised. His eyes melted whatever anger I had. He reached over and touched my cheek with the back of his index finger, "I really want this to work, Callie. Forgive my eccentricities?"

I nodded, hoping I could forgive them. He changed the subject, and I spinelessly let him. I'd figure him out somehow, but now wasn't the time to press.

He took me to a tiny hole-in-the-wall restaurant that, from the outside, appeared shady but, inside, was beautiful and elegant.

"You like Greek food?" he asked as we entered.

"Yee-aas." I hesitated.

"But?"

"Authentic or Americanized?"

"As authentic as you can get in America. If you tell me you've been to Greece, I'm walking out that door." He didn't believe that I knew about Greece or about their food.

"But I have."

His mouth dropped.

I added, "For a bit," to downplay the fact that a portion of my childhood had been spent there after my mother died.

Archer spun on his heel and made a beeline for the door. I hurried after him and grabbed his arm to stop him from leaving, shocked he was going through with his goofy threat. He whirled around, capturing me in his arms, and stared down at me. "I like that." I wished I knew what he was thinking, what he meant by that comment.

A man came out from behind the counter. "Archer, geia! Kalós óra kalí!" I recognized the Greek greeting.

Archer let go of me and shook the man's hand. "Kai esý."

"Any seat in the house." He motioned for us to take a seat in his thick accent, switching to English for me. He and Archer made a few more comments in Greek, but they spoke so fast, I could only catch a couple of words here and there such as "gorgeous," "lamb chops," and "beautiful girl." I needed to brush up on listening to Greek. It was simple enough on the page, but aloud at that pace...

Archer chose a comfy booth in the back of the little restaurant. The place was empty, but it wasn't primetime dinner hour because we had left the movie so early.

"You speak Greek?" I asked him. "Now *I* like that."

He looked at me, confused.

"You can tutor me."

"You're taking Greek?" He stifled a laugh.

"To make my dad happy. He still thinks I will follow in his footsteps one day: archaeology in Greece and Rome."

"But you don't want to?"

"Chasing the unknowable past always seemed to be a waste of time to me," I explained. *But I can't tell him that.*

"Is that why you went to Greece? Archaeology?" he asked, extremely interested.

"Yes. It was fun as a child, I have to admit."

The same man came over to take our order.

"Do you like lamb?" Archer asked me. "They have the most amazing *kléftiko* here."

"I trust you," I told him. "As long as we save room for some *baklavá*."

Archer ordered two *kléftiko* dishes, which I assumed were lamb—as long as it wasn't eel or octopus, I'd be content. The man smiled widely and left us to it. People began to trickle in.

"Where were we?" Archer pondered casually. "Oh yes. Where did you go in Greece?"

"Gosh, all over. Macedonia as well," I told him.

"What was he looking for, your father?" Archer seemed to slightly lose interest and was now merely making polite conversation. His mind was half with me and half someplace else. He nervously picked at a roll.

"Okay, well, don't laugh. We were at Oros Olimbos," I said, trying to fake the accent properly.

Archer almost choked on his water. "Mount Olympus?" He coughed. His full attention was back on me, those eyes probing, measuring me.

"You know Greece well. He was searching for the palace of the Olympian gods," I explained, not wanting him, of all people, to laugh at my father as well. In a way, I was testing him, which wasn't very fair, but Dad was the most important person in my life. I couldn't date a guy who could laugh at my dad.

"Did he find it?" Archer studied me, his expression blank, masked, trying not to react—trying not to laugh most likely.

"That's odd."

"What?"

"Most people laugh. Mount Olympus is a myth."

"Then he didn't find anything?" he concluded wrongly.

"No, he did. Took him half my life to find something, but he did. Inside Mitikas, the highest peak, he found the opening into a very ancient settlement. Of course, there's no way to *prove* who it belonged to, but he's trying to."

"How does one go about finding something that no one has found, even when they searched for it for thousands of years?" Archer raised his eyebrows. He was interested again and a bit shocked.

"It was well concealed."

"How did he find it then?"

"Well, technically, he didn't." I smiled at him. "I did. I was eight."

"That sounds like a fascinating story." He eagerly awaited more.

"Well, we were camped out at the mountain range, and my father left me with the helpers as he went up in search of the entrance. Obviously, I couldn't go all the way up with him because of the altitude—he had to use oxygen and everything. He left me a little archaeology set, an old worn one of his, and I was simply playing. I chiseled away at the ground, not knowing that below me was hollow. It caved in, and I fell into a cavern, which ended up being the foyer to a large palace-type dwelling inside the mountain.

"You see, he was looking for an entrance up in the clouds. I was playing where a cloud was carved into a crag. The entrance in myths was supposed to be in the clouds, see, but it wasn't."

"You fell into Mount Olympus? You stood where the gods had?" Archer laughed tightly, picking at the roll with his fingers more anxiously and shaking his head in disbelief.

Now I felt stupid. He was only keeping his laughter at bay, and here would be the ridicule of my poor father and I.

"I never said it *was* the house of the gods!" The anger leaked into my voice.

Archer's smile dropped. "I'm sorry. I do believe you."

"No, you don't. You're laughing at me."

"No," he said quickly, reaching across the table to take my hand in his. "I believe you. I have family from Litochoro, and myths are very important there. Some still believe them," he told me, mentioning the name of the town at the base of Oros Olimbos. Then he let go of my hand quickly. "Obviously, they're mythological, and that must've just been some ancient settlement, though. Did he share his findings with anyone?"

Archer met my gaze, and he was challenging me to say the truth. I wanted to tell him my father's harebrained ideas, but I didn't like Archer's cold, calculated change in tone. He was shutting me out and trying to get me to admit the truth. I felt protective of my dad.

"Of course, it was just an ancient settlement," I scoffed.

"Did he share them?" Archer pressed, his face tight. I didn't like the way he was pressing for answers. And why? If he wasn't going to laugh, why did he want to know if Dad believed in the gods or not?

"The Aegis is in the British museum, thanks to him."

"The Aegis?" Archer asked, shifting his posture.

"I thought you knew all about mythology."

"I said I knew myths were important to people in Litochoro."

"So, you're Greek?" I asked him.

"Yes," he said hesitantly. "Family from all over the country. Crete, Athens, but Litochoro mostly." He then relaxed and smiled roguishly. "I was born there, but I haven't been there in a long time."

"It's some really old shield," I told him, leaving it simple. "Tell me more about you." I was eager to change the subject.

"Like what?" he asked.

"I don't know." I felt myself blush. "What do you do when you're not showing new girls around the town?"

"Is that what you think I do?" He smirked playfully.

"Girls are crazy about you. You must've had a lot of girlfriends."

"Must I?" He laughed, surprised. "I assure you, it's quite the contrary. Let's just say I enjoy watching others fall in love rather than do it myself. I live vicariously."

That seemed a strange thing for a boy to say, but perhaps he was afraid of being hurt and didn't want to admit it.

"What about you?" He changed the subject back to me. He took my hand in both of his again, squeezing it. Then he gave me an irresistible and intense look. I couldn't say no to eyes like his.

"I had one real boyfriend a couple of years ago but more disastrous first dates that I'd rather forget."

"I hope this doesn't fall in that second group?" He suppressed a smile.

"I'll let you know," I teased.

"Did you kiss all of them on those first dates?" he asked.

"Very few of them." I tried not to laugh, seeing where his line of questioning was headed.

He sighed. "Mmm, how nice for those lucky fellows."

"I won't be kissing you tonight," I told him smartly.

"No?"

"Because I never make the first move," I bantered.

"What a shame for us then."

"I can have rules too."

"Then we're doomed."

"Unless I can make you break yours." I toyed with him, trying to be alluring, twirling my hair and biting my lip.

"I wish you wouldn't," he said solemnly, peering down to his hands. All the witty banter vanished from the room. We had just gotten back on track after the whole mythology bump in the road. His smile was too much of an asset to see him frown.

"Why *is* that?" I asked quietly.

He ignored my question, stayed silent for a moment, and then his eyes shot up at me with an evil, mischievous look, and a wicked grin spread across his lips. "I could always make you break yours," he said so sinisterly that he gave me chills (of pleasure if I'm honest) for a moment.

"We'll see." I gave him an equally wicked glare. We began to stare one another down. Then the food came, interrupting our staring contest, and we both laughed.

As he drove home, the sun began to set. Traffic was a nightmare, something I wasn't quite used to yet, but I was relieved to have more time with Archer. I felt like, when we reached the apartment building, the perfect dream I found myself in would end, and reality would come back with a large slap in the face.

"You all right? You're suddenly very quiet," Archer asked, concern in his voice. He was forced to focus on the road again as traffic crept along.

"Sorry, not ready to go back to reality yet."

"Then don't. Come over," he said.

"I should check on my father."

"He has his assistant, doesn't he?"

"I *want* to check on my father," I rephrased.

"Then invite me over." He smiled roguishly.

"Fine, come over?" I growled, having to ask again. I was sure, no matter what, that Archer would win this game. I just couldn't deny him.

"Thought you'd never ask. So, is this one of the first dates you'd want to forget?"

"Well, it's not really a 'first' date until you have a second, is it?" I teased.

"Well, we'll have to do something tomorrow so you can properly evaluate today." He smiled.

"I suppose that could be arranged." I smiled, despite the fact he had managed to ask me out again without actually asking. "Only for part of the day."

"Tired of me already?"

"No. Limited time left with my dad, remember?" I answered.

"Yes," he said quietly. "How selfish of me to take up all your time. I'll come over another time."

"No, come over. I didn't mean it like that," I said too quickly. "If there is a second date, maybe you should meet my dad."

"Should I be scared?"

"Not a mean bone in his body."

"Lucky for me then."

My dad was shocked I brought a boy home, because I never had in the past, except when he'd insisted on meeting Jack, my ex-boyfriend. My dad was nice enough to Archer. After Dad had his supper, he turned in early to do some writing. He was looking much better, to my relief, and the doctors were optimistic. I was glad the side effects had subsided.

The moment Dad had gone into his study, Archer put his arm around me and pulled me closer as he had in the movie theater. We sat watching a terrible made-for-TV movie and, as in the movie theater, his hands clamped on my shoulder and my hand. He tickled my palm, making me squirm, and instantly, he was continuing where the movie theater snuggling had left off, nuzzling his nose beneath my jawline.

I gathered up every ounce of bravery in me as his lips brushed my neck. I turned my face toward his, our cheeks touching. Archer's hand gripped my neck, and his lips pressed slightly against my cheek, close to my lips. I gasped, surprised, as every fiber in my body yearned for him to kiss my lips. His arms tightened around me, and mine instinctively pulled him closer. I felt his lips on my neck, my ear, my cheek; he wasn't technically kissing me but brushing my skin gently with his lips, which drove me crazy. Then he pulled away, my face in his hands, holding me away but still close. His glowing eyes danced across my face, and he leaned to kiss me but stopped, his thumbs gently rubbing my jaw.

"You could kiss me, you know." He breathed on my lips, his honey-sweet breath tickling me.

I leaned in closer until our lips were almost touching. "Not a chance," I whispered, not pulling away.

"Callie, you are cruel." He enunciated each word slowly and then tickled my sides, making me squeal and twitch. Archer tickled me again, and I couldn't help but quiver and flail about. Somehow, I ended up on the ground with Archer on top of me, both of us laughing.

"I think I broke my hip."

"No, it's mine that's broken." He laughed once more, and then the smile faded from his face.

Archer's expression changed drastically, his face sunk into a serious expression. His eyes bored into mine, probing, wanting to read my thoughts. I tried to understand the dozen emotions that flitted through his luminescent eyes. It was clear he wanted to kiss me, that he really did like me, and that he didn't want to abide by these foolish rules. But why keep up the pretense?

"I should go," he said, color leaching from his face as he backed away and sat up. He offered me his hand and lifted me up without making eye contact with me. The joking about kissing had gone too far, and now he was avoiding me (his stupid rules!). He headed toward the door. "I'll show myself out. I'll...call you tomorrow," he said quietly.

Before I could follow him, he was gone. I opened the door and peeked out. Archer was walking quickly away down the hall, too far away to have walked the entire way at that pace. Was he running away from me, literally? He appeared downcast and frustrated, with his head down and his hands in his pockets. I regretted it now. I'd kiss him the next time I saw him. I would forgive him for his eccentricities. I just hoped I hadn't completely blown it.

The next morning, I awoke early and made breakfast—and when I say early, I mean early—I was up by six AM on a Saturday. Dad came out in his robe, looking even better than last night.

"You look good, Dad."

"I feel good." He smiled as he answered. "And that smells good. What are you doing up so early?"

"Couldn't sleep."

"What are your plans today?" he asked, pouring himself coffee.

"I dunno. You?" I tried to act relaxed about doing something with Archer, but I knew it would drive me mad waiting for him to call. I hoped one of his rules wouldn't be the typical boy-rule of saying they'll call but waiting days to do so. I needed to see him today, but I didn't want him to realize that.

"Raphael is taking me into town, shopping. Lost too much weight, and I can hardly appear in public looking like a bum." He pointed at the baggy jeans he had on.

"Do you want me to come?" I asked.

"You're not doing anything with that nice boy today?" Dad asked, using his typical laissez-faire attitude when questioning me about my life.

He thought if he acted aloof, then I would tell him. And then there was that awful sixth sense of his: he *knew* I wanted to hang out with Archer.

"Who? Archer?" I asked, trying to act aloof myself.

"No, all the other boys you brought by." He chuckled.

"I might be if he calls me, but I can't see why we can't go shopping, and I'll do something with him later, *if* he even calls."

"Is he your boyfriend or something?"

"Dad," I groaned, not wanting to talk about boys. "Really?"

"What? He is a handsome kid, seems very nice, very mature, and polite to the old man."

"Why don't you go out with him then?" I shot back.

"Ha-ha. I approve."

"I'll tell him you said so."

"Just be safe and hard-to-get and all." Dad wore a mischievous grin, awaiting my potential outburst.

"Da-ad!" I groaned. "We are not having the sex talk again. He's not even my boyfriend yet."

"*Yet.* So, it is headed there!" he said triumphantly.

"May-be. I dunno, Dad. Just eat." I plopped the plate in front of him. Seriously, no other teenage girl had to deal with those talks from their dads. Guess they had moms, though.

I tried to stay busy all morning by unpacking the last of the boxes, cleaning, doing laundry and dishes, but I kept thinking about Archer calling. The hours ticked by so slowly. I kept checking my phone, getting annoyed that he hadn't called, and then getting annoyed at how pathetic I had become. I rearranged my closet and then showered. I'd hoped he would have called while I was in there, but he hadn't. But it was only noon. Perhaps he slept in? Perhaps he wanted to go out at night? Uuuugh! I was officially a loser in my book.

My phone came alive. I leaped at it and read the text: **What are you doing tonight? I'm having a party.** It was Emily.

I texted her back, telling her I'd let her know. Finally, around one o'clock, I decided to go shopping with my dad. A few new shirts couldn't hurt, and maybe an outfit for a future date. Dad and I were headed to the car when I realized I'd actually forgotten my cell phone after obsessing over it all morning. I had left it on the bathroom sink, hoping to hear from you-know-who while I did my makeup.

I ran back up to the apartment, grabbed my phone, and made my way back to the elevator. When it opened, two gorgeous figures almost bumped into me. It was Archer and Lucien in shorts and sneakers only, topless, with their rippling muscles exposed, making it hard for me to focus on their faces. Archer's cheeks were pink, and he wiped his face with the t-shirt in his hand, although he wasn't sweaty.

"Hi...hey," he said, trying to sidestep to let me in.

"Hey," was all I could say as I entered the elevator.

Lucien squeezed out past me with a small nod.

"Lucien and I just went for a run," Archer said, fidgeting with the shirt as he stepped out of the elevator. I tried to stare at his face and not his perfectly ripped chest or his washboard stomach. It was actually quite difficult.

"Oh, really?"

"You headed out?" he asked, concerned.

"With my dad, clothes shopping," I told him.

Then the elevator doors began to close, threatening to cut off our conversation. I pressed the open button. He was doing the same on the other side.

"I...did you still..." he stammered awkwardly.

"Yes," I told him. "Let me know."

"Callie," he said as the elevator doors began to close again. "You really are cruel." He winked right before the doors shut. My heart leaped into my throat. I was positive about one thing: I would kiss him by the end of the night if he didn't kiss me first.

CHAPTER 9

Archer

All it took was Callie's body crashing into mine, and parts of me that had been dormant for centuries came to life. I could hardly resist her any longer, and the thoughts that went with those feelings were too obscene to let myself think about them for too long. I could hardly keep my hands off her or refrain from kissing her. I was addicted. I was acting...too human. Emotions and hormones clouding every rational thought, acting more on impulses than on logical choices—none of this was me. I was beginning to understand this human trait, these human weaknesses, all over again. It had been ages since I'd felt like a mortal.

I tossed and turned all night, thinking of Callie. In between sleeplessness and thoughts of her, I worked on mortals' love lives, which frustrated me more because I wanted to work on my own instead, damn it. It had to slow down, but part of me begged to speed it up. I even mentally visited Callie once in the night, just to see her sleep, but she was wide awake, unable to get comfortable. The improper thoughts began again, so I left.

Around seven, I couldn't take lying in bed any longer, and I called Lucien. Even though the sun was already up, I had woken him. Long ago, he had learned to make the sun rise unconsciously, like breathing. I annoyed him until he agreed to go for a run to burn off my energy.

I ran into Callie and, not expecting to see her, acted like an idiot, which Lucien immediately mocked. Sometimes, I wanted to kill him. That is, if I could; we were quite difficult to kill.

"Shut it," I told him.

"You've got it bad. What are you going to do?"

I shrugged. "I could always ask Grandpa."

"You think he'd do it again?"

"I've been dutiful, and I haven't asked for anything in a long time."

"He spoils you, really." Lucien tried to mask his resentment but failed miserably.

"He'd do the same for you. You're his son after all, Uncle Phoebus," I mocked him using the part of his name he hated. Officially, he was Phoebus Apollo and my dad's half-brother. He was always bitter about how Zeus favored my dad, who was the legitimate son, over him.

"You'd shut your mouth if you had any sense left," he growled at me.

"What? You are my uncle," I countered.

"Yeah, you know she could die trying to become immortal. Ambrosia is sometimes too strong for mortal blood," he said. Drinking ambrosia is the only way for demigods to become immortal. However, it doesn't always work, and when it fails, it is fatal. The ambrosia simply attempts to bring the immortal recessive gene out, making it dominant to override the demigod's system, making them stop aging and essentially live forever. My grandfather keeps ambrosia under lock and key. Of course, he was the only one who understood the science behind it, since he tested ambrosia on himself first and created our race.

"Callie must be part god. I mean, look at her," I protested, and it wasn't merely in reference to her appearance. This immortal recessive gene had to explain the powers Callie had over me. "Maybe she's one of yours," I joked to Lucien.

"Ha, ha. She's not. Maybe she's one of yours," he shot back.

I gave him a look of disgust. "I've only ever had one child."

He examined me, most likely trying to ferret out a lie. No matter how many times he asked, he still couldn't believe it. Unlike my mother, I thrived off love. It made me stronger and made me feel complete. Lust never came to me until I was...in love. That meant I had to be in love with Callie. It had happened so fast, I hadn't recognized it.

"Aroha?" he shot out then.

Quickly, thoughts of love went to disgust. I'd have to sort out my feelings later.

"Technically, she could be your sister." Lucien was grinning as I unlocked my door.

I couldn't help but cringe. "You are really enjoying this aren't you?"

"You have no idea." He laughed.

When we entered the apartment, I heard a female voice and shuddered. Had Aroha returned already? I was counting on Dad to be more obstinate, hateful, to hold a long grudge. She was going to kill me if Callie wasn't in love with Vinnie, but I was beyond obeying anyone at this point about Callie. Even Zeus himself couldn't tear me from her.

Another female voice answered the first, then a third. It wasn't Aroha, but it was much worse. I looked at Lucien in horror. He grinned smugly and said, "You can't ignore them forever." He really enjoyed my misfortunes, the ass.

"Oooo!" a high-pitched squeal greeted me as I walked into the living room, which was brightly lit with the sun shining through the full wall of windows.

"Aglaea, Euphrosyne, Thalia. To what do I owe this pleasure?" I feigned a pleasantly surprised tone as three beauties rushed up to me. They were alike, except one was blonde, one brunette, and one a redhead. I grew nervous at the thought of the past clashing with the present. How could I hide the Charities from Callie? My old life was trying to integrate itself into my new life, and it was too dangerous for Callie to get mixed up in it all.

I glanced behind me and realized Lucien, the snake, was hiding. The only possible place was wedged between the wall and the still wide-open door.

"Oh, we couldn't stay away from you much longer," the blonde Thalia said in a blissful tone.

"We needed to see you. You always fill us with delight," redheaded Euphrosyne protested.

"You don't need me for that. You always feel ecstatic. It's your job." I sighed. "Look, I thought we all agreed to keep our separate ways for the time being."

"I told you he'd be mad," Aglaea, the beautiful brunette, scoffed, picking at her vermilion nails.

"I'm not mad. It's just not good timing." I tried to be kind. These girls were each a Charis, or together, the Charities, the goddesses of charm, beauty, and happiness, instilling these attributes into humans. The girls had been given to us to be attendants and an entourage of sorts for assistance and companionship. There were a few more in our old retinue, but a fallout many years ago broke up the group, and the other three rarely spoke to us, or more likely, they were afraid of my mother and stayed away.

"Oh, Archer, please don't send us away," Aglaea whined, trying to wrap her arms around me. I pushed her away gently, which would be almost impossible for a mortal to do since Aglaea was the embodiment of beauty, so strikingly beautiful that she drew most beings in. Grandpa originally wanted me to marry Aglaea, but I could never resign myself to be interested, despite her beauty, nor was she truly interested in me that way.

"Gimme a minute. I need a shower," I protested. I needed to buy myself time to think of an excuse to send them away.

"I'll wash you!" Euphrosyne boisterously came over to me. I had to remove her hands from my chest.

"Atlas's burden, you can't stay here. There's hardly room. Aroha will be back soon." I tried to intimidate them with the thought of Ma. The girls were always afraid to upset her, because she was so tenacious and held long grudges.

"Let us stay until then. We'll play high school too," Thalia suggested.

Lucien, who watched smugly from his hiding spot, ignored my imploring stare. He was such an ass sometimes.

"Lucien, don't be so shy. Come greet our guests," I said. "More importantly, close the door so we're not overheard."

Lucien pushed the door, slamming it closed with little effort, as he gave me a death-stare and a smirk that promised he'd retaliate someday. The girls attacked him with hugs, squeals, and kisses.

"I'm getting a shower. Have fun," I taunted Lucien. Then I hurried into my bathroom, shutting out the noise, and locked the door for good measure. I took a long shower to digest the fact I had to deal with part of our love entourage.

When I came back, Lucien had ironed everything out. They were to be my visiting cousins. Lucien would take them around the city while I was with Callie, and we'd all meet up at Emily's party. I was nervous they'd scare Callie away with their silly and overbearing natures or, worse, expose us for what we were. They weren't as conditioned to mortalling as we were.

We caught up. They wanted to know a lot about Callie and me, since I never seriously dated. I played it off as just a mortal fling, and thankfully, Lucien didn't object. He knew me well enough that he could tell I was serious about her. I felt protective of Callie, that the girls were prying for info to give Zeus. I shifted subjects by asking about the rest of the family, and we were bombarded by useless gossip from Fiji. Only once did they mention Ma being there—they left the day she arrived. That timing was strange, like the Charities had been sent to babysit me. When Lucien started asking about his estranged sons, I escaped to the bathroom.

There was a knock at the front door. I hesitated, hoping Lucien would answer the door, but I heard the knock repeated. I washed and dried my hands at immortal speed and came out.

"I was just looking for Archer," I heard a familiar voice say.

"He's indisposed," Euphrosyne insinuated, giggling.

"Am not!" I scolded. I'd almost shouted out the Charis's name in fear

Callie would take that comment the wrong way. I had to watch myself before I became the one who would expose my own immortality.

Euphrosyne turned, glaring at me, twirling her red tresses as she sauntered away from the door.

"Callie." I went to the door. The old and new collided, but Callie still seemed ignorant to who these silly girls were. Her ignorance would be the only thing that could save her from my kind.

"Lucien, big boy, let me in!" Thalia shouted, banging on Ma's bathroom door.

The water was running, so Lucien must've escaped to shower once he'd heard about his kids. I hoped it wasn't bad news. Thalia tried the doorknob, probably trying to get a glimpse of him in the shower. Knowing Lucien, he'd welcome her in. I slipped out and closed the door behind me, embarrassed. I didn't want Callie to be involved with this side of my life. The Charities were the most ridiculous girls in existence, despite all their charms. Callie's eyes were calculating, judgmental, and hurt. It was obvious where her mind was wandering. She was instantly jumping on the jealousy bandwagon.

"Sorry about that," I told her. "I was in the bathroom." Gods, I was embarrassed admitting that to her. "My cousins are visiting, and they're a bit...strange," I said for lack of a better word.

"*She's* your cousin?" Callie asked, her brow raised, insinuating she didn't believe me.

"Yes. I must prepare you. There are three of them, and they're the biggest pains ever." I tried to joke with her, but Callie didn't even smile. Instead, she crossed her arms in dissatisfaction. She didn't believe me. And she shouldn't because it was a lie. I wasn't at all related to them. The Charities were the daughters of Eurynome, a Titan-descended sea nymph, and a mortal man, and the triplets had been made immortal by Zeus later. But they might as well have been my cousins because that was the kind of love I had for them.

"Callie." I took her hand and forced it out of her defensive stance.

She didn't object but was still hesitant.

"Callie, they came into town unannounced, and poor Lucien's going to take them sightseeing so our day isn't ruined, but would you object to meeting up with them at Emily's party?"

"Oh, no, that's fine. If you need to hang out with your cousins..."

"No, I need to hang out with you," I said. This made her finally smile. "I was just about to call you. Is everything all right?"

"Yes. I..." She turned red. "Never mind."

"No, what?"

Callie stared down at her feet. "The moment's gone."

"What moment?" Why was she being so vague, toying with me? What had my idiotic fellow immortals ruined?

"Oh, Archer?" The door popped open a crack.

I withheld my urge to groan.

"Can we meet her?" Aglaea asked.

"Lucien says she's your *girlfriend*." Thalia pulled the door open to further inspect Callie. I guess she'd successfully gotten into the bathroom to annoy Lucien.

I peered at Callie, embarrassed as all Hades, and then to the girls, while Euphrosyne reappeared as well. "Callie, these are my cousins..." What names could I call them without Callie recognizing them from the myths her father had programmed into her brain? I hoped Lucien had warned them.

"Thalia." She nodded to Callie.

My heart skipped a beat. It was a common enough name, but the others... I shot the other two a significant act-human glare, but they were staring at Callie.

"Belle," Aglaea said.

"Ada," Euphrosyne added.

Of course, symbolic names, like my own. We gods were suckers for irony.

"Girls, this is Callie, my girlfriend." The last words were said with pleasure. After all, I hadn't said it first, technically, so she wasn't bound to me. Callie's hand tightened on mine.

"Aww!" The girls giggled happily with doe eyes, treating us like a bunch of cute bumbling puppies to fuss over.

"Nice to meet you," Callie squeezed out uncomfortably.

"She's so pretty," Euphrosyne said to Aglaea, and the latter was smug as if she were the one responsible for bestowing Callie with so much beauty. It must have been her because Ma sure hadn't.

"And seems so sweet," Thalia added.

"Can you stop talking about her like she isn't here?" I was mortified. They had no clue how to act normal in front of mortals. I led her away from my apartment, away from the annoying and immature Charities, whom I always tried to get as far away from as I could. "I told you they're pains." I pulled her closer as we walked, draping my arm around her shoulder.

"They're lively creatures." She was exactly right. "So, you're my boyfriend?" Callie asked, smiling.

"Well, if you're my girlfriend, that's usually how it works, right?"

"You're a snake." She laughed at how craftily I'd asked her out without actually asking. I'd have to thank Lucien for his big mouth later.

"What moment was lost?" I remembered.

Callie glanced over her shoulder to see if we were alone or if my "cousins" were still watching. We turned the corner, and she stopped, pushing me gently against the wall and leaning her body against mine. Indeed, she was torturously cruel. I was unsure if I could resist her for much longer, especially if she wanted to be this close. Callie hesitated a moment, then went on her tiptoes to wrap her arms around my neck, and pulled me down toward her. Then she kissed me. I froze, unsure if I could kiss her back yet. Then she kissed me again, harder, and pulled away to gaze at me. Surely, that qualified as a first kiss, and if it didn't, I didn't care anymore.

"Now that that's out of the way," she whispered.

It felt like someone had snapped the chains of restraint I had imprisoned myself in. I pulled her to me and kissed her with a pent-up passion. I kissed her again and again, not wanting—unable—to stop.

The elevator signaled its approach with a bing, so I tore my lips away from hers, realizing someone would interrupt us in just a moment. I held her hand and led her down the hall, unable to take my eyes off her. She was beauty itself, more beautiful to me than Aglaea. I was no longer in danger of falling in love, but instead, I was done for. What I hadn't wanted to admit earlier was coming back: I loved her. I had no idea what the future would hold for her or for me, but I never wanted to let go of her soft, warm hand or break my gaze from her dark mahogany eyes.

Once we were in her apartment, I pulled her to me again and kissed her, compensating for each urge and wish to do so since I had first beheld her.

"My dad," she breathed between kisses.

"Sorry," I told her, kissing her forehead and letting her go.

"If I knew that's how you'd react, then I would've broken down sooner," she said with a wicked grin. Then her face and tone shifted. "Do you have to get back to your cousins soon?"

"No, I have to be wherever you are."

We decided to spend the rest of the day in Central Park because it wasn't too cold. Callie wanted to see the zoo, so I humored her, and afterward, we sat down in the waning sunlight.

I began to think of the future again, something I rarely worried about until meeting her. Callie would age. She was a fragile mortal. She could die; I had to grasp that she *would* die one day. How long could I stay with her? I could never tell her who I truly was. How could I constantly hide such a large piece of myself from her, especially if she was fully honest with me? I was absolutely torn: What would you do if you could live forever? Could you hide it from the one you truly loved, especially if her life depended on it?

"Archer?" Callie touched my cheek. "I've been saying your name."

"Sorry," I said, being sure to add a chipper note to my tone, although my thoughts were anxious.

"What's wrong?" she asked, worried. How in Hades did she notice something was upsetting me? I was purposely acting happy.

"Nothing." I smiled cheerfully.

Her hand remained on my cheek. "Your eyes don't lie when your mouth does."

"My mouth doesn't lie," I said, leaning in to kiss her.

She stopped me with her fingertips, scrutinizing me.

I sighed, wondering how I could tell the truth. What words could I use to tell her enough but not expose her to harm? "Callie, you know those silly rules—"

"I know they're not yours."

I stared at her, shocked, and awaited more. I had to see how much she perceived. I must've foolishly given myself away.

"The way you kissed me back. There's no way you didn't kiss me because of your 'virtuous' principles. I don't pretend to understand you, but I want to."

I toyed with a long blade of grass between my fingers, thinking hard on how to word things. When I finally formulated the words, they came from the heart: "What if I told you I could never tell you everything about me, Callie? Would you still want to be with me? What if knowing these things would put you in danger? Could you live without knowing them?"

"What? Just remain in the dark about some things?"

"Precisely." I tried not to laugh when it brought naïve Psyche to mind, who'd failed to remain literally and figuratively in the dark. It had been so long since I'd even thought about my former wife.

"Not because you don't want to tell me, but because it's dangerous for me?"

"Exactly."

"Like you were in the witness protection program or something?" she asked.

"Good analogy."

"Then I would say, if I can understand you and care about you without the whole picture, then it's all right for now."

"For now?"

"Well, I don't know how I'll feel in a year, or two, or three, or twenty. As long as it doesn't matter then…"

"Can you promise me something?"

"Depends." She eyed me suspiciously.

"Will you promise you'll never purposefully pry, that you won't try to find out the silly things I can't tell you?"

"The things that could put my life in danger?" She gawked, telling me she found me odd.

"Yes."

"Why would I seek information that might get me in trouble, hurt, or killed?" Now her gaze proclaimed me insane.

"Because curiosity killed the cat."

"I'm not a cat." She frowned stubbornly.

"Just promise me. Please."

"I promise I won't go looking into the hidden facets of your life for some mysterious information that might get me killed." She rolled her eyes. "Happy?"

"Immensely." I kissed her.

"So, were you involved in the mob?" She suppressed her smile.

"Callie." I grabbed her wrists, restraining her as she laughed. I pulled her closer.

"I was kidding." She giggled. I couldn't laugh with her. My throat tightened, and I was unable to swallow. The sunlight had struck one side of her face, illuminating her beauty like one of Rembrandt's paintings. She was so stunning that it was painful. It was at that moment in Central Park, watching the setting sun shine on Callie's cheek, when I realized there would be no going back. I'd never leave her willingly, and after a while, she'd discover the truth. I somehow would need to make her immortal or die trying. That sunset, that cheek it was cast upon—that was my new reason for existence. I didn't want to exist without Callie.

Despite these overwhelming feelings, despite my frigid heart rekindling after years of inactivity, the things Lucien had said overpowered any urges I had. I would be careful with my words. Although I wanted Callie forever, I had seen many times how fickle the heart could be, mortal and immortal alike. I needed to give Callie the choice, without forcing her to love and desire me and only me. I would not bind her to me, but let her love me for the person she believed me to be and not the god whose powers could force her.

After the sun set, it quickly grew chilly, so we went to our respective homes to get ready to go out. I was more than happy the cousins were out with Lucien. I must have dressed too quickly and eagerly, because when I reached Callie's apartment, she wasn't ready.

Their servant let me in and motioned for me to continue into the living room. I found myself waiting with her father, who was on the sofa with a blanket wrapped around him, piles of notes and books strewn about.

"Where are you taking Callie tonight?" He pored over his notes, only giving me half his attention. We'd had our awkward introductions previously, but I still didn't feel comfortable around him. Something irked me about him, but it could've simply been my worry over his godly expertise.

"Oh, uh, dinner." I sat down across from him. "And to um...Emily's house," I responded, unsure whether he knew Emily or not. I wasn't sure what to say to him. I had little experience in dealing with fathers, especially concerned ones.

"Emily, yes. So, a party?" He glanced up at me over his spectacles.

I swallowed the lump in my throat. God that I am, I was terrified. What had Callie told him? "Well, yeah," I let out. Better not to get caught in a lie, and reading his mind in front of him might be a little obvious and awkward.

"You driving?"

"No sir. Got a driver." Not that it mattered. Ichor burned off the effects of mortal liquor pretty quickly. Nectar whiskey was a whole other story.

"Be sure she doesn't drink too much, and have her home by midnight," he instructed.

I was taken aback by his leniency, the lack of strict rules most mortal kids complained about. I slightly recalled the days when my parents had had rules, but I couldn't remember what they were exactly. "Oh, I didn't intend to—"

"Archer, I cannot be strict with her. I am not the typical parental figure. I must shock you, I'm sure, but I will not be on this earth much longer, and I feel when one is used to rigidly strict rules, once free from that restraint, the child goes wild. My daughter tells me almost everything. There is an uncanny trust between us."

I wondered how much he surmised about Callie and me. "You seem to have a great relationship," I told him, trying not to think of what they would say about me.

"Do you and your parents?" he asked, going back through his notes.

"I don't with my father, unfortunately. He's...in the military." I told him vague truths. "But I have a great relationship with my mother when she's not away."

"What does she do?"

"Besides live off of alimony from her previous marriage? Not much of anything. But she's in school." The half lies were so easy to tell, it made me feel guilty.

"School is good. I hope Callie goes to college," he mused. "What on earth is this?" He pulled up his notes, squinting. "I've never heard of this before." He picked up a Greek-English dictionary and then closed it a moment later, stumped.

"May I?" I asked him.

Dr. Syches's expression was skeptical. "You can read Greek?"

"Didn't Callie tell you I was born in Litochoro?" I asked, taking up a photocopy of an old manuscript.

"No, she didn't. I wonder if you were there when we were," he mused.

"I don't think so. I left when I was young, but my parents made sure I kept up with my heritage. Which part?" I scanned, reading the document easily. It technically was true. We moved on to Rome when I was fairly young, for a god.

"Fourth line down," he told me. I read it, not noticing anything odd, but he might be referring to the ambrosia part. It wasn't in reference to the food of the gods, but the high-altitude berry ambrosia was squeezed from: *ambrosía moúro*.

"It literally translates to immortal berry." I told him. He was bug-eyed. I had to expand. "Some believed it was a juice from some mystical berry."

"Interesting." He eyed me. Why was he so suspicious?

"That's what this writer seemed to believe at least," I told him, handing it back, wondering who wrote it.

He studied me carefully and thoughtfully. Surely, I hadn't revealed too much.

Then my stomach dropped. Callie had said he knew Greek, so he hadn't needed me to truly translate. "Ambrosia" was a common enough word, and "berry," simplistic. Had I been the first to reveal to mortals that immortality came from a berry? I couldn't be. Mortals thought of us as a myth. Even if this one thought we were real, that ambrosia was real, he could never prove it. Just as he could never prove our old palace was actually Mount Olympus.

"I heard you climbed Oros Olimbos." I wanted to test him, just as he was assessing me, to see how much he knew.

"Yes, some of the artifacts are in those glass cases over there. The ones museums weren't interested in," he told me vaguely.

I got up, highly interested, to examine the glass cases along one wall. I scanned, looking for things I might recognize. There were a few arrowheads, broken jars, and my attention came to a couple of figurines of ancient soldiers and tiny arrowheads. Faded old memories of my childhood came back to me, dim distant memories that were hard to recollect because they were so long ago...

I could remember my dad sneaking into my room to see me when he thought I was asleep and leaving me soldiers he had carved for me. Those were the tiny arrows my mother made for me to teach me archery. My parents had a secret love affair back then, and I was the result. But when I was six, her husband Hephaestus found them out and that I wasn't his son. They had been so happy then, Ares and my mother, until that fateful day when Heph found them...

"Recognize anything?" Dr. Syches asked.

"Pardon me?" I turned toward him, confused. What did he mean? Callie mentioned he was very perceptive, but this was impossible. No mortal could fully read someone's mind, especially us gods. We were the hardest to read.

"You're from the area. Have you seen similar items in museums over there? They refused to take them because they could not date them, so they thought they were counterfeit. The experts believed them made much later and placed there. Too high tech for the era to match the architecture."

I half listened to him, examining the rest of it. An all-too-familiar carved ivory box, a bronze flute, a couple cosmetic pyxides, and a bronze lyre without strings—that last one would amuse Lucien, as it most likely had been his. It wasn't his first lyre—that Hermes invented with a tortoiseshell—but Lucien used to have quite a collection.

"What I believe is that the inhabitants of the dwelling were far more advanced, despite being so secluded," Dr. Syches went on. At least he wasn't telling me outright that they were gods. At least he didn't dare say it out loud and look crazy. Yet his tone suggested that he was onto me, onto what I was.

"You ready?" I heard Callie ask. "Oh Dad, he doesn't care about your old toys."

Dr. Syches turned to gaze upon her, and his face beamed. "Her beauty was so great and illustrious, that it could neither be expressed nor sufficiently praised by the poverty of human speech," he translated Apuleius's description of Psyche's beauty from the myth as he crossed the room and kissed his daughter's cheek. "Gorgeous."

I tried not to react, not to let my eyes, which Callie could read so well, betray me. It was too familiar, too coincidental, too close to home to have him quote ancient literature about my first and only love before Callie. Apuleius was the first to record Psyche's and my love story, thanks to Dionysus's loose, inebriated lips. Syches spelled so similarly, how I sensed she must be a demigod or at least a descendant of one, her unrivaled beauty—all these factors were making my mind hatch wild and frightening theories.

Callie didn't notice my expression. She was much too mortified by her father to notice me. I really had to watch myself around these two mortals. I composed myself.

"You look amazing," I told Callie, and it was the truth. She was stunning, and it scattered every fear in my mind to the four winds.

Dr. Syches beamed at us with a sense of pride. I turned away, unnerved by his probing gaze. I rushed Callie out of that apartment as fast as I could.

No matter how I tried to shake the feeling, Dr. Syches's words wouldn't leave me. A fear grew in the pit of my stomach. Were the parallels a sign that history would repeat itself? I couldn't deal with losing Callie. The emotions from hundreds of years ago resurfaced—the grief, the anguish when I saw my ex-wife's and daughter's ashes. I tried to repress the thoughts by paying all of my attention to Callie, but the fear of losing Callie became paramount, and I had a sinking sensation that it wouldn't be long until this fear was well-grounded.

CHAPTER 10

Aroha

I naively believed that going to Fiji in Autumn would be like a holiday since it was practically summer in the southern hemisphere, but I was very wrong. Zeus ranted, raved, yelled, and bellowed at me about all sorts of nonsense, half of which was really not my fault. He scolded me about Ares, Hephie, and Archer, as if I were the one who was supposed to keep track of them. They were men and did as they pleased; men had forever attempted to control the world, despite all the feminine efforts to thwart them. When they acted all high and mighty, whose job was it to contain them? Mine? I think not. He was the god of gods—deal with it!

At dinner, Zeus appeared more civil. He had to be in front of everyone—all nine Muses; his sister, Demeter; and his wife, Hera. Sure, most of them hated me—jealous of my beauty—but they wouldn't stand for him screaming at anyone as he used to. He had my favorite dishes made, served nectar wine and ambrosial cakes and berries—just like the old days. Zeus was quiet and sulking behind his feigned civility. Hera's gaze volleyed back and forth between us, sensing the tension from our fight, or perhaps she was creating one of her little jealousy schemes. Hera was jealous of every female, mortal and immortal, and she had her reasons. Zeus was as unfaithful as the sky is blue, but Hera stayed with him anyway, and now she constantly struggled with his infidelity. Plus, I mean, what man could gaze upon me without adoration anyway? I couldn't help that I was the most beautiful being ever to exist.

"Zeus, please don't be angry. I'm at your service. Whatever you want, I'll do." I finally crumbled. There would be no peace until Zeus got his way. That was the way it always went. Selfish and obsessively controlling Zeus.

"First, you need to convince Ares to peace," he began.

"Zeus, he's your son. You know how hard it is. He's in love with fighting, with battle." I looked to Hera for help. Her cold expression told me I would get none. She had never liked me.

"He's the difficult son," she scoffed, "but you did leave your husband for him." Bitter old Hera was still upset that I left *her* son,

Hephaestus—Hephie—the god of fire, for her and Zeus's gorgeous and powerful son, Ares. Ares and Hebe were their only legitimate children, but she always favored Hephie because he was hers and hers alone due to her one and only fling with a mortal in revenge for Zeus's many conquests. Zeus later made him immortal in hopes of gaining Hera's forgiveness, but Hephie was in his early thirties by then. Created gods appeared the age they were made immortal, while us born gods were frozen when the body stopped growing, around eighteen.

"You will try your hardest. Bring him home with you for a while."

"Ares in New York." I laughed. "Disaster."

"You will obey or suffer the consequences!" Zeus commanded. By the beard of Zeus, he had no sense of humor.

"What are those consequences in case I fail?" I asked quietly.

Hera choked on the soup she was daintily consuming. She wouldn't dare speak to him that way. Then again, she was spineless.

"Then you will stay here under my supervision for as long as I deem necessary."

That was enough for me to obey. No one wanted to live with Zeus breathing down her neck. He wasn't as peaceful and laid back as he had been back when we all lived together in the original Mount Olympus. The world was much more complex, and mortals harder to manage, these days. Plus, with all of us scattered across the world, it was difficult for him to keep tabs on us.

"I'll give it my all," I told him.

"As for Hephaestus," Hera began.

"You will find someone for him. A temporary mortal solution to make him happy," Zeus finished.

"He is still brokenhearted. It pains me," Hera mused. "Over three thousand years, and he still loves *you*."

I swallowed my soup, trying not to choke. I always felt horrid for what I had done to Hephie. Back then, after the affair with Ares expired, I had wanted to reconcile, but Hephie wanted my darling Eros dead, and being the god of fire, he could easily do so. I could never trust Hephie around Eros, and I loved my son best of all.

"I'll find someone," I told him. I'd fail at this task yet again, but I didn't want to be stuck with Zeus.

"That reminds me. You need to stop making Eros and the attendants do everything. You've been letting them pick up all the slack. *You* are supposed to find the matches, and your son, enforce them. Your attendants inform and keep track of people for you, instilling beauty, happiness, jollity, lust, to reinforce the matches you make. The other boys are to make sure the love you instill succeeds in marriage or to have it thwarted. *You*, along with Aglaea, are to instill beauty in the world of mortals. But no one has been working together. Eros is doing it all, the others sometimes lending a helping hand. Tell me, Aphrodite, if things continue as they are, what use do I have for you?"

"None." I told him what he wanted to hear. "But I will make myself useful again." Holy Hades, Zeus was an old bore.

"Last order of business is your son," Zeus said.

"What about him?"

"He's falling for a mortal," Zeus told me.

"He's not falling for her. It can't be serious. Plus, aren't we all entitled to our little mortal toys?" I scoffed. The hypocrite could hardly tell me Archer couldn't be with a mortal when Zeus himself had been with so many mortal and immortal women over the years. After all, that's where Apollo, Artemis, Dionysus, Hermes, and most of the hybreed-turned-gods came from.

"I do not like this mortal," he said vaguely with a flourish of his hand. "Surely, he can have his games with a different one."

"I should go directly home. I ordered him to make her fall in love with someone already." I didn't like the idea of Archer ignoring my wishes. As my son, he was supposed to be obedient; there was a tie that binds, as the saying goes, meaning he couldn't outwardly disobey Ares or me.

"He disobeyed," Zeus told me.

"He can't."

"Did you order with selfish intent?" Hera interjected, as always, where she wasn't wanted.

I didn't answer at first, and they took it as an affirmative. "She has beauty beyond what is right for any mortal," I protested on seeing he expected an answer. "I should go home and stop it." This Callie was indeed another wench who was wedging herself between my son and me. Stupid kid to let feeble mortals rule his heart and mind. I swear, the boy lived to embarrass me.

"No, I'll keep an eye on him. I've sent the Charities as a distraction. Eros isn't irrational. He doesn't make a habit of toying with mortals, like some others," he added, insinuating me.

What. A. *Hypocrite*. I was seething but trying to keep my temper under control.

THE IMMORTAL TRANSCRIPTS: QUIVER

Zeus was well aware of how angry he was making me and was gloating about how I couldn't retaliate, much like a pig rolling around in its own filth. He was purposely doing this to distract me. I wasn't sure what Zeus's "keeping an eye" on my child would mean. Nothing good, and most likely, he would meddle. I wasn't in a position at the moment to ask questions, though.

He continued, his expression brightening. "You will take care of your ex-husbands, and then I want a list of a minimum of a thousand couples *you* have found for your son to enforce. You get those men in your life in line, and you'll be handsomely benefited. Did you not say you wanted another child? Try that on my son, and see what he says. He still laments Phobos's and Deimos's deaths. And I know you miss Harmonia," Zeus suggested.

I held my breath in order not to react. Jerk, jerk, jerk! Was Zeus devoid of all parental feeling? How could he casually bring up Ares's and my deceased children? After our affairs and big split, Ares and I got back together from time to time. About four hundred years after the hybreed mistakes were made immortal, Zeus granted us a baby, which resulted in twins. Our daughter followed not long after. Yes, the twin boys Phobos and Deimos I found to be awful creatures, being gods of horror and dread respectively, but I adored dressing them alike, and their father loved them more than anything. We lost them in the Battle of Thermopylae, when they were hardly more than four hundred years old, and our dearest and only daughter died trying to save them: Harmonia, goddess of peace. To talk of her pained me more than anything. Our children lived on in the world through humanity: their presence was always felt among the mortal world still, but if Harmonia had survived, I imagine this world would be a much kinder place.

I was brought back to reality when Zeus handed me a bank card. "Fifty thousand for your troubles." He smiled. "I will also cut Hermes's last transgression and wire it to yours and Eros's accounts." Hermes was an eternal thief, and his last heist was so huge and mind-boggling, it disrupted the mortal world and enraged Zeus.

I thanked him heartily. If the cut was as much as I suspected, it would keep me afloat for a decade. Plus, Archer never burned through his money like me. He'd keep us afloat much longer if I could keep him with me.

Hymenaios walked in. The sight of that immortal made my heart race because he was always accompanied by the other two: my and Ares's mistakes. I wanted to forget my little offspring and murder Ares's. In a moment of weakness, I'd fallen for the mortal Adonis. To love a being who can die is ludicrous, and I'd learned my lesson the hard way.

Zeus observed me with a smirk as the two little wretches entered, and I attempted to compose myself. They gave me anxious stares, and I forced myself to give them a small smile of recognition. Their uneasiness always made me perturbed, and I assumed my indifference to their existence was what made them uneasy. It was a vicious cycle that I had no clue how to remedy.

"Aphrodite," they said in unison, bowing at my feet. I bowed my head and addressed them out of civility, not wanting to snub them in public, "Anteros, Himerus." I tried not to hiss the second's name. After all, it wasn't their fault they existed, but Ares's and mine alone, and Zeus's as well for making them immortal.

"Don't worry, dear." Hera patted my hand reassuringly. "Zeus has them on a mission. They were just leaving," she whispered demurely. I hated her condescending attitude toward me.

The boys looked away from me sheepishly, probably having heard Hera's stinging remark. I felt myself relax as Hymenaios hugged his mother Euterpe, a Muse, and the three of them said goodbye to others as they were leaving. Anteros, who was mine, glanced back at me with a strange expression and then continued on. I kept a stoic mask upon my face but met his gaze. What was his look? Longing? Bitterness? Regard? I couldn't tell. I didn't know a thing about the little wretch. A wave of guilt washed over me for my lack of maternal feelings.

The last three of my "love retinue" left. Ha! Companions and helpers for us? More like, here are your sins to haunt you for eternity. I swear Zeus enjoyed torturing us.

I tried to banish thoughts of the foundlings and the painful memories of the past, but they kept creeping forward. Despite my desire to suppress such memories, they came back: the infidelity Ares started and I ran wild with in attempts to rouse his jealousy; the fights with Ares, the pubescent Archer stuck in between; the astounding level of anger and wrath that erupted from Ares that terrified Archer and me. With all these reminders, it appeared hopeless. Our history was against us. How was I to overcome that in one visit? Why must I love the one god who would not only complicate my life and feelings beyond any reasonable understanding, but also the one who would hurt me the most in the end? Every time Ares and I parted, I felt a piece of me die.

I excused myself from the festivities and retired to my room. I stepped out onto the balcony and watched the waves crash upon the beach. I found the lulling of the surf a strange comfort that helped me think clearly. I had to do what was asked of me, and deep down, I had to admit, it was not at all a chore, but a deep-seated and repressed desire. Part of me would forever long for Ares. He was my soul mate, which was why we had married immortally; we would be linked together the rest of our existence, and I could never force myself to regret that decision. He had insisted we do so to prove our bond stronger than the one I'd had with Hephie, which it was.

I needed to call Ares. I closed my eyes and mentally tore down the layers of stone walls that surrounded and protected my all-too-sensitive heart. Love would fall in love again, whether she wanted to or not.

I pulled out my phone to look up the number I had saved but never yet used. Phones were always supplied by Zeus, and our new aliases, numbers, and emails updated through encrypted group messaging. I was nervous, feeling like an adolescent calling my crush to ask him out. My hands shook as I selected the name "Ari" in my phone that I pored over almost every day yet never had the guts to call or text. My finger trembled as I pressed the call button, and I felt my stomach stir sourly and my heart palpitate. I hadn't heard that voice in so long...

"Dite?" I heard his voice whisper in disbelief.

"Ares," I breathed back, the nervousness ebbing away. "I want to come see you."

"S-sure," he said awkwardly, "Is everything all right? Eros?" I could tell he was surprised and worried at the same time. Leave it to Ares to think the worst.

"He is fine and in New York, but I'm in Fiji, visiting your parents. You ought to come see them, you know? I think your mother misses you. She'd hardly admit that, but I could tell. She still hates me, the old cow. Anyway, it just brought back memories. Reminded me of our Olympus days. Thought maybe, since I was on this side of the world with Hermes at my disposal...would you mind me coming? Just for a few days?"

"No, I think that would be nice...yeah," he said softly. He didn't sound at all like the warmongering madman I'd stormed out on so long ago. This was the side of the sly fox that I had trouble denying, the one who had led me away from my first husband.

"Are you sure? I wouldn't want to impose."

"Impose on what, Dite?" He laughed. Imagining his bright smile made my stomach flop.

I wanted to say that I didn't want to interrupt him and his favorite lover, war, but I was supposed to be coming in peace. I had to gauge the competition, although I could easily win him from any woman. "I mean, if you're, you know, *with* someone..."

"No," he answered quickly. "There's no one."

I sighed, relieved. I don't know why I was so relieved, but I felt myself relax. Ares laughed lightly again. It was always games with us. He could see through me; it might become one of *those* visits. He had craftily established that I did not need help nor wish to fight.

"How and when are you arriving, darling?" He broke an uncomfortable silence.

"Hermes will deliver me to an airport to keep up appearances, but which is the closest one to you?"

Ares gave me the details and said he'd take care of all other arrangements for me. His businesslike tone made me fear that this trip might be made in vain. But how else did I expect him to be? The last time we were together, in the 1930s, I'd left him in the middle of the night and never looked back. In my defense, WWII was on the horizon, and I could tell he was being pulled and inflamed more by the conflict than his wife.

The next morning, Hermes took me to Afghanistan, where my Ares was camped out, creating havoc. By the beard of Zeus, mortals would tear each other apart limb by limb without Ares's help. I had no idea how I would convince him to stop interfering with mortals and their ridiculous wars and politics, but I had to try.

Ares surprised me by showing up himself. He usually sent a car, some random goon to take me into some horrid battle campground. He was exactly as I remembered: a staggering six-five and about two hundred and eighty pounds of pure brawn and muscle; truly terrifying on ancient battlefields. Nowadays, he passed as an average high school football player since humans were evolving over the ages, getting bigger. Ares was olive in complexion, always beautifully tan, his hair thick, wavy, and the color of kohl mixed with henna, which he had let grow long. His eyes were large and set deep in his brow, with a fiery brownish-amber hue that eerily glowed when he felt profound emotions. He had a prominent Greek nose, large, but fitting with his other angular features, a strong square jawline, and thin, serious lips that rarely turned up in smiles—except when he beheld me. Naturally.

"Aphrodite." He blinded me with his gorgeous smile and those intense eyes. He pulled me into a hug and then gave me the once-over, smoothing my hair.

I felt my frigid heart spark to life, and the walls began to crumble. "Aroha Ambrose," I corrected.

"Lieutenant General Ari Ranjit," he told me the alias he was going by. "To what do I owe this pleasure?"

"Can't a woman want to see her husband every now and then?" I stroked his face with my fingers, feeling the need to touch him. He was a magnet to me. I was enticed and immutably drawn. How had I denied seeing this face for so long? All thoughts left my mind, except ones including him.

"Ex-husband, I thought," he replied, twirling my hair between his fingers. I tried to dispel memories of him doing the same to my hair in warm, cozy beds and focus on his words. Ex, he had pointed out. He was being cautious.

"Well, immortally married means bound forever, whether you like it or not," I told him teasingly.

His jaw tightened as his eyes searched my face for something. He swallowed hard. He was just as simultaneously terrified and tempted as I was, which comforted me. He wanted to jump right in and kiss me but was holding back. He was afraid of getting hurt, which we constantly did to each other. Ares, for all the strife, anger, aggression, and hate that fueled him, was actually a teddy bear on the inside. Aside from our son, he was probably one of the most romantic gods in existence.

"I never said I didn't like it. Just thought you considered 'us' over with. You were the last one to walk away, so the ball's in your court." He was smug and so cunning to force me to make the move. It was always a game with him.

However, I had tricks up my sleeve too. "Could you blame me? World War II, Ares?" I sighed sadly. Trick one: guilt trip.

"Quite the masterpiece, wasn't it?" he said proudly.

"You wiped out a good portion of the human race." Trick two: the artful pout. It made me even more irresistible. I shouldn't start the bickering already, but it irked me how he could justify war and death so easily.

"You don't condemn Demeter, Zeus, or Artemis." He frowned as we made our way to his car. I tried to ignore that the car was armored and bulletproof. I couldn't help but be as frightened for myself as I was for Ares in every modern battle. The intensity of heat created by these modern bombs could be enough to kill even us immortals.

"You always try that card," I coyly bantered back.

"Yes, well, the human race needs to be limited from time to time. You know what happens to too many rats in a cage—"

"Yes dear," I cut him off before continuing his lecture for him, "—war, pestilence, famine, and natural disasters. Let us not talk of war."

He opened the car door for me and climbed in after. He had a driver.

Tricks one and two hadn't panned out too well. Onto tricks three and four: flirt and flatter.

"It was nice of you to meet me personally." I peeked at him from the corner of my eye, bit my lip, and twirled my hair.

Ares grabbed my fingers to make them stop twirling. The ephemeral light in his eyes dimmed down. He caught on, now that I was being too artful, and his dazzling grin dropped. Had I lost all my charisma?

I changed the subject. "Where will I be staying?"

"I've got a hotel room for you." He played with my hair himself. No campground tent, another surprise: he wanted my stay to be comfortable. "The war front is too dangerous for you. And please, please, keep yourself covered in public." He handed me a beautiful scarf.

"I truly think these people quite odd. Why hide beauty?" I protested.

He took the scarf and wrapped it for me over my hair. "All different people have their ways. I suppose they wish to keep their wives' charms to themselves. I could understand that." He pulled my lightweight jacket closed and buttoned it to cover my chest and neck.

I acquiesced that with a nod.

"You're still amazing," he murmured.

Trick five: show you care.

"I still worry about you," I told him softly. "These nuclear weapons and all."

"I'd never die darling. I couldn't allow it. Your soul is bound to mine. If I am harmed, you are. That thought keeps me from being rash." He ran his finger along my cheek. Every time he touched me, I felt alive, vulnerable, and smitten.

"Good thing then. Someone's gotta keep you in line."

He turned away with a laugh and peered out the window. "How I have missed you, Dite."

THE IMMORTAL TRANSCRIPTS: QUIVER

Once he had me settled in my room, he ordered room service. Ares always, at least in the wooing phases, went all out for me. Five-star hotels, lobster dinners, and champagne. Tonight, he didn't let me down. I started to suspect Zeus likewise ordered him to reunite with me. Zeus was all about control. Any direct order from him was almost impossible to deny; some force within all of us, like the ichor in our blood, demanded obedience. And he most likely wanted us together to control Archer better, but why did he dislike Callie?

Best trick of all: be yourself. That one would have to work.

"Ares, you shouldn't have," I told him as he pulled the chair out for me at the table on the balcony. "This is all too much. This is new."

"You being spoiled to death? Oh, that is something you've never experienced," he said with heavy sarcasm.

"Ha ha."

"I know how you love seafood," he mused as he sat down before pouring the champagne. He was forever fascinated that I'd sprung from the sea fully grown.

I honestly cannot remember my childhood, but imagine I was one of Oceanus's children who somehow broke through the barrier. Each of the three Olympian brothers had his domain—a territory—and his offspring and subjects remained in that domain: Zeus had the sky and surface of the earth, Poseidon had the seas and Atlantis, and Hades had the Underworld. None of us are meant to enter another's domain without Zeus's permission, besides the rare teleporters, but somehow, I had slipped through. Athena, the smartest of us all, believed that I had to be a descendant of Oceanus and some Olympian or Titan god, able to break through Zeus's barrier that was meant to oppress and contain Poseidon and his descendants. No one came forward to claim me, so I gave up searching for my parents a millennium ago.

"So, darling, are you going to cut to the chase? Why are you here?" Ares broke me from my wandering thoughts.

"To catch up. To see you. To talk."

He eyed me suspiciously but dropped the subject and rolled his neck, letting loose the tension with it. I felt the tension in the room ease off a bit. He had a way of transmitting his emotions onto others, purely accidentally of course, but rage, anger, hate, sorrow—all devastating emotions that radiated from him. It came in handy for him in warfare, I suppose. If you were lucky, like me, he'd radiate love and passion.

"How's my son?" he asked.

"More like you every century."

"I doubt that. He's your son through and through."

"He acts like you. I'm glad you brought him up. You should come to see him in New York. The truth is I need your help with him. He stopped obeying me."

"I'm busy at the moment here. Why don't I just call him, give him a talking to, command him to listen to you," he suggested.

"There's more. He's falling for this insipid mortal girl, and we have to stop it."

"Wait," he interrupted. "Why can't the kid have his fun?"

"Your father says no. Something about her he doesn't like. You know your father never embellishes on anything. All orders—no explanations."

Ares laughed, throwing his napkin down, and then glared at me with those fiery eyes. "I knew it. Zeus sent you to stop me. To stop the wars. But you can tell him these mortals would have war without me. The Afghanistan Conflict has been fueled for forty years now."

"I have no idea what you're talking about. I never meddle in your little games. I sent myself. I came here to ask you to come back to New York for me, for Eros. He goes by Archer now. I thought, why not try again to be a family?" My words bothered him but did not sway him. I had gone with the truth, since it would be the only way to win him over.

"Just the three of us?" he questioned.

"Apollo's in New York too, but he's itching to leave."

"What of your entourage?"

"No. I only deal with them when forced to. Your father paraded those mistakes around in front of me just to irk me."

"Don't call them that," Ares groaned. "Those kids are our responsibility, but I agree. I don't think there's room for more in our family."

"I disagree," I said, pausing for dramatic effect, "I think it's about time you give me another baby. Your father said he'd permit it."

He almost choked on some lobster. He coughed, swallowed, and downed an entire glass of champagne. His hands tightened on the table, denting it.

"You're breaking the table, darling," I warned him, waiting for him to calm himself. "You know we make beautiful babies."

"Could you do it all again? Raise them and then lose them like the others? I don't know if I can. Isn't that why we never asked Zeus to let us have any more?"

I unlatched his hands from the table. They had left molds of his strong fingers in the metal.

"Times are much different now, my love. The world is much safer than our Greecian days, and I will not let them go to the battlefront if they take after you." I tried to reassure him by squeezing his hand.

Ares digested the conversation, relaxed, and poured us more champagne. The gears were grinding in his head. I could tell he was plotting, scheming, measuring my strengths and weaknesses against his own. Everything in life to him was evaluated like a battle.

"You know, I might be able to help you with that tonight, love." He raised his eyebrow seductively.

My stomach flopped. This was so sudden, so rash. It all was true: another child to raise and care for after Archer left, another little one to fill up my half-empty heart. I wouldn't be alone, but now? That would ruin some of the plans in New York. I'd have to give up Dan and my games that I thoroughly enjoyed.

"Will you come to New York?" I pressed.

"Is that the condition?" he bartered, the warrior in him trying to write up a treaty.

"If it is?" I answered his question with one of my own.

He tried to suppress the smile playing on his lips.

"What?" I asked coyly.

He shook his head. "You haven't changed a bit." Ares stood up, crossed to me, and offered me his hand. I gave mine to him. He pulled me up and drew me to him. "Dance with me."

"There's no music."

"Be creative, darling," he breathed into my hair. "I know you better than you know yourself." I tucked my head under his chin as he wrapped his strong arms around me. He was the strongest god of all of us, physically. It was his strength that won me over, but it was dancing in his arms that first stole my heart from Hephie. "You don't really want to settle down, do you? You've always been more about the chase."

"Can't a girl want two things?"

Ares pulled me out from under his chin, leaned down, and kissed me. It felt like millennia since those firm lips had touched mine. It felt like coming home. I couldn't help but kiss him back. His arms held me in a tight embrace, his body against mine. He was so warm, with his rock-hard muscles pressed tightly against me. I felt my heart flutter as if a butterfly were trapped in my chest. I was in danger of falling under my own spell. All the doubts about our future vanished. I could do this. I could succeed in this mission and win him over, and after that kiss, I wanted to succeed.

"You always want two things." He smiled at me, cradling my chin in his hands.

"And so do you," I countered, pouting. I could tell the pout swayed him at last. Trick two always worked in the end. "Come with me," I pleaded.

"Stay," he countered. Then he sighed, anticipating my answer. "You knew coming here and begging me to come back wouldn't work. Why'd you try?"

"To make you want me again," I told him honestly.

His jaw tightened. "It worked," he said glumly. The gears in his head were turning again, perhaps devising a strategy to keep me here with him. His eyes bored into mine, and what I had been waiting for shone through: love. His eyes glowed brightly, almost orange, like a fire was burning within him. I had succeeded in that task, but I needed to get him to come to New York with me, or all could be lost.

"Why deny it, Ares?" I touched his cheek.

"What?" he said, his voice soft and cracking as he ran his rough fingers over the smooth skin of my cheek.

"That you love me."

He pulled me almost painfully tight against him and leaned in. "I *never* denied that."

"Then come with me." I threw him the most pitiful pout I could muster.

Then he kissed me but quickly pulled away. "Say it," he begged, holding my face in his hands.

"What?" I toyed with him.

He then gave me an intense and intimidating glare.

"That I love you, Ares of Thrace, god of war, the most stubborn being on—" I was cut off with another kiss.

"It would have to be a real chase," he said, suddenly letting go of all but my hand. "You'd have to be really hard to get. Challenge me; tease me; make me jealous; make it really difficult. Deny me again and again." His grip tightened on my hand, insinuating this would happen.

"Hmm, this sounds like it'll be a lot of fun."

"And our son?" Ares asked.

"Another game for you to win, darling. I can't help you with him. If I knew how to manage him, I wouldn't need your help on that front."

And that was how the game began. I left Afghanistan without Ares, but he promised to relocate to New York as soon as possible. To ensure this would happen sooner rather than later, I made a list of soldiers from each side and chose people they'd fall madly in love with, hoping it would at least distract them from war for a while. I had over my quota for Zeus.

And so I went to deal with my son, dreading how far his disobedience had taken him in my absence. I hoped for his sake that Callie was in love with someone else.

CHAPTER 11

I kept thinking of the prophecy. Every day, it plagued me, yet I could not figure out how Callie could change our entire world. That did not seem feasible. For one beautiful, but not exceptional in any particular way, mortal to change us forever was not plausible. And Zeus? He'd never fear a mortal being, but what in the vision had him cowering? I was beginning to wonder about my own high level of intrigue. Why was I so drawn to her? The fact I was so interested in my best friend's girl was depressing and made me feel like a rotten friend.

When I pondered on it, she and I did have amazing conversations; she was clever, outgoing, and kindhearted, not to mention beautiful. There was something about her deep, dark eyes; her soft, glowing skin; and I adored how her lips broke around her teeth when she smiled. I had always been led by my eyes before my heart, but Callie captured both without even trying. She enraptured me, even though she was only ever friendly to me, never flirtatious.

The Charities, although a chore to entertain sometimes, were a well-needed distraction. I took them—my darling friends of beauty, jollity, and charm—through Central Park, trying to keep them away from stores. I knew how dangerous they were when it came to shopping. I'd honestly once watched them drop ten grand in one outing between the three of them. Whose money it was or where it came from, I was afraid to ask. They could cajole money out of the tightest of men. After that, they had to see all the typical sightseeing attractions, and then we ended up at the mortal Emily's party.

Emily's house was packed with students from our school, but I found Archer immediately, just by scanning for Callie. He was by her side, their hands glued together. They were standing inconspicuously in the corner, oblivious to the people around them, talking in whispered, hurried tones. They were intimate already, their body language so drawn together and at ease, like they had been together for ages. I tried to conquer my jealous feelings, to not be annoyed by my friend when it wasn't necessarily his fault. Plus, it wasn't my right to be angry with him. My intense anger alarmed me. Was I truly falling for Callie?

The jealous feelings were easily suppressed when he saw me, smiled genuinely, and waved me over. How could I hate the one true friend I had in the world? I couldn't let a mortal girl, no matter how beautiful and charming she might be, get between us. I walked over to them. Callie was glowing with happiness. The three "horrors," as Archer called them, followed me, eyeing up all the boys as tasty treats.

"You survived. I owe you," Archer told me.

"You do." It honestly wasn't such an atrocious day with Archer's entourage, but I wouldn't let him know that.

"What are you doing tomorrow?" he asked me. "You should come around Callie's. Her dad has some interesting artifacts from Litochoro." I wondered exactly what he meant by his coded comment.

"Oh, don't pretend to be interested to please my dad, Archer," Callie said, laughing.

"No, I really was interested." Then he directed his attention back to me. "You should come around with me, check 'em out." He really wanted to impart something to me, but it would have to wait.

"I can't. I'm going to France."

"How do you guys just do that, skip class and everything?" Callie protested.

"Permission slips. I'll fake you one, and we'll go to Paris." Archer told her, his tone completely serious. He needed to act more human around her and stop showing off. The last thing he needed was to levitate or run like the wind in front of her and expose what he was.

"My dad would like that one." She shook her head at Archer's facetious comment.

"No, I'm not going to Paris. There's something I need to look into in Nice. A family matter," I said vaguely.

Archer gave me a concerned and quizzical stare. He wouldn't pry in front of Callie, but he might ask for more detail later. I'd have to avoid him, or he'd pry the truth out of me.

"Not a big deal. My mother," I said, rolling my eyes. I threw Archer off with a lie. It came out so fast that I didn't realize I could do it. I lied to an immortal. How was that possible? My pulse spiked at the realization, and my stomach did an elevator drop. How could I lie? It was one thing to omit where prophecies came from, but normally, the truth came out of my mouth, no matter how painful or damaging it could be.

"Everything all right?" Archer gave me a critical glance. He knew something was up.

"I think so." I tried to hide my shock from him. I stuck to being vague because this lying thing was new to me. "So, you'll have to deal with this lot tomorrow. Sorry."

Archer gave me a grimace.

Two of the girls went on their merry little ways, easily mingling, but Belle stayed with me. Usually, these mortal parties were a bore, but this time, I was actually having a lot of fun just catching up with Belle. What guy wouldn't when talking to one of the most beautiful creatures ever born? Our reminiscing was interrupted by Emily when she sat down on the sofa on the other side of me, crying. The girl was full of drama, inventing it wherever she went. Linda came to soothe her.

"Emily," Linda said quietly.

"Leave me alone!"

"Look, you've had a bit to drink. You're rightfully upset, but let's take this upstairs where no one will hear," Linda pleaded.

"What do you think *they're* doing up there? What a slut! Both of them!" Emily cried, tears streaming down her face.

"Who?" I ventured, forcing myself into the conversation.

"Your buddy and *Callie*," Emily said Callie's name with scorn. "They're up in *my* room doing you-know-what."

"No, they're not." I laughed. I closed my eyes for a fraction of a second, picturing myself up in Emily's room, and was there mentally. Archer and Callie were lying across the bed on their stomachs, side by side, talking. He touched her cheek gently, she blushed, and they kissed. It was a scene far more innocent than what Emily assumed. I left them alone, trying to dispel the image from my mind. I hoped, for Callie's sake, that she had kissed him first. "They're a couple of prudes, honestly. Making out maybe but not what you're suggesting."

"How would you know?" she lashed out.

"My cousin Archer is a gentleman," Belle said defiantly.

This wasn't good. If it came down to defending Archer, Belle would kill Emily—literally. I squeezed Belle's hand to calm her down.

"Why can't it be me?" Emily wailed. "I was saving myself for him," she muttered in drunken slurs.

"Emily, quiet," Linda begged.

Linda observed me and my hand on Belle's. I instinctively let go. I didn't want her to think Belle and I were together. I'm not sure why.

"I need to put her to bed. Can you help me clear her room out?" she asked Belle and me.

"Yeah, okay." I was aware Linda had as big a crush on me as Emily had on Archer. Boys aren't as insipid as girls make us out to be. We can tell. Linda wasn't bad at all, and if I had to drown my sorrow for not having Callie, then why not Linda?

We went upstairs together, and on opening the door, we found the "fugitives" in the same position I had seen them in, watching TV and flirtatiously chatting. They were surprised at the interruption.

"You're in Emily's room," I told Archer.

He got up quickly, taking Callie's hands and helping her off the bed. The others approached behind me with a ranting Emily.

"Skank!" Emily directed at Callie. "I hate you!"

Callie gasped. "What?" The look of horror on her face was heartbreaking.

Emily pressed her finger sharply into Callie's chest and said, "You stole him. He was mine. I love him!"

"Emily, I'm sorry—" Callie began.

"Don't." Archer put his hand up to silence Callie. "We have nothing to apologize for." He took up her hand, squeezed it reassuringly, and led her out of the room.

I began to follow them as Belle forcefully pushed Emily into the room. Archer eyed me to stay away, so I remained awkwardly in the doorway.

"Gosh, you're really strong, Belle. She carried me up here," Emily slurred and stumbled.

"Okay, Emily, go to sleep," Linda said in a tone that betrayed she didn't believe her friend and was equally embarrassed in the present situation.

"Who does Emily like?" Archer asked Callie. I couldn't help but overhear the lovebirds.

She scoffed and said, "You."

"Besides that," he pressed.

"What?" She was confused.

"I mean, who would she be good with? We could play matchmaker, you and I." He smiled at her. What was he doing?

"Um...Pete maybe," Callie mentioned. "He's really nice, and she thinks he's cute."

Archer closed his eyes for a moment, most likely matchmaking in his head, and kissed her at the same moment. I was sure Emily would be in love with Pete soon enough. What a bloody show off. What an idiot to expose himself. I wanted to strangle him. Didn't he realize every little hint that he gave her to what he was put Callie closer to danger? Or was he too blinded by love?

"We'll work on it on Monday," he told her, feigning how they would talk Pete into going out with Emily.

I glared at him.

Archer noticed, gave me a confused and questioning glance, and then pulled Callie protectively against him.

I shook my head at him.

"I didn't," Archer mouthed at me. He claimed he hadn't shot Emily or Pete, but he probably would.

I went back downstairs. I was sure he was clueless as to why I was bitter, which was a good thing since it was more than his carelessness that upset me. Since our welcome was overstayed, I gathered up the girls to leave. When we walked out into the cool night, Archer, who walked out first, abruptly stopped. Callie bumped into him and me into her, almost tumbling us like dominos.

"Archer?" Callie asked in a worried voice, her eyes darting to him and then to a man standing between our cars and us.

It was Hermes, his arms crossed, looking, as always, arrogantly pleased with himself. He always felt privileged at being Zeus's go-to man, servant of sorts, but in all honesty, I didn't find honor in constantly following through on Zeus's every whim. Everyone knew, except for the knave himself, that Zeus kept him occupied so he'd stay out of trouble. His service was a punishment.

Hermes eyed us all, barely acknowledging Callie, and then said, "We should have a talk...Archer." I thought for a moment he'd call him Eros, but he was simply toying with us.

"Now?" Archer challenged, gripping onto Callie's hand, reminding Hermes we were in mixed company.

Hermes examined Callie like a specimen and shot her an obviously fake smile. "It'll just take a sec," he said pleasantly back. His gallantry was unnerving. He was never nice.

"Callie, get in the car. I'll be there in a minute," Archer told her softly.

"No," she said worriedly, eyeing Hermes as one would Tartarus himself, a primordial god who named a part of the Underworld after himself, the place no being would ever want to end up.

"He's my grandfather's servant. Grandpa's private about things," Archer explained craftily, not lying to her.

It was clear Callie didn't believe him.

"I swear." He put his hand up. He shot a silent but commanding look to Belle.

Archer's driver watched from the car with an anxious expression. My car was parked behind Archer's. I handed my keys to Ada.

"Come on, Callie, we'll talk about them while we wait," Belle said in a bubbly tone and opened the door to the car. The two girls climbed into his car, while Ada and Thalia climbed into my car.

Hermes raised his brow, questioning my presence.

"Witnessing," I answered his unspoken question as we walked away from the cars.

"Oh, I don't think there will be a need for that." Hermes laughed in his haughty way.

"Oh, I think there will be," I countered. "Only half the time do your messages make it back verbatim, and even then, there are high exaggerations to one's tone. I can't lie, and so I make the best witness."

"Have it your way." Hermes turned to Archer. "Zeus says stop meddling with the mortal. He wishes you to give her up."

Archer's fists clenched, and his face went deathly pale. I wasn't sure what he would do, but Hermes awaited an answer.

"Did he say why?" I ventured, trying to buy time.

"Does he need to?" Hermes challenged.

"Might help Archer's decision if there's a grounded reason behind it, that's all."

"No, it won't." Archer glared at me stubbornly, his eyes an eerie blue with the ephemeral light that shimmers when he feels any intense emotion. Archer was going to go wild. His anger was building and seething. I was afraid he'd expose his powers in front of Callie.

"It would still be nice to know why," I said slowly to Archer, hoping to put the point across in my tone for him to stay in control.

"It can't be hard to let a toy go, no matter how appealing it may be," said Hermes.

"She's not a toy." Archer's glare shifted to Hermes.

Hermes backed up a step. "Don't shoot the messenger."

"I will shoot you, throttle you, strangle you. I'll do whatever I want to you," Archer growled through clenched teeth, stepping closer to him.

"The mortal is watching," Hermes said smugly.

Archer peered into the car, then turned quickly away. He focused on the ground and, struggling to be calm, said, "Tell Zeus that I regret I cannot acquiesce to his wishes at the present moment."

"He's not going to like that," Hermes said in a singsong voice.

"That's your problem," Archer hissed and stormed toward the car.

I looked at Hermes sheepishly and shrugged.

"You'd tell him to ditch her if you wanted what's best for him," Hermes warned as I walked away.

"And you'd tell me why he should if you wanted me to help Zeus," I countered back as I knocked on the window for Thalia to lower it. "But I'm sure you have no clue, just always blindly following orders without knowing why."

Hermes glared at me, his jaw set, and I turned my attention back to the girls. "Ladies, I better keep an eye on Archer."

I let them take my car, and I squeezed into Archer's. Belle made room by sitting on my lap. Out the window, I saw Hermes walk away toward the nearby alley so he could inconspicuously disappear.

"What was that about?" Callie asked me.

Archer stared out the window away from her. She must have tried him and Belle and received no answer. Belle stared at Archer, frightened and astounded. I really wanted to figure out what she knew about the situation. The Charities had come from Fiji. Had Zeus ordered them here for some specific reason besides spying?

I shook my head at Callie to warn her not to press him at the moment, and she sighed in frustration.

"Rupert, home," Archer commanded.

The car lurched forward. We were all silent.

Callie suddenly turned to Archer, grabbed his chin, and pulled him to face her. She searched his face for something. "What is it?"

His eyes were still alight. "Nothing," he said, trying to put on a smile.

"Your eyes don't lie," she said quietly. She met his gaze shakily but determined.

They stared at one another for a while, neither breaking the stare or blinking. The internal fire in his eyes dimmed down and simmered out. Her gaze appeared strong and probing, making me fear for her own sake how much she could perceive. It was eerie that she could behold our gaze. Usually, people could only glimpse at us, unconsciously overwhelmed by our intensity. And she was so perceptive, her comment exposing that she could see the light in his eyes most mortals couldn't.

THE IMMORTAL TRANSCRIPTS: QUIVER

Archer took her face gently in his hands. "Stay in the dark, Callie. Please?" Archer begged her. I couldn't comprehend what it meant on a personal level. What had he told her? It seemed painfully similar to Psyche, who had failed to remain literally and figuratively in the dark when Archer visited her.

"What is going on?" Callie pressed. "That man upset you."

Archer tried to smile, but the effort was futile. He was feigning his upbeat and positive attitude for her. His rage and fright were seething beneath the surface. Belle shifted uncomfortably on my lap. She turned to me for answers. I shrugged.

"Callie, please. Stay in the dark. You don't want to know anything about my grandfather. You agreed not to pry," he warned her. His tone was no longer soft or joking. He was dead serious, and from Callie's reaction, he had never reproached her like that before.

I didn't understand what he meant exactly or how much he had told her about his life, but Callie nodded solemnly, seemingly understanding him. Somehow, they had encoded silences already. He kissed her passionately to appease her, which forced me to look away, so I turned my attention back to Belle, who bit her lip trying not to laugh at the awkwardness of the situation. I squeezed her hand, happy to not feel alone in that moment. She thought they were adorable, but she might change her mind if she found out Zeus's order.

Belle's eyes searched mine for an answer, and I couldn't ignore her forever. I pulled her closer, her ear to my lips, and whispered in immortal speed so that if Callie somehow overheard, she could not discern my words. "Zeus ordered him to quit her. He refused. I don't understand why the demand was made in the first place, do you? Obviously, you were all sent here for a reason."

Belle shook her head to suggest otherwise. Then, taking the same precaution not to be overheard as I had, she said, "We were told to simply watch him, observe him and the mortal, and report. I have no idea what is going on, I swear. I don't know what to do if he won't give her up."

I sighed in frustration. She did as well.

"I won't do it, Lucien," Archer said, his attention still on Callie, smoothing her hair. He must have been listening to us as he kissed Callie. "I won't," he repeated, glancing at me over her shoulder with conviction. They were the last words he said to me before I left for Nice early the next morning.

I was beginning to see how the "everything as we know it will change forever" prophecy would unfold. If Zeus did anything to Callie, I could imagine Archer lashing out against him. His mother would defend him and, by default, his father. No one messed with Ares. He, if anyone, was a match for Zeus's power. I could imagine this going horribly wrong. I needed to discover who Callie was in order to understand Zeus's command. The question was, could I find the answers in time before the prophecy occurred, before Zeus would cause irrevocable damage?

CHAPTER 12

Callie

I hardly wanted to get up. There was something I had to do that I was dreading (well, a few things that I dreaded). First on my agenda was to go over to Emily's and make whatever amends I could. I had known she liked Archer, but she never bothered to notice (or cared) that I did as well. It wouldn't be a pretty situation.

Second, my schoolbooks were staring me down. I hadn't finished any of my homework, and I was still behind since I'd missed the first six weeks of the school year. Every time I made a good attempt to catch up, I'd slip behind again because Archer was sucking up all my time (don't get me wrong; I enjoyed the distraction). I had at least three hours straight of homework due tomorrow and a lab report due on Wednesday, and one of our lab partners was AWOL, having fun in France.

On top of this, I had been neglecting my dad. I needed to spend more time with him, so we were going to dinner. I felt childish and selfish because all I wanted to do was be with Archer. As much as it pained me, I needed balance in my life. I couldn't fight with or dismiss friends and family for a boy.

I got up. Better to get the day over with so I could enjoy dinner with Dad.

I dialed Linda's cell. "Hey, it's Callie."

"Oh." She was surprised to hear from me.

"Are you still at Emily's?"

"Ye-ah," she hesitated. This was not good. They must have been trash-talking me all night. I could tell from her tone (great, just great).

"I need to talk to her."

"Uh...hang on." Linda covered the phone. I heard muffled voices (so childish).

"Callie?" Emily's voice came on the phone.

"I was calling to see if you needed help, you know, cleaning up and all." I felt so awkward. I was afraid she'd start yelling at me.

"Uh, sure. Come over if you want," she said just as awkwardly. Maybe I was lucky, and she forgot everything that happened last night. The phone was silent for a moment, and then she sighed deeply. "Look, I'm sorry, Callie. I was ridiculous last night. I drank way too much and said some terrible things, but I am a little upset. I've had a crush on Archer since the first time I saw him in ninth grade. Then you show up, and he's with you right away."

"I'm sorry," was all I could say.

Emily sighed again. "Just come on over." Then she hung up.

Great, now I felt guilty for my attraction to Archer when it was natural and just. Emily couldn't have claims on him when Archer wasn't interested. She didn't seem like the kind of girl who would understand that, though.

I nervously headed over to Emily's house, but the anxiety was pointless. She was nice to me, almost too nice, as if last night had never happened. My intuition told me she was being fake. She was keeping me close, perhaps to get closer to Archer, and then she'd try to steal him. Her mind was like an open book—her thoughts so apparent and so loud that I wondered why Linda did not question her behavior. I would keep her close as well to make sure she wouldn't try to break us up.

The house was a mess, and we chatted about nonsense while we cleaned up. Emily's parents had gone away for the weekend, so it was vital that all party evidence be removed. I could never dare to defy my dad like that, but I wasn't really like Emily at all. Our differences were becoming obvious, and while I wasn't sure I really wanted to be her friend anymore, I didn't have many close friends yet. I had many acquaintances but still felt a bit like an outsider. Even with Archer's friends, I felt like I was kept out of their secret, weird society.

At one point, I found myself alone with Emily while Linda was out on a dumpster run. Emily lost no time and got right to the point: "Did you know I liked him?"

"No. I mean, I thought you might have a little crush on him, but a bunch of girls do." I told her the truth. "You never said anything to me about it."

"Did he tell you I asked him out last year?"

"No," was all I could say. Obviously, he must have refused her.

"He *said* he didn't date. And he never has until now." She wasn't mad, but hurt, which was even worse. There was nothing I could possibly do to make her feel better. But what did she expect? It wasn't as if they were together before I came along.

"I didn't know that. I'm sorry." I focused on picking up plastic cups.

"Do you really like him, like a lot?"

"Yes," I told her firmly. Better to play it straight.

Emily smiled then. It was a forced smile but a smile nevertheless. "Good. You are nice and so very pretty. He deserves someone like you."

"Um...thanks," I muttered awkwardly as I got her unnecessary permission. My uncanny intuition told me I wouldn't want to know her private thoughts, so I didn't try to further read her.

"In other words, let's forget about last night," she added.

"Yes, please!" I sighed and then attempted to be kinder. "You should come sit with us at lunch, you and Linda."

"Aroha doesn't like us."

"She doesn't like anyone. Girls at least," Linda said flatly, joining us again.

"And she's visiting her dad overseas. You should usurp her little throne while she's out of town." I grinned wickedly at them.

They loved it, laughing.

"And if she throws a fit, we'll start a new table without her."

"Deal!" Emily smiled, shaking my hand. All seemed repaired between us, for now.

My homework took me ages that night, so long that I had to cancel dinner with Dad, and we had pizza delivered instead. I had to listen to a lecture about budgeting my time and not spending all my time improving my social life. He wasn't mad, though, which was good. Dad hardly ever got mad. As of late, he didn't have the energy to waste on anger.

The next day, I found myself alone with Archer in chemistry class since Lucien was away. We'd even become accustomed to riding to school together since Aroha was still visiting their father, who was stationed overseas. When questioned why he didn't go as well, Archer was a little too curt, telling me that he didn't get along with his father but using a string of curse words instead of "father." I was forced to let it drop for the time being. I hated to admit that I was glad Lucien and Aroha were both gone. I enjoyed being alone with Archer, even though we were going over the periodic table and not working together on a lab. If we were working on a lab, it would be a glorious uninterrupted tête-à-tête, something I never got enough of at school.

"Go out with me tonight," Archer said as soon as I was seated and the late bell chimed.

"Is that a request or a demand?"

"Demand." His eyes narrowed into a very intimidating scowl.

"Where are we going?" I tried to suppress the smile that threatened to expose my deep-rooted weaknesses when it came to him.

"Not the movies," he sighed, his cheeks blushing red and making him adorably school-boyish.

"No," I said too quickly, "not the movies."

Mr. Montgomery pulled down the periodic table chart with a loud bang, most likely to stop us chatterboxes who refused to quiet down after the bell. The room grew silent in obedience.

Archer wasn't paying attention to the front of the room, but staring at me, which I found extremely distracting. I dared to peer at him from the corner of my eyes, but he refused to look away, even after I shot him a glare.

"Stop it," I whispered, trying not to be heard by Mr. Montgomery.

"Stop what?"

"Staring at me."

"I can't."

"Yes, you can." I gave him another defiant glare, warning him he would be in trouble if he continued. "It's very distracting."

"So are you," he shot back smugly. "You shouldn't be allowed in public places. You could cause all sorts of mischief, distracting us guys."

"Archer," I scolded.

"What?" He played dumb.

"Shush, we'll get in trouble."

"Who cares?" He shrugged. Then he said, not as quietly as our previous conversation, "Let's do something different tonight. No cafes, pool halls, movie theaters, homework in front of your ever-watchful dad—I dunno—like ice skating at Rockefeller Center, go to a club, or a museum—"

"A museum?" I asked, my curiosity sparked by the idea.

"Art, I dunno." Self-consciousness crept in his voice and mannerisms. He was worried that I thought he was weird, almost ashamed at such a suggestion.

"I do like art," I answered to alleviate his anxious ego.

"And I like you," he mused in an odd tone, like an actor reading lines.

"And *that* was cheesy." I laughed.

"It was from that atrocious film you tried to put me through."

"*I* tried to put *you* through? *You* suggested it."

"It really was awful, wasn't it?"

"Yes," I affirmed, trying to figure out where I had left off in my notes, only to find I was now lost. "I never want to see that film again."

Archer looked away, his posture going rigid and his brow wrinkled. He shifted silently in his seat twice, and then his eyes shot to me. I couldn't read his mood swing, so I was expecting another joke from the movie we had seen when he said, "Callie, what do you *want*?"

My mind whirled through what slight memories I had of the movie, but after his face didn't crack into the familiar mischievous grin, I realized he wasn't making a joke at all, but was serious. But what did he mean? His stress on the word "want" didn't give me any insight. And why was he suddenly so serious after cracking jokes a moment earlier?

"What do you mean?"

Instead of answering, he sighed in frustration and turned his attention to the front of the room. Despite my brilliant gift of intuition, I couldn't fathom what he meant.

"What...like in life?" I shot out a wild guess. Then it dawned on me that he might have meant us. All these silly rules, the thing he wasn't going to do that his grandfather asked—perhaps he needed to know how serious I was about him? I had been afraid to say things, held them back to not scare him off. "Oh, do you mean...er...with us?"

Archer's head turned so quickly, I wondered how he didn't get whiplash, "I..." he stopped himself, his eyes illuminated abruptly with astonishment. Then he looked back to me, those alluring eyes drawing me in, "I really—"

"Mr. Ambrose. Miss Syches. That's enough!" Mr. Montgomery barked at us, interrupting whatever Archer was about to say.

I felt my face flush brightly from embarrassment as the class's eyes all turned to stare at us. I'd called it. We were in trouble.

"Sorry, sir," Archer said dutifully.

"Detention after school for both of you."

I sighed, annoyed. What a fascist! Detention without a warning first—so unfair! I felt my anger flare up, and the unfortunate Archer was the recipient of my bitter glares. His apologetic eyes met mine, and then he turned forward to pay attention to the lecture, which resumed in the front of the class. I felt his hand seek my own under the table, and when he found it, he gave it a squeeze and then let go.

I longed to hear what he would have said if he hadn't been interrupted by dreadful Mr. Montgomery. I could've sworn he was about to declare something profound. That he loved me? I felt my heart race at the thought because I realized that I loved him already too.

Once we were in the hall after class, I grabbed Archer's hand in mine, hoping to continue the conversation. He studied our hands, then gave me a crooked grin. He intertwined his fingers in mine.

I decided to be blunt and just ask him what I was dying to know. "Archer, what were you going to say before Mr. Montgomery yelled at us?"

"Oh...uh...just that I really enjoy spending time with you," he said a little timidly. However, something else in his voice set me off. He was lying or had decided against what he'd planned to say. "Sorry about detention."

"At least we'll be together."

"Mr. Montgomery will probably make us sift through old books and catalog them. That's what he usually does. He's sweet on Miss Hutchens, the librarian."

"Good, I was worried he'd make us clean Bunsen burners or feed mice to snakes," I said, cringing.

After school, we showed up to Mr. Montgomery's classroom, but instantly, as Archer had predicted, he whisked us away to the library's basement. Our punishment was to sort through old yearbooks and organize them on shelves by year. Apparently, Miss Hutchens was attempting to open an archive in the basement, which appeared to have been renovated lately, although the smell of mildew and dust remained.

Archer and I set to work opening boxes and emptying crates, agreeing to first compile them into decades and then arrange them on the shelves by year. As soon as Mr. Montgomery was satisfied we were working hard, he slipped from the room. Archer sighed, put the books down, and pulled me to him, kissing me gently and smoothing my hair down my neck.

"Come on, Casanova," I teased. "We'll be here all night if you keep that up."

"I don't care." He held me tight and kissed me again.

"Didn't you want to go to a museum?" I wasn't about to let his honey-sweet scent or addictive charisma get me into any more trouble.

Archer sighed, torn, then kissed my forehead and let go. We grudgingly got to work, quietly at first, before Archer broke the silence. "So where do you go after graduation?"

This was random. "What do you mean?"

"Colleges. Your dad said something about you continuing your education. Where'd you apply?"

"Why do *you* want to know?" I teased him. So, this was what he had been digging for earlier. He wanted to know my future plans, like I ever made them.

"Might want to visit you someday...maybe," he wittily bantered back with a smirk while still stacking books. He was feigning a lack of interest, telling me in a roundabout way that he really was contemplating a future with me. I wasn't sure if I should fess up my feelings or make him squirm.

"I'm not sure where yet. Applied to NYU, Berkley, Hunter, and King's, but it all depends on what happens with my dad. Have to stay close in case...he needs me."

"So, you might put off school and spend time with him?"

"I want to, but he is very insistent that I get an education, no matter what. So this was best. I could commute and still live at home." I didn't add my thoughts about how it all hinged on whether the doctors could give us that much time.

"He also wants you to be an archeologist, take Greek—"

"Your point, Archer?" I didn't like anyone talking about my dad that way, not even Archer.

"I'm just saying you should do what *you* want to do, not be at your father's mercy. I know he's ill, but you shouldn't make a martyr of yourself for him. That has to be the last thing he'd truly want. What do *you* want to be, Callie?"

"I don't know," I mused. It had been a long time since someone had asked me what I wanted. I remembered taking a career aptitude test that said I should be a psychiatrist, lawyer, or historian. Dad, of course, only supported the last option. I never wanted to think about my future, almost as if putting it off would allow Dad to live longer. I would have time to decide what was best for me later. "I've thought about psychiatry or something else in med. school maybe. I'd like to help people."

"You seem to have a knack for that. Helping people, I mean. You do it too much already. You're too selfless, Callie. What else do you dream about? What do you expect out of life?" He was getting awfully philosophical for detention. These questions were building up to a more important one. He was oddly cautious.

"Oh, the usual," I said, sorting through another box. "Is that pile you're making the 1930s?"

"Forties," he corrected. "What's the usual?"

"Oh, you know, a good job I'd actually like doing, nice husband, a nice house, a couple kids...oh, and I want to travel all over the world as well..."

Archer broke into a wide smile, shaking his head, laughing quietly at an inside joke.

"What?"

"Nothing." He composed himself. "Tell me more."

"Well, what I want most in life is to be happy."

"And you're not right now," he insinuated more as a fact than a question. His voice was again layered with various emotions, trying to verbalize all the multitude of sensations he believed I was feeling.

"I am happy at times," I insisted vaguely so as to not hurt his feelings. His presence made me happy. The only time I felt happy was when he was around, but it felt too soon to admit that. Again, I felt torn between admitting all my feelings and the fear I'd scare him off. It was a tight balance with boys; sometimes they bolted like deer at the L-word.

I wanted the subject off me, and I wanted to hear about him. "So, what about you?"

"I haven't a clue. Probably take some time after graduation to travel, settle somewhere incredibly warm," he said nonchalantly, flipping through one of the yearbooks, barely glancing at the pictures.

"No college?"

"Maybe NYU, Berkley, Hunter, or King's." He gazed at me with his dazzling eyes. He sounded serious yet simultaneously joking, so I wasn't sure what to think.

I laughed it off and then flipped through a yearbook, examining the photos. "Look at these people!" I laughed, pointing at a couple dressed in cheesy '70s prom attire. A change of subject felt necessary.

Archer peered over my shoulder and laughed a bit. "I will never understand the evolution of style. How did they actually believe they looked good?" he murmured as he went back to sorting.

I flipped through some more albums, well aware that I was wasting time, but any time with Archer, even detention, was worth it (sad but true). I came across a very old album, one tattered so badly that the spine was cracking. I opened it carefully, trying not to damage it any further. It was a book from Ithaca High School, a school in New York dating back to 1912, and was by far the oldest one I had come across.

"Oh, wow," I said quietly. "This one's really old."

Archer peered over at it briefly without much interest as I began leafing carefully through it. The people were in old-fashioned clothing, all unsmiling, like when cameras were so old that the flash took a minute or so to fully capture the scene. I remembered seeing some blurry old family photos of my great-great-grandparents, and Dad had explained to me about the long flash.

I flipped through the senior class photos of serious-looking students: the girls with wispy, voluminous hair culminating in a knot atop their heads, with dresses buttoned up to their necks; and the boys with severely parted hair slicked down on their heads, suit collars showing. Then, right in the middle of the page, I came across a photo that made me freeze.

I don't know how long I had been inspecting the photo when Archer's voice broke my trance: "Callie. C'mon, let's get this over with." His voice was oddly commanding, his eyes full of worry, yet he was masking it, not wanting me to know he was troubled. He tried to take the book from my hands, but I refused to let go, daring to stare again at the specter on the page.

"You'll ruin it," he urged, trying to unlatch my hands. "Callie, what is..." He stopped as he peered down at the cover of the album. He instantly went pale, his body rigid, and his eyes locked on mine. The shock left him just as quickly as it came, and he had on a laughing smile again. "What's wrong?"

I peered down at the photo again, willing it to change or to just be a trick of my sometimes overactive imagination, but I saw exactly what I had seen previously: a young man in a suit with a small smile barely on his lips, his light hair parted and slicked into smooth waves. The eyes, although gray, shone eerily off the page. It was Archer, or an exact replica of him as if he'd walked into an old-time photo shop where they dress you up in Wild West clothes and take your black-and-white photo.

My mind reeled, attempting to make sense of what I saw. How was this possible? It was too accurate to be some uncanny coincidence. It was my boyfriend, only drained of color and planted in 1912. My gaze darted from the book to Archer and then back. The only differences were the hairstyle and the clothing. I inspected him, realizing that it *was* him; somehow, this was Archer. Then his words from the weekend echoed in my mind: *"What if I told you I could never tell you everything about me, Callie? Would you still want to be with me? What if knowing these things would put you in danger? Could you live without knowing them?"*

Archer gave me another forced smile and took the book away from me. I let him, unable to say a word to stop him. He peered at the book again quickly, closed it with a hard bang, and dropped it in the earliest pile we had formed.

"Archer?" I finally found my voice as he silently sorted more yearbooks, ignoring the photo entirely. He could not pretend that the photo meant nothing. I wouldn't let him get away with it.

"Hmm?" he murmured nonchalantly.

"Um, that photo?" I reminded him with agitation.

"What photo?" He was extremely guarded again, which made me even more suspicious.

"That photo. That guy. He looks exactly like you."

"That's absurd."

"Look at it!" I insisted, grabbing for the book again. Archer prevented me by grabbing my hands in his.

"I did!" he said a bit sharply. Well, this was a sudden shift in mood. "He sort of did. 'Exactly' is a bit of an exaggeration, don't you think? Maybe he's some long lost relative?" His voice was jagged. He was deeply annoyed at my line of questioning.

"'Exactly' is not an exaggeration. 'Exactly' is *exactly* the right word."

"A coincidence." He shrugged.

"It's a bit too coincidental then." I gave him a glare to show him he was far from off the hook.

Then a huge smile spread across his face as he squeezed my hands gently. But his eyes were unsmiling, with fear behind them. He was exposed and vulnerable behind this mask of feigned ease. For once, I felt I had the upper hand—the power to unlock his eerie secrets.

"So, what you're trying to say, Callie, is that someone alive in—" he paused to pick up the book to ascertain the date and dropped it in a different pile "—1912 is the same person here now before you, at roughly the same age, unchanged by time?" The way in which he worded it made me feel foolish, but something deep down within me couldn't let it go.

If he'd play these little games and deny me some real answers, then I could too. "You're right. What was I thinking?" I laughed, hiding the doubts in my mind.

"Just a coincidence," he said, gently drawing me toward him. He kissed my lips softly at first—one of those kisses that built up and made me never want to pull away. My body went limp in his arms; he had kissed away all my doubts, fears, and shock, making me feel foolish for the ridiculous conclusion I had jumped to.

We continued to sort the rest of the books, forgetting about the entire incident. Before we knew it, Mr. Montgomery came back to dismiss us. As we were leaving, I felt the urge to take the yearbook, just to examine it one more time. I'd return it—I only wanted one more peek to reassure myself I wasn't going mental. But when I went to find the book again, it wasn't in either of the two piles I'd seen Archer place it in or on the shelf.

I suspiciously scrutinized Archer, but his hands were empty. His eyes studied me and were firmly set, most likely willing me to forget everything. He knew what I was scanning the room for. I'd never be able to forget it or fully let it go. It would fester in the back of my mind, my imagination creating more layers on top of it. And if I didn't get to the bottom of it all, the very idea would ruin everything. But how can you question someone about things that are utterly impossible? The glowing eyes, the strange rules, the necessity for secrecy, and now this photo?

It was impossible. The logical part of my brain acknowledged that. Archer couldn't have been alive and eighteen in 1912 and be here today at the same age. But the logical part of my brain had to admit that no one could look so identical. My mind was not one that could live in the dark as Archer had made me promise. I was born with an innate intuition and a curiosity that was unquenchable.

I felt his firm, warm hands in mine, and again, as if by magic, the doubts began to drift away. His eyes puzzled me—he was upset, confused, angry, and torn, yet all the while, they shone with love for me.

"What are you thinking?" he asked, his voice on edge as if my answer determined everything.

I didn't want to let it go, but I didn't want to lose him either. "How utterly complex you are."

He smiled at this, the answer satisfying him. "Hardly."

"No, really, when you say things, there are so many meanings in your voice. I can hardly tell what you really mean."

"You really do have an active imagination, Callie," he said with a genuine smile and pulled me tighter to him. "Let's use that to our advantage. Hmmm, you have to make up an interesting story about every piece of artwork we come across."

"We'll be there forever."

"If only we could have forever," he mused, his thoughts far away.

At the museum, he didn't ask me to tell him stories, but we enjoyed silently viewing the paintings. He held my hand so tightly the entire time that I thought if I tried to pry it loose, I wouldn't be able to. He had a stone-set grip on me, but I didn't test the theory, wanting to hold on to him tightly as well. I had this idiotic feeling that if we let go, our relationship might slip away.

When I finally got home, Dad was eager for my help. He was attempting to draw out a diagram that showed the gods he discussed in his book in a family-tree sort of set up. He was having trouble because his arm was tired, making his hand cramp and his fingers shake. So instead of doing my homework (as I should), I helped him. After all, it proved more interesting than labeling the periodic table or translating Greek.

With a ruler, I copied Dad's scribbled diagram. It was kind of odd. His chart did not match the one in my world mythology book. I wondered if he had done this on purpose or if the meds were affecting him negatively.

"Hey, Dad?"

"Hmm?" His eyes were closed and his head back, almost asleep.

"Why do you have the family tree all discombobulated?"

"I have it correct. History books have it discombobulated."

"But..."

"Do you believe everything you read?" He sat up straight. "You move from one text to the next, and the mythology changes. Take the lesser gods, Hymenaios for example. Is that god male or female? Is this god a child of Apollo and a Muse, Dionysus and Aphrodite, or the other combinations the ancient poets professed?"

He was getting annoyingly Socratic on me, so I attempted to stop him. I shot a question at him to prevent him from questioning me further. "How do you know you are right?"

"I don't know if I have it *all* right, but I do know I *am* right. They did not all descend from Zeus."

I guess it was another one of his harebrained ideas. You never know with Dad, though; he could be right. I let it go and finished the diagram for him.

Afterward, I stayed up until two finishing all my homework, except for my Greek translations, but Archer could do them during lunch for me in minutes. If Dad had known my homework wasn't done, he would've refused my help. To avoid explaining detention and my date with Archer, I told him a small fib of being at Archer's the entire time doing homework, which I felt a little guilty about.

Despite the late hour, I couldn't fall asleep. There was this feeling that crept over me that was hard to describe. I was sensing some impending doom, like anxiety for a test I hadn't prepared for, or that these moments with Archer that were so amazing were about to come to an end without warning. I tried to calm myself by thinking about Archer, but that only compounded my anxiety even more. I tried to shake the feeling, but then memories flashed before me: the eyes glowing brightly after our first passionate kiss, the eerie photo from long ago, the ridiculous rules made by someone else...

There was Archer, staring at me, his eerie eyes shining brightly with love. Thunder boomed. There were a bunch of crazy images flittering by repeatedly: a knife covered in blood; thunder booming, rattling my bedroom balcony doors; Archer screaming, and fire, smoke. I saw them again and again until I couldn't handle it.

I grabbed my head to stop them, but two hands grasped mine. Archer was terrified and upset. "You should've stayed in the dark," he lamented. Then I saw Aroha, Lucien, some stranger...and the Grim Reaper in a black cloak. The figure came flying at me.

I woke up before the dream could go on any further. The sun shone through my window, announcing a new day. The brightness of my room contrasted with the dark mood of my dream. One thing was for sure: I was glad I wasn't psychic because if I were, the dream showed it was likely someone would die. The dream seemed to point to me.

CHAPTER 13

Archer

Just as I feared, the clash of my old world with my new one began to get more complex. Yes, they admitted it: the Charities had been sent by Zeus to babysit me, to protect me from myself while Aroha was gone. Only, Zeus hadn't planned on them becoming as smitten with Callie as I was. Ada, Thalia, and even the more down-to-earth Belle went from watching me to letting me have my own way. They were "quite taken in by her," "absolutely besotted," and "adored her eternally."

It seemed clear that Zeus couldn't stop me from being with Callie. No more messages came, so my confidence grew daily—until the yearbook debacle. Callie started asking questions. I smuggled that yearbook out of school by sliding it into my bookbag at immortal speed. When I got home, I went up onto the roof and torched it. So stupid. We never take photos, but Aroha had been dying for one back when they were still a novelty, and she was the one who'd insisted on coming back to NY now, just over a century later. What were the odds anyone would see an obscure old yearbook? It was ridiculous and virtually impossible, and yet Callie somehow found it. The Fates were against me. How much longer could I pull off the lies? The worst part was, I didn't want to. I was tired of hiding part of myself from the woman I loved, yet her finding out who I was could give Zeus reason to hurt her.

I was walking past the intersection of Fifth Avenue and Forty-sixth Street, holding Callie's hand while the retinue of the Charities, Linda, and Dan roamed ahead of us. We were merely window shopping, only going inside when the Charities burst out with squeals that they needed one item or another, which was often. Dan doggedly followed, carrying all their bags. I was a bit annoyed that Callie had even invited him, but he was safely in love with Aroha and naturally infatuated with the Charities.

"Are you okay?" Callie asked me.

I nodded.

She sighed.

Damn it. I wish she'd stop prying, as she had promised me. Pointing out that promise would make her even more suspicious, though.

"Hey, Belle!" Callie called, waving around her phone. "Can you take a pic of Archer and me?" Callie asked in such a way that made me realize she was suspicious and expectant that we would deny taking a photo. It irked me that she somehow concluded the truth.

Belle hesitated. We were to be in photos sparingly ever since Dionysus became a famous actor in the 1920s and was later recognized in the 1950s after his "death." Zeus had several gods busy destroying evidence and memories of our existence. Evidence much like the artifacts in the Sycheses' apartment.

Callie was suspicious, and a photo would put her at ease. A few photos here and there would do no harm. I could destroy them later if necessary, although the thought of erasing Callie and our time together made me feel ill.

I gave Belle a nod, and she took the phone, snapped a photo, and gave it back. Callie viewed the photo and showed it to me. We looked good together, just as we did the day I met her, seeing the reflection of us in the elevator doors.

With that hiccup gone, I thought all would be well, but then I spotted *him* across the street: Anteros, the avenger of slighted love, my enemy and, unfortunately, my half-brother. He glowered at me across the crowd, unmoving as mortals bumped into his shoulders like waves breaking around a steadfast rock. Before I could wonder why in Zeus's name he was here, Anteros raised his hand, his finger pointed like a gun. He aimed it at Callie, and he pulled the imaginary trigger. He then met my glare with a smirk and blew on his fingertip. He was here about Callie, and I didn't like his threats.

I gave him a glare as we walked on, and he nodded down the street ahead of us to where I noticed another familiar face. It was the other family outcast, my half-brother Himerus, god of lust and longing. I was sure Hymenaios, one of Lucien's immortal sons, was somewhere close by. The three of them were inseparable. The entire love retinue was in New York—save my mother, the one who could pull rank on all of us. Great.

This could be a problem of catastrophic proportions. Anteros could stand in as my double, almost identical, but with hazel eyes and poker-straight sandy-brown hair. He was a good three inches shorter than me too. Ma called him her "sullied Eros." Hymenaios was problematic as well. He was the god of the wedding feast, and now he had taken over Hera's role as the guardian of marriages since she was too lazy to do her job. The dilemma was the fact he looked a whole lot like Lucien but a softer version—paler, thinner, without as much muscle tone. Himerus was much safer as he had our dad's darker eyes and hair, was extremely tall, and took more after his mother—if Ma's jealous rantings in the past had merit.

And here they were in NY, ready to threaten my entire world again, this time through exposure. I let go of Callie's hand and tapped Thalia on the shoulder. When she turned, I nodded in Anteros's direction. She was genuinely as surprised as I, so the girls hadn't known about this.

"Take care of it," I said quietly to her.

She nodded, skipped over to Belle, and grabbed her arm. "Oooo! Belle, look at that dress! It is absolutely fabulous!" She pulled Belle along with her. "Go on, guys. We'll meet you at home." They skipped across the street and disappeared into the crowd.

Nervous, expecting a full-on ambush, I clasped Callie's hand, futilely hoping the act might protect her from them. They might jump out and attack us at any moment.

Twenty minutes later, safe at Callie's apartment, I received a text from Thalia: **Meet them at the Grapevine around 9. Just curious.**

I had to look up the place, and as I assumed, it was a bar. It was a good fifty blocks from my apartment. Meeting them a distance away from Callie was a good thing.

It was almost impossible to get away from Callie. She sensed I wanted to give her the slip, but that night, I met the three stooges at the Grapevine, Belle going with me for moral support. I was glad to have a friend with me, yet I couldn't help but reflect that Lucien would have been best in the present situation. His son was always in awe of him, striving for Lucien's approval. He would have been easily persuadable if Lucien were with me, and my brothers would've followed in kind. Ma would've been great too. They were scared of her. Zeus took her from me and sent six—seven counting Hermes—immortals; this was a major threat from the god of gods.

I told myself, like a mantra over and over, that at least I wasn't alone. I was a legitimate son. I had nothing to be scared of. Except they had Callie's life in their hands and could easily enlighten her to our existence, and then Zeus could smite her. I shook off the horrid thought.

They were sitting in the back corner of the bar in a booth, staring out. The bar was a dilapidated hole-in-the-wall and was full of shady mortals. It appeared to be a formerly posh wine bar that hadn't been renovated or even cleaned since the early 1980s. It smelled of musty spilled wine—rotten grapes with a sour hint of vomit.

I stood in front of them with Belle at my side, not making a move to sit.

"Eros," Himerus sneered as a greeting, as his eyes undressed Belle.

"Himerus, Anteros, Hymenaios," I greeted, trying to remain neutral and relaxed in tone. "To what do I owe this pleasure?"

"Pleasure? I wouldn't go that far, *Bruv*," Anteros said sullenly. I tried not to flinch at his slang use of the word "brother." He did it merely to annoy me because we were never close or acted like brothers.

Annoyed, Hymenaios elbowed Anteros and said, "Please, Eros, Aglaea, sit." I had forgotten how melodic his voice was; he was the child of music, it being the very thing that had brought Lucien and Euterpe together.

I silently obeyed, sitting closest to Hymenaios, feeling that he was the one I was least likely to throttle. Belle slipped in next to Anteros, while the lustful bawd Himerus eyed her up. He was hopeless when it came to decency.

"Holy Hephaestus! You get prettier every time I see you," Himerus blurted out to Aglaea.

"You say that every time I see you," she complained.

"Cut to the chase," I told them, trying to hide my nervousness. "Why are you here?"

Someone came to the table with five drinks.

"Relax, *Bruv*, have a drink," Anteros forced a smile.

"I'd rather not."

"Go on, lad." The bartender patted my back roughly. I peered at the face of, not an ordinary bartender, but Dionysus himself. "Nectar. Seventeen-hundreds stock. Not bad stuff."

"Uncle D." I shook his hand.

He examined me thoroughly. He and my dad were never on good terms. That's the problem with being an Olympian: we were as dysfunctional as beings could get. "How's your old man?"

"How in Tartarus would I know? Haven't seen him in ages." I shrugged.

This made Dionysus smile widely as he patted my back again. "Your mother?"

"She's here in New York. Well, away at the moment, but she lives here."

"Tell her to stop on by." He still eyed me suspiciously. I wondered if he was here to spy on me. It was doubtful since the place must've been there for more than thirty years. Had Dionysus been in Manhattan all along, and I had never run into him in the last four years?

"I will."

"You guys behave," he warned, walking back to the bar.

I took a big swig of the sweet nectar. Feeling everything was instantaneously perfect, I relaxed a bit. Nectar does that—burns away every bad feeling and thought, making you happier than ever, like liquid euphoria. It's actually quite good for us, like vitamins or medicine when we are weakened. Aroha drank it daily to keep up her beauty.

Hymenaios sighed and stared at me with the same honest eyes Lucien had. "We were curious about the mortal girl. Zeus is pretty angry, and we just had to see her."

"I'd say she's worth it all." Himerus's eyes bored into mine. "Is she?"

I almost stood up to throttle him, but instead, my legs hit the table. Belle threw her hands out to keep the table from toppling over, and Hymenaios gently forced me back down. Dionysus shot us a glare, and a few mortals eyed us suspiciously.

"Ooo." Anteros laughed mockingly. "Love has fallen in love."

I tried to keep my temper under control, but I must've been turning red, for Himerus chided me, "Tsk. Tsk. Dad's temper is rising."

"You've seen her. Can you go now?"

"Where's the civility, *Bruv*?" Anteros challenged.

"If she sees you, she'll know something's up, and Zeus might destroy her. The same for you, Hymenaios. She's well acquainted with your father." I purposely brought up Lucien.

"My...my dad's here?" His eyes widened, and his mouth twitched into a small grin. The seed of doubt in whatever their plan had been was now planted.

"It would be a shame to have Zeus kill something so...beautiful." Himerus had paused, most likely searching his vocabulary for an appropriate word. More doubt. Whatever plans they had were crumbling.

"I could just avenge Emily's slighted love," Anteros hissed.

"Like you could make Eros love someone," Belle scoffed at his lack of powers.

"I could make his little prize love—what was that mortal's name? Dan?—or any other mortal who pines futilely after her."

"It won't work," I told him. I wasn't quite sure if that was true, though. That was another issue. Like I could, Anteros could see who each mortal loved, but he could only make slighted victims be loved by the one who had forsaken or spurned them. I didn't think his "arrows" could defeat mine, and Dan loved Ma.

"Are you so sure?" Anteros shot out.

"Try if you must." I faked bravado. "This is why Zeus sent you anyway, isn't it? A little mission for you to try to please him." The guilty expressions on their faces told me I had guessed their true motives. I was no longer afraid, though. It wasn't just the nectar making me confident; it was a fact. Callie would always love me, and if Anteros somehow changed that, I'd win her back.

"Better not be too confident," Himerus sneered.

"Yeah, or I'll end up with another *brother*," I shot back.

The two of them scowled at me, tensing up. Zeus had made them immortal when I was a boy to try to keep my only-child syndrome in check. I hardly warranted it. I hadn't been spoiled, but overconfident as a kid because I had been one of the few gods to develop my powers soon after birth, when most immortals went through a rocky power-gaining stage during puberty, some not having powers until eighteen even.

"Look, why can't you boys all just swallow your egos and get along for once," Belle interjected. "The jig is up. Zeus sent you for some purpose. He sent us, too, for intel, but the truth is, we all like her, a lot. I, and my sisters, support Eros and this girl. There is nothing scary or troublesome about her. I don't understand why he's all upset that Archer chose her. I honestly think he should make her immortal. If you'd only just talk to her, you'd see how wonderfully charming she is."

I put my hand up to stop Belle. "Don't take Aglaea the wrong way, guys. I'm not going to ask Zeus to make her immortal. He'd never... The most important issue here is keeping her safe, which means ignorant of what we are. That last thing I want to do is give Zeus a reason to smite her."

I was pleading with them. I was taking a chance here, a big gamble. I was counting on the hope they wanted my respect rather than to avenge their feelings of jealousy due to being unloved and unwanted. The trio studied me intently and then looked at one another in turn. With them, most likely, I was on trial, awaiting the verdict.

"Are you so confident she won't love another if I try to make her?" Anteros was wavering.

"Yes." And if not, I'd bind her to me.

"Well then, I'll do it to please Zeus, but if it doesn't work, he'll be even more angry," Anteros said.

"It's nothing against you. We just don't want to get in trouble," Himerus added.

"I understand."

"Or"—Anteros smiled mischievously—"we could always make sport of it, like the old days."

I smiled, despite the gravity of the situation, recalling the days when we were highly competitive about our abilities. There had been a time we got along, in a sort of sibling rivalry type of way, but it hadn't lasted long.

"A race?" Himerus smiled broadly.

"Well, you can't be seen," Belle said.

"Rooftops?" Anteros grinned wickedly.

"If I win?" I asked.

"I do nothing, and we leave immediately. But if I win, I make her slight you. If Himerus wins—"

"I get her," Himerus cut in.

Anteros gave him a chiding glance and continued on, "Himerus makes her lust for a *mortal*."

Himerus growled in defeat, and I cringed as I thought of Callie having those kinds of feelings for anyone else. I was beginning to get worried about this, but if I didn't play their little game, they'd follow Zeus's orders. In the end, I really had nothing to lose.

"Deal."

Anteros and I shook on it.

"First one to Callie's front door wins," Himerus officiated.

I gave him a leveled look. That would defeat the purpose. I didn't want her to see them.

"We won't knock or bother her or anything," Anteros conceded.

"I will tell you when to start," Belle added, stopping the others from jumping up at that exact moment.

We all stood up, and my brothers eyed the drinks, then me. Great, they were mooching off me. I rolled my eyes and threw down a few twenties for Uncle D, and we left the Grapevine, entering the chilly night air. We walked in silence a couple doors down until we reached the perfect spot, an alley out of the way of prying mortal eyes.

"This ought to be interesting," Hymenaios scoffed. "Archer always wins."

"Yes, but how long has he been mortalling? How long has it been since he stretched those immortal limbs? Bit rusty, eh, *Bruv*?" Anteros mocked.

"You wish," I retorted, feigning confidence. Was he right in a way? It had been a few years since I'd pushed my body to immortal limits.

"Shut your traps!" Belle smirked, lining us up in the empty alley. "Ready, steady." She paused for dramatic effect. "GO!"

I "flew." No, I don't have wings, but it was probably the easiest way for the Greeks to explain how I was able to momentarily defy gravity. Using my unique ability, I had jumped as high as I could but barely caught the roof's ledge under my arms. I had misjudged, being, as Anteros predicted, a bit rusty. Anteros landed on top of the building, stumbling a little and laughing at me as he began to run across the rooftop. As my opposite, he embodied gravity, or he had magnetism—and not in reference to his personality. When he wanted to be somewhere, all he had to do was see it, and he could draw himself to it, like a pair of magnets. I wasted no time in launching myself up onto the roof as I heard Himerus struggling to climb to the top behind me. Himerus had only the normal immortal traits, but much more potently: abundant strength and speed.

I leaped into the air, pushing off as hard as I could, thinking only of Callie. I shot over the next two buildings, passing Anteros, who glared up at me as he stopped and focused, squinting ahead. I landed and ran to gain some speed to launch myself up again. If Anteros could see our building, he could bypass all the others. I listened intently as I launched myself again, my legs fresh and back to their full potential. I heard footsteps behind me: one set far in the distance, one closer.

This time, I cleared five buildings, much to my surprise. I don't remember being able to defy gravity for that long ever, but now that I had stretched my "wings," it was almost effortless. I pushed on, thinking only of keeping Callie safe, keeping her in the dark. I had to win, not to appease my ego, as Anteros was trying to do, but to keep her safe. I couldn't lose her or see her with someone else. The sounds behind me disappeared under the loud pounding of my accelerated heart. Love gave me power.

A moment later, I found myself on our building's roof, where I swung down onto my balcony, entered through my window, and raced through the hallway. Just as I approached Callie's front door, it opened. I tried to put the brakes on, but I was going much too fast. I collided roughly with Callie, who wasn't—bless the Fates—looking up at the time. She'd suspect something if she saw me moving down the hallway at about eighty miles an hour. I pulled Callie to me to prevent her from falling and kissed her.

I pulled away.

"Archer," she gasped as I steadied her.

Her quizzical expression put me on alert. Before I had time to invent an explanation, two figures appeared, one crashing into me while laughing hysterically and the other slowing down to a mortal pace. I hoped my body had blocked their approach from view because I wasn't sure how to explain away superspeed.

"He always wins," Himerus complained, panting.

They both looked at Callie, then quickly away, most likely unable to withstand her probing gaze. They were a little taken aback by her and suddenly very shy.

Anteros took a step forward, and I was glad because I had no idea what to say. I didn't want to lie, and Callie already was noting the eerie similarities between us. Her eyes shot back and forth between us rapidly.

"Antony. I bet Archer's never told you a thing about us, has he?" Anteros offered one hand for her to shake, while the other rested on my shoulder.

"No, he hasn't." Callie was confused and, unfortunately, a little hurt as she shook his hand. Damn, the power of her eyes when she was sad almost killed me.

"Russ." Himerus waved awkwardly, struggling to stare at her face and not her chest.

"Callie, these are...uh..." I began thinking of how I could word it to still be the truth "...my...well, family. My half-brothers. My parents are complicated people."

"I'd say." Himerus laughed.

"But you all look the same age," she studied us. Too perceptive, Callie. I needed her to stop digging so deeply.

"Same age?" Anteros, or Antony, laughed nervously.

"Archer's the oldest," Russ told the truth. "But only by a year." Okay, that was a lie, more like four years.

"I'm the youngest by two more years," Antony interjected. I supposed he could pass for as young as fifteen with his hair so long and shaggy. The truth was, he was about six years younger than me, but that didn't matter now.

"Ma and Dad weren't exactly always faithful to one another," I tried to explain to Callie, who still had a skeptical expression written across her face.

"Antony is my mom's son, and Russ is my Dad's." The truth came out quickly. "We're as dysfunctional as you can get."

"Good to meet you, and no, he never mentioned you two at all." She crossed her arms, a clear sign of annoyance.

"We don't see Archer often," Himerus said, trying to stick up for me. They were playing their roles so well, and I had been worried they'd spoil everything. It was awfully generous of them, which was not a common occurrence when it came to those two.

"You having a family reunion or something?" Callie asked.

"Guess you could say that. Are you guys staying?" I asked them. It wasn't a deliberate invite; too late, I realized it sounded like that. But they were behaving, and I could probably deal with them for a couple days rather than retract the invite and insult them.

"Nah, we're just pit-stopping, staying here overnight on our way overseas. Got a flight out of LaGuardia in the morning." Anteros shuffled his foot impatiently.

I could tell he didn't like the probing, the questions. Callie was too curious for her own good. That was the last message I wanted sent back to Zeus.

Russ poorly hid the fact that he was ogling her.

"When will I meet your mother?" Callie frowned.

"Whenever she decides to grace us with her presence?" I shrugged.

"Good luck with that." Russ scoffed at me, then remembering we were among mixed company, added, "She's never around."

"Where were *you* headed?" I asked Callie, changing the subject before more questions could bombard us. One day, I would have to hire someone to act as my mother, or Callie would get even more suspicious.

"To see you, actually. I need help with my translations." She held up a notebook and a Greek textbook that I hadn't noticed before.

"Right." I looked at the others, questioning whether we were finished with our bet. Would they leave without doing anything to Callie?

Anteros gave me a nod, and Himerus winked at me as they said a few awkward goodbyes and headed back toward my apartment. But they had done so much, were risking so much on my behalf, that it felt rude not to say something.

"Hey," I said to stop them, and they turned. "Thanks for everything. I'll see you later, and I, uh, mean it. Don't wait so long to visit next time." It wasn't much, but it was something. I was trying to tell them so much in a vague statement that I was unsure if they understood what I intended. I wanted them to know that this act of charity was not lost on me, that perhaps we didn't need to be enemies. True, I despised things about them, like Himerus's lust and disbelief in true love, and Anteros's rationality about matches and his cruelty in revenge for those slighted. Love shouldn't be rational, and not every human being can have whom they desire—it all needed the delicate balance of a multitude of feelings. But I could put these differences aside if they truly supported me, if they truly wanted to protect Callie.

"Okay." Himerus gave me a wide and genuine grin. He understood completely.

"See you soon, *Brother*." Anteros smiled tightly, refraining from his mocking slang.

I left them and went back into Callie's apartment to help her with Greek homework. If she still was suspicious, she didn't act like it, but she was holding a grudge and acting severely disappointed that I hadn't told her I had brothers. At least this time, I could honestly answer her that I had no other siblings.

When I got home that night, my brothers were already gone. The Charities were still hanging about, and Hymenaios hadn't left. He awaited Lucien's return, and the girls only stayed another day, leaving to avoid Ma's return. I found I wished neither of them would return. I couldn't face Lucien or my mother.

CHAPTER 14

When I arrived in Nice—the city once devoted to the victory goddess Nike—it was evening. The difference in time zones made it impossible to visit La Bibliothèque Louis Nucéra, the municipal library in Nice with one of the most impressive collections. I stayed in a clean and quaint hotel in Vieux Nice, or Old Town, with a beautiful view of Place Rossetti, the pedestrian square full of cafes, restaurants, and shops with some of the best ice cream I had ever tasted. However, my downcast mood prevented me from truly enjoying it. All I could think about, while I tossed and turned in the crisp linen sheets, was how I could break all this news to Archer. If Callie was truly Psyche's descendant, how disturbing was this going to be for him? Or would it matter at all? Some of us married and procreated in pretty taboo ways, yet this wasn't too bad. If I admitted it to myself, reflected in my honest heart, he wasn't committing any social faux pas. Callie had no blood ties to him, and it was clear they loved each other immensely.

I hardly slept and woke up early, so I decided to walk across the Old Town to Place Garibaldi, where the library was. Although it was a good walk, I still showed up at the doors to the library as they were opening to the public.

Immediately, I found the same records I had on the internet of Marshal Psyches, who had been left on the Grâce de Dieu church's doorsteps, baptized on March 12th, 1571, and raised in the orphanage. I also found his death logged in 1638. I found many sources about Grâce de Dieu because the place was infamous for burning down in 1590 with the children inside. The fire that consumed a large portion of the city was one of the worst events in the city's history and took up a lot of historical concern. I pored over a few books about the church, frustratingly reading at a mortal pace, for there were people milling about, and they'd notice rapid page turning.

Nothing much caught my interest until the mention of a Sister Jeanne Jacques occurred frequently in one book around the years I was researching. The book mentioned a surviving journal of this nun. It was a shot in the

LISA BORNE GRAVES

dark but worth a try. I had an eerie feeling it would be useful, especially because the last name Jacques was ringing a bell, but I couldn't quite place where I had heard it.

I went back to the library to ascertain whether or not they had a copy of this journal and was told I had to make an appointment at a specific archival library. I hopped on a bus to La Bibliothèque Patrimoniale Romain Gary, not because it was far but because the bus was much quicker. I found a sweet old woman, who assisted me and took me to where the most historical records lay, but the original manuscripts were locked away, and I would have to wait until three so a curator could assist me. The woman's face was so lined with wrinkles that I thought for a split second that maybe she had been alive the last time I was in France. Then again, my kind are not good judges of time; when time is endless, watching it so closely seems pointless.

I couldn't find much more information without being able to read the actual journal, so I walked around, searching for a place to get a bite to eat. I stopped at a little café, sat outside, and nibbled impatiently on a croissant. I hardly touched the coffee in front of me as I read more books about the city's past.

"You look deep in thought," a strikingly familiar voice rang. I perked up; that voice subconsciously both comforted and enticed me. I glanced up at the speaker: Euterpe. She was Hymenaios's mother, the one and only immortal true love of my life, and my ex since the Olympian days. Things never worked out for me in the love department.

I felt a chill of guilty pleasure shoot down my spine just from beholding her beauty. I wasn't the only one mesmerized, for the few men walking down the street all had eyes only for her. It used to drive me insane with jealousy. Staring at her beautiful form, I realized I was definitely in danger of being distracted from my self-appointed quest.

"I am," I replied. "Please sit."

Euterpe sat elegantly, all smiles.

I grew suspicious at once. "Why are you here?"

"Can't I enjoy Nice? I am as surprised as you are at meeting you here. What are the chances? Aren't you supposed to be in New York?" Her eyes wavered to the left, although she tried to hide it as being bashful. Instantly, I could tell she was lying. She never was very good at it, not that anyone could fool me.

"I was."

"What brings you here?" she asked, overly disinterested.

I couldn't keep up the charade. "Don't lie to me. I hate it more than anything."

"What makes you think I'm lying?" Her tone bordered on flirtatious.

"Umm...the fact that our son is in New York right now and knows I'm here. Don't act so surprised. I talked to Archer today. Zeus sent you for some ridiculous reason." I took her hand in mine. "Euterpe, stop the pretenses. I'm the god of truth. You know you can't lie to me and get away with it."

She stared at our hands for a moment, slipped hers out of mine, and then met my gaze as she said, "Our son is there waiting to see you. I hope he's all right."

"Archer will look after him."

"Archer's younger than Hymenaios," she mused quietly.

"Yes, but a bit more mature," I began but was given a censorious glare, and then added, "well, when it comes to mortalling."

She swallowed her pride about our boy and then watched the mortals going about their day in the square. Compelled by some deep-seated emotion within me, I clutched her hand and squeezed it. "I'm sorry."

I had her attention again, but she didn't squeeze my hand back. "For what?"

"Because I'm so bad at all this."

Euterpe awaited more, batting those seductive eyes. How did she always do this to me? Reel me into her power with just a gaze? A toss of the hair? A shift of her posture?

"Being a proper husband to you, a proper father to our son. I can't...I don't know..." I faltered, the words not coming to me.

"The god of truth is speechless!" Euterpe's sardonic tone mocked me. She laughed a little, tossing her silky hair flippantly.

"Sometimes the tumult of feelings we undergo cannot be truthfully rendered in a couple of words," I defended myself. From Euterpe's reaction, it must have come out a little angrier than I had intended. Her face sank, and then she apologetically touched my face gently with her palm. I closed my eyes, not wanting to see her pain, her love for me—I didn't deserve it.

"So, why are you really here?" I asked her, trying to shift the subject off me and onto her.

"I'm supposed to see what you're up to." Euterpe gave up the charade and withdrew her hand.

"And Zeus figures I'll have a harder time hiding things from you than anyone else? Does my father forget I can't lie?" Except that omitting the truth that I was able to suddenly lie was, in itself, a lie.

She shrugged. "I volunteered to come. He was going to send Hermes to spy on you."

"Why'd you get yourself involved, Euterpe?" I groaned. She was so innocent, so unaffected by the years. It wasn't like her to involve herself in Zeus's games.

"To protect you," she said sheepishly, avoiding my gaze.

"After all these years, how can you still...after all I've done to you, how can you want to help me?"

"You know why."

"I don't deserve it."

"Then get your 'buddy' to make me love another," she said grimly. "This is all about him, isn't it? I overheard Zeus and Hera arguing about him."

"Euterpe, please, don't get involved. Zeus's anger is irrational, and he's being vague. There is something strange going on, and all I'm doing is trying to figure it out."

"Please don't." Her lips trembled as she begged.

"I can't help it. God of truth. I need to know."

"Please, come with me, Api, for a little while. Come home to us?" She used my old nickname, bringing back memories of playing music together, of stolen kisses when our mothers weren't watching and nights on Mount Olympus spent looking at the stars. She had been my first everything. Hymenaios was my father's way to force me to marry, but I was not the marrying type. I was unfaithful to her and broke her heart on more than one occasion. It was quite difficult to maintain a relationship when your response to your wife's inquiries about your day led you to expose exactly whose bed you'd spent it in.

"Just come to Fiji for a little while before your father turns against you as well," she said.

I was torn. There she was, gorgeous and caring, her hand on my knee. I reached out to touch her face; she was so soft, so vulnerable. She would love me forever, no matter how many years I'd forsaken her, no matter how many times I'd broken her heart by saying I didn't reciprocate that love anymore.

Before I realized what was going on, I had leaned across the table to kiss her. It had been almost a year since I had kissed anyone and centuries since I'd felt immortal lips. She kissed me back eagerly. I wanted more. I was all too aware of her hand creeping hesitantly up my leg, of her warm lips on mine. I didn't have the self-control Archer somehow cultivated over centuries of celibacy...

Archer. He was why I was here, and Callie. I had to figure out who she was and why Zeus dreaded her union with Archer. All this, those lips, her wandering hand, her entreaties to come home with her—these were pulling me away from my quest. She was a distraction. Going to Fiji with her would be exactly like turning my back on my best friend. Even if he didn't realize it yet, Archer needed my help.

I tore myself away from Euterpe and her beguiling lips. "Stop," I commanded her, not daring to behold her lest my willpower would falter.

"You won't come, will you?" Her voice was shaky.

I dared to look at her. Her eyes were welling up; it was almost too much to bear.

"I can't. Archer needs me." It sounded so weak and pathetic of me.

"I always keep thinking you'll come back to us, day after day, year after year, and yet you never come. Am I foolish to still have some kind of hope that we'll be together one day?" Her voice was hardly more than a jumble of whispers.

The answer was so complicated, it couldn't be phrased properly. "Euterpe, I can't answer that. I hardly know my own mind and heart, let alone what the future will bring."

"But you dream prophecies, for Zeus's sake!"

"I can't lie." I shrugged her comment off. "Plus, like I've told everyone a million times, I'm not sure exactly where the prophecies come from or exactly what they mean."

"But you told me! One of the visions was that I'd love one from the sun line!'" She was close to hysterics now.

"Euterpe!" I put up my hand to silence her. "Shh, the mortals will overhear. I've thought about that prophecy over and over again. What if...what if that part of the prophecy was about Hymenaios? Maybe I was just a pawn of the Fates to give him to you. He's my son, and I am the sun god, and it's clear that he adores his mother—"

"Typical," she scoffed. "I should've known you'd take the blame off yourself. Never your fault, huh?"

"Euterpe—"

"No, and I suppose all that nonsense you fed me ages ago about you believing we were meant to change the world together, that we were the *Spírto Teleíos*, was all lies to win me over?" She referred to the prophecy I had made ages ago about a perfect match, a couple who would somehow change the world forever. I had believed back then that the prophecy was about myself. Certain clues had seemed to point in my direction, but now I wondered if it could be Archer and Callie, although the signs didn't quite line up. Prophecies were vague and usually were told far in advance of when they actually occurred. I had volumes of them written down, where I crossed them off after they happened. There were hundreds, if not thousands, that hadn't happened yet.

Euterpe stared me down with her dewy eyes and little scowl.

I swallowed hard. "No, I believed all that then. I can't lie, remember?"

"And now? Do you believe it now?"

I couldn't say the word, so I shook my head.

"I can't believe you!"

"Euterpe, I don't think we'll ever be together again. Please stop hoping. But...I will start trying to make it up to the boy. I'm a terrible excuse for an immortal, and I know it. I wish you'd never fallen for me. All I do is hurt you. I'm so sorry."

She took it wordlessly, staring down at her hands. I couldn't keep stringing her along, allowing her to wait in the wings for a slight chance in the future.

"If I miss Hymenaios again, tell him I'll send for him soon. That is, if he wants to come to New York."

"I won't give him any more of your empty promises," she muttered.

"Fine then, I'll tell him. I *am* sorry, Euterpe. What else am I to say?"

She nodded, but I wasn't sure what she was agreeing with. Then she stood up and walked gracefully away. I watched her disappear into the crowd, where she most likely would meet up with Hermes, Iris, or one of the four Winds. How else could she get to Nice on such short notice? I regretted hurting her again, but I hoped it would be for the last time. I would ask Archer to try again to make her love another. Maybe this time it would stick.

I stood up, but before I could head back to the library, another familiar voice broke me from my reverie. "Sit back down, little sun god."

Iris stood before me. I wouldn't have recognized her if it weren't for the husky voice. She always sounded like she'd screamed herself hoarse. And she was always just as disrespectful to her elders, but we needed her abilities often, so we rarely reprimanded her.

I relaxed as she sat down and took up my untouched coffee. "Thanks," she said as she took a sip.

I shrugged off her petty theft and awaited her message.

Iris was a goddess of...well, her title is kind of tricky—she was the personification of the rainbow, and like Hermes and the Winds, a sort of teleporter. Only, instead of being a messenger by punishment, she was a free agent and traveled for profit, leaving a rainbow trail behind when she traveled. She was the UPS of the gods: she delivered messages, news, and physical items. Also, she had the ability to morph herself, which was why I didn't recognize her. Iris could change her hair, eyes, and skin color, but she always remained human, female, and limited to the tiny five-foot frame her genetics dictated. Today, she had short-cropped black hair, purple eyes, and pale skin devoid of any blemishes or freckles.

"So, what's the message? I'm kind of in a hurry," I pressed, losing my patience. It was half past two, and the curator would be back soon.

"Whatever you find in that library, you mustn't tell anyone. If you find you must tell someone, then trust Athena and only Athena. Do not tell your friends or Father."

"What am I going to find in there?" I asked.

"Holy Hades, Apollo, how would I know?" She giggled, judging my question as outrageous. "I'm just delivering a message."

"From whom?"

"Now, that's a secret." She smiled. "And before you try to bribe it out of me, he or she made me swear on the Styx."

"But obviously, someone out there already knows the answers to what I seek. Why can't he—or she—tell me?" I asked, annoyed. I knew she couldn't tell me, but this trip was pointless if I could've gotten the answer through a phone call.

"Maybe because you're the god of truth. Apollo, you could be forced to tattle, now couldn't you?" She took a large gulp of the coffee. "You mustn't tell anyone, though. Force yourself to withhold the truth. Many mortal and immortal lives depend on secrecy, especially the one of whom you are searching."

"But—"

"My client said nothing more, and my client didn't want a response. So, if I'm done here..." She faded into thin air, leaving only a rainbow behind her.

I looked around at the mortals, but no one was acting as if they had seen a girl vanish into thin air. Fearing yet another interruption, for it seemed gods were on the go these days, I got up quickly and hurried toward the library.

This wasn't good. Somewhere out there, some other god knew what I was up to. He or she already had the answers I was seeking about Callie and didn't trust me. I felt exposed and vulnerable.

It wasn't Zeus because Iris never worked for him. And why should I trust Athena above my mother, my twin sister, or even Archer? Athena was just and noble, but she was always in cahoots with Zeus, working for him and often by his side. Why her? Worrying about whom to trust was pointless until I found out the information that needed to be kept hidden. The problem was, could I truly hide this information? What if someone directly asked me about it? Could I keep lying?

I pushed the worries from my head as I entered the library. I was led by a stern middle-aged man, who was very businesslike and strict about the rules, into a lower room, where he unlocked many doors to get to our destination: a pressurized and temperature-controlled archive room. He pulled out a book that barely held together and placed it gently on an old desk. He made me put on latex gloves and told me to be careful.

"Pas de probleme, monsieur," I told him, eager to search the book. Carefully turning the pages, I skimmed for the date of March 12th, 1571, which I found midway through the bound journal. The old days of using Middle French easily came back. The nun was talking about picking vegetables in the garden when a beautiful creature floated down from the heavens. She truly believed it was an angel sent from god. The angel carried a baby and went to leave it on the steps until she noticed the nun. The angel begged her to take in the child and then floated back up to God.

My fears were confirmed if this woman truly had seen what she'd described. There were only so many goddesses who were "winged" ones, and Psyche had had powers similar to Archer's. This had to be baby Marshal.

I read on. She took the child in, and a letter was in his blanket. After reading the letter, the nun changed her mind about the angel. She proclaimed the woman was mad or, worse, that she could be a witch sent by the Devil. They baptized Marshal immediately to save his soul, and the nun was instructed to burn the witch's letter. But she did not. She copied it into her journal and then let the priest burn the original. The woman wrote:

> To the honorable sisters of Gràce de Dieu, please take this child in good faith, for his mother fears for his life as well as her own. We live in desperate times where neighbors bear witness against one another in hopes of saving

themselves from condemning eyes. The term "love thy neighbor" has fallen by the wayside, and the unpredictable judgments here on Earth are not justified as your God's mercy. In haste, I must leave my child under your protection in hopes...

I turned the page, but the words were concerning the lack of potatoes for stew. Why didn't the journal have the rest of the letter inside? I studied the page numbers to find four were missing, two pages front and back. There had to be something incriminating on those pages. Why else would a devout nun go from believing an angel to thinking she was a witch? I kept on reading, hoping for answers. Here and there, Joan mentioned certain children by name. Once or twice, she mentioned Marshal Psyches, but only in passing and of how beautiful a child he was. I found only one more passage pertaining to Marshal:

> I have always believed Marshal's mother deranged, but there are things the child can do that no human possibly could. I must write about this because I cannot tell a soul for fear they may murder this child and me, as they must have done to this child's mother. Such subjects fall under the crime of heresy in these troubling times. He sees beyond what we see, reading our hidden thoughts. I do not know how it is possible. My faith cannot allow it, yet God wouldn't create this boy and his gift without a purpose. I cannot believe the words of his mother because there is only one God. Marshal was given his gift by God, and for a certain purpose, he was left here. If only we could ascertain how or why he was given this gift. I fear it may not be for good or, more properly, that he may not use it for good. I must watch him, guide him to use it well and to hide it. God does not give us trials we cannot overcome or endure.

"There is only one God" meant Psyche had told them about us. Maybe that was why Zeus let her burn at the stake and never intervened. But I was still missing that definitive proof and her signature. The rest of the journal was useless. It did continue for the rest of her life, so Sister Jeanne was never killed. She'd told no one about the gods, or Zeus didn't see her as a threat. Or maybe, he wasn't as all-seeing as we thought? I flipped back to the missing pages, inspecting the crease, but it didn't appear to be cut, torn, or ripped. However, it clearly wasn't the original. It had been printed in the seventeen hundreds from the look of the paper. It must've been printed at the expense of her family or someone who wanted to preserve this information.

I asked the preoccupied curator where the original could be found. "Museum, but it is a perfect copy."

"It's missing pages," I told him and showed him the evidence.

"The original had missing pages." He took the book back and gently put it back on the shelf. He motioned me out of the room and into an office.

"Are you sure?"

He gave me a look that could kill. Apparently, I was impertinent for questioning his very ability to perform his job. He quickly typed into the computer as he answered me, "Yes." He sniffed at me snobbishly. "They appear to have been cut out. The original was part of the private Jacques collection and sold to the museum in 1785. This copy was then made because it was deteriorating rapidly, and it was moved to this archive in 1996." He showed me the computer screen with the information pertaining to the book.

"Merci, monsieur. Bonsoir," I told him, masking my disappointment. When I left the library, it was already dark.

I decided to meander toward the hotel so that I could digest the information I'd learned. It did all point to a goddess leaving her child, a goddess who couldn't return to retrieve him or decided not to during the Inquisition and the heretic hysteria in France during the sixteenth century. Psyche and Hedone were burned at the stake during the Inquisition's heretic purge. The mother of Marshal, who alluded to polytheism, did not return, and the nun believed her to have been a victim of the times. It was highly doubtful that Hedone had a child. The goddess of pleasure preferred her own gender when it came to love. It all fit: the portion of the mother's letter and Sister Jeanne's journal all hinted at our world and our abilities. Marshal must have been a demigod, descended directly from Psyche herself. A half-mortal with the ability to read minds, like Psyche's ability to "read" souls, to understand someone fully, instantaneously, and not in the way all gods could by entering one's mind. Psyche had done it through eye contact. His last name was Psyches before it was changed. It was as bright as a neon sign now: Psyche's. She was signaling to us gods to find her child, knowing she would die. And we failed her.

Others would doubt, deny. I needed tangible proof, real evidence I could show them when the time came. The missing pages were the key. I doubted they'd be there, but the next day, I made my way to the museum mentioned in the records and instantly sought out the original journal. It was tattered, crumbling, and the particles all around it were its own decomposing dust. It stood perched on display in a long glass case with other items from the area and time period, most having to do with artifacts from Grâce de Dieu. I read the simple caption printed on the card beside the book: "Diary of Sister Jeanne Jacques of Grâce de Dieu (1532-1590)." As I thought, there was less information here than in the copy. I examined the other artifacts inside the case: charred toys, a hairbrush without bristles, some old books, an old city map that outlined the city previous to the devastating fire, some old bricks, and many other trivial items. At the end of the case was a caption explaining that everything was donated to the museum by Jean-Charles Jacques III. There was a painting of the Jacques family, consisting of about ten members, and underneath it, a small plaque labeled them. There was Jeanne, and oddly, next to her name was Marshal Syches with no p. Marshal in a family likeness? Then it hit me why the surname of Jacques was so familiar: Marshal's wife's maiden name had been Jacques.

I pored over the plaque on the wall next to the family portrait. It was a sort of biography about the Jacques family, who had been wealthy. There were a few sentences about Marshal, explaining that he was raised in the orphanage, then schooled in law under Geoffrey Jacques, who was Sister Jeanne's brother and the second son, not the heir. Marshal proved a successful attorney—because he could read the minds of those on trial, I assume. He then immigrated to the American Colonies with his wife, Émilie Jacques, who was his benefactor's daughter. There they lived, prospered, and had three children—two sons and a daughter, with only one son surviving childhood. Marshal died in 1638 in Jamestown. I skimmed over the rest of the information about the family but found nothing important about any of them. The entire Jacques line diminished and disappeared by 1900.

Marshal's son survived. This much I'd seen in Callie's family tree. Something still bothered me. It was the missing pages of the nun's journal. Marshal Syches and the Jacques family had had access to the book prior to its donation. Someone had removed those pages, and they'd done it for a reason. Had it been Marshal himself trying to hide his identity?

I needed someone to talk to, to work it out. My instincts told me to call my twin sister Artemis, but the mysterious message I'd received stopped me. Instead, when I pulled out my cell, I dialed Athena.

"Hello, it's been a while, Lo." I could hear the smile in her voice.

"Where are you right now?" I asked.

"London. You?"

"France, Nice. Look, I've been doing some research, and I'm stumped. Could I come see you?"

"No need," she said, so businesslike, you'd think we had only just met. She always was standoffish, like an old hermit preferring her books to our company. "Subject?"

"Marshal Syches."

"Spell it out, please," she instructed.

I spelled out the name for her. The phone was silent for a moment. "Thena?"

"Wait, as in I add a *p*, and I get Psyches, like Psyche's child," she whispered.

"That is my concern."

"Tell me everything," she said. I could hear her typing in the background.

"Can you keep this secret?" I asked, hoping she'd agree to keep it from everyone else, especially Zeus. Something inside told me that he wouldn't favor the discovery that Psyche had descendants who still existed. I had always questioned how no one had stepped in to save her or Hedone, but it was a question I couldn't truly voice without Archer going mad. There were many gods around at the time of their deaths who could be implicated. With Prometheus's foresight, Zeus's omniscience, and with several gods having the ability to teleport—it seemed almost like a choice to let them die.

"Yes." Her conviction allowed me to continue. If there was one thing Athena wasn't, it was dishonest. "The question is, Lo, how can you?" Athena questioned.

I wasn't sure if she meant it rhetorically—pointing out the obvious fact I couldn't lie to others—or if she was onto my newfound ability to lie, but I hung up, not giving her time to question me further. I had wanted answers but stupidly overlooked the fact that she would too. And now I'd pointed Athena—the wisest of us all—to Psyche's mysteriously hidden line; it wouldn't take her long to figure out who the last descendant was. Hiding the truth was essential now, and I had to figure out how to go home and lie to my best friend...to his face.

CHAPTER 15

Callie

I tried to buckle down on my homework, but as much as I tried to concentrate, Archer's piercing eyes kept coming back to haunt me. As did the strange dreams of my possible demise. There was something in my constitution that was utterly wrong. I should've been frightened, upset, repulsed. I should've seen my dreams as dark omens. Instead, the dreams were puzzles to solve, and I was attracted, mesmerized, drawn in by his alluring eyes. Archer's eyes, whenever he was upset and angry about something, were amazingly bright. They were brilliant and luminescent, as if his anger and love shone through them. I could no longer ignore that something was amiss. The weird yearbook photo, his eccentric rules, and his overbearing family who kept cropping up—and I sensed a power within him that he kept hidden but that surfaced accidentally in front of us. What kind of power? I didn't know, but I wasn't frightened by it. Instead, I was drawn in by it, like a magnetic force that irresistibly pulled me in.

I wanted to see those eyes light up again. Forbidden thoughts began to creep forward from the recesses of my mind (but I welcomed them).

My cell phone rang, interrupting thoughts of great blue eyes, soft lips, and perfectly chiseled abs. Archer's name flashed onto my cell's screen.

"Hello," I answered. "I was just thinking about you."

"Yeah, what were you thinking?" His voice rang out with complex emotion, confusing me as to what he really felt.

"I'm not telling. I can keep you in the dark about things as well."

"Touché," he said quietly. "I want to see you."

I sighed. "I have homework and dinner with my dad..." I began.

"Afterward?" he ventured.

"What power do you have?" I blurted, thinking of those intense and iridescent eyes, the perfection of his face, the multitude of emotions he held within him that only seeped out in his voice.

"Come again?" he asked, the melody in his voice gone. He was guarded. I hated when he put up the defenses, because he appeared fake.

"You must have a power, a power so great that I can't resist you," I said.

"Yes," he said softly. "You have it too. I can't stay away."

"Oh yeah, what is it then?" I flirted with him.

"Love," he said simply.

What did he mean? (Oh my God!) He loved me? (Oh my God, oh my God, oh my God!) He knew I loved him? This was all so sudden but so right.

"Callie, I need to see you now." He wasn't asking to see me but needed to, a tortured and longing demand. I wasn't sure what was more powerful: my longing for him or the thought that my absence might cause him any suffering. I had somehow lost myself in him. Although I mocked those girls who lived for their boyfriends, I was on my way to becoming one of them. I had underestimated love, and now it was making a fool out of me.

"Yes," was all I could say, unable to deny that compelling voice.

"Come over," he pleaded.

"Your cousins?"

"Left yesterday."

"I'll be over in a second," I said too quickly.

"Okay," he replied just as quickly.

We hung up. I gave myself a once-over in the mirror, brushed my hair and my teeth, and raced out of my room. There was no time to touch up my makeup or change into a cuter outfit. I had to see him then and there. It was a physical need, almost an addiction.

"Where are you going in such a hurry?" my dad asked (eek, an unforeseen obstacle).

"Oh, didn't I tell you? I have a chemistry lab to write up with Archer and Lucien."

He raised his eyebrows at me, knowing full well I was lying, and he and Raphael exchanged a conspiratorial look.

I rolled my eyes at them. "Not a lie, it's just not due until Wednesday. I'll be home for dinner," I told him, kissing his cheek. I didn't want to get into the other lie: Archer and I would be alone. Aroha and Lucien were living it up abroad.

I shot Raphael a feigned glare. He smiled and gave me a conspiratorial wink. I turned quickly to leave. He and Dad shared everything. Freaked me out (seriously).

"Six on the dot," Dad shouted as I tried to pretend I wasn't racing.

I grabbed up my chemistry book for effect and left. I had to keep myself from running down the hall. Before I could knock on the door,

Archer opened it. Either he had been waiting, watching out the peephole, or I must've sounded like an elephant stampeding down the hall.

"What took you so long?" he asked breathlessly, but he didn't wait for an answer. He pulled me in roughly, kissed me, and slammed the door shut with his foot. It rattled in the doorframe loudly.

I dropped my book, stopped, and looked at the door in shock.

"Don't know my own strength." He shrugged, wrapping me closer to him in his arms, and kissed me wildly like we might run out of time. He kissed my lips, my cheeks, my neck, my jaw.

I felt my heart leap from my chest—he must have heard the pounding, it felt so loud. Every nerve, every fiber in my being, was alive and flared in anticipation. I couldn't get enough of him. His hands wandered, making my stomach flop in nervous desire. He kissed my lips with a kind of fervor I hadn't experienced before, and I found myself suddenly on the sofa with the full weight of his lean, muscular form on me. How had he gotten me across the room so fast? I must've lost track of time in those kisses.

The feeling of his lips on me, his hands edging up my sides, the weight of him upon me, and his heart beating in tandem with my own made me want so much more. Yet I was a rational person (although struggling at the moment), and I reminded myself we had only known each other a month and that he had so many secrets he kept from me.

It took all my willpower to turn my lips away from his and push him off me. Archer didn't get up, but propped himself up on his elbows, easing the burden of his weight from my chest. He had to catch his breath, its honey-sweetness assaulting my senses and trying to destroy my resolve to behave. When I met his gaze, his eyes were wild, dilated, and with that eerie, incandescent blue that aroused my earlier fantasies.

All willpower to deny him vanished, and I pulled him back down, kissing him with reckless abandon. Those eyes were irresistible, literally. I felt his rock-hard stomach under his shirt, then his chest. I pushed him away again, squeezing my eyes closed so his own couldn't tempt me again.

"Callie," he gasped.

"I have rules too," I said.

He was back up on his elbows. "Callie, open your eyes."

I obeyed but refused to look at him. Archer moved my chin back and forth to try to force me to meet those alluring eyes, but I avoided his gaze.

"Look at me, or I'll never kiss you again," he threatened.

I caved in, and his eyes were still mesmerizing me, glowing. I bit my lip to hold back the urge to kiss him. He was smiling and chuckling at me. He touched my cheek softly.

"It's hard to look at you and not kiss you when your eyes do that," I mumbled in embarrassment. I felt stupid, but it was time to press him about his eyes. It was not normal, nor was it...human. But how could I say that to his face?

"Do what?" he asked, biting his lip. Was he biting back the urge to laugh at me or to kiss me?

"Glow," I told him.

Archer's smile faded, and the quickest whiplash of shock went through him. Then, a split second later, he was smiling and laughing again. He sat up, pulling me into a sitting position. "I love your imagination." He laughed it off.

I had hit a nerve, another secret, which I was now seeing as a threat to our relationship. How long could I endure this? I didn't think I could handle a blatant lie to my face again. "They do," I protested. I needed to put my foot down. It was a harder issue for him to dodge than the yearbook photo.

He kissed me, most likely to silence me.

"Don't try to distract me with kisses. Seriously, what's with the eyes?"

Archer sighed, closed his eyes, and leaned away from me. This, I didn't like, so I snuggled up under his arm, which he draped around me. He opened his eyes. They were dim again, normal.

"What about my eyes?" he said reluctantly.

"You turned them off!" I couldn't help but say it disappointedly.

"Turned them off?" He gave me the classic you-are-looney look. "It's not like I have a light switch in me. What is with your wild fantasy about my 'glowing' eyes? They lock people up for saying less than that, you know." He was teasing, but there was a slight edge in his tone. There were walls between us I wanted to break down, but he kept building them up.

"You do have a switch," I told him, leaning in to kiss him. Surely, he knew exactly what would happen, but he couldn't resist kissing me back. The kisses became more passionate, and then I pulled away to see his eyes glowing softly.

"Stop it, Callie," he said sadly, closing his eyes as he leaned his forehead against mine.

Realizing that I was right and not imagining it was enough at the moment. I (very, very) reluctantly let it go. "I know, the dark." I referred to my promise not to pry.

"Yes, I am so sorry." He sighed, clearly torn. He kissed me gently and then pulled away. He struggled to smile. "So, what are these rules of yours?"

Now I regretted opening my mouth at all. This was about to get very embarrassing. I stared at his wiry fingers, running mine along his, avoiding his gaze. "Well, I always told myself I'd never, you know...before I was married," I mumbled.

"Oh, *that*," he said, comprehension flooding him. "I wasn't trying to... I mean I didn't want you to come over to... I don't want to... I mean I do *want* to, but I don't want you thinking that is *why* I wanted you to come over," he stammered nervously. He was adorable in his floundering.

I finally dared to meet his gaze. His eyes were back to their normal aquamarine blue, nervously seeking my approval. I smiled at him and touched his face gently. "I didn't think you were trying to get me to— It's just that we've only known each other like a month and all..."

"But it feels like forever," he finished.

"Yes."

Archer pulled me closer. "I hope you want to get married young," he said in a whisper.

(Whaaaaat?) I kept my head on his shoulder, trying to comprehend what he meant. "What is that supposed to mean?" Was a seventeen-year-old girl supposed to get excited about a guy talking about marriage or run immediately in the opposite direction?

"Only a month, and we're already at the 'talk' stage. What will we be like in a year?" he mused, so calm and nonchalant about it. Archer nuzzled my ear.

My heart began to race a little bit at his comment. He anticipated us being together in a year and even mentioned marriage, even if it was as a joke. Boys never brought up things like that unless they were in love. But he hadn't said the L-word yet. I wanted to hear him say it badly, mainly because I wanted to say it back.

"A year from now, huh?" I commented, in hopes he'd elaborate.

Archer propped my chin up so our gazes aligned. His eyes searched mine for something, most likely, my meaning. A smile spread across his face. Whatever he saw gave him his answer. "I'm not going anywhere, Callie. You're stuck with me forever."

"Forever is a long time to refrain from..." I smirked at him.

"I would wait forever," he said to me with conviction. His look was so serious that it was clear he meant it. It was a declaration of sorts, so I kissed him. As always, one kiss was never enough, and he kissed me more and more. He was the one who pulled away from our lip-locked embrace. "Or I'd try at least." He laughed.

"It seems a hopeless rule, I know. I'm old-fashioned," I apologized.

He pulled my face up to meet his. "As am I," he said, kissing me again. "I'd be much too scared of the consequences."

"Consequences?" I asked.

Archer blushed a bit. "Children."

"Children? Well, there are ways to prevent that."

"Ways that don't always work," he said sternly. "Anyway, no worries. I'll at least wait until we're married," he said, kissing my forehead.

My stomach dropped to my knees at that comment. He was completely serious. Who was he? Archer was not like any other boy I had ever known. There was definitely something wrong with him. Refraining from sex, talking about marriage while still in high school—not to mention all the other weird stuff—were not normal for a teenage boy.

Archer snuck a peek at me from the corner of his eyes. He then turned on the TV and shifted his attention to it. "Any more rules?"

"I'll let you know after I invent them," I teased.

Archer began to tickle my sides, and when I tried to tickle him back, he pinned my hands down and began kissing me. Suddenly, he yanked himself away from me, pulling me up to a sitting position as if someone had walked in on us. Then someone pounded on the door loudly. He somehow sensed someone the moment before he or she knocked. Perhaps Archer could sense people or had really good ears? Maybe that was how he had known I was outside before I knocked, and I wasn't as loud as an elephant after all. Archer sat frozen, his eyes growing bright. Now did not seem the time to point out to him that I was right about his eyes.

The person knocked again. Archer finally got up to answer. He opened the door to reveal an ugly, chubby man, perhaps in his mid-thirties, with bulbous pink features, fiery tangles of long red hair, and bloodshot dark eyes. He looked like a creepy stalker type.

"Heph," Archer said quietly, shocked to see the man.

"Can I come in?"

"I uh...I have company," Archer replied, opening the door farther.

The man inspected me, blushed even redder, and then focused his attention back on Archer. I had never seen someone turn as scarlet as this man did. Archer was on edge, worried, almost frightened by this man. His muscles were rigid, ready to pounce. I sensed that he was scared, not enraged or enflamed like the other times his eyes had lit up.

"Is your mother home?"

"Actually, she went away. My grandfather wanted to see her." Archer spoke carefully. He was making me feel on edge. Was it my imagination, or was Archer purposely standing an obvious distance away from the man?

"When will she be back?"

"Heph, honestly, she didn't tell me when. I swear. Want to leave a message?" Archer asked.

"Yes. Could I come in for just a moment? I've been traveling for twenty-four hours," the man asked with a tired sigh.

Archer hesitated. "Can I trust you?" he said so quietly that I could hardly make out his words. Maybe the man really was a shady character, or as always, I was reading too much into things.

"I'm over you, kid. Won't lay a finger on you or your...little friend," the man growled as he spoke. He reminded me of Beast of *Beauty and the Beast*.

Archer opened the door widely, letting Beast in. The man shut the door behind him and stood awkwardly, gawking at me, until Archer handed him a pen and paper (creepy Beast). The man tore his eyes from me and walked toward the breakfast nook that overlooked the kitchen. He walked with a limp, and I noticed the strange large shoe and realized he must've had a clubbed foot, with one leg much shorter than the other. Beast caught me staring, and I diverted my gaze guiltily. He sat down on a stool much too small for him, the wood groaning in protest, and began writing a note.

"Uh...Callie, this is my mom's ex-husband Heph, and, Heph, this is my girlfriend, Callie." Archer seemed a little worried as he performed the introduction.

"Girlfriend?" Heph's gaze met Archer's.

Why did he think it odd that Archer had a girlfriend? It was yet another puzzle, another mysterious family member. How big was his family? And how many times had his mother married? I mean, I'd heard of dysfunctional, but this was over-the-top.

"Yes, girlfriend. Need a drink, Heph?" Archer wanted to change the subject.

I didn't understand this strange beast of an ex-stepfather's behavior. He didn't seem the social type.

"Water," he growled.

Archer took a large water bottle from the fridge and placed it next to his strange guest.

"How's your mother?" Heph asked.

"Fine, I suppose," Archer said awkwardly. His eyes darted to me unconsciously and then back. He was still nervous.

It was a little odd that they never mentioned Aroha at all. I guess this Heph guy didn't care since they weren't his kids.

"My *sister* is here much more than Ma. Ma's never here."

"Ah," Heph said, his face comprehending some inside secret.

Yet again, I was to be left in the dark. How long could I endure not understanding every little thing, every person in Archer's life? People just randomly popped up in his life; there were his beautiful cousins, then the brothers, now an ex-stepfather who didn't appear quite old enough to have fathered any of them unless he had been pretty young.

"Well, just give this to her when she returns," the man said, taking up the water bottle while pushing a note across the counter. "Bye," he said simply and let himself out.

Archer locked the door behind him, picked up my forgotten book, and placed it on the counter. "Sorry about that." He sighed in relief, running his hands through his gorgeous blond hair and making it sexily disheveled. It was growing out into full curls that made me want to twist my fingers around them.

"I need to go," I told him, checking the clock.

"No." He pulled me up off the sofa and held me. "Don't go."

I groaned. "Dad said six on the dot."

"I'll walk you home, get an extra minute," he said, leading me by the hand.

"My book." I stopped, grabbing it. I couldn't help seeing the note next to it on the counter. It was addressed to "Aphrodite, my love."

Archer turned my face away from the note and toward him. "Aren't we nosy? Heph's a cheesy romantic, the old git. It's nauseating." He kissed my forehead and took up my hand. "It's 5:59," he warned and urged me out the door.

Archer delivered me to my door, where my father waited outside, inspecting his watch. Dad looked at our hands, which were clasped. I let go self-consciously.

"Just made it," he teased, sighing in feigned disappointment that he'd lost an opportunity to punish me.

"Bye," Archer told me, smoothing the back of my hair and kissing my forehead. His eyes glowed for a moment before he turned away. Archer loved me, and I loved him.

"Bye," was all I could say as he walked away, regretting that I couldn't muster the courage to tell him how I felt. Having Dad there made it impossible as well.

At dinner, Dad began to pry, "You really like that boy, don't you?"

"And from your tone, you don't."

"On the contrary, I like him a lot. You two seem a little too close too fast, but besides that, I couldn't leave you in better hands—"

"Dad, I hate when you talk like that. You're improving."

"Callista, I'm on borrowed time. It's not a cure." He held up his hand to stop my protests. "You'll say now that time may make a cure available eventually. Callista, just let me speak my heart, my mind, for once. Archer has money. He's extremely intelligent, and it is clear he cares deeply for you."

I groaned. "Why do I feel a 'but' coming on?"

"Not a 'but,' but a 'don't you think.'" He smiled.

"Don't you think..." I prompted him.

"He's a bit...different," my father finished.

My mouth dropped. I was offended, but deep down inside, I knew that Archer wasn't normal.

My father proceeded after he realized I wasn't capable of answering, "Callie, there is something odd about him, and before you get offended, I do not mean that in a bad way."

"Do you have one of your harebrained theories?" I asked, not bothering to mask the dread in my voice.

"Yes, but theories are sometimes wrong." He eyed me for a moment, using his keen perception to weigh whether or not I could handle his ridiculous theory. He peered down at his hands. "Never mind my harebrained ideas. I want to talk more about you..." From there on, my father wanted promises from me to finish high school, even if he passed away soon, and then to go on to college. Of course, I promised both easily to make him happy. Why wouldn't I go to college? The third promise he asked was unexpected: "Could you promise me to publish my book if I pass before it's finished?"

"Dad, stop talking about death. And isn't Raphael in charge of all that?" I asked.

"Yes, but you will be Raphael's employer when I'm gone. I have a lawyer I want to introduce to you as well. I trust him with everything. I want you to trust him likewise. He'll teach you all the things I can't be bothered to waste our time with, such as all our money, stocks, my company, all the business side. Besides that, Callista, there are things I need to tell you before I go."

"Dad, we have time." I protested.

"Yes. This last item should wait," he agreed.

Great, more secrets from another man I loved. Why was I to be left ignorant? What was everyone trying to protect me from? And why did they think I was too fragile to handle it?

Before I could press, he shifted the subject. "Would you mind helping me with my book? I'd like you to wrap your head around it in case you have to deal with the editors and, God forbid, if you must finish it."

"Whatever you need, Dad," I said hesitantly.

He raised his eyebrows at me. He knew that I was guessing he had ulterior motives. There were no secrets between my father and I. There had never been any room for them.

CHAPTER 16

Archer

Time alone with Callie was like a dream, when I could get it, since I was busy entertaining Hymenaios, who was camped out at his father's apartment so Callie wouldn't see him and be exposed to yet another immortal who looked exactly like someone she knew. Uncle D was nice enough to keep him company when I was busy. I wanted to spend all my time with Callie, but Hymenaios's presence prevented that. I knew it was a good thing; it gave her much-needed time with her father, but I wanted to spend every moment of every day with her.

Hymenaios eagerly awaited Lucien's return. I couldn't say the same. Aroha would be home soon too and would be very upset with me and my disobedience. I was lucky that the first family member to return was Lucien, although he was in a foul mood. He must've had a crappy trip to Nice. I wondered what was going on with his mother. It was extremely odd of him not to come see me on his return and talk about it. Instead, Hymenaios met him at the airport, and I didn't see them again until Lucien showed up on Monday at school. Perhaps it was an unintentional avoidance because he had wanted to spend the weekend with his son.

"Who kicked your puppy?" I teased.

Lucien didn't smile. "Remember Daphne?" he asked quietly. Daphne? Why would he bring her up after 3,200 and then some years? I mean, I have heard of grudges, but this was ridiculous.

"Ye-es," I said hesitantly.

He looked at me sharply. "I wish I could do it to you now, hurt you like you hurt me then."

This was unexpected, to say the least. "How many times can I apologize? I was a kid. You always picked on me. And I honestly did intend to make her love you after I had my fun at your expense. You don't still..." I broke off, for we were no longer alone, other students beginning to mill into the classroom.

"No. I just..." Lucien stopped, scowling. "Never mind."

I didn't know what was going on in his head. I wasn't sure what questions to ask him to force the truth out of him either. This wasn't about

Daphne. When I was ten, Lucien, who was an adult, picked on my archery abilities, my powers, and me. One evening, he claimed that my powers were too weak to really make mortals fall in love and that, to prove my powers, I should attempt to make a god fall in love—something thought to be impossible because even my mother was unable to do so. In bitter childish resentment, I made him fall in love with a nymph named Daphne. I won't lie. It usually takes just one arrow for a mortal, and on him, I used ten. Lucien was violently in love with her, scaring the wits out of the girl. We all got a good laugh out of it, but before I could make her love him back and end his anguish, her river-god father interceded—turned her into a laurel tree. Hence, Apollo, god of truth and light, spent years obsessing over a tree. After about ten years, my poisoned arrows lost their power. Each arrow lasted about a year on immortals, while their effect could be eternal on mortals. I never tried that many arrows on an immortal again, not even my dad.

I didn't comprehend Lucien's attitude or what he did over the next few days. Ignoring Callie and me, even after Hymenaios left, he began spending time with Linda. Linda must have been ecstatic. There was no need to poison her to be in love with him, but he had always rolled his eyes at her and Emily's obsessive stares.

I minded his distance, but it gave me more alone time with Callie. I had to constantly be with her, kiss her, hold her. Her presence would turn something innocuous like watching TV into something so lusty that I could swear Himerus was poisoning me. The way she kissed me back drove me insane, igniting the ichor in my blood.

Today, alone in my living room, was no different. I turned her to face me and kissed her again and again, not wanting to ever stop feeling her lips against mine. I gripped her shoulder and the pillow under my head tightly to occupy my idle hands. I was honestly glad Callie had her scruples when it came to being physical. One of us needed to be rational.

Between my reveries and the warm kisses, I hadn't heard the front door open, but I did hear a female gasp. I tore myself away from Callie to see Aroha, eyes wild, suppressing the fury that threatened to overtake her in mixed company. She dropped her suitcase, turned away, and muttered, "Don't let *me* interrupt you."

Well, this was damn awkward. This was my mother catching me with a girl, one she'd forbidden me to be with, and yet Callie thought she was simply my sister. Callie sat up, her cheeks flushed, mortified. Surely, Aroha wouldn't dare say a word in front of Callie.

My mother picked up her case and headed to her room, "Seems like I missed a lot since I've been gone." Unfortunately, she didn't bother unpacking and came back out, seating herself on the other sofa.

"Dan has been asking about you every day," Callie told her, trying to be friendly.

"Is that right?" Aroha said pleasantly, her ego being pampered. Then she shot me a reproachful glower before turning to Callie with a superficial smile. "I thought he liked you." Aroha stared Callie down.

Callie kept her gaze steady, not intimidated at all. I wondered how she did it, since most girls cowered under Aroha's daunting gaze. "He must have been trying to make you jealous." She shrugged.

Aroha looked away first and gazed unfocused at the television. "Dad wants to see you."

"He can go to..." I stopped myself from saying, "the Underworld for all I care," in front of Callie.

"Yes, I told him you'd say that. At least make an effort. Call him," she scolded, sounding a little too maternal.

"Heph came to see Ma. He left her a love letter," I mocked.

Aroha's head whipped around, deeply shocked.

"I should go." Callie shifted uncomfortably.

I gripped her hand tightly. What would Aroha say to me, do to me, after Callie left? Would she forbid me to see Callie, and if so, could I disobey her again? I got up, helped Callie up, and walked her to the door. "I'll see you tomorrow," I told her, kissing her.

She nodded. It pained me to see her walk through the door. I grabbed her hand and pulled her back to me, kissing her passionately. Callie backed away slightly, touching her lips, confused, and then looked me dead in the eyes. "You're saying goodbye," she whispered quietly.

"Don't be silly." I kissed her again, being careful not to give my emotions away. She was much too observant for me to give so much away.

"Your eyes don't lie," she muttered.

"Then learn how to read them correctly," I tried to tease lightly. "See you tomorrow."

At last satisfied, she left. I closed the door and turned regretfully around. Aroha stood, hands on hips, her eyes locked on mine with anger. This wasn't going to be pretty.

"How cute," she taunted.

"Shut up," I grumbled. I tried to walk past her.

She used all of her strength to push me into the door with a thump.

"Where's Vinnie?"

"I couldn't."

"You mean you wouldn't," she insisted.

"Dan's in love with you," I tried to point out.

"Zeus said no. You have to give her up."

"I can't," I insisted, getting heated. I kept my fists clenched so I wouldn't attempt to hurt her. When it came to Callie, I wasn't sure what I was capable of anymore.

She was confused and shocked at my outburst. "You have to! He will send an ultimatum if you don't listen to me."'

"He already did."

"Oh, Archer, did you tell him no?"

"Of course, I said no!"

"Are you insane? Defying a direct order from Zeus? Defying me? What will become of you? You must go to Zeus. Beg forgiveness!" she ranted.

"Forgiveness? I've done nothing wrong! You are all allowed your toys. How many mortals have you messed with? How many hearts have you and all our fellow kind broken? I ask for one girl, and I'm being threatened in every corner," I cried out the injustice.

"Zeus said anyone but her." Aroha was calming down, which was good because I could not still my racing heart.

"Why not her?" Being defiant might set her off, but I couldn't bear the thought of breaking up with Callie.

She shrugged.

"I can't give her up," I told her, feeling defeated. "I'd rather die."

"Die?" Aroha looked at me oddly. Then her face went pale and sank. "Oh, my poor boy." She came over and pulled me into a hug and rubbed my back. "You've fallen in love, you silly little thing. How could you be so foolish?"

I pushed Aroha gently away. "I won't leave her."

"And if he threatens to kill her if you don't?" Aroha raised one concerned eyebrow.

"Then your little boy will be no more. I may still exist, but I won't feel alive without her." I sat down exhausted, cupping my head in my hands.

I felt Aroha's fingers knot through my hair like when I was a boy, combing my hair and trying to soothe me. "Archer, I don't know what to tell you."

"There's nothing you can say."

"I'll consult your father about this. See what he says—"

"Don't involve *him*," I spat out, letting her see all the emotions I felt: anger, fury, hate, fear, desperation, and dread. I sure didn't want the god of war involved in my love life.

"Well, I have to. We're going to be spending time together. He's coming to New York, darling. It was the only way to get him to stop fighting. Oh, and here." She plopped a stack of papers in my lap. "Zeus is angry at me for not working, so these are for you to follow up on."

I stared down at names coupled together. Finally, she was working again. I was thankful for the welcome distraction they'd give me that night.

Aroha went to the counter and read Heph's letter with a sigh. "Oh, and Hera wants Heph in love with some mortal."

"I've tried before. He burns off those arrows. He's like a wild boar that won't go down."

"Try ten arrows. That worked before. And someone he can't refuse," she mused.

I got up to get to work. "Oh, who's he coming as? My father, I mean?"

Aroha shrugged. "The new boy?" Then a smile crept on her face. "He wants to win me over again."

I rolled my eyes at her. The last thing I wanted was to see my dad. All my parents did was play mind games. All he and I did was fight. But my biggest concern was what he'd do about Callie and me. Apparently, I could disobey Ma and Zeus. Could I disobey him as well?

For a few days, we were safe from the appearance of any other immortals. Not since Rome had I seen so many other gods in such a short span of time. Then Chase Gideon, an appropriate alias for a warrior, showed up in mid-November. Without warning, he just waltzed into AP Chemistry, came up to us, and asked, "Is this seat taken?" pointing to the chair next to Callie. We just shook our heads, and Lucien stared at me in shock. Because he had been so distant, Ma and I had forgotten to warn him.

He sat down and said to Callie, "Hey, I'm Chase." He offered his hand, and I wanted to cringe. What teens shook hands these days?

"Callie." She shook his hand.

"Callie," he repeated like he had heard of her before. This was weird. "A girl in homeroom was talking about you. Friend of yours, Linda?" My dad, Chase, smiled. Where had this nice, civil behavior come from? I remembered him as gruff, militant, serious, and strict.

"Your friends?" Chase pointed to us.

"Yes. This is Lucien, and this is my boyfriend, Archer." I could kiss her for her amendment. "Oh, and Lucien is with Linda," Callie added.

Chase nodded at Lucien, then me. His gaze lingered on me for a moment, and he said, "You're a lucky guy."

"Don't I know it," I told him, pulling Callie protectively closer to me. I had no idea what else to say to him. This was damn weird as it was, reuniting with my father in front of mortals, but his easygoing, almost flirtatious tone with my girlfriend was unnerving.

"What's there to do around here?" Chase asked Callie.

"Well, on Mondays, they shoot pool, but they're much too good. I wouldn't bother if I were you." She laughed.

"Oh, pool sounds excellent," he said, inviting himself. He tagged along with us to lunch too, talking to Callie constantly. Lucien raised his eyebrows at me, and I shrugged in return. I pretended it didn't bother me.

"So where are you from, Chase?" Lucien interrupted.

"Florida. Miami," he answered vaguely, making it up on the spot, most likely.

"I'm new here as well," Callie told him. "I moved here in October from Minnesota."

I shot Chase an angry stare, and he smiled back at me smugly. He was enjoying trying to make me jealous. Everything was always a game to him. He sat down on the other side of Callie, pushing Lucien and Linda down a seat. She and Emily had drifted from their adjacent table to ours while Aroha was gone, but Aroha didn't seem to care.

I propped my elbow on the table, my chin resting in my hand, thinking about what to say to my dad when he caught me alone. What was he doing, stepping in and chatting up my girlfriend? Ma observed him like a specimen. He caught her gaze and then turned back to Callie, asking her who Aroha was as if he didn't know. I picked at the bread on my sandwich, no longer interested in the conversation and nervous about talking to him alone, awaiting some reprimand or command.

I felt eyes on me, and I glanced over to see Callie gawking at me. You could never tell what was going through her head, but I sensed she was scared.

"What?" I asked.

Callie's brow wrinkled. Her gaze oscillated between Chase and me. Her expression seemed to accuse us of looking alike, but I looked nothing like my father. Could she have been picking up on how Himerus sort of took after him? But she would've noticed that as soon as she met him. No, it was something here, now. I quickly assessed the scene and noticed that he and I were sitting with the same *The Thinker*-type posture, both picking at the crusts of our sandwiches. She recognized a similarity in us, one not very obvious to most others, but her mind was jumping to confusing conclusions.

I subtly shifted my posture. "What?" I asked, touching her cheek. She went slightly pale. She couldn't possibly guess the truth, could she?

"Nothing," she said quietly, clasping my hand as if it were a lifeline. I would have to be careful about my mannerisms around Chase, especially if they were so noticeably similar. I surveyed the table, but no one else was staring at us. Callie was paranormally perceptive, and it terrified me that she might see much more than I wished her to.

Thankfully, she didn't bring it up again for the rest of the day.

At the pool hall, I was alone with my father for the first time in centuries. He was preoccupied, staring at Dan, who was flirting with Aroha.

"I wish I could kill that little whelp." Chase glared at Dan, his eyes glowing bright with an amber fire.

"Your eyes," I warned him.

"Mortals never notice such things."

"Callie does." Damn it. I'd accidentally broached the subject I should stay away from. And yet, he had befriended her. Why? If he was here to command me to abandon her, why would he bother?

"She is a very beautiful girl. Very exceptional," Chase said as he broke the set, knocking in a few balls.

"But?" I pressed. When parents offer praise, they are likely to qualify it.

He looked up at me. "But what? I wasn't saying anything else."

"You mean you're not here to yell at me, punish me, or try to make me obey you?" I shot back defiantly.

"You wouldn't anyway." He gave me a mischievous grin. "You're too much like your father."

"Grandpa's not happy. I'm awaiting punishment every day."

"Oh, he won't bother you for a while," he told me, finally handing me the cue stick. "I saw to it."

"What do you mean?" I asked, shocked.

"I saw to it. Convinced him to leave this be for the time being. I'm to watch over you." He smirked. That little twitch of his lips told me he believed the idea ridiculous. "Still, he wouldn't tell me why, but there must be something about her that threatens him. I'm not sure what, but I only bought you time. Time was all I could give you."

"Why did you do it?" I asked, stunned.

"What do you mean, why?" He was confused.

I didn't answer. What could I say? That he was a warmongering, pathetic excuse for a god and a father? He never loved Ma and me, just war, and there was no room in his heart for anything else? I was angry with him, wanting to lash out at his treatment of us, but I just couldn't. I'm embodied love; hate just can't take root in my heart.

"Oh," he said, sadness registering in his face. "I see. Well...I see how you view me. I know I'm not the best father, but...don't you remember any of the good times?" He shifted his weight and avoided my gaze uncomfortably. Any time he ventured toward expressing emotions, he always stopped. I supposed it had to suck to have a wife and son who were all about feelings, when those kinds of words were difficult for him to speak.

The little figurines popped into my mind, him secretly touching my head, kissing my cheek when he thought I was sleeping, then later teaching me to count by tickling my toes, his sweet words to my mother, his always kind instructions to me.

"I do," I murmured. "Sorry, and thank you," I managed to squeeze out.

"I did it for you, Archer, because I do care. If she is what you want, need, then...I'm on your side."

He had won the game, and I had hardly noticed. Chase shook my hand as any two men would in good sportsmanship, but we were shaking on much more than that. He had talked to Zeus in order to reconcile with me, and it would be wrong of me to refuse him. I'd be guarded, cautious, and let him mingle in my life without any expectations. Every time in the past when I had trusted him, he had let me down.

"So how exactly did you get Zeus to change his mind?"

"I left a prime warfront. He wants the war to close. Alliances he's trying to make with others, I suppose." He referred to the "others," a subject we rarely talked about and rarely dealt with. There were way more gods out there than just us Olympians. "The point is, being in the good graces of the others was more important than his dislike for Callie. He needed me to stop fighting. When he sent your mother, I realized he'd do anything to get me to quit fighting. I used that to my advantage."

"Thank you."

He nodded and glanced over to my mother. "Now, introduce me to this broad Aroha?" He winked, and I couldn't help but smile about how ridiculous my parents were.

Callie seemed to let things go when it came to my dad, the eye thing, and my messed-up family. The truth was, between her father and my mother, Callie and I were hardly ever alone anymore. We decided one day to just go walking, explore the city, merely to be on our own. We had been chatting and sipping coffees, meandering on the side streets that weren't packed, when I noticed we weren't too far away from Uncle D's place. When we turned the corner, onto an even more deserted street, Callie gripped my hand tighter, and that was when I felt it...like someone brushed ice against my neck. Chills shot down my spine. A feeling of being hunted, as if an enemy had me in his scope, washed over me.

I scanned the street to find it desolate, extremely so for a side street in Manhattan. It was lunchtime, which made it even odder. Callie rubbed her arms, shivering, her eyes searching for this unseen threat. It was cold out, but this was something more than the normal chill from the weather, which never really fazed me, the ichor in my blood doing what was necessary to keep me comfortable. The eerie feeling was real. No wonder the mortals were steering clear of this street at the present moment. They could feel the impending danger.

My sharp eyesight caught the figure ahead before Callie could. He stood in a doorway to our right, conspicuously dressed in a trench coat, looking very much like he was trying so hard to blend in that he stuck out. I recognized him from the scar across his face: Zelus, god of rivals and one of Zeus's attendants. He was a "winged-one," just like me, which made any escape tricky. Zelus had many purposes, like filling mortals with zeal, but Zeus used him for his other role: the ice daemon. He hadn't been sent for a friendly chat.

He stared me down with an icy glare, his irises a crystal white that eerily contrasted with black pupils. His gaze then flickered to Callie, and he smiled. His scar, which had been acquired when he was still mortal, stretched, making his grin elongated, lopsided, and creepy.

Then Zelus closed his eyes, and I knew what would ensue. I reacted instantly. I pushed Callie into a doorway under an overhang and kissed her.

I felt the sensation of several sharp icicles plunging into my back. I tried futilely not to wince or cringe so she wouldn't notice. Zelus wasted no time and went into full attack mode. The pain was excruciating, the invisible icy knives slowly being pushed farther into my body.

My mind spun. How could I fight back? Where could I go? How could I get Callie out of here without exposing everything?

Callie pulled away, her face frightened, her hands touching my temples. She searched my face, her eyes flittering and her face wrinkled up in concern.

"Danger," she whispered, her lips shaking. I didn't know how she could sense it so clearly, like she was reading my mind, but I didn't have time to worry about it. We had to move, to run to a safer place.

"I'm so sorry, Callie," I managed to squeeze out, poorly masking my pain. I took her tightly in my arms as more daggers penetrated my back. This time, I couldn't hold in the agony, and I writhed in pain.

There was no way to get out of this acting like a mortal. I held her and attempted to push off the ground and jump as high as I could. Instead, my legs buckled under me, and I fell to the ground, pulling Callie with me. I was now powerless, as helpless as a mortal. I realized my folly too late. He wasn't after her, but trying to incapacitate me so he could easily get Callie. He had anticipated I would protect her.

"Archer," Callie gasped, trying to help me up. The pain was spreading, my entire body solidifying, as if ice were beginning to replace the blood in my veins and the ichor becoming solid and useless. Without the ichor, not only did I have no power, but I could also die—ichor is the essence of immortality. Damn it, I was dying. Icy sludge moved through my heart. It was becoming hard to breathe.

"Stop it!" Callie screamed. "Whatever you're doing to him, stop!" Her voice wavered in my ears as they throbbed with the sound of a slow sludging pulse. My body began to uncontrollably shake from the intensity of the pain, like being electrocuted, as anyone who's pissed off Zeus knows.

"I came for you, child," Zelus said sinisterly.

"Oh," Callie gasped, clutching her chest as she swooned and slumped on top of me. For the split second Zelus's attention was diverted, my pain lessened slightly. It was now or never. I used what strength I had left to jump up and grab him by his head. I simply twisted it, snapping the son-of-a-nymph's neck like a twig, and let his body sink to the ground. He'd be paralyzed momentarily until he healed and would be after us again.

I scooped Callie up in my arms and ran at human speed, looking for

Uncle D's bar. I didn't run slowly because I wanted to. I had no power. I feared Zelus would heal before I could shake off his curse. Whatever he had done to me appeared to be lasting.

Then I saw it: the Grapevine, not far ahead on the left. I hoped Dionysus was in, because my body grew heavier by the moment. I burst through the front door, crumbling to the ground, Callie dropping with me. My eyesight began to wane, and the light began to fade. The pain pierced my head. I could no longer feel my body. Was this how it felt to die?

The next few moments were a tangle of impressions that I could barely register. Dionysus forced my eyes open, his face a blur. Callie weakly asked me what was going on, the pain in her voice apparent. Her hand was still clutched to her chest, her heart hurting. My own voice sounded detached from my body, whispering, "Zelus." My eyes closed, I felt myself drifting from my body. I didn't know death, but I sensed I was permanently leaving my body. Something wet and warm hit my lips, burning. I almost choked on the liquid in my throat before I could swallow. Warmth spread through me, thawing my ichor and strengthening me. I was being pulled back into myself. I could feel the weight of my body, hear Callie's frantic breathing next to me.

I opened my eyes to see Dionysus sigh with relief. "Close call there, kiddo." He sat back, beginning to relax, and drank some nectar whiskey from the bottle. He had to have given me a great deal to save my life, because now I felt woozy.

I sat up, trying to formulate a sentence, "How...What..." I stopped, seeing Callie next to Dionysus.

She took the whiskey from his hand and took a swig.

"Enough of that, little darlin'. How old are you anyway?" He took the bottle back.

"Old enough to realize that that thing was not human. He was torturing Archer just by looking at him! Then he looked at me, and I was cold, so cold, my heart was full of ice. What was he? What are you? And why do you smell like flowers too?" She eyed Dionysus suspiciously. "And what is that exactly?" She pointed at the bottle of nectar.

"We got a problem here, Archer." Dionysus's eyes narrowed at Callie as if she were a bug to be squashed as he helped me up. My joints felt oddly loose, and I knew my powers were back but slightly hindered from my nascent intoxication. I shook my head, trying to focus.

"Is anyone going to tell me what is going on?" Callie asked.

"Iris," Dionysus called.

She walked in the front door instantly, the shape-shifting teleporter, in the form of a schoolgirl.

"Cute," he sardonically commented about her appearance.

"Go tell Father to cease fire and that I'll clean up his mess. Then get Mnemosyne. We need to alter a few memories here, especially this one," Dionysus said, blatantly forking his thumb in Callie's direction. Then he flipped Iris a gold coin, which she caught, bit to ensure it was real, and then vanished right before our eyes.

Dionysus shuffled around, muttering, "In broad daylight! Mortals everywhere. What was he thinking?"

"Um, Uncle D, a little obvious."

Callie stared aghast at the spot Iris had been standing. "Mnemosyne..." Callie's eyes flickered, meaning she was deep in thought, jumping to hasty but probably accurate conclusions.

"I'll take care of that. But kid, how long are you gonna keep this up?" he asked.

"Forever," I asserted. I should've been thankful for his assistance. I could have died or had been so ill that something could have happened to Callie, but Zelus had gotten me into fight mode. Odd for me, the lover, to be violent.

Dionysus examined me and sighed. "You are a nightmare when you're in love, you know that, kid? This is your one and only get-out-of-jail-free card."

"What are you going to do exactly?" I asked warily.

"Erase the last fifteen minutes from her mind is all."

"No, you'll make her crazy," I protested. One of his godly talents was the madness of mortal minds.

He rolled his eyes. "Give me a little more credit than that Er—Archer. Anyway, Mnemosyne should be here in a minute. She's erasing it, not me. I'll fabricate a nice sweet romantic conversation to fill up the void."

The entire time, Callie was watching us, and then her mouth dropped open in a sudden epiphany. "You're...you're..." Her eyes darted back and forth between Dionysus and me. "Wait, what are you going to do to me?"

Iris reappeared with Mnemosyne in tow. The latter gave me a haughty glare of annoyance and whisked Callie away into the back room. I turned away, unable to watch as Callie struggled, protested, and called out for me to help her. Part of me wanted to race back there and stop them, to let her know the truth. I was tired of hiding, tired of lying to her. The other part of me realized that if Callie remembered all this, then Zeus's attempts would never stop. Forcing her to forget would be the only thing that could save her. I told myself this several times in order to assuage my guilt, but it never left me, even after her memory was erased. What had I done by involving her in my world? The damage would be irrevocable.

CHAPTER 17

Aroha

Chase was instantly popular with the girls at the school, which did not surprise me in the least. Dan was as loyal as a puppy dog, which was driving Chase insane already. But I wasn't completely finished with Dan yet, so I'd stretch out the chase to make it last longer. What girl wouldn't want two attractive boys fighting over her and for the entire school to know about it? This would be so much fun.

A couple days after his arrival, Chase randomly appeared at my door.

"What are you doing here?" I raised my brow at him.

"I wanted to see you. Can I come in?"

"I have a boyfriend," I toyed with him.

"So? Just wanna hang out." He was adorable when mortalling.

Regardless of my protests, I opened the door wider to let him in.

"Archer home?"

"Out about the town with Callie. You've found me utterly alone," I flirted. Did I imagine a little spark of pleasure in his eyes at that comment?

He walked up closer to me, and from the look on his face, I could surmise his next move. He took me in his arms and tried to kiss me. I turned so all he could reach was my cheek. "What is it you want, Chase? Why are you here?"

He let me go, a little disappointed. "I felt something amiss with Archer, so I came to check on him. Then I got distracted."

"Amiss?" What was he talking about? "How can you sense what is going on with him? You hardly know him, really."

The comment wounded him, and his eyes revealed as much. "When Psyche and Hedone died, I felt his anguish. It was unbelievable, the amount of pain he went through. My own pain is one thing, but my child's pain..." He shivered at the thought.

"How?" was all that came out of my mouth.

"I don't know. Athena explained it as 'a tie that binds.' Because he is mine, I will forever be connected to him. It was only ever him," he expanded, answering my unspoken questions about our other children that were formulating in my head. "It's gotta somehow be connected to the eye thing."

"The eye thing," I repeated. "Why have you never told me this? I mean you've had over three thousand years to tell me."

Chase examined me for a moment, and then he looked away. "I never had a relationship with him like you did. It felt like my own bond to him that no one else could have. I didn't want anyone, even you, to ruin that."

"He's never said he felt something like that."

"He knew Hedone was in danger before she truly was. How else could he have made it halfway across the world in that day and age to arrive only moments too late? With he and I—" he shrugged, struggling for words "—perhaps because I technically am always in danger and not upset about it, he can't sense it. I truly don't know."

Then Chase cringed and held his head, hiding the fact he was upset. I thought he was about to cry until I saw his face tighten in physical pain.

"Chase?"

"He's in imminent danger, right now. He's in pain."

"What?" I screeched. I was pulling Chase up by his collar and shaking him. A tumult of questions flew out of my mouth that even I could not make sense of. I shook him violently, and he gaped at me, bewildered and astonished at my behavior.

"I don't know where he is or what it is. I can only feel what he feels," he tried to explain, overpowering me with his strength. I felt his arms restrain me in a bear hug.

"What help is that?" I shouted, not caring how my words hurt him. "Archer is my son, my only true child left. I can't lose him!"

Chase pulled me to him, hugging me tightly and kissing my forehead. "We will not lose him," he said with conviction.

We sat down, holding hands together and scanning the city for Archer. He was in Dionysus's bar. I couldn't fathom why Dionysus would touch a precious hair on my son's head, but before I could curse him, Chase relaxed and explained that the pain was subsiding, that Dionysus must be helping him.

I called Dionysus, but it went to his voicemail. The same with Archer's phone, so we waited impatiently for his return.

Archer entered, looking as if he had aged five years overnight. His face was pale, and he walked awkwardly in the door, his legs not working properly. Callie was not with him, so we pretty much attacked him with affection. I pulled him into a hug and then gave him a good once-over. I forced his chin up to see his haggard face and smoothed his hair back. He was ice cold, which is odd for our kind since the ichor works as a temperature gauge, always balancing out our internal temperature to keep us warm or cool as needed. His eyes were dull, with dark circles under them.

"Are you all right? My darling boy, we were so worried!"

Archer then turned his head to acknowledge Chase. "How'd you know?" he asked in a frail and scratchy voice.

Chase tapped his head. "Built-in emotional homing device."

"Forgot about that." Archer plopped exhausted into the armchair.

"What on earth happened?" My curiosity was piqued, but my maternal instincts overcame me, and I began to pamper him. I wrapped him in a blanket, made him tea, and put on soup as he explained the attack by Zelus.

I was appalled. I was disgusted. How could Zeus attack without a warning or an ultimatum? He promised us time with the Callie situation, but here he was, sending Zelus to assassinate the mortal. We all were similarly astonished.

"This is unacceptable," Chase growled, standing up and taking out his cell. He dialed a number and walked into the other room.

"Is Callie okay?" I asked Archer, running my hand through his hair. He felt a bit warmer, the heat eradicating the last remnants of Zelus's poison.

"Uncle D and Mnemosyne wiped her memory clean and fabricated new ones. So, I guess she is technically okay and still ignorant of the truth," he said quietly. I could tell he wasn't happy at all about altering Callie's mind.

"It's what's best."

"How so? She knows nothing, and he still tried to kill her."

Before I could give him feigned assurances that everything would be fine, Chase's angry voice distracted both of us. With his voice raised, we could hear a muffled but intelligible side of the argument.

"C'mon, Dad, you expect me to believe that? I may not be Athena here, but I do have a brain. You had Zelus deliberately attack her in broad daylight, in front of mortals... He attacked my son! You should see the state of him!... Lies! I'll believe it if you tell that story to Apollo... Yeah, I didn't think so... You promised me time to sort all this out... I am sorting it out... You aren't to hurt a hair on that girl's head, you hear me?... If anything happens to my son again, there will be a war like Olympus has never seen."

Then Chase's voice was quiet and muffled, but I had a feeling the conversation turned to my son.

Archer's eyes went wide, frightened.

"Only your father can talk to Zeus himself that way and get away with it. He will sort everything out, Archer. If anyone can, he can." I tried to convince myself of the same. I could not believe the gall Ares had in standing up to his father, even going so far as to tell him what to do. It made my blood heat up with passion, thinking of how utterly powerful a being he was. He could defeat Zeus himself; I was sure of that.

Chase came back out, ranting about how Zeus claimed he'd sent Zelus just to spy, not to attack, and that, apparently, Zelus's attack was unsanctioned. "I know now what he is up to here. I accused him of it, and he was livid. He's agreed to not attack the girl unless given a reason, and thankfully, he has agreed not to send any more spies."

"What was he up to?" Archer asked, perplexed.

"The Charities, your...siblings, and then Zelus, they were sent under false pretenses; Zeus was counting on them to expose themselves to Callie," Chase explained.

"So, then he'd have a reason to..." Archer swallowed hard.

Chase finished for him, "Zeus sent them all, while Lucien and I were occupied, in hopes to expose Callie to our world and therefore have a reason to kill her."

I wanted to know why on Mother Gaia he'd want her dead, but the question that came out instead was, "Why does he need spies?" After all, Zeus was omniscient, always keeping tabs on where we were and what we were up to.

"That is the real question isn't it? Dad's sight is waning, apparently, but what that means, I have no idea," Chase said.

The day after Archer was attacked, I found a note in my locker, which was simply Sappho's "Hymn to Aphrodite," signed by my "secret admirer." Each day from then on, I received poems. Then the flowers came, little presents, and chocolates. Chase was really going all out. It became the talk of the school, and the attention from everyone was euphoric. Everybody had a guess as to who it could be, but only Dan suspected the real culprit. Dan hated Chase's guts, and he made it clear to everyone and anyone who would listen.

Dan took me to the wretched, ridiculous homecoming dance with the cheesy gods theme. I went as myself, of course, and Dan went as Ares. Chase was livid at the imposter, but to irritate me, he took Emily, who really wasn't too bad looking for a mortal. Emily also was a desperate flirt, and I was unsure how far Chase would take that flirtation. He might use her to anger me.

The dance was like any other of the modern hundred or so I had been to, except that the decorations were nicer, the punch was never spiked, and the coatroom was make-out central.

I was dancing cheek-to-cheek with Dan toward the end of the evening. It was utterly romantic, and I was still waiting for Dan to kiss me, since of course, I wasn't supposed to make the move—Zeus and his silly rules to try to cut back on our mortal children. I didn't understand him. During our days in Greece, he spoke of making more gods, of expanding, always urging us gods to have children together, and even making our halfbreeds immortal. Then he suddenly stopped. Whatever control he had over us spread to our fertility. I never heard of a full Olympian god born after the fall of Rome. And now, he offered us a baby if we complied with the Archer situation. It was tempting, yet it rankled me. Why was he so bitter that my son had found someone? In the past, he had always urged Archer to find a new love, promoting the Charities each time, but now he wanted Archer to be forever alone. Asking me to give up one child's happiness to have another was utterly cruel and impossible to choose.

Archer was home with Callie, which worried me, but I tried to focus on the mortal in my arms. Dan licked his lips nervously. "Kiss me, you fool!" I nearly shouted. It would drive Chase mad. Maybe he'd start a scene. It was taking the warmonger longer than usual to start a fight. I attempted to make myself look even more appealing, but Dan pulled me closer to him, forcing me to rest my chin on his shoulder. So much for a kiss at the moment. For how adorable the boy was and how much he talked to the boys about his conquests, I was beginning to think it was all talk and no walk. Not that I intended to take it that far.

Suddenly, Dan let me go and turned to someone behind him. Chase stood there, his hair slicked back into a sleek ponytail. He must have tapped Dan on the shoulder.

"May I cut in?" Chase asked Dan politely.

"No, you may not," Dan mocked him.

"Dan, play nice. It's just a dance," I soothed, taking up Chase's hand.

He was so strong, so appealing in a *chitóniskos*, sandals, and his hoplite armor and shield. He dressed more realistic than anyone else there. Most of the boys appeared foolish, wrapped in cotton bed sheets, but Chase looked as he had over 3,300 years ago—give or take—when I first saw him in this same situation. I was at the festival Aphrodisia, the celebration held in my honor. I couldn't help but love to see all of Athens rejoice in my splendor. I was still within my first century and was with my husband Hephie at the time, dancing with many different mortals, none of whom knew we were gods. Hephie, being lame, allowed me my fun, but then I saw Ares from across the courtyard, and I knew instantly that he was one of us. He didn't stop staring at me as I danced, and then finally cut in to dance with me...

"How is my father?" he asked in the present, replicating the day we met as closely as possible. I clutched his arm, realizing what he was up to, pulling at my heartstrings with the past.

"Your father?" I asked, playing along, trying to recall the words from such a long-ago scene. I found, because it meant so much, it had been ingrained in my memory. "You must be the elusive Ares."

"And I know who you must be. They didn't lie," he whispered.

"Who, and what did they say?" I stared at him, mesmerized as I had been when I was still naïve in godly terms.

"Everyone, and how you are the most beautiful being to grace this earth."

I didn't blush as much as I had back then. I looked deeply into Chase's eyes; the soft glow was building within them, the trait that stole my heart—to see, to actually *see* the love he had for me without having to wait for words. It was the same trait my darling boy had. I remembered how his eyes had glowed during the first hours of his life as he beheld his mother with filial love. I knew then that he was Ares's child, and I never knew a love stronger than being loved by the product of love. I swallowed the guilty lump in my throat. I had given my son's girlfriend a hard time, when Callie must've felt this love when his eyes lit up, just like I felt staring into the depths of Chase's eyes.

I turned away from those enticing eyes. He chuckled, pulling me tightly to him.

"Your puppy looks awfully angry," Chase whispered.

"That's not in the script," I bantered.

"Adjustment of terms for different times and significant others. What had I called Hephie then?"

"Mmm...my minotaur troll, was it? You were mean," I pouted.

"Aroha, you should leave all this behind and run away with me...again." He smirked, his eyes even brighter.

"Give all this up? Never," I mocked. Back in the day, I'd meant it. I'd loved my ugly little broken husband. Poor Hephie. He had adored me, worshipped me, and given me everything I ever wanted at the time. But it had been Ares who'd made me a mother and introduced me to lust and longing.

"It's not working, is it?" Chase dropped the charade.

"It's not exactly the same," I told him. "But I wouldn't say it is completely failing."

"Kiss me," he demanded.

"Here?" I asked, astonished. Dan was staring at me.

"Later then?" Chase asked, disappointed.

"Go to the apartment. Wait for me there. I'll ditch the mortal," I told him, trying desperately not to kiss him as his eyes glowed a bright amber. "Enough." I pushed him away.

"What's wrong? Can't you take it?" Chase smiled smugly, well aware I couldn't, that he drove me crazy.

I could hardly pay proper attention to Dan the rest of the evening. After the dance, a bunch of people were headed to a late-night breakfast diner. I lied to Dan, telling him I felt sick, so he took me home. He pulled up outside my building and put the car into park.

"Aroha, do you like Chase?" he asked. From his tone, I could tell it took all his courage to ask it.

"What?" I played confused.

"Do you like him? 'Cause he likes you."

"What, are you promoting him or something?" I teased him. "I like you, Dan," I lied to see if he'd ever step up to kiss me. After it was all over, I'd get Archer to make him love someone else; for Archer's sake, he should choose Callie and save himself. Something told me if we hadn't been in NY, Dan and Callie would've made a good couple.

Dan leaned over and finally kissed me, a slobbery, terrible, hormonal kiss. I kissed him back, regardless of being completely turned off. He went for more slobbery kisses, but I pushed him away gently.

"Don't push your luck, Dan," I told him coolly, climbing out of the car. He sighed in frustration.

"Thanks for tonight. See you tomorrow," I told him, walking inside. I was leaving him angry and frustrated, but I'd end the relationship tomorrow.

I opened the door to see Chase sitting patiently on the sofa, carving something over the trashcan. He smiled and held up his finger for me to be quiet. He put down the knife, blew the dust off a little marble figurine, and stood up.

"The kids are asleep," he whispered, nodding to Archer's room. His bedroom door was ajar, the television still on, the light flickering against the walls.

Chase walked into Archer's bedroom like it was his own, with the completed figurine in his hand. It was the shape of an archer with his bow poised for action. I stopped in the doorway as Chase went all the way in. Archer was asleep, still fully dressed on top of the sheets, his arms around a sleeping Callie. They looked like two beautiful angels asleep. I hated to admit it, but Callie was a beautiful girl. They were peaceful and innocent. Perhaps my Archer was being a good boy after all.

Chase placed the figurine on Archer's nightstand and touched his head gently. Archer stirred a little, burrowed his face in Callie's hair, and sighed, not waking up. Chase tiptoed to me, shut off the TV, and then closed the door on them.

"What time is her curfew?" Chase asked.

I shrugged, taking a guess. "Midnight?" She usually left around then on weekend nights. "He's not a child you need to protect anymore. He'll get her home or deal with a measly, frail mortal father."

He sighed, pulling me into his arms. He stopped abruptly. "Are you crying?"

"No," I said sheepishly, wiping away the evidence. I hadn't realized I had gotten emotional until he said it.

"What's wrong?" he asked, worry lacing his voice.

"I don't know." I tried to suppress my silly tears. "You playing the family man, I guess."

"I'm not playing anymore," he said seriously. He grabbed my face gently in his hands and leaned in to kiss me.

I backed away.

"What?" he entreated me.

"Dan kissed me."

"He couldn't have done it right, or you wouldn't be up here with me." He smirked confidently and wrapped me in his arms. His kisses were like coming home, and I couldn't refuse them, kissing him back.

"Stay," I pleaded, my weakness for him bubbling to the surface. I was crumbling to his every whim.

"That was a short hunt," he teased. "Easy prey."

"Not if I refuse to make it public," I bantered back, walking toward my bedroom. I looked over my shoulder at him, seeing his eyes smolder with their amber light.

The next morning, I woke up to the smell of coffee and frying bacon. I stretched in my bed, not wanting to get up, but the smell was intoxicatingly inviting. I rolled over to see if Chase had stayed. He was gone, and there was no note. I smiled regardless and smelled the pillow he had slept on—musky earth and sweet nectar, the smell of a god. He had wowed me last night and not in the naughty way. We cuddled and kissed and talked until the sun was about to rise. Chase claimed everything had to go in the right order, the right way; he truly believed we never worked out because Archer had been born from our affair, the child before the marriage. He could have said the same about the other children, the ones we lost, but he didn't bring them up. He wanted to do it right this time. He would woo me, remarry me, and then the baby. I had never seen him so sentimental, so restrained, so...in love with me. No, he had always loved me to distraction. What was missing was his love of war, conflict, fighting. He was a lover right now, not a fighter.

I padded barefoot out into the living room, expecting to see Miss Whittle cooking breakfast. Instead, I saw Chase, clad in sweat pants and a T-shirt that were much too tight for his large muscles, ones belonging to Archer, I assumed. He glanced up at me and smiled.

"Cooking?" I was skeptical. He had never been known as a good cook. In fact, he was challenged in all that was culinary.

"Bacon sandwiches?" he asked innocently. "Can't manage eggs...yet."

"It sounds perfect." I poured myself a cup of coffee and kissed his cheek gently. I sat at the table. "Where's Miss Whittle?" I mused.

"Called her, pretending to be your father, and told her to have the day off because you two would be at my place," he told me, picking bacon out and burning his hand. He hesitated, waiting for it to heal, and did it again.

"Darling, use some kind of utensil," I scolded.

"Oh, yeah." He pulled a fork out as if I were a genius. How did he ever manage on his own? Lots of servants, I supposed.

"Are we spending the day at your place?" I countered.

"If you'd like," he mused in an easygoing tone. This felt so easy, so right, like a perfect household. For the first time, I began to feel optimistic about this venture. It could work this time.

Archer came groggily out of his room, clad in his pajama pants, looked at me, then at Chase, turned, and went back into his room, slamming the door.

"What was that about?" Chase asked me.

"Just because we're starting up where we left off, I hope it doesn't mean he is. He was a nightmare through the first set of teen years." I sighed, sipping my coffee.

Archer came out, his face astonished. He gawked at me, then at Chase, opened his mouth to say something, thought better of it, and went back into his room. The door didn't slam this time.

"How much nectar whiskey did Dionysus give him the other day? It's like he's still drunk," Chase asked, his tone only half joking.

"Of course he's not." I laughed. "Archer!"

He took a second but came out.

"It's not what you think," Chase told him.

"Yeah, sure." Archer sat down uncomfortably at the table.

"I told you your father and I were going to start over again. I warned you," I said.

"I didn't think you were serious," he muttered, put out about something.

Chase began, "And you're going to have a brother or sister—"

"I see you didn't waste any time," Archer interrupted.

"Archer, shut up for a second," I scolded him.

"Here, put that in your mouth as a muzzle." Chase put a plate of food in front of Archer.

He squinted in bewilderment at the sandwich, then at Chase but picked it up and took a bite out of it.

"No brother or sister yet. Perhaps a few years from now," I told him. I didn't want to think about it. Chase and I hadn't truly talked about it. I should've told him the baby hinged on getting my men in line, keeping him from Afghanistan and Archer from Callie. "I'm not blind, Archer. You're restless. You're getting ready to leave again."

Chase sat down with our food.

Archer swallowed. "I don't know what I'm doing now," he murmured, not meeting my eyes.

"What do you mean?" I searched his features for answers and, finding none, waited for him to speak.

"It depends...Callie," was all he said, looking at me guiltily like he had when he was a child awaiting my temper after he had done wrong.

"Archer, whatever happens," Chase cut in before I could blow up, "we're not booting you out. There will always be a place for you."

Who was this man? This was another side of Chase I hadn't seen before.

"Er...thanks," Archer said awkwardly. "And thanks for the thingy, the figurine...and, uh, for breakfast and all." His face was red.

This could work. Archer was at last on speaking terms with his dad. No fists were thrown, no tempers overwrought. The chase was definitely on, but as Archer innocently pointed out, his, mine, and Ares's futures really came down to Callie. How had a simple mortal taken control of our lives, our destinies?

CHAPTER 18

When I'd returned from Nice, my son eagerly awaited me. It was great to see him after quite a few centuries; plus, I was in need of a distraction from all my discoveries. As always—since I was such an absent and incapable father—it was an awkward reunion, but I tried to make the best of it. He was so eager to please, and the insurmountable guilt that only a deadbeat parent feels rekindled. Once I let go of the past and treated him as I would Aroha or Archer—as a friend—things got better. It wasn't long, though, until his bitter mother insisted he return home. I wanted to tell him I loved him, that I was proud of him, but as always, the words never came. I watched the smug Hermes vanish with him, wondering if I'd see him again. I had to find a way to get him away from Zeus if things turned out badly.

Even after he left, I kept my distance from Archer, only seeing him and Callie in school. Then Aroha returned, followed shortly by Chase Gideon, the new guy. It was odd having Ares around, and he was behaving even more strangely—almost peaceful. He didn't rise at my bait when I tried to get him arguing. We used to fight a lot. When it was wits, I'd won, but when it was brawn, he'd won. Chase was my half-brother, but I had never felt close to him at all. And now it felt very much like he had replaced me among my friends.

This loneliness consumed me as much as the other problem: Callie. Knowing now who she was, of what she could one day be—it no longer mattered that she was with Archer. If she were made immortal, she and I could be something one day. And that hope made me feel wretchedly guilty. In AP Chemistry and at lunch, I'd find myself mentally logging things about her instead of paying attention to the teacher: Callie's hair smelled of lilacs; she used a strawberry lip gloss; her skin was bronze and radiant, matching my own; her eyes endearingly welled up when talking about her father, but she was strong enough to blink them back; she had exceptionally thin wrists that made her attractively dainty; she chewed her lip when confused.

I hated myself for this masochistic weakness.

And then I finally asked Linda out. So help me Zeus, I don't know why, but I did it. It wasn't for love—she was a nice girl—but I did it because I desperately needed some outlet, some distraction, and I wanted to rid myself of my loneliness and desire for someone I couldn't have.

Poor Linda. Poor me. I'd stooped so low as to use a mortal to ease my own pain. The guilt was overwhelming, but I convinced myself that it was better to hurt Linda in the end to stop myself from acting on my urges for Callie; that would ruin an eternal friendship.

One thing that drove me craziest of all, that made me want to tell someone about everything I found, was how unfair this was for Callie. Archer didn't love Callie for Callie, but loved her because destiny would have it, because the Fates, the Moirae, had dictated it be so. He loved her because he had loved Psyche, and she was most likely a part of Psyche. I love Callie for herself and herself alone—the past had nothing to do with it.

I met up with Archer at the pool hall. It was the only place I thought I could find him without Callie. When I entered, Aroha and Chase were playing pool, and Archer looked bored and grossed out by their flirting. She had just cast aside Dan.

When he saw me, Archer grinned wholeheartedly.

"I'm so glad to see you." He shook my hand and pulled me in for a half hug. "These two." He rolled his eyes.

"They are pretty sickening."

"Where have you been?"

"Since France? I hung out with my son, and then the Linda thing happened. Sort of seeing her now." I danced around the truth.

"Is everything okay with you and me?" Archer asked, examining me carefully.

"Of course," I lied. Again. Somehow. "Play a game?" I shifted subjects, not sure how long I could lie.

Archer smiled. The guilt churned in my stomach as I put in the money, and Archer racked the balls.

"I need a favor."

"Anything," Archer said straightaway. That was the kind of friend he was. He would do anything for me, and I would not do the same for him. I was a horrible god.

I pressed forward since the favor wasn't about me. "I'm toying with Linda right now. I bound her accidentally. Just asked her to a stupid movie. When the time comes, when I ask you to undo it, will you? I mean, no matter what our relationship is, even if you hate me, will you do it?"

Archer looked at me oddly. "I would never *hate* you, number one. Number two, you're a stupid hypocrite. And number three, why did you do it?"

"To forget about the most beautiful mortal we know," I blurted out, revealing everything. It was guilt fessing up the truth, although Archer would think it was my anti-lying problem.

"Oh," he said, his posture awkward. "Sure. Of course, I will."

"Have you done the same? Bound her?" I challenged.

He sighed, frustrated. "No. I'm like a starving infant staying away from mother's milk."

"How do you do it? Can you keep it up?"

"I don't know, and I don't know." He buried his face in his hands.

"Archer..." I began, ready to tell him all, but I hesitated.

"Don't," he said. "Whatever you'll say will be the best advice ever, but I'm beyond listening to any rational advice. I *can't* part from her. I will be with her for the rest of her life and whatever that comes with. It sounds like you understand a shred of that at least. I'm sorry you feel that way about her, but at least you understand me."

I couldn't say a word to dissuade him or negate what he was saying. If they weren't together, I would be with Callie. And the envy of her choosing him consumed me.

I played nice and suppressed my jealousy while we played pool and in the days that followed. I made excuses every time Linda tried to set up double dates with Archer and Callie, and I used Linda as an excuse to stay away from my happily coupled friends.

And then, my son's name popped up on my cell phone not two weeks after he had gone home. Unfortunately, I was with Linda at the time, who was trying to playfully grab my phone. I had his name under a codename, of course; the last thing I needed was a nosy mortal, such as Linda, picking up my phone to see Zeus or Aphrodite as an entry.

I wrestled the phone away from her.

"Who's Sonny?" she asked, laughing.

I ignored her and answered, "Hello?"

"Lucien?" he asked hesitantly.

"It's me. I'm not alone," I warned him.

"I need to speak to you. Meet me at Seventy-seventh and Lexington Avenue in twenty minutes," he instructed, then hung up. It sounded serious.

I had a million questions for him, one of which was why he had returned to Manhattan so soon. I made many apologies and excuses to get rid of Linda so I could meet my son, who was acting strangely mysterious. He sat on a bench in the subway station, awaiting me with a small pale nun by his side: Iris. This meant that neither did my son have Zeus's permission, nor was Zeus aware Hymenaois was here. Iris would only be employed for secrecy.

"What is it? Your mother?" I asked him, worried.

Hymenaios looked at Iris, who rolled her eyes and stuck her tongue out at him. "Just call me when you're ready to go home." Then she vanished.

"My mother is fine. Everyone is well in Fiji. I came because I needed to tell you something. I'm worried about Archer mostly, with all the talk back home. But now I'm worried about you. He's your best friend, and I fear anyone linked to him might be in danger," Hymenaios blurted out, his tone terrified.

I realized straightaway how much guts it took him to come here to see me. "They don't know you are here, do they? You could get in a lot of trouble." I patted his shoulder. It seemed an awkward gesture, but it made him smile slightly.

"Aww, don't worry about me, Dad. I had to tell you that all of Fiji is in an uproar. Zeus is angry, cursing Dionysus and Eros, but mostly Ares. He wants her dead. Callie is all he talks about. But all the others tell him it will begin a war. Who would dare wage war against Ares? But Dad, it is obvious. Behind Zeus's back, they are all claiming that he is losing it, both his mind and his powers. Hera is running everything. She begged Dionysus to come heal his mind, but he refused, claiming 'Zeus is not insane, but a stubborn, ridiculous, old man,' and that's word for word. Everyone's left; even some of the Muses went on a holiday..." He paused to breathe.

"Your mother is faithful to him to the end, is she not?" I asked.

"She won't leave, and she forbids me to move here. She's afraid I'll tell you things," he smiled mischievously. For a moment, I saw in him the man I always longed to be—carefree, able to lie, cajole, be free from the bonds of truth and my powers. "But, Dad, I came because I overheard Zeus speaking to my mother last night. He's searching for your oracle. He thinks you are withholding a prophecy. He said he's going to punish you if he has to, just as he did Prometheus, in order to get it out of you. I had to come, to warn you."

"You shouldn't have," I murmured. Although a thousand years of getting my liver eaten daily by an eagle wasn't appealing, I worried about my son. "You are now in just as much danger as I am." I'd hate to imagine what Zeus would do to him if he found out he was helping me. I made a mental note to move my current oracle to Manhattan so I could protect her. Why hadn't I already? She might be able to decipher more of the images for me, put them into words.

"I don't care," Hymenaios said stubbornly.

I reached out and touched his cheek; he was my flesh and blood, my boy, and my paternal pride was finally apparent.

"Dad, is there a prophecy?"

I instantly withdrew my hand, wondering if he was trying to get it out of me to use it against me. Was this all staged? It only took me a second to read him, and I saw the truth. He would never set me up.

"You're involved enough," I told him gently.

He smiled weakly.

I realized why he was doing this. He wanted my approval. It was all he ever sought, but I could never formulate the words to express my pride in him. Didn't he realize I was proud of him?

"You don't trust me."

"No," I insisted. "I don't want anything to happen to you. I'd trust you foremost with my life, Hymenaios. For you are the one who would do anything to help me, not hurt me. You have proved as much tonight."

He smiled broadly, nodding as his eyes met my own.

"I like how you can't lie. I know you mean it."

I didn't think now would be the proper time to tell him I had somehow found the ability to lie, but it wouldn't have mattered. I had said the truth. "Thank you for telling me all this. You must get back before they find you missing. If anything happens, and I mean anything that leads you to believe you're in danger, come back here. I will protect you."

"Dad?"

"Yes?"

"Never mind," he sighed. He whistled loudly, and then Iris instantly appeared. He might've been about to tell me he loved me. I wasn't sure what I'd do then if he had. Probably, I would have very awkwardly told him the same. He had done so much, risked everything; he deserved some kind of praise.

Iris looked at me, interested, which made me wonder how much she knew.

I wasn't sure what to say, but when I saw him walking away, I called out, "Oh, and Hymenaios?"

"Yeah?" he asked, his voice filled with eagerness.

"I am proud of you," I said.

Before he vanished, a smile spread across his face. Perhaps being a father was not as hard as I had always believed.

In early December, we all met up for Linda's birthday in a little restaurant with boring Americanized Italian food that was horribly overpriced. She was turning eighteen, a landmark for both gods and mortals. We came fully into our powers by our eighteenth year. However, some get them early, like Archer. It had been absolute chaos when the spoiled brat unexpectedly made mortals fall in love with the wrong people at the tender age of three. I'd hated him then, and it took a few hundred years and him maturing for us to be friends.

Callie and Archer arrived late and had to take the only seats left, which gave me some inward satisfaction. Archer was stuck at one end with his parents and Dan, and Callie at the other end next to Linda and Emily. In the center, I was torn between two conversations, so I missed the beginning of what was going on with Callie.

"Don't you think he's a little weird?" Emily said in a hushed tone, unaware immortal ears could pick up everything.

Callie's face was in a stone-set mask, not showing any emotion. "If I remember correctly, you liked him. You were mad at me and jealous," she said, her tone light, but there was a strain in her voice that betrayed she was upset about Emily's line of questioning.

"Not anymore." Emily sniffed, her gaze darting down the table at Archer and then back. "He's mysterious. I used to like it, you know, find it attractive, but..." She hesitated, pretending she didn't want to hurt Callie's feelings. "...he's sort of creepy."

Archer's gaze flickered to me and then Callie, most likely disturbed by Emily saying such things to his girlfriend yet being unable to do anything about it since he wasn't supposed to be privy to a conversation that far down the table.

"Creepy, whatever." Callie tried to laugh it off.

"Back me up, Linda," Emily whispered.

"Oh yeah, well, I did always think he was a bit unusual," Linda began hesitantly, gauging our reactions, "but now that I know him a little better—"

"He looks at you like one of those stalker types. Like obsessed and all, and he's always watching you... Oh, he is right now." She glanced down at her plate dramatically. "How much do you *really* know about him?" Emily asked, feeding the seed of doubt that I was sure already had been planted in Callie's mind. "No one has met his parents. They email Linda's parents excuses when invited to all the parties, don't they Linda?" Emily didn't wait for an answer but continued, "Oh, and he and Aroha always look at each other weirdly, like she controls his every move. What is with that? Oh, and..."

I didn't say a word. I didn't want to be involved in the conversation, so I observed the others. Callie must have been doubting herself because, no matter how close she and Archer appeared, there were secrets between them. It was just like the abyss of secrets between Linda and me. They didn't really know us since we were hiding our true selves. But Archer didn't hide enough, apparently, because even Emily was noticing things.

The other side of the table's conversation was worse. Dan and Chase were having a tête-à-tête about sports, which was getting heated since Aroha had dumped Dan for Chase, and the former was in denial, but what interested me more was Aroha and Archer's whispering.

"Drop it," Archer growled.

"I won't. It's time to give her up. The longer you draw this out, the more painful it will be for you later."

"I won't be leaving her later," he said.

"Stop being such a... I swear, it's like you're sixteen all over again. Stop this." She actually hissed.

This was about to kick off, but I wasn't sure which argument would flare out first.

"I will stay with her for the rest of her life," he said to her.

Now Dan's attention came back to Aroha. "Is everything all right, babe?"

"Don't call me that anymore," she whined.

"Lucien, what do you think?" Linda suddenly squeezed my hand, giving me a look. I hadn't been listening, but she wanted me to take her side. "You're his best friend," she prompted. "There's nothing wrong with him."

"Archer? No, nothing wrong. Why?" I asked.

Callie stared down at the table, deeply troubled.

"Emily's trying to tell Callie to break up with him," Linda whispered to me.

"That's because Emily wants him for herself," I said loudly enough for Emily and Callie to hear.

Emily's cheeks went pink, and Callie's, a shade paler.

The food came out, and everyone let go of earlier conversations, yet the tension didn't leave the table. The cake came out, the wait staff sang a ridiculous birthday song in badly pronounced Italian, and Linda opened a few presents some of us had gotten her. She opened the Tiffany's watch I had gotten her with eagerness, most likely disappointed that it wasn't a necklace or earrings, but it seemed too intimate to get her anything else. Linda, always eager to please me, smiled wholeheartedly and made me fasten it to her wrist instantly, claiming how much she adored it. At least she'd stop constantly bugging me about what time it was when her cell was right there in her bag or pocket. I would never understand women. Not even another few thousand years would help me.

Another argument erupted between Archer and Aroha, with Aroha storming off. Archer, Chase, and Dan went after her. A moment later, Dan came back, dejected. It was a family thing, apparently, so I stayed out of it.

"What was that about?" Linda asked, concerned.

"Aroha and Archer are fighting about something." Dan's eyes flickered to Callie. "Oh, Archer was asking for you, Lucien."

I rolled my eyes and got up, getting a glimpse of Callie before I left. She was pallid, anxious, and her eyes brimmed with tears. She knew exactly what was going on, or at least had enough insight to make an educated guess.

Out on the street, Archer was seated on a bench that lay against the restaurant's front window. Chase and Aroha were arguing with one another over him.

"He needs to stop this," Aroha insisted.

"But he's happy. I can't ask him to give up what makes him so happy," Chase pleaded Archer's case.

Archer noticed me. "Lucien, what do you think?" He was as pale as Callie, and his hands shook, all his feelings ready to burst from him at any moment. His eyes shone with suppressed fury.

"Well," I shuffled my feet awkwardly. "You have to think what is best for her, Archer. And that is a mortal life with a mortal guy. If you really loved her, you would let her go."

"Not you too." He glowered at me, let down. He hadn't been asking advice at all, but testing our friendship, and I had failed him. "I thought you were my friend!" He stabbed the knife deeper into me and twisted it.

It was true, and it hurt, but something in me snapped. "How can you be so selfish?" Someone had to say it. His parents spoiled and coddled him, so it was up to me to point out the truth. "You *know* letting her go is the right thing to do!"

"I can't!" He stood up, shouting in my face. I had never seen him so angry, so enraged; his eyes lit up with an eerie energy, and his muscles tightened. I could see Chase in him, war-hungry and love-crazed.

"You are unbelievable," I groaned. "You're willing to give up your friends, your family, thousands of years of strong relationships for this girl? Do you realize how ridiculous you are being?"

He grabbed my jaw in his hand, gripping tight, and growled in my face. "I'd do *anything* for her." Then he shoved me away with more force than I'd known he could muster. I'd bet he was stronger than me at the moment, and I was his elder. "I'd trade my existence to keep her alive," he murmured, sitting back down. Trying to calm himself, he put his head in his hands, and I took a step closer.

Chase put up his hand on my shoulder to stop me and shook his head. Archer was losing it. I couldn't fathom his behavior, yet I could see how much he felt for Callie, how deeply in love he was. If I had met her first that day, could this have been me? But the answer was no: Archer was placing over three thousand years of love on this mortal—too much—and it was utter madness to give oneself completely away to something as unstable and fluctuating as love.

"Archer," I tried again in a soothing voice.

He looked up at me, his eyes defensive.

"She won't live forever."

Archer swallowed hard, the fact being too hard to digest, and nodded that he understood. Then he peered up at me, his eyes eager. "She could if—"

"Archer!" Aroha cut in, cautiously watching the mortals who walked by.

"No Archer, it would kill her," I told him. He couldn't know the truth. It should be impossible for me to lie among all three of them, but I was doing it.

"Not if..." He looked to me, suspicion in his features. "Why did you go to France?"

"To see if..." I began with the truth but stopped myself, switching to a lie. "Archer, she's human through and through. The beauty is just a mistake made by nature." The lies came out so easily.

I wasn't being vindictive in my actions, although Archer would see it that way. I was trying to save Archer from himself, from Zeus coming down hard on him, from Zeus killing Callie and destroying Archer's life. I was trying to save Callie from the overbearing love he had for her, a love too strong for a mortal to bear for long. Archer did not need to learn that he loved Callie only because she was one of the last fragments of Psyche in the world.

"You're lying?" Archer seemed confused and hurt.

"How is he lying?" Aroha shot back as if Archer were being ridiculous.

Chase just stared at me, scrutinizing my every move. "Enough of all this for now. Let's go back inside and not ruin Lucien's girl's birthday."

We went back inside, Archer as quiet as a mouse. We all sat down, except Archer, who didn't return to his chair but went straight to Callie. She met his gaze, nodded, and then got up and entwined her fingers with his.

"We're going now," Callie announced. "Happy birthday, Linda."

I wasn't the only one to notice the seemingly telepathic exchange between Archer and Callie. It took only a simple glance, and Callie figured out what he needed, that he wanted to leave. She was very perceptive as Archer claimed, but their connection was uncanny. Chase, Aroha, and I all exchanged looks of bewilderment.

I had a small hope in my chest that he would do the right thing and break up with her tonight, but it was most likely futile. The connection, the way he gripped her hand as they left, made me realize his words outside weren't for dramatic effect. He would end his existence for her if it came down to it. What Archer didn't think of was how Callie might do the same. That little detail might sway him to break it off—he had to want her to live.

The rest of the evening was a bit morose after the pair left. Dan and Chase battled over spending time with Aroha. Emily broke down crying—hopefully, from guilt—and stayed in the bathroom. Linda went in after her, taking a half hour to get her back out. In all, Linda's birthday was a disaster.

Back at my place, I apologized to her for it. She was more interested in what occurred outside than the apology.

"Just an argument." I tried to be evasive, but that brought on more interest.

"It was about Callie, wasn't it?" she prompted.

I kissed her to try to get her to drop the subject.

"Why does everyone give them so much trouble?" she asked.

"We weren't," I lied, holding her in my arms. "It's just Aroha. She doesn't like her."

"I like Callie," Linda told me. "I didn't at first. We were all jealous, but I'm over it."

"That's because you are kind—" I kissed her lips, "—generous—" her cheek, "—and forgiving—" her neck. She was finally distracted enough to let the subject go. She was so warm, soft, and fragile... Ignoring my immortal problems in the arms of a beautiful girl was always the answer, right? Nothing could possibly happen that couldn't be solved by the morning.

CHAPTER 19

Callie

It was late and dark. Archer gripped my hand as we walked, looking every now and then for a cab. He walked quickly, and I had to almost run, stumbling in my heels to keep up. He was silent, his jaw still set in anger at his sister and our friends (ha, if that's who they really were). I had been noticing things, observing too much, logging each out-of-place detail in my mind. But I couldn't confront Archer about any of it. He wished me to remain eternally in the dark about his rich grandfather, his elusive mother, his controlling sister, and his strange cousins and half-brothers.

There were other factors: no family photos around the house, no personal items from childhood like drawings or a tattered teddy bear, no school photos or souvenirs from vacations—no personal details of his past and nothing of his parents. I doubted the third bedroom in their apartment was used for anyone but guests. It was eerie (wrong).

But the eyes were the thing that bothered me the most, how they glowed inhumanly, just like Chase's. They moved the same, spoke the same—although Chase's voice was deeper and rougher—and had the same mannerisms and posture, from picking at their food when nervous to walking with their heads down and hands in pockets. They came from the same mold, like brothers who looked nothing alike except for the intense glow of their eyes when feeling a strong emotion and the way they moved (impossible, I know, but there it was all the same).

The dreams I had, especially the one where the Grim Reaper was coming for me and my most recent nightmare, where we were attacked by a man with a scar, were uncanny. And the old yearbook photograph—it was all adding up to something that made no sense to me. I couldn't figure it out, but something was completely off. Emily was right, and I desperately didn't want her to be. The secrets Archer was keeping from me had grown into an uncrossable chasm between us.

Archer didn't speak or slow down.

"Say something," I commanded.

"Something," he muttered, avoiding my gaze.

THE IMMORTAL TRANSCRIPTS: QUIVER

"Archer, you just fought with all our friends and your sister, over me," I complained. "It's not right."

"They are not right. None of them. We belong together," he said with conviction. His eyes were bright.

"Don't fight with your sister because of me," I pleaded. When he didn't respond, I asked, "Can we slow down?"

Then, I felt a terrible pull on my other arm, and I was falling. This time, it wasn't my heels; it was a man, his hands on my purse, the strap pulling me off balance as he tried to steal it. He tugged again, and I saw the ground coming up to meet my face. At the last second, two strong hands caught me and pulled me upright. The purse was gone, and the man was running down an alley with it.

"My purse!" I cried out.

Archer was down the alley before I could blink, going after the man. He was out of sight quickly, impossibly quick. I ran after them, my heels slowing me down. When I entered the alley, Archer had pinned the man on the ground and pried the purse from him. The mugger struggled to get away but couldn't break free from Archer's hands. The man was bigger than Archer, thicker and stronger, but he couldn't move under Archer's pressure. Archer turned to me and tossed me my purse. I caught it and put the strap over my head and across my chest to make it harder to steal.

"Sad excuse for a human being!" Archer snarled at the man.

The man scrambled around, frightened. I saw shining silver in the dim light, and then the man lunged. Archer fell to the ground, a maroon stain spreading across the abdomen of his white shirt. Archer stared down in shock, touched his stomach, and then looked at his hand. It was crimson. Blood. My knees went weak. Archer might die over my stupid purse! We needed help, but I was frozen, unable to move due to shock.

The man dropped the pocketknife and ran farther down the alley. Archer was up and chasing him, alarmingly fast for even an unwounded track star, and tackled the guy. Archer grabbed him, letting out streams of curse words mixed with ones that did not sound like English, and then pinned him up against the wall.

"I should kill you right now!" Archer shouted.

"Wha...what are you?" the mugger whimpered.

"The Devil," Archer growled, putting his hand on the guy's face.

The guy screamed as if Archer was inflicting some kind of horrific pain upon him (what the...).

196

"Archer," I cried out, scared for him, for the thief, for the things I was witnessing that didn't make any sense.

Archer looked to me, his eyes perceptibly glowing with fury, making their own light in the darkened alley. His angelic face was distorted in a frightening grimace of rage that sent chills down my spine. He took his hand away. There was something odd on the man's face, like a handprint had been burned into his flesh.

"Lucky for you, we're not alone," Archer snarled, his features more inhuman and more terrifying than I had ever seen them. All my fears, my worries were well grounded. He could not be human. He *was* not human. He had said he was the Devil (I could not believe that).

Archer let him go, and the man ran off.

"Archer, we have to get you to the hospital," I cried, running to meet him.

"No, it's just a small scratch," he insisted, wiping his bloodstained hand on his shirt (liar). I tried to touch him, but he pushed me away with one hand and covered the wound with the other. He was trying to hide the wound by pulling his jacket closed to block my view.

"It's not. There's too much blood," I insisted, trying to grab his jacket to lift it away and see how bad the wound was.

"No, Callie. Stop!" he shouted, pushing me away with great strength.

My face must have sunk or taken on an angry grimace, because he then amended, "Please, I'm fine. Just please, give me a sec." He turned away, took off his jacket, stripped off his shirt, tossed it on the ground, slipped his jacket back on, and then zipped it up.

"Just give me a second. I don't want to hurt you," he said quickly and nervously.

Hurt me? What did he mean? My mind whirled with the impossibility of everything I had seen. Was his temper so out of control that he could hurt me?

Archer breathed a deep sigh, his eyes wide, scared (of me?). I crossed my arms to show him he should be.

"Okay," he said, coming closer, taking my arm out of my angry stance and leading me toward the street. "Are you okay?"

"Physically, yes," I said, scrutinizing the shirt he left to see if there was as much blood as I thought. I saw no blood, but there were charred holes in his shirt, with smoke rising from them. The man's face was burned; the shirt was burned. He didn't want me hurt. Archer's blood burned; it ate away at things like an acid. Inhuman eyes, poisonous blood, running too fast, too strong, perhaps healing too quickly, and never aging...

Dad's research and harebrained ideas came to me like a slap in the face: all the mythology he believed was factual history, the ancestor who believed he was a goddess's son. "Ichor," I thought aloud, remembering in mythology how the mineral in the gods' blood poisoned mortals and burned their flesh. But dad's ideas were crazy, ridiculous, weren't they? Archer, a Greek god?

"What did you just say?" Archer stopped, staring at me as his face drained of color (crap).

I would not back down though. It was time for answers. "Show me your stomach."

"No." His jaw set firmly. "What did you just say?"

"Nothing." I set my jaw in anger. "Take me home."

"Callie." His voice broke, his anger turning to desperation. "Please?" he begged.

"It matters now. I want the truth."

"Callie," he said softly, his eyes pleading. They were welling up with tears. "I don't want to give you up." He wrapped his arms around me.

I felt my willpower begin to go mushy. How and why did he destroy any strength I had?

Before my determination crumbled, I pulled up his jacket to see his perfectly sculpted stomach uninterrupted by any wound or cut. He had completely healed, and the dried blood on his skin was the only evidence of the wound.

Archer grabbed my hand roughly, looking at me with stern eyes, and he silently shook his head back and forth once. I let go of his jacket. His expression terrified me. His eyes weren't just angry, sad, desperate, and in pain, but they said goodbye (I wouldn't let him).

I grabbed him by the collar of his jacket and pulled him closer to me. "Then don't give me up," I whispered.

"Don't worry. I can't."

"Your eyes don't lie." My own eyes moistened with tears.

"They'll have to tear me away," he whispered before he kissed me.

I gulped. "Will they try?"

Archer nodded solemnly. I wasn't sure if he was speaking of our friends or of something beyond them that I was unaware of. I was too afraid to ask. Without another word, he took my hand in his and hailed a cab.

The cab ride was silent, and my mind churned trying to make sense of everything. Archer gripped my hand tightly but did not look at me for the entire ride. When we got out of the cab and entered the building, a foreboding feeling crept over me. I wouldn't see him again.

"This isn't goodbye, is it?" I pleaded. "Forget it. I don't need to know." (I was pathetic, desperate.) I was afraid he'd slip out of my life overnight. I couldn't imagine life without him. We had arrived at my apartment door.

"I'll see you tomorrow." He kissed me and touched my cheek, still in his morose mood. Then he tore himself away and began to walk down the hall. He stopped, not turning, and said, "I would tell you anything and everything if I could." Then he walked on.

I walked into the apartment, trying to suppress the tears. However, if I were considered uncannily perceptive, my dad was psychic; there was no lying to him.

"Callie. Is everything okay?"

"It annoys me when people ask that question, Dad. I mean, when you ask it, you know something is utterly wrong, and it just makes the person break down in hysterics." And that was exactly what I did.

Dad got up with great effort and gently seated me on the sofa next to him. The medicine wasn't improving him any longer; he was becoming tolerant to it. The doctors gave him two or three months if he were lucky. I shouldn't have been crying about my oddly superhuman boyfriend. I should've worried about my dad more. That guilt made me cry even more.

"What is it, Callie? Did you fight with Archer? Your friends?" The questions brought more tears.

"I was mugged," I cried, trying to catch my breath. "And Archer went after him..." The entire story came out then. The burning blood, disappearing wound, his strange eyes, the ridiculous rules—everything came out in a torrent of tears.

He wiped my tears with a tissue and said soothing words about how fear and shock might have heightened my imagination, because such things were impossible, but his thoughts were very different, and somehow, I *knew* that. His thoughts were speaking to me aloud. He was recalling all his harebrained theories about supernatural people, mythology being real, and of Mount Olympus.

I pulled away from him, staring. "Dad, not you too. Don't lie to me. You know something. You've been trying to hint to me all along. Translating, helping you with your book."

Dad sighed, stood up, and crossed to the wall, studying the blown-up picture of him and me with the Oros Olimbos mountain range behind us. He put his hands on his hips and sighed.

"Don't measure what you should and shouldn't tell me. I'm too involved now. I love him, Dad, and he isn't...human," I said the last word so quietly.

"I had my suspicions Callie, but I was not one hundred percent sure. From Litochoro, the glowing eyes, knowledge of Greek. Callie, I believe he is a Greek god." My dad turned to see my reaction. "That was my harebrained theory."

I'm sure he was disappointed. I wasn't necessarily shocked, and the gears in my head were turning too busily for me to react. I put my hand up to tell him to wait, to give me a moment. The affirmation from Dad slipped the last puzzle piece into place. All the jokes, all the vague answers that Archer gave me were partial truths: how he had moved so many times that I wouldn't believe him, the weird rules he was supposed to abide by, the military father—Ares, god of war, or Chase as they called him—it explained the matching mannerisms and the incandescent eyes. The absent mother, Aphrodite, who was the most beautiful being on earth, had to be Aroha, pretending to be his sister. If they didn't age all these years, she would have to pretend, and her maternal, controlling tone at times confirmed it. Then Archer, their son, my Archer, the "bowman." How obvious his name was when I knew what to look for. Ambrose, like ambrosia, the food of the gods. Archer was Eros, the god of love, the archer who shot mortals with arrows of love.

"Eros," was all I could say to my father. I hadn't noticed him move about, but my dad had sheets of old parchment in protective plastic in front of me.

"I believe so. It is so strange that I spent my entire life searching for the gods, and when I must give up my search to welcome death, they appear right in front of my eyes. Callie, there's something I want you to see. It's a letter addressed to Marshal Syches from his mother—Psyche, the goddess."

I took up the letter and read. If it was possible that we were supposedly descended from a goddess...

My mind reeled, thinking of the myths: Cupid and Psyche. My Archer was Cupid as well, wasn't he? If so, that meant Archer was with her, my ancestor?

"Dad?" I said, feeling sick.

"No, I am positive we aren't related to Eros. These gods don't seem to age, so they must have immortal children, Callie. I think Psyche had a child with a human, a demigod. Marshal wasn't immortal, since he died. And I don't think Archer knows about any of this either," he continued, dispelling my sudden fears.

"Is she alive?" I tried to hide my fear, my contempt that Archer could still be married as he was according to myth, or history as my father believed. Was there a woman (well, a being) whom Archer belonged to? Would she want him back? Kill me for stealing her husband? If so, I wouldn't let her. Then I realized my jealousy outweighed my shock or fear. I needed to see a psychiatrist, since my first concern was another woman, not the fact my boyfriend was a god.

"I don't know, Callie. And where is Hedone as well? They might be dead."

"Gods can die?"

"It seems possible, but how is a mystery. Why wouldn't she come back for her son?" He sighed. "Was it wrong of me to tell you?"

How did my dad know all these things? "No, Dad, I just need to digest all of this. I can't even believe it. What should I do?"

"Do?" He stared at me, confused. "I hope to leave you in the most capable hands possible. I couldn't be happier."

Of course, my dad wholeheartedly accepted things that were impossible. He would gladly leave me with Archer. I wasn't so glad. I wasn't at all happy to find out Archer was a...god. I was dating a god? It was so unbelievable. Then my mind kept returning to Psyche.

I went to bed, exhausted physically and mentally, but of course, I couldn't sleep. I turned the light back on and took out my world mythology book from the closet. I flipped to the myth of Cupid and Psyche as recorded by Apulieus after the Greek gods moved to Rome—literally—as Dad had always said. The myth came quickly back to me, but I read it over completely, just the portion where the old woman tells the story about Cupid and *her*. In my head, I had to substitute the names with those whom I knew now.

Basically, Cupid (Archer) accidentally poked himself with his own arrow after Venus (Aroha), jealous of Psyche's beauty, ordered him to force the girl to fall in love with a vile creature (knowing Aroha, I could definitely believe that). So Cupid stole Psyche away and secretly married her, only visiting her in the dark so that she couldn't know who he truly was. (I felt the sting there of a sickening parallel—I was to "stay in the dark," wasn't I?) She stole into the room with a lamp to see his face and dripped oil on him, which woke him. He then fled from her (of course). She begged Venus for help, who tortured the lovesick girl with impossible trials, which she miraculously succeeded in with help (I was beginning to truly despise Aroha). Psyche opened Persephone's box, which was supposed to be full of beauty, according to Venus, and fell into a deep, eternal sleep. Then Cupid finally forgave her and woke her. Jupiter (or Zeus—this controlling grandfather) made her immortal by giving her ambrosia. She and Cupid had a baby, and they lived happily ever after. (So where was she then? And the baby?)

I couldn't help but be jealous. Psyche had been with my Archer. I was not his first love as he was mine. He had been married, had at least one child; I was just some naïve little human he was using for the moment. I believed this only momentarily, until his comments came back to me. He said he'd wait until I was ready, until we were married, *forever*...

I shut the light off and finally fell asleep. My dreams were haunted by the mythology I had read: Archer screaming, Aroha's judgmental glaring, and Chase challenging the stormy lightning-streaked sky.

I shot awake in bed. My dreams hadn't disturbed my sleep but what had? A noise. I scanned my dark room. There was a soft tap on the French doors that led out onto the balcony. I slipped out of bed and peeked out the curtain. Archer stood outside, his breath making clouds in the cold, and the wind violently whipped at his clothes.

I opened the door, letting him in. "What are you doing here?" I asked, closing the door and the cold wind out.

"I had to see you. I couldn't wait until morning." His gaze danced across my face.

"How did you get on my balcony?"

"The roof." He smirked, slightly embarrassed.

I gasped. "You could have fallen." I couldn't fathom him as a god. He was just my Archer, so human.

"It's only a story." (If he only knew the story I just read.)

"With twenty-nine others below it!" I scolded.

"I'll sneak out the front door when I leave."

"Don't leave."

"Never."

He pulled me to him, burying his face in my neck. I held him. I was scared, feeling odd and wrong to be holding a god in my arms. What should I say to him? Should I act like everything was normal, that he was like me?

"Archer," I began but couldn't finish a thought. Everything was surreal.

He came out of his hiding spot in the nape of my neck and gazed at me. I tried not to betray myself—my sudden insecurities and my new knowledge. Archer kissed me, pulling me roughly against him. He kissed me with a new passion, as if he were afraid this might be our last time together. It wasn't goodbye, but there was fear apparent in his lips and in his eyes. Archer was as scared as I was, but about what?

"I don't want to lose you," he gasped between kisses.

"You won't, you won't," I told him, my voice wavering and tears forming. I couldn't lose him. It wasn't an option. What he was, the fact that he was different and so much more than I, did not matter at all. Our dependence upon each other, the love between us, made us equals. God or no god, he needed me as much as I needed him.

Archer kissed me even more wildly, his hands pulling at my clothes in frustration. He was kissing his way down my neck. I tore off his shirt to trace those stomach muscles I'd had a glimpse of in the alleyway. I traced my finger along the tiny white line on his abdomen where he had been stabbed only a few hours earlier, then ran my fingers up until I wove them through his short curls.

Archer regarded me with his bright blue eyes glowing with love, passion, and fear. I am sure my eyes matched his, only humanly duller. That's when I crumbled. My defenses came down. I loved him too much to express it with looks or words; all that was left were actions. I needed to show him how I felt.

Without a word, I took his hands in mine and walked him to my bed. I lay down. Archer slipped off his shoes. He followed me, his face in pain as if he had no choice but to follow me. He knew it was wrong, but he couldn't walk away.

"The rules?" he asked, toying with the hem of my pajama shirt. He kissed me wildly, almost not letting me answer. His body weight crushed me in a pleasant way.

"Forget. The. Rules," I said between kisses.

This made his hands and lips go crazy. He stopped, clutching my pillow roughly. His jaw was set, trying to suppress all feelings. I didn't want him to. I touched his cheek.

"Okay," he said to me, defeated.

"Okay what?" I asked, not sure where his mind was headed.

"Forget all the rules," he said. Then he looked at me, his eyes shining more brightly than I had ever seen them. His hand cradled my cheek, and he said, "Callie, I love you. I've been dying to say it. I love you." He kissed me then, a long, slowly building kiss.

I could hardly break myself away from it, but I had to. I had to give him back what he had given me. Obviously, loving me was against the ridiculous rules, his grandfather Zeus's rules, I supposed. The puzzle was slowly completing itself in my mind.

"Archer, I love you too." The moment I said it, it felt as if someone squeezed my heart, pulled it from my chest, and put it in his. My heart was no longer mine, but belonged to him. But it still wasn't enough. I wanted him to know he no longer had to hide or to feel guilty about lying to me.

Archer looked at me quite sadly at first, but then he smiled and pulled me against him, kissing me. Then he kissed his way down my neck again, giving me chills.

"I love you...Eros," I said so quietly, I wasn't sure he heard me.

He froze. He had heard. Then his body began to quiver like he was shivering, laughing, or sobbing deep inside his body. "What did you just say?" he asked, his voice cracking, his face still hidden in my neck, his body shaking all over. I heard no laughter or smile in his voice.

"Eros," I said under my breath.

He shook more and pulled back, his face completely in shock, his eyes wide. I touched his paling face, but he took my hand, removed it, and backed away from me up on his knees. "No," he said sadly, his fists clenching up.

I was terrified that I would lose him, that he would slip out of my life as quickly as he had entered it. But with this new knowledge, there was no going back to a normal life. I needed him now as much as I needed air to breathe. And a growing dread in the pit of my stomach told me that my air supply was about to be cut short. I had to stop him from leaving me. I knelt up to get closer to him again. "Yes." I pulled him closer to me, kissing him.

He remained frozen at first, but I kissed him again and again, running my fingers softly over his back. I heard a groan escape his lips, a defeated one, and before I could kiss him again, he slammed me down on the bed while he wildly tore at my clothes and kissed my neck with an unstoppable passion.

Thunder clapped in the distance.

"No," Archer said stubbornly. Who was he talking to? He began to kiss me faster and rougher, as if he were running out of time.

The thunder clapped louder, seemingly closer.

"No, leave us alone," I heard him beg quietly, kissing my stomach. He was moving very fast, as he had earlier in the alley. My eyes could not quite keep up with his movements. Perhaps it was a Greek god thing.

Then a deep, booming peal of thunder clapped outside, so loud that the windows shook.

Archer tore himself off me so fast that he lost his balance and fell over onto the floor; his eyes closed in concentration, and then they shot open. He had his shoes in his hands, slipping them on before I realized he had moved. "Get dressed, Callie," he commanded.

I wasn't sure what he meant. I was comfortable in my pajamas. "Archer," I pleaded, scrambling to catch the sweater and jeans he tossed to me. I hadn't seen him go into my dresser. He was moving insanely fast.

"Now, Callie, now!" he barked. He rushed from the room.

I changed quickly and slipped on my shoes and followed, almost running into Dad.

"What is he doing here at this time of night? In your bedroom?" Dad demanded. (Just great.)

I had no idea what to say, so I avoided his chastising and disappointed gaze. I wasn't typically a rule breaker, and boys in my bedroom was definitely a big fat no.

Archer was going through cabinets and drawers, dumping and knocking things about.

"Archer!" I hissed.

"Callie?" Dad asked, pressing for an answer.

"Callie, go pack a bag right now. Necessities only. You should've stayed in the dark," Archer lamented. He moved so quickly that I couldn't see his hands. Finally, he stopped, slipping an item into each back pocket of his jeans. I hadn't seen what they were.

"What's going on?" Dad asked, his tone edging into a furious frustration I had never heard from him before.

"You just put your daughter on the worst hit list possible." Archer glowered at my father.

Dad sank, paling. "And so did you." He buried his head in his hands. "Get her out of here, then."

What was going on? What had happened? Hit list? Then it all came back: *"What if I told you I could never tell you everything about me, Callie? Would you still want to be with me? What if knowing these things would put you in danger? Could you live without knowing them?"* I was in imminent danger.

"Pack, Callie, now!" Archer ordered forcefully. "Didn't you realize what's killing you?" Archer snapped at Dad.

Thunder clapped again.

"He is." Archer pointed to the window. Zeus.

The idea of the god of gods wanting me dead snapped me out of my shocked state. I hurried to my room to pack. I opened the door and screamed.

CHAPTER 20

Archer

I had crossed some unknown imaginary line, and now Zeus was furious. The third peal of thunder scared me so badly that I fell onto the floor. I closed my eyes and then saw him. How could Zeus act so rashly and send him without a proper warning? Delegations? A phone call? I had been told I had time; apparently, that was a damn lie. As I scrambled around, looking for any means of protection, Dr. Syches kept nagging and asking questions. I found lighter fluid and a BBQ lighter. They were the only weapons I could find against a god, but I hoped I wouldn't have to use them.

Before I could formulate a hasty escape plan, Callie screamed. I flew to her doorway—immortal speed. I grabbed her and forced her behind my back before I even saw what had frightened her.

Then I saw him. Thanatos's pale form was standing there with his sunken eyes, consumptive pallor, wax-like skin, and thin, frail frame. He was only frail in appearance. He was actually quite strong. He wore a dramatic black cloak—playing up his Grim Reaper role—and let his hood down, exposing thin wisps of mousy blond hair. The moonlight reflected in his dark gray eyes. When he came for people, his appearance was the last thing they ever saw. It was by no means comforting. And the sick creature relished this fact.

Dr. Syches came in behind us, pulling Callie close to him protectively. He could not protect her from Death. No mortal could escape him.

"Eros," Thanatos greeted me with a greedy grin.

"Thanatos," I snapped back without any of the politeness he used.

"Death," Dr. Syches's hushed voice said in awe.

Callie's breath caught in her throat. I couldn't let him take her. My mind whirled and panicked, searching helplessly for a way out.

Thanatos had left the doors open behind him, the wind whipping the curtains and rippling his cloak, making the scene eerie and cold. He was always melodramatic, staging his soul conquests for effect.

"So nice to see you," Thanatos said in a hissing tone.

"Can't say the same for you, my friend," I told him.

He took a step closer to us. I tried not to move so as to not provoke an attack. I, an immortal, was suddenly terrified of Death; he could take everything from me.

"Don't come any closer," I warned him, balling my fists to stop myself from attacking him. What could I possibly do? I thought of Chase. He would feel my panic, sense that I was in danger. Could he get to us in time to help? I willed him to feel my fear, grasping desperately at some invisible lifeline I never knew how to control.

"I'm here for the mortals. Both of them. Orders, you see. Surely, you wouldn't harm brethren over a couple of frail toys. I'm merely...doing my job." He steepled his fingers together and gave me a haughty grin.

I wanted to smack that grin off his face. "You sure take pride in your job, joy, some might even say." I tried to stall him with words. It was the only option I could think of. We couldn't run from him, or at least, Callie and her father couldn't outrun him. I could jump far enough to safety, but he'd just find her again. It was hopeless.

"As do you."

"Yes, but I create love. I give. I don't take." I fumbled with words, trying to sort out an escape route. My mind contemplated the myriad actions I could take and their possible outcomes. None of them would save Callie, and I wasn't sure how long I could stall him. If I could only get to Chase, the strongest of us all, maybe he could protect us.

"Don't take? Your silly, selfish behavior took her life. Rules are rules," he sneered, stepping closer.

"I never told her anything," I insisted, but the truth was painful to hear. I had shown her too much, been my immortal self, but how could I hide a huge facet of my being when I wanted to give all of myself to her. I loved Callie. I had to let her in.

"But she knows." He shrugged as if that comment explained everything. "Step out of the way, Eros."

"She won't tell anyone."

"Doesn't matter."

"You can't have her."

"Now, now, now, Eros, let's play nice. I don't want to have to hurt you."

"You couldn't if you tried." I feigned bravado and flashed him a smile.

Thanatos laughed sardonically. "Physically, maybe, if you take after your daddy deep down. I've never actually seen you in a fight." Then he cocked his head in thought. It gave him a sinister predatory appearance.

He was right. I wasn't a fighter, but I was strong. I had my father's power, and no one had ever been able to stop him.

"It has been a while, Eros, since I saw you last." He began to slowly circle around us like a cat ready to pounce on its prey. "When was it?" he mused in fake thought, his playacting atrocious. He obviously was going to hurt me mentally in any way possible.

I braced myself.

"Ah, yes. Back in the late fifteen hundreds, wasn't it? After Psyche and your poor little darling daughter—"

"Your point?" I tried to ignore him, needing to stay focused. However, the memories I had suppressed came flooding back. I tried to never think of Hedone. It was always too painful, and even though the memories had begun to fade after all this time, I still remembered the last day I saw her. I remembered her waving and blowing me a kiss from the back of a coach destined for Nizza back then—Nice, France these days—and supposedly under the protection of her mother. And then it hit me hard. Lucien, Nice, Psyche's and Hedone's deaths—it was all connected. He had gone there about them, not his mother, but why?

"Yes, I was summoned to collect them without warning. Boom! There they were at the top of the list. I hurried to collect those precious souls. I didn't want them to wander the earth till the end of time. When I got there, they were in such pain and agony. They begged me to take them."

"Shut up!" I growled.

"I really did end their suffering. It was a kindness. Don't worry about your girlfriend here. I'll see to it Hedone can care for her. I'm sure you can see both of them again in the Underworld if you like. If Hades lets you. He usually keeps the pretty souls for himself, and my, she is pretty." His sunken face laughed haughtily.

Something in me snapped. Either envisioning Callie dead, imagining never holding her again or kissing her warm lips; imagining Hades never letting me see her image again, even her translucent soul; being reminded of my daughter, having to think about her and Callie together in the Underworld—one of these reasons or all of them snapped me into action.

I leaped at Thanatos and tackled him to the ground. The floorboards cracked and groaned in protest. I closed my hands around his throat and tried to squeeze, but he wedged his knee under my abdomen and shoved. We collided with the ceiling, my back making popping noises as it broke with the plaster of the ceiling. We fell back to the ground, me incapacitated but healing quickly. Thanatos shoved me off of him and got up awkwardly, his injuries hindering his normal nimbleness. I lay there helpless, unable to even move my neck. I was momentarily paralyzed.

From the corner of my eye, I saw Thanatos walk over to Callie. She stared at me in horror and then at her attacker as he grabbed her by her wrist. Callie's intake of breath was sharp and painful. She struggled to free her wrist, which made Thanatos both perplexed and bitter. He pulled her closer to him, and she gasped, going limp and falling to the ground. If she were dead, I'd...I'd be capable of the worst. Anxiety bubbled up in me. Rage bashed around in my brain. And a desperate helplessness that I had only felt once before filled me up. She would not die like my ex, like my daughter, not Callie.

I finally felt the tingle in my fingers that told me I was almost well again. Seconds felt like ages, just watching, without being able to do a thing to help. I saw Raphael, the servant, appear with a wooden baseball bat. He swung at Thanatos, who stood over Callie, ready to extract her soul, his fingertips on the back of her neck. Not ready for the blow, Thanatos was thrown backward next to me. Despite the fact that he was a mortal, Raphael had momentarily overpowered a god. I took a chance with my building strength and rolled onto Thanatos, pinning him down. I squeezed his neck tightly, thinking only of revenge. Callie might not have lived through his touch. No mortal could, a demigod maybe. I wanted vengeance.

I tried to look away and think of something else as I squeezed his neck, his face turning purple. Could Chase feel my strife? If so, then where in Hades was he?

I heard a moan and glanced over to see Callie coming to in Dr. Syches's arms. I must have relaxed my aggressive stance in shock, for I was thrown off Thanatos and landed on my back again. My mind whirled around in circles as Thanatos stared me down, regaining his breath. I could not escape with Callie. I had to end this. The only way to save her was to get Death away from her, permanently.

I used all my strength, thinking of my love for Callie, and leaped at Thanatos, catching him off guard. We tumbled onto the balcony through the still-open French doors, exactly where I wanted. I had my hands around his bony little throat, squeezing. Somehow, he couldn't fight me off. He should have been stronger than I was, since he was older, but I had heard of instances of adrenaline rushes, of becoming stronger in situations of great magnitude. It was primal, instinctual. I had to stop him, or I'd die trying to protect Callie. Love pumped through my veins, empowering me to continue fighting.

Thanatos's instincts kicked in; with his shock now gone, he fought back, knocking me off balance. I grabbed him, taking him with me as we went over the balcony railing, plummeting twenty-nine stories, the blistering winter wind cutting through my clothes.

I heard Callie screaming, "Archer," but her voice faded as we fell. The ground wouldn't come fast enough, falling while trying to push one another down first. This was going to hurt. I put on the brakes, defying gravity, falling much more slowly and gracefully than Thanatos, which was my plan. But he reached out and yanked my foot, gripping it, making me plummet at his rate. I had Thanatos under me when we hit the ground in the alleyway. I heard shattering and crumbling beneath me, and I fell onto my side, piercing pain shooting through my legs.

Thanatos twitched in a hole in the cracked pavement, his mouth bubbling with blood. The ichor hit the pavement in droplets as he spit and rasped, trying to breathe through burst lungs. The blood scorched the pavement, corroding it. It would only take him a few minutes to fully heal; me, much less. Every bone of his was likely shattered, every organ burst.

I dragged myself away from him with my arms, my broken legs dragging painfully and uselessly behind me. His gray eyes searched for mine. I met them as I tried to dig for the contents of my pockets, hoping I hadn't broken them in the fall. I felt my legs already warming. I was healing.

"Why?" Thanatos spit out blood with his words. His fingers moved slightly. His nerves were healing.

"Love."

The lighter fluid was still in the container, which was not even scratched or cracked. I tested the lighter, which lit. Thanatos gawked at me, his eyes wide. He was utterly helpless.

"W-what are you doing?" he gasped.

I dragged myself a little closer, testing my legs. I could move them now. I squeezed the entire bottle of lighter fluid all over him.

"No...no...don't!" Thanatos pleaded. He was helpless, yet in moments, he would heal and take Callie away from me forever.

"Will you take her?" I challenged.

"I...I...have to," he whimpered.

He would never stop. He would kill Callie because he was ordered to, and he wanted to because he enjoyed his job. Seeing him touching her, trying to extract her soul and to take her away from me forever, had made me realize with a crushing finality that I couldn't live without her. I had to do whatever it would take to keep her alive.

"I am so sorry, Thanatos," I told him, meaning it.

Then I touched the lighter to him and pulled its trigger, which lit him instantly on fire. I dragged myself away against the wall, between two dumpsters, far from harm. I closed my eyes, but his screams were piercing. I covered my ears, but I could still hear his screams of pain, his suffering. I could visualize his broken and bloody body, his gray eyes pleading. Then chaos literally filled my mind, reminding me of the last time I had seen it. The last Olympian immortals to die had been Psyche and Hedone. Then, I had been too late. This time, I was able to save my love. *It was Callie or him,* I thought over and over again like a mantra to assuage the sick feeling in my stomach that I attributed to rising guilt, struggling not to lose my mind as the images and memories flickered by relentlessly. Every sensation, feeling, event, every possible piece of matter, flesh, plant, tree, the light, the dark, life and death, pain, suffering, mortal, immortal—it all flashed before my eyes. Like the mortals who profess their life flashes before their eyes in the moment of their own death, for each immortal death, every moment of all time flashes before our eyes, each one with its array of feelings, thoughts, details, senses, and imagery. It is chaos, too much information for even the immortal mind to grasp, let alone process.

The screams stopped, and then chaos vanished. I opened my eyes to see a pile of rubble on fire that no longer held a human form. I slipped the lighter back into my pocket in case I needed it again. It all seemed so surreal. I couldn't believe what I had just done and witnessed.

I closed my eyes and just lay there, letting my legs heal more. It would just take a minute for them to fully mend, but I felt vulnerable and out in the open, and there was Callie's safety to consider. Zeus could send someone else after her while I was incapacitated. She'd live without there being a Death, but he could do much worse to her.

CHAPTER 21

I raced down the alleyways of Manhattan to Archer's building. Chaos meant someone was dead. I hoped it wasn't Archer, but I had a sickening feeling in my stomach. No matter who it was, one of us had died, and that was something to mourn.

As I reached their block, I stopped when I saw them in the alley: Chase and Aroha helping a limping Archer, with Callie and her bat-wielding servant behind them. A smoldering pile of ashes told me it was someone else who'd died. The truth etched across Archer's face told me he was the one who'd done it.

I hurried to them, desperate for answers. Archer's gaze met mine. He was pale, shaking, and in shock. "Thanatos came for Callie and her father."

His comment ignited a fuming anger, and Archer could sense my thinly veiled emotions. I was jealous and angry, and I feared for Callie's life. I loved her, and he had almost gotten her killed by exposing his powers or identity—something had to have set off Zeus to order this. I was silent and followed them as the servant led us back into the building and into the elevator, up to the top floor, and then into Callie's apartment. Dr. Syches was there, and on seeing all of us, he let out a relieved sigh and sank onto the couch.

I stayed quiet as they discussed what had happened and what still might happen, how Zeus might punish Archer. I didn't care anymore. I cared about Callie's well-being, and I wasn't sure how I'd let a mortal girl destroy my longest standing friendship, but it was done, and there was no way to undo it. The prophecy haunted me. Callie had truly changed us all forever.

Callie's father pumped us for info and told us about the things he'd found that were housed in his glass cases. When he was over all the excitement and was about to keel over on us, Callie sent him to bed. The conversation continued with Archer's worried parents, while the lovers held hands and stared silently at each other.

A tap at the door made me go rigid, Ares and Aroha alert, Callie quiver in fear, and Archer slump in defeat. The visitor knocked louder. No one moved at first to get it, but Aroha snapped to attention first. She headed to the door with a snarky, "Well, it's not Death."

Hermes's smug I-told-you-so mug came into view, followed by Aroha, who childishly made a face behind his back.

"Well, here we are again, Eros." His beaming smile belied his message. "You're wanted in Fiji in four hours. I was sent to ensure you arrive promptly." More like ensure Archer actually went.

"What for?" Archer asked. He was feigning a calm mood and tone, but I could see the fear in his eyes.

"Your trial," Hermes said as if it were nothing.

"I'll go pack," Aroha said quietly. She wasn't joking around anymore, the gravity of the situation finally hitting her.

"Zeus said he goes alone," Hermes countered.

"No, he doesn't. I'm going with him." Chase stood up, towering over the short Hermes. Chase was a pretty intimidating guy, although I was loath to admit it.

"This isn't a war, Ares, and I'm not your soldier to command." Hermes sneered at him, but his eyes darted around at all of us. He was scared under all that fake bravado.

Chase's fists tightened. "If he harms a hair on my boy's head—"

"You'll what, Ares? Fight your own father?" Hermes laughed.

Chase simply stared him down. The staring contest lasted for a full minute before I finally had enough. "Hermes, if Eros has to attend a trial to receive a punishment, it only makes sense that his parents need to be there. Why don't you send good ole Dad a text instead of throwing down the gauntlet to the god of war. I think we all know who would win."

"Admitting he's your dad, Apollo? Progress," Hermes said.

"It'll take me another three thousand years to admit we are even related." I never saw Hermes as a half-brother.

Callie's mouth dropped at hearing my real name and my age, but Archer didn't meet her quizzical gaze. He was staring at the messenger still. Her reaction made me wonder how their age gap conversation would go.

"Why don't we just stay quiet if we can't be nice," Aroha said. She was met with silence, so I guess no one had anything nice to say back.

Hermes made himself at home by pulling a dining room chair over in front of the door as if to prevent us from leaving. We sat in silence. Only Aroha asked questions now and then to try to be somewhat polite to Hermes, or more likely, she was trying to break up the uncomfortable silence. Callie's shock began to wane, but she must have been overwhelmed by everything. Then she started nodding off due to pure exhaustion. Archer led her to her room, entreating her to sleep. He seemed torn leaving her room. I think he was more afraid of what would happen next. We were all about to confront him about his stupidity, and I had to go first before I burst.

"You ruined her life," I said simply.

Archer kept his gaze steady with mine. "I know."

"How can you be so calm about it? You're going to be summoned to Olympus for only Zeus knows how long. What is she supposed to do without you? She's better off dead than the state you're leaving her in," I protested.

Given the state of Archer, I wasn't ready for what happened next. Archer grabbed me by the collar of my shirt and, with great speed and exceptional strength, slammed me into the wall, leaving a large dent in it. I heard and felt my collar bone and a couple ribs break on the impact.

"I've already killed one immortal tonight. Don't push me into making it two," Archer growled through clenched teeth.

I shoved him off but doubled over in pain, still healing. "What? Don't speak the truth? It's what I do! You didn't bind her? Do you realize she'll never have a chance for happiness ever again? Love anyone else ever again? Think of how selfish you have been!" Let him deny it all. I'd see the lies in his eyes.

"You would have let her die?" Archer laughed dryly like a madman.

"Don't avoid my question!"

"Which one?" Archer shouted, shoving me down.

"Stop it now," Chase tried to command us. As our elder, he should've been able to command the situation. But something was off. I could lie, the god of love could kill, and Death had died. It had something to do with Callie, but what?

"Just answer one question." I glared at Archer. I stood up to my full height, healed, and pushed him back with my finger.

"What?" Archer glared me down.

"Did you bind her to you?"

"Does it even matter at this point?" My question had confused Archer, but then his face fell. "You're hoping with me out of the way, you'll have a chance with her." His accusatory tone made me feel like a scumbag, but it was unfair to force Callie to love him.

"This isn't about me."

"I think it is, Lucien." He glared at me. "I bound her, yes. At least now I know she'll be safe from you."

I gave him a hard right hook that made his jaw crunch. He wouldn't be able to talk for a minute. He had bound Callie, ruined her life, and ruined any chance I could've had with her in the future. He would refuse to undo the bind under some false pretense to protect her from me, when really, he was selfishly claiming her while shutting me out.

Chase's arms snaked me into a full nelson. There was no point fighting against the strongest god, so I gave in. I was thrown into a chair and ordered to stay there. Aroha gave me a glare and tended Archer's jaw. I could see I was now on my own. The absentee parents were now going to fully support their criminal son.

"This is hardly productive. Why are you so mad at him, Archer?" Aroha asked, completely confused.

Chase sighed, exasperated. "Shouldn't we be figuring out why Zeus wanted Callie dead?"

"No, wait, dear. I want to figure out what is up with these two." Aroha shifted back to the fallout between Archer and me. "You don't seem surprised by any of this, Lucien, just angry at Archer. Tell me, Lucien,"—Aroha looked at me slyly—"have you not had any prophetic dreams of late? And exactly what was France all about?"

Archer sat down, calmer but still glowering at me. "Go ahead," Archer muttered through his clenched teeth, his jaw still healing.

"There was nothing going on in France. Just my mother," I lied, trying to stay vague.

"He's lying," Archer accused.

"Not this again," Aroha rolled her eyes. "He can't lie."

"Or can he?" Chase pondered.

"What?" All three of us said in unison. I was astounded that he'd surmised the truth. Chase, the bullheaded fighter, my half-brother, had never been celebrated for his intellectual abilities.

"Think about it. Why am I away from war? Why did Archer fall in love? Why does Zeus need spies to see what is going on? Something is amiss with all of us." Chase paced as he spoke. Then he turned to me. "And why is Lucien taking secret trips, hiding things, and lying?" He challenged me to contradict him.

They were all staring at me. It was time to fess up. "I had a dream. I saw Archer upset and angry, fire, Zeus afraid, and Callie's face. That's all. I hadn't made sense of any of it until now."

"How long have you been sitting on that?" Archer's eyes narrowed, the accusation apparent in his gaze and voice.

"A couple days before she came here," I retorted.

"And you never felt the necessity to tell us, to warn us. Poseidon's trident, all of this could've been prevented!" Aroha lashed out at me.

I wished she would redirect her anger toward the deserving. Archer had created this mess. "Really, Aroha. Would it have mattered?" I taunted back.

Before she could answer, Archer cut in, "No, it wouldn't have. I was in love with her the moment I met her by the elevator. I never would've been able to stay away."

"We could've better protected Archer, her, if we had known." Chase gave me a reprimanding shake of his head.

"From an omniscient god?" I laughed.

"He's not. His powers have weakened or, at least, his sight. It has something to do with Callie, but I don't know what. How could a mortal..."

"She's a demigod," Archer proclaimed.

All of our mouths dropped. How in Mother Gaia had he figured it out?

"Isn't she, Lucien? Isn't that why you went to France? To prove that?"

"But why would Lucien even care?" Aroha threw her arms up, lost. She plopped onto the sofa like the drama queen she was.

"Because he has to understand the prophecies, and more importantly, he wants her immortal one day as much as I do. He wants her after we tire of each other, but we never will. This is true love, Lucien. Bound or not, she never would've loved another, and neither will I," Archer said.

I wanted to punch him again for his big head. She wouldn't only love him. He had just gotten to her first. There would be a time for Callie and I to be together, despite his ridiculous notions of true love.

So, out of jealous resentment, I prepared to use my last piece of ammo that would most likely forever sever our friendship: Callie's godly ancestor. "I did go to France to research her lineage. And I did find it. She is—"

"A demigod, yes. My father has the proof in a letter written by one of your kind." Callie was standing there. She shot me a significant look that begged me not to reveal it. I was powerless to deny her wishes.

"Who?" Aroha's perceptive gaze darted between us.

"It doesn't matter," Callie said.

"Never thought I would ever say this, but the mortal is right," Hermes piped up.

I had forgotten he was there. Idiotically, I had been about to reveal something huge in front of Zeus's pet because of my temper. I should've been thinking about protecting her, not giving Zeus the info he longed for.

"As much as I love to watch you squabble, Zeus will never make her immortal. Her heritage is a moot point, but I'm sure he'd loved to know that ancestor."

"The letter isn't signed," Callie lied.

Chase and Aroha also had forgotten about him, because they now were hounding him for information and arguing with him. Thankfully, they turned Hermes away from the subject we'd almost exposed. My attention was turned instead to the couple. Archer had crossed over and pulled Callie into his arms. They were doing that annoying speaking-without-words thing they did—simply looking into each other's eyes, communicating what they needed. Archer let her go and took up her hand. He led her toward her bedroom door.

"Eros," Hermes called over Chase and Aroha's conversation. "I'll be watching you." He punctuated with a leering grin, his innuendo not lost on us, then added, "No desperate attempts to escape either."

Archer said nothing but followed Callie into her room and closed the door. We all heard the door lock. That click sound spoke volumes. He would not be escaping, but he sure was going to use his last hours here in the arms of the most appealing mortal I had ever met. I didn't think Hermes would let them take things too far, but I still burned with envy.

CHAPTER 22

Callie

As soon as I locked the door, Archer was kissing me as if he would never see me again. I kissed him with the same fearful lips. I couldn't tell what was weighing more on my shattered heart: fear or passion. Only, Archer was trying to leave off where we had been before Zeus's powerful thunder clashes, pushing away from the door and slyly kissing me toward my bed. Despite knowing what he was up to, I fell victim to his kisses, wanting to let go and forget all the unwelcome interruptions: Zeus, Thanatos, Hermes, and all the pending consequences. Consequences? Could I endure it? To give myself so completely to another being, knowing he might never come back? Could I bear that much love and then let go? Last night was different. He was going to stick around then. Today, however, the chief of all the gods was summoning him for trial and punishment. The messenger god was watching us (gross). I was so lost. (Who wouldn't be?) I could only wonder what Archer was thinking. I needed to see what was going on in his head.

Then, as if I had jumped out of my own mind and gone into his, I could see what he was really thinking: he wanted me to have a baby. He believed a child would solve all our problems. Zeus would never keep him from his offspring. Archer loved me and wanted a future with me. Zeus would never hurt a woman with child...

I opened my eyes, and I was myself again. (What just happened?) Archer's thoughts were all wrong, the circumstances, the situation. (What was he thinking?) People who want babies should be married and in love and older (waaaaay older) and... How could I read his mind? Had he done this before? Impregnated Psyche to get her to be immortal? This was wrong on so many levels.

"Stop." I pulled away from his kisses. "Stop!"

Archer grabbed my hands in his, squeezing them, and buried his face in the pillow by my neck.

"I can't." I shuddered, crying silently.

"I'm sorry." He turned and kissed my temple.

"I can't have a baby now, not unless you stick around." I quivered all over, crying uncontrollably. What was I telling him? That I, at seventeen, would do even that for him, that I loved him so much I would put college on hold and start a family with him if he stayed? It wasn't at all like me (crazy, really).

"What?" He froze, taking my face in his hands, searching my eyes. "How... You are beyond paranormally perceptive, Callie." Then he lay next to me, cradling me in his arms, pulling the covers around us tightly. "Shush," he soothed me. "Please don't cry, my love."

I suppressed my emotions. How could I ruin our last hours by crying the entire time? I needed to be stronger, to show him I was not such a frail and pathetic human. I had to show him I could bear the hardship of our parting. He had enough to worry about.

"I'm sorry," I told him, wiping away my immature tears.

"For what?" he asked softly.

"For not staying in the dark."

"I would've given it away eventually. I never would've left you, and you would've realized. I will always look like this. I always have, since I was eighteen."

"Oh." I realized what he meant. A million questions filtered through my brain, preventing me from focusing on one to ask.

"I wasn't going to, you know, try for a baby. It was just a thought you weren't supposed to hear. Hermes and Zeus wouldn't let me."

"Because you tried that move before?" It was out before I realized what I was saying, and my tone, quite accusatory. I felt like I couldn't control myself; my emotions were everywhere. All in one night, I'd discovered myths were real, and I was thrown into them. I couldn't process and was in awe that the being in my arms was a god, a god whose face was squinting in confusion.

"What move?"

"Did you get Psyche pregnant so Zeus wouldn't kill her?"

Archer let out a sigh. "I don't want to spend our time together dredging up the past. If—*when* I come back, I'll tell you everything. To satisfy your curiosity, the answer is no. Zeus had no issue with Psyche and made her immortal out of pity for all the crap my mother put her through. We had a baby later."

"And they died?"

"I really don't want to talk about that. Just know, Callie, that I don't think I ever knew the full extent of love until you."

My heart soared at hearing this, and I wanted to tell him how important it was to hear those words, to know he loved me more than Psyche. I was about to tell him the truth about my ancestor, but his lips on mine distracted me. By the time he pulled away to stare at me with those incandescent eyes, my resolve had shifted onto another concern. "Promise me you'll come back," I pleaded.

"Callie." His voice broke slightly, and he buried his face in my hair. "Please don't force me to make promises I may not be able to keep. I don't leave willingly."

"Promise me," I pushed. He was supposed to be a god. Didn't divine beings have powers beyond the norm? That was another arsenal of questions I had.

He leaned over me and turned my chin so our gazes met. "I promise you, I will try to come back to you one day. I can't promise how long or hard it will be. I may die trying, but I will try. I could never stay away from you." He kissed me to seal his promise. "And you promise me something, Callie: no matter what you hear, no matter what anyone says, no matter what happens, you must promise me you won't hurt yourself in any way. If anything happens to me, I want you to keep on living. You hear me?" He held me so tightly that it was hard to breathe. His eyes danced across my face in their electric blue hues.

"I promise," I told him solemnly. How could he ask me such a thing? How could I easily accept his request? He didn't realize that I couldn't live without him. If he didn't exist, then how on earth could I go on? Without my father or him, I really had no one who loved me. As these thoughts crossed my mind, I began to feel so helpless. How had I let my rationality slip away to be replaced by an overwhelming love that made me quite ridiculous? My rationality returned ever so slightly to remind me that it would be worse if something happened to me and he wished to follow. I wasn't immortal like him. I wanted to ensure he would not hurt himself without me as well. "I promise. But you can't either."

"I can't die." He laughed, kissing me. "You of all people should realize that—seeing me get stabbed, falling off a thirty-story building," he tried to joke. I could see he was really just dodging the promise.

"Archer, don't pretend you don't know what I'm talking about. I saw how the gods can die."

He went quiet for a moment, staring at the ceiling, then at me from the corner of his eyes. "It's a redundant promise anyway." He cracked a smile. "I'm not going to let anything happen to you." Then he kissed me

221

several times, most likely to prevent any of my protests. "Sleep, my love," he murmured in my neck. He began to softly whisper a song. From what I could tell, it was in Greek, but I couldn't keep up with the words. My Greek had improved vastly, thanks to Archer's tutoring, but this sounded different.

"What's that? I can't keep up."

"A lullaby in Ancient Greek. My mother sang it to me," he said, then he stared off at the ceiling, deep in thought.

"What are you thinking?" I prompted.

"Honestly?" He peered at me.

"Yes, honestly."

"It would've been nice to have a baby," he said simply, closing his eyes. "Sleep, Callie. If you are as tired as I am, it won't take long."

I did not want to dwell on his comment. Had Hedone been his only child like the myths claimed? I had so many questions, but I could not sully our time together with them. I was exhausted—lack of sleep compounded with an emotionally epic battle where Death had actually knocked me out. I closed my eyes, thinking sleep was impossible, especially after my short-lived nap earlier (disrupted by Archer and Lucien trying to prove who knows what), but Archer had been right. I was asleep instantly.

Again, dreams came to me. These days, I couldn't sleep without the newly vivid dreams, and they were getting easier to recall:

Archer was humming and singing the same lullaby, but I could only see the back of him in the dim light. He sat in a wooden rocking chair in a room with vibrant yellow walls, detailed with white molding and skirting. The room was glowing faintly from a chandelier that looked like candles, yet I could tell they were bulbs shaped that way. It was decorated like the personal home of someone wealthy, yet with a strange blended style of modern homes mixed with something from a distant past. Archer's hair was cropped very short, shorter than it was at present. He turned on seeing me enter and smiled brightly. "He's fussing."

Then I peered down into his arms to see a little bundle wrapped up in them. I took a few steps closer, putting my hand on his shoulder. In his arms rested a beautiful baby with fuzzy wisps of warm brown curls, of varying shades of russet and burnt sienna, and the same bright blue eyes that Archer had. The baby cried out a couple of times, and Archer shushed him, rocking him in his arms and singing again. I leaned over to kiss Archer's forehead, my hair cascading over his shoulder, but instead of my dark brown waves, they were strawberry blonde.

I woke up in bed. I was back in my own room. And I was alone. Archer had left while I slept. How could he leave me without a goodbye? And why did I have to have a dream like that? I bet Psyche'd had strawberry blonde hair, a nice reminder that this fantasy life I dreamed about had already been lived by Archer before.

The sadness was overwhelming but not nearly as bad as the waiting.

The dream and the multitude of questions I had about Archer and his world haunted me for the rest of the day. Lucien helped subdue my fears, let me hear about a sliver of what their world was like. He was a good friend for that, clarifying some of my confusion when trying to grapple with this complex world of immortality. He explained their telepathic abilities to help mortals, some of their common and uncommon superhuman talents, and how they'd willingly left the limelight when the rise of Christianity occurred, which led to an awkward age conversation—they were thousands of years old, so I had heard them correctly Friday night (weirded out to the max). I learned Archer had never married another nor had any more kids—never actually fell in love naturally until me (no pressure there). In all, learning details about the world Archer had tried to keep me from to protect me made me feel closer to him. I still worried about what Archer was going through.

We hadn't heard anything from Archer or his sis—his mother (thinking of Aroha as that was weird). It hurt to wait. It was as if Archer were in another world where I wasn't allowed to follow. I went to bed Saturday night, distraught that I hadn't heard anything about Archer.

Sunday, I almost canceled meeting up with my friends, not only because Archer was gone, but also because we had made the plans to meet up prior to Linda's disastrous birthday dinner. Lucien showed up at my house, surprising us, claiming he didn't want me to have to face Emily and the others alone. It was thoughtful of him, and it was one issue I had been dreading all morning: showing up alone and having to explain where Archer was. I didn't know if I could hold myself together, and if I broke down, what on earth would I tell them was wrong? My god-boyfriend Eros is in trouble with the god-law because they tried to kill me, and he wouldn't stand for it and murdered someone? (Yeah, that would go over well. They'd locked me up.)

"I'm not sure I'm going," I told Lucien. "I've got a fever."

"It'll be a good distraction," Lucian insisted. "Come here."

I walked over to him, confused. He took my head in his hands, laid his fingers on my temples, and closed his eyes like he was concentrating. My

223

head began to feel very warm for a moment, like heat was emitting from his fingertips. Then I felt clarity, like the fog of my fever had lifted.

Lucien let go, suppressing a smug smile. "Ready?"

"What did you just do?" I asked him, grabbing the thermometer and putting it on my temple.

"Callie, you're fine now." He crossed his arms and tapped his foot impatiently.

I slid the thermometer across my forehead and gave him an I'm-not-going-anywhere look.

He sighed, shuffling his feet. "I can heal people, at least of minor things, like bruises, scrapes, cuts, *fevers*. God of healing, remember, among the other things I told you about? Let's go," he urged uncomfortably.

I awaited the beep on the thermometer and then read it: 98.6. I had just dropped three degrees.

"Fascinating." I gathered my books since we were heading to the coffee house to do homework. I was sure we'd all talk more than study, but maybe it would be a good distraction.

Dad protested my going, but I showed him the thermometer, and he merely shrugged, confused. Then he turned his attention to Lucien. "The healer. Could you...an illness like mine?"

Lucien swallowed hard. "That, I'm afraid, is far out of my league. I might be able to see how far it has progressed. Measure out your time left."

"No," I protested, tugging Lucien toward the door. Finding out the day I would lose my father forever was more than I could bear. "I don't want to know."

"I do." My father looked at me, shocked, as if I should understand why. "It could help me plan out my last days better."

"Dad. It isn't natural. We both would've died two days ago."

"Callie, wait outside," Lucien ordered.

It felt awkward to deny a god, even when I told myself it was just Lucien, but I regretfully stormed outside.

Two minutes later, Lucien came out, avoiding my gaze.

"Tell me," I begged.

"You didn't want to know," he said quietly.

"Lucien," I insisted, hitting his shoulder hard, aware there was no way I could truly hurt him. After all, if one of them could fall twenty-nine stories and temporarily have a slight limp, then what could my measly fist do?

"Unfortunately, you were right. His time was already up Friday night. It is a miracle he lives at all."

I swallowed hard. "Archer saved his life, but for how long?"

Lucien let out an uncomfortable breath. "Until another Olympian Death is born or made."

I contemplated that as we rode in the elevator down. When we were out on the street, I took his hand to stop him. He peered down at our hands. I quickly let go, realizing how it could be misconstrued. I tried to ignore the fact that I'd overheard their conversation the other night where he didn't deny he had feelings for me.

"Will you..." I paused to catch my breath and suppressed my rising emotions. "Will you warn me? When one is made, will you please tell me?"

Lucien's eyes met mine, and it was as though he were thinking about his own father's death. He was that sad. He nodded, gave my hand a quick squeeze, and led the way toward his car.

Walking into the coffeehouse without Archer was atrocious, but at least Lucien fielded the questions about our missing friends, telling everyone that their father flew Archer and Aroha out to Fiji for a vacation, and Chase wouldn't come with us because it wasn't his scene. I was amazed how it still was sort of the truth. These gods were so good at hiding the truth without truly lying. Everyone was envious of a winter vacation in Fiji, where it was summer, but if they knew the real circumstances, then they'd shut their jealous mouths (yeah, I was bitter).

I was in a daze, and Linda and Emily kept asking what was wrong. They must have thought I was pathetic, claiming I missed Archer and was worried about the long flight. Linda was the only one to truly sympathize with me. It was clear, since she'd made it that way on Friday, that Emily only played nice to me to be able to sit at our popular table. I could no longer rely on her for anything. Linda's disastrous birthday party felt like a lifetime ago.

I went up in line to get another coffee. Emily's sparring words were too much for me right now.

"You look flushed again. Go sit down and take something. Your fever's probably back, and I can't do anything about it for you at the moment," Lucien commented quietly as Linda followed him a second later, acting a bit territorial.

I nodded and followed his orders because he was right. I felt dizzy, spaced out, and my vision spun. And Linda, my only real friend, was jealous, when she had every right to be. This sucked. I never asked for Lucien to like me.

"You okay, Callie?" Dan asked as I sat back down.

"Dunno," I murmured. "I almost didn't come out because I had a fever. I think it's back." I fished into my schoolbag for medicine.

"You and Lucien came here together, didn't you? He's been oh-so-very attentive, hasn't he? How nice," Emily mused in a catty tone.

Thank goodness, Linda wasn't around to hear her thinly veiled accusations.

"She's sick," Dan defended me. "Lay off, Emily."

"I'd play sick too to get one of those boys' attention. One superbly hot guy isn't enough for you? You need the whole set now? Who's next? Chase? Or maybe you've already hooked up with him and got him sick. That's probably why he's not here," Emily shot out.

I couldn't respond, the room spinning. Linda sat down, followed by Lucien, who was carrying a tray of snacks and drinks.

"Callie?" Linda sat down next to me. "You're right, she doesn't look good." Her gaze was focused on Lucien. Linda touched my forehead and withdrew her hand quickly. "She's burning up, Lucien." Her voice betrayed horror.

"I already took a Tylenol," I murmured, my voice sounding odd to my own ears, as if I were outside myself, listening in. My head was like a balloon detached from my body and floating up to the ceiling.

"She's just being a drama queen," I heard a voice say, Emily maybe.

"We should take her to a clinic," Linda protested. "That's a high temp for sure."

Lucien touched my head, and his eyes went wide. I felt the healing heat come out of his palm, but nothing happened. He was frustrated as he removed his hand. "No. Hospital. I'll drive," Lucien told her.

I felt my arms being lifted, and I walked, following where they led me. I was on autopilot. My legs moved without my mind telling them to.

The rest of the day was just foggy images I could hardly recollect. I never had felt so out of it: riding in a car, Linda holding my head in her lap; a nurse taking the thermometer from my mouth, gasping; someone saying, "I need cold water, sponges...one-hundred cc's of dantrolene"; holding someone's hand—Lucien perhaps; being in cold, damp sheets; needles and queasiness...

I woke up in a cold bed, shivering, with someone holding my hand. I looked at the hand, then to the face. It was Dad. He was so frail and worried.

"Hey, pumpkin." He tried to smile. "You gave us quite a scare there."

"Where...what..." I was confused. Something was in my nose; I went to pull it out, but another set of hands stopped me, much stronger ones. My gaze flew to the owner of the hands: Lucien. I was disappointed. I had hoped it had all been a nightmare, and those hands belonged to Archer.

"Stop it," he scolded.

"You're in the hospital. You had a fever of 106, Callie. They've got you down to 101, but it was very scary there for a while," Dad explained.

"I'm so cold." I shivered.

"And you'll be sweating in a minute." Lucien leaned back against the wall.

"Wait, you said a while."

"Callie, you've been out of it for almost twenty-four hours." Dad patted my hand.

"Archer!" I tried to sit up, but Lucien was pushing me back down again. I felt the IV shift in my arm and almost gagged.

"Rest, darling," my dad instructed.

Lucien and Dad exchanged a look. Did I see my dad shake his head slightly?

"What's going on?" I pleaded. They were hiding something from me. There must've been news while I was out.

"Well, you have some kind of infection. They have no clue what it is, but the idiots are claiming food poisoning. I sent some of your blood to the most intelligent...'person' on earth, but she's busy at the moment, so hopefully, we'll know the truth in a week or so," Lucien told me quickly. He was trying to distract me from the subject of Archer.

"Infection?" I asked. "Food poisoning?"

"Her brain's fried," Lucien mocked me.

"Shut up." I scowled at him.

"There she is." He chuckled.

My dad's hand touched my hair. He looked so sad, so scared, so frail and vulnerable.

"I'm okay, Dad," I told him.

"You really did give me a scare," he said, brushing my hair from my face.

"How are you feeling?" I asked him, concerned.

"Hanging in there, kiddo. Hanging in there." He tried to force a smile.

I was released from the hospital a couple hours later with a prescription for antibiotics. Dad insisted I stay home from school the next day to make sure the fever was kept at bay.

Lucien had stopped by the school to pick up our missed work and delivered it to me. We hung out in my new camp out, the living room sofa. I hadn't slept in my bed since Friday. It reminded me of the last moments I'd had with Archer. Dad hung out with us, and he and Lucien talked all about history and mythology. I was hardly interested, so I got started catching up on schoolwork. But my mind was elsewhere, on the other side of the world, to be exact. It had been almost three days since Archer had left. What was going on for him not to call me? Or had he called while I was unconscious? I hoped he hadn't, because if it were good news, Lucien would have told me. If it were bad news, he wouldn't because I was ill. I looked at them both, my dad and Lucien. What were they hiding from me?

"What is it, Callista?" Dad perceptively studied me, concerned.

"Something's happened, and you won't tell me." I glanced at them both. "It has to be bad, or you would've told me to cheer me up." I kept my voice strong to prevent them from using my sickness as an excuse to further hide things.

Lucien and Dad looked at one another. Dad nodded, giving permission, and Lucien said, "He called while you were...out."

"You told him I was sick?" I asked, shocked. That was the last thing Archer needed on his plate, to hear that I had been deathly ill.

"He knew you wouldn't...without Death around and all," Lucien defended himself. "I had to anyway. He wanted to talk to you."

"Call him," I pleaded. "Call him back now," I said, finding more strength in my voice. "Where's my phone?" I frantically searched the clutter in my sick campsite, but it was lost in the mess.

"I can't. He's in a complex negotiation with Zeus. There is more than one life on the line here, Callie," Lucien said, talking down to me as if I were an obstinate child. "But Callie, we will know today." He glanced at his watch. "In fact, he should've called by now."

I felt dizzy again, staggered that I would hear something soon. My entire future, my life, might be on the line as well as Archer's. It all crashed down on me and overwhelmed me.

"So we cannot die until there's a new Death?" Dad asked.

"What?" Lucien was confused by my father's shift in topic. "Oh, no. There are other Deaths out there, the others—"

"All religions, the gods are real?"

Lucien froze. "Let's not talk about them to get you on more hit lists, but no one dying isn't as good as it sounds. You have a human body. That body can stop working. Without Death, your soul will be trapped in a body that doesn't function.

"Meaning?" My father prompted. I didn't like this conversation.

"A coma, life support, trapped and unable to communicate. No picnic."

Dad paled.

"I don't want to hear this," I said in an attempt to cut off the morbid conversation before I could envision what might happen to Dad.

On cue, Lucien's phone rang. We all froze. Then Lucien got up fluidly, with such speed that when I blinked, he was already in Dad's office. I muted the television to hear his side of the conversation. My father looked at me but didn't scold me for eavesdropping, probably because he was curious as well.

"She is better, yes, and at home now," Lucien said, then waited a moment. "What's wrong? What's happened?"

A long silence.

"What?" Lucien's tone was disbelieving.

Silence again.

"Are you sure? Are you positive?" Lucien's voice was firm.

Another pause.

"Okay, all right. Bye." He hung up the phone and came back out into the living room.

I stood up, awaiting the sentence. It was my own as well. My dad got up and crossed to me, then placed his arm around my shoulder. I didn't know who was supporting whom more.

Lucien stared at the floor and shook his head solemnly, grappling for the words. When he raised his head, he avoided my gaze, instead, fixating on the area a foot above me. He cleared his throat and shuffled his feet.

"Archer...um..." Lucien swallowed hard. "Callie, he's gone."

"What do you mean, gone?"

"He's gone. He's dead. Executed. It was his life or yours, Callie. He died to save you." Lucien's voice cracked, and he was trying to reel his emotions in.

But why wouldn't he look me in the eye? The god of truth should be able to look someone in the eye.

As the words set in, I felt myself quiver from head to toe. I couldn't believe it. I felt my heart and mind crumble from within. All my hopes, all my dreams were shattered. Everything I wanted in life had been torn from me. Didn't he realize that I'd rather die than be without him? Archer had called me cruel, but this was beyond cruelty.

"No," I heard my own faint voice gasp. "Impossible." I could not believe it.

Lucien placed his cell phone down on the coffee table and pulled me up into a hug.

I pushed him away and turned. "I want to be alone."

"Callie," my dad said weakly.

"Please, just give me a moment," I said.

Lucien awkwardly led my father into the office. Something in me wouldn't click; my mind would not process the information given to it: Archer, gone. It was impossible.

I tried to take in a deep breath, but my chest constricted painfully. I heard their concerned murmuring. Then I noticed Lucien's cell phone sitting there. I picked it up and went into the call log to see the last caller. Expecting to see Chase's name or even Aroha's, I was shocked to see Archer's name. My heart skipped a beat. If he were dead, how could he call? I hit the Talk button.

The phone was torn from my hands, and I looked up to see an enraged Lucien glaring down at me. "What are you doing?" he demanded as his thumb quickly ended the call.

"He's alive. You're lying." I lunged to get the phone back. "He called you!"

"Stop it!" Lucien shoved me back a bit roughly.

I went in attacking him, hitting him. I wanted to hurt him as he had just wounded me with his deceitful words. How could he possibly say those things?

"Stop it!" he repeated. I felt my feet go out from under me and was slammed on the sofa. Lucien had me pinned down and restrained with his immortal strength. His face loomed only inches above my own as he growled, "Chase used his phone, Callie. It was Chase."

The scent of flowers tickled my senses, reminding me of my mother, of Archer—all my loved ones taken from me, dead. I stopped struggling.

After he realized I had stopped fighting, he let go of me and got up. I stood back up defiantly. "You didn't look me in the eye when you said it," I protested. "Why wasn't he allowed to say goodbye, then?" My voice sounded weak to my own ears. The fight was leaving me.

Lucien's eyes met mine. "He is gone, Callie. Archer is gone, and he's never coming back." It felt like a slap in the face this time, acute and painful. "I am so sorry..." His voice cut off in his throat, and he choked back tears that formed in the corner of his eyes.

My head swirled in realization, and I had that floating feverish feeling again, like everything was happening around me, but I couldn't focus directly on any of it. I felt my knees go weak, and darkness closed around me. I felt my body slump to the floor, and then the sounds around me went faint. I heard panic in my father's voice and Lucien's commanding tone, but I could not make sense of their words. Then all noises ceased, but in the comforting cocoon of darkness, I heard my heart still beating strong.

This wasn't right. It was all wrong. If Archer were truly dead, my heart should have died with him. I clung to that thought. It was the only gleaming object in the obsidian darkness. It was left in Pandora's box for mankind to behold: hope. It was mine, and Zeus couldn't take that away too. Archer had promised he'd come back to me one day, and he would somehow, at some time, come to me. He could not break that promise. Gods can't die. They just couldn't. I would see Archer again. I knew that was true, somewhere deep down, and I would *never* give up that hope. It was all I had left, and I concentrated on clinging to it as I sank further into the abyss, an unconsciousness from which I did not want to wake.

CHAPTER 23

Archer

In the wee hours of Saturday morning, Hermes whisked my parents and I away, in two goes since he could only bear so much matter when teleporting. Fiji was hot and beautiful, or so my father exclaimed. I saw no beauty around me at the moment. We checked into my grandfather's vacation resort and were sent a message to report to his office in the morning since it was already night in Fiji.

I didn't sleep at all and went down with my somber parents the next morning as instructed. The hearing terrified me. At the moment, despite being a god, facing Zeus felt very much like facing the firing squad. He sat behind his corporate-looking desk in a tailored suit, looming and intimidating and not at all the doting grandfather he had been to me years ago. It had been a few hundred years, so I'd forgotten how pale he was, so pale that the veins showed blue through his almost transparent skin. His hair and beard were platinum blond, making him appear older than his thirty-six mortal years. He had been the first of the Olympians, the one who figured out how to become immortal. I didn't know how old he truly was, and I wasn't sure if he still kept count. He also had piercing pale blue eyes that felt as though they sliced through you, and if you beheld them for more than a moment, which was difficult, you could see how old and wise they were. The pale skin, hair, and eyes were not the most intimidating thing about him; Zeus was an exceptionally big man, muscular, thick, and tall. My dad was the only one who was as big as him. Zeus's demeanor and status demanded our submission and respect.

I, the defendant, sat across from him, and Athena, my defense lawyer, next to me. My parents stood behind me for moral support and ready to beg mercy, I was sure. But this was no ordinary trial with a jury to deliberate. Zeus was prosecutor and judge. I was to be the only witness, the only one to tell any side of the story. Dr. Syches's and Callie's views didn't count. In Zeus's eyes, they were as insignificant as ants, ones he could crush if this all went horribly wrong.

Zeus sighed and studied me. I swallowed with difficulty, waiting to hear what would happen to me, to Callie. I feared his wrath because no one had an anger like his: tornadoes, hurricanes, thunderstorms, cataclysmic events.

"You look terrible," he said. Harsh, and not at all what I expected.

"I feel terrible." I felt ashamed. What I had done finally caught up with me. I felt guilty. I had taken life. Unlike my father, this was something I had never done before. There were people who did love the god of death, and he would be missed by a few. I was conflicted, though. The guilt was kept in check by justification. I could not regret killing Thanatos. He would've killed Callie, and I couldn't live without her.

"Where do we begin?" Zeus mused, drumming his fingertips on the desk. "Perhaps with what happened on Friday."

I sighed and then told him everything. The truth was the only way to get anywhere with Zeus. I told him my strong feelings, how much I loved Callie, how I had to protect her, that I had given Thanatos ample opportunities to back down. I explained how I had been prepared to defend her no matter what but never wanted to kill. I had felt forced to do it.

When I finished, Zeus sighed and said, "But I explicitly told you that I did not want you to get attached to that particular mortal. I allowed you time to have your fun with her and discard her, not fall in love with her." He shook his head as if I'd breached some deal we had drawn up.

I wondered for a moment what deal my father had made to get me more time.

Athena jumped in to my defense. "Let me remind you, Zeus, how much of a shock it was to hear you'd ordered the mortals' deaths without a second warning. Plus, Hypnos was keeping Aphrodite, Ares, and Apollo asleep, from the sounds of it. It was an intentional, covert, and planned mission. Very unjust and unlike you. We should have discussed this, come to a compromise. The mere and sudden surprise to be forced to part with someone he has attached himself to defends his rash actions. If he had been prepared to let go, had a stern order from you, a direct conversation, then perhaps we would not be here."

"Noted Athena." Zeus scowled at her. "I thought my thunder peals were enough of an order. He was trying to lie with her."

I felt my face burn; I should've been used to not having privacy, for Zeus sees *everything* we do. According to what my dad had said, that might not be true anymore.

"And you seemed extremely eager to prevent that," my father cut in, pushing the interrogation back onto Zeus. "Why is that?"

Zeus simply glared at my father, and the silence grew stiflingly awkward.

"What Ares is trying to point out, Father, is that if we knew why you dislike and prohibit him from this specific mortal, then we may better understand your wrath," Athena said.

"Zeus, he's an obedient boy. If he had known why, he would have obeyed," Ma chimed in, trying to wheedle him with a coy look. Mortals might fall victim to my mother's charms, but Zeus wasn't buying it.

I bit my tongue to prevent myself from bursting out with the truth that I never would've given up Callie. Even if she would bring the end of my existence, I would never leave her. She had become as necessary as the air mortals need to breathe.

"How I feel about a particular peon is none of your business. The point is, I wanted Eros to leave her alone. I wished her to remain ignorant of our secrets, and she wouldn't stop meddling until she found you out. This knowledge is enough for me to execute her without warning. I want her dead, and I did not want him procreating with and creating another creature like her." He paused and cleared his throat. "But enough about her. Eros killed an immortal being to protect his plaything, and I still want her silenced. Before I decide on a punishment and make my verdict, I want to see all of you privately, beginning with Eros."

Zeus dismissed everyone else, which made me nervous. I swallowed the large lump that was forming in my throat.

"What do you want, child?" Zeus asked me. His tone was softer, and his eyes sympathetic. He transformed into my grandfather right before my eyes, caring, loving, the man I had idolized growing up.

My instincts warned me it was a trick. "What do you mean?"

"This is called negotiating, Eros. I do forget that you rarely get yourself in trouble. At this stage, you tell me your wishes, I present mine, and then we reach a compromise, a few options we can both live with," he said in a pedantic voice, treating me like an ignorant child. Something was wrong. Underneath his feigned sincerity, I sensed he was more than merely mad at me. It was a seething anger he was holding back. Not a good sign. I would get no compromise.

"I want Callie to live," I said quietly.

"Is that all?"

"I don't want to push my luck." I finally dared to meet his gaze. His face was blank, merely trying to read my own expression. I wondered how I looked: ashamed, depressed, desperate, afraid—I'm sure they were all clear on my face.

"Try me," he said simply.

"I want her made immortal," I ventured, awaiting an outburst. "I want to spend eternity with her."

"I've heard this all before." Zeus rolled his eyes, telling me I was foolish. Just because he was too damn cold-blooded to truly love someone else didn't mean we were all victim to the godly indifference for others he exuded.

"It's different this time. Look, Grandpa, I never ask many favors. I've been obedient for all my existence. I know I've done wrong, and I feel terrible about it. The guilt is overwhelming. I've hurt many, especially Hypnos." I tried to persuade him. I did feel terrible. It was true that very few of us would miss Thanatos. He was Death after all and relished too much in his role, but his brother, Hypnos, god of sleep, would miss him dearly.

Zeus's face remained stoically unconvinced, so I continued, "But I've had my losses too, without any retribution to other immortals. Let me add, a few of our kind could be implicated in their deaths, but I did not point fingers or seek revenge. No matter how Psyche turned out, she didn't deserve to die. And my daughter, Hedone..." Her name was so hard for me to say. "...you were fond of her. She was my world—you remember, after her death, I could barely go on. It's taken me over five hundred years to fully grieve, to enjoy living again. Callie is the reason I'm happy again, that I thrive and exist. If I could get what I want, I would begin a life with Callie, have a family again." I had said more than I wished. I had given too much away, but by showing him how important Callie was to me, I hoped it would persuade him to allow her to live.

"Why this mortal?"

"I don't know. I feel so intensely and did so instantly. I had no choice in the matter, as if someone used my arrows against me. I'm irrevocably drawn to her."

"Eros," Zeus said with a sigh.

Whatever he said, I wouldn't want to hear. I braced myself, pushing my temper down so I wouldn't react.

"What I would prefer is for this girl to cease existing. Just as you are irrevocably *drawn* to her, as you say, I'm irrevocably *annoyed* by her presence. She is a threat to us. If she must live, because you've made it clear that it's your greatest wish, then I'd rather her procreate with another mortal, not a god. Second, her father must be silenced ASAP."

I tried not to flinch when I thought about how much Callie's father's death would hurt her, when Zeus discussed her death with ease, and when I envisioned her marrying and raising a family with another man. My stomach dropped at the thought. Zeus was going to make me give her up. I felt weak and sick. I couldn't protest because the worst punishment, the option he wanted, was her death.

"I will consider your wishes with my own. You're dismissed. Send Athena in." And with that comment, he waved his hand to dismiss me.

I stood up, my head spinning. Had I told him too much? By giving him so much, would he take more from me? Had I begged too far? Would he use my wishes against me? The only thing I was positive about was that Callie obviously must live.

The verdict did not come in that day. Zeus had heard from them all. Despite her jealousy, even Aroha admitted Callie must live. Athena agreed that it was unjust to kill a human without probable cause, particularly since I had singled her out as my mortal. All four of us demanded that. Surely, Zeus would listen. It all depended on the verdict, the options Zeus would present to me.

It had been over two days since I had slept or eaten anything. I lay in bed for hours with my eyes closed, unable to sleep. Back in New York, it was still daytime, the end of the morning if my calculation was correct. If it all went wrong, it could be the last time I ever heard Callie's voice. But I had no idea what to tell her. It would hurt to tell her it all might be hopeless, that my promise to come back might be broken. She wouldn't understand that I couldn't disobey Zeus. She would ask too many questions, perceive too much. She would cry. I couldn't deal with that in the state of mind I was in.

I lay there until the sun rose high in the sky, which made me think of my best friend, who was with her right now. Masochist that I am, I called her. Lucien answered. Callie was in the hospital, sick. I hung up, feeling utterly helpless. What was the point of being a god, a divine being with supernatural powers, if I couldn't be with the woman I loved, to nurse her when she was ill?

I went down to Zeus's office. I didn't knock, but burst in to see Athena and Zeus having an intense discussion. Zeus gave me an odd look, which made me worry about what was to come.

"I need to go back to New York." It came out a bit more demanding than I had intended.

"Absolutely not." Zeus motioned for me to sit down. Athena did as well. Zeus sat on the edge of his desk, intimidatingly looming over us.

"Callie is ill. In the hospital."

"And you are being punished, so no. You are to stay put. She'll pull through with Thanatos gone and Apollo there to heal her." Zeus looked like he enjoyed the news and my pain.

I looked to Athena, my rational aunt. Her normally stoic countenance was looking at me with a pained expression. What had they been talking about before I burst in?

"What's wrong?"

"You look awful." Athena leaned over and took my face in her hands, a loving gesture unlike her standoffish nature. "Zeus, he's wasting away."

Zeus hit the intercom on his office phone. "Hebe, bring me a bottle of ambrosia and three glasses." Hebe was my full aunt, meaning Dad's sister and Zeus and Hera's other child. Besides Zeus, she was the only one who could access ambrosia. But she would never disobey Zeus, so any ideas of pleading with her to help me make Callie immortal disappeared as soon as they began.

"I don't want any. What is the verdict?" I sat down only because I was too weak to stand. The last thing I wanted was ambrosia for myself.

"Still negotiating, Eros," Zeus said.

Hebe entered with a tray, her youthful face vibrant and cheery as always. In my mood, I wanted to wipe that smile off her face. As soon as she left, Zeus directed his attention to me.

"Drink," he said, pouring me a champagne glass of ambrosia.

My mind focused on the size of the bottle of ambrosia. Even after he poured three glasses, there was one more left in the bottle. If only I could get it to Callie...

"It's not a request, but an order." Zeus pushed the glass even closer to me.

I drank down the delicious elixir. It reached every nerve in my body and strengthened every fiber of my being. I instantly felt more alert, stronger, and healthier than before. The hunger vanished, and I felt well rested. Too bad ambrosia didn't improve moods. My mind instantly went back to a smuggling plan.

"First punishment is nonnegotiable. You will choose three hybreeds to make into gods. You have brought it to my attention that we have lost a few immortals here and there, with what happened to your family and your recent crime. One will replace Thanatos as the new god of death, a second will be Hypnos's companion or mate—as your charitable act of asking his forgiveness—and the last will be your companion to prevent any more of your mischief. However, none of them can be your beloved Callie, her father, or any of her descendants in the future. Is that clear?"

"Yes, Grandpa." Nonnegotiable? And he had claimed we were in negotiations. He'd thought of every loophole as well. Only, in his punishment, he gave something away: he assumed Callie had a chance at immortality, meaning he was aware she was a demigod.

Athena recorded everything, typing like a fiend on her laptop. It distracted me. The gears in my mind switched to what the next punishment could be. I awaited his words, my fear growing worse as he took a moment to thoughtfully sip on his ambrosia. He was stalling on purpose.

"The second is a choice, Eros, and I do not expect an answer right away. You can have Callie for one full year, no rules or interference from me, but after that full year, she is to be destroyed. She is not to be made immortal, and if a child happens to be born in that year, it is to die with its mother."

My stomach lurched, and I forced the bile back down. Only one year? Destroyed like she was a condemned building, not a living being? I wanted to protest, to pick up the chair I sat on and smash it over his head for suggesting such a horrid compromise. Instead, I kept my poker face frozen in place and simply asked, "What is my other option?"

"To never see her again. She will remain alive for the duration of her mortal life as long as you never see her again, no other god mates with her, and she never tells another mortal about us," Zeus concluded.

I swallowed hard. The choice was painfully obvious: Callie must live. "I've made my decision." I had to see it through before I changed my mind.

"Take some time to think about it." Zeus was nervous. He was afraid of the choice I would make. He was depending on my history of being spoiled, which meant he wanted Callie dead.

"I don't need time." I pressed forward, trying not to think about what I was agreeing to.

"I insist," Zeus hissed. "You drink your ambrosia, go eat something, and sleep." It was a direct order.

I didn't want him to change his mind for the worse, so I drank the ambrosia, then went to the hotel restaurant with my parents and ate some food. I went up to my room and lay in bed, pretending to sleep in case I was being watched.

"Wake up, Archer," Ma said. She was shaking me.

I felt as if I had sand in my eyes, and I wiped them vigorously until I could see. "What time is it?" The sun was still up, but I felt fully rested.

"Tuesday." She was wide-eyed. "Nine in the morning."

I sat up quickly. "I slept a day?"

"Hypnos," Chase said with distaste. He leaned against the wall, arms crossed.

At least Hypnos *let* me wake up. I couldn't be angry at the guy after what I had done.

"Archer. Zeus demands your answer now," Ma said.

Of course, he did, on his terms and time.

We headed down to his office, where I was told to enter alone. Athena was there again, looking grave.

"Well?" Zeus asked. He motioned for me to pull up a chair.

I refused to sit, not wanting to stay longer than it took to utter the words I might regret one day: "I will never see her again in exchange for her to live out her mortal life." My voice shook, as well as my entire frame.

Zeus's brow wrinkled, and his shock was apparent. He neither expected that answer nor was happy with it. My suspicions were well grounded. He put too much faith in godly selfishness and not enough in the power of love.

"She lives then," he said quietly.

"And I get to see her one last time one day," I amended, thinking only of the promise I had made to Callie. I promised her I would come back someday, somehow.

"On her deathbed only, and, Eros, no plotting for loopholes. I mean the moment she dies, when the new Death is sent for her," he said demurely.

"And I get to see her in my mind, I mean. I need to see she is okay and happy."

"Can't see how that would hurt anything. It will torture you, but we are speaking of punishments, aren't we?" His sadistic grin showed me he enjoyed my pain. I was no longer a favorite of his, that was clear. "All I ask is that you do not physically see her."

"Deal," I said before my resolve left me.

He offered his hand, and I shook it. The terms were now set.

"If you break the terms of punishment, she will die," Zeus warned me as I left. I gave him one last look over my shoulder. He was rubbing his beard, thinking deeply, his eyes troubled.

I sought my father out instantly and told him all. I added that I needed to leave Fiji before I did anything stupid, like change my mind. It was strange that I sought him out and not my mother, but I had a feeling she would not be able to refrain from her I-told-you-so tendencies.

"Where are we going?"

Now, this comment I wasn't ready for. You wouldn't think my father, who had been absent for most of my existence, would follow me to the ends of the earth in my punishment, but here he was, offering. It wasn't what I wanted. No one deserved to be punished with me.

"You...don't have to go with me," I said awkwardly, realizing too late that it sounded as if I were rejecting him.

"If you prefer your mother's company, I understand. I just thought...never mind. I'm always too ambitious. Part of being the god of war, I suppose." The way he rattled on was unusual for him. Through his tough exterior, I had wounded him.

"I didn't mean it that way. I'm just not going to be good company."

"Archer, you can't be alone. You don't know how terrible that is," he said, avoiding my gaze.

I felt sorry for him and all the years he'd spent without us. True, he'd never reached out to me, but had I ever tried to reach out to him? Feeling bad for him made me a little less sorry for myself, and that was necessary at the moment.

"I'm gonna stay with you, Son, as long as it takes for you to get over this."

"It may take forever."

"Well, it's a good thing I have forever." He gave me a sympathetic look. "So, where shall we start?"

"Somewhere warm and far from New York. In fact, not the US at all; I don't want to be tempted."

"I'll get us out of here in an hour."

I went back to my room and packed, quickly putting off the hardest deed of all: breaking the news to Callie via Lucien. There was no way I could talk to her, and Lucien had told me she had been sick the last time I had called him. I dialed Lucien.

"Lucien." My voice cracked, despite my best effort to stay strong. "Is she okay?"

"She's better, yes, and at home now. What's wrong? What happened?"

"It's done. I can never come back, never see her again, or he'll kill her. It's over." As I said the last word, I almost lost it.

"What?" Lucien was surprised.

"I could've had one year with her, and he'd kill her. Or I could give her up completely, and she'd live. Lucien, take care of her." I swallowed the lump in my throat. "Tell Callie...tell her...no, tell her I'm dead. Tell her Zeus executed me. Make her realize there is no possible hope of ever seeing me again."

"Are you sure? Are you positive?" he pressed.

"Yes. I am. And Lucien, she can't tell anyone about us. Make sure she keeps the secret, or he'll kill her. I guess I'll see you in the next century."

"Okay, all right. Bye." I could tell from his tone that he was upset as well that it had gone so badly.

I hung up, lamenting over losing my friend as well. I didn't know when I'd see him next.

He most likely was with Callie right now, or he would be in a moment. She would not be alone, but always have a friend in him. I lied to help her move on, but I felt as if I were truly dead. I was, in a way, my own executioner; I made the decision to save her by sacrificing myself, my heart, the essence of who I am. For without love, I could hardly exist.

I had to resign myself to my fate and pray to Anteros that Callie wouldn't suffer from heartache too long. I would suffer from it for all eternity. The only consolation I had was the fact I would get to see her one more time and fulfill my promise. Somehow, deep down, I believed I'd see her again much sooner than that. Part of my devious mind was already trying to hatch possible plans to work around Zeus's decree. I wanted that part of me to win, damn it. I would see her again. I just needed time to figure out a loophole. It was a good thing I had plenty of that: time. With time, Love will always find a way.

CONTINUE THE STORY...
AVAILABLE NOW!

THE IMMORTAL TRANSCRIPTS II

FEVER

BOOKS2READ.COM/ITFEVER

OLYMPIAN FAMILY TREE
(from the journal of Dr. David N. Syches)

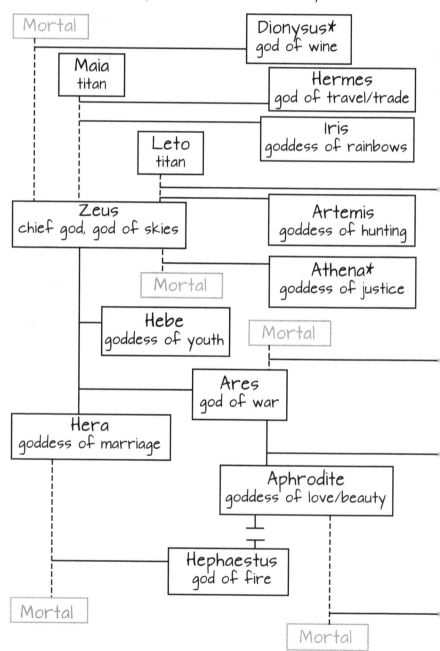

Mortal

Dionysus*
god of wine

Maia
titan

Hermes
god of travel/trade

Iris
goddess of rainbows

Leto
titan

Zeus
chief god, god of skies

Artemis
goddess of hunting

Mortal

Athena*
goddess of justice

Hebe
goddess of youth

Mortal

Ares
god of war

Hera
goddess of marriage

Aphrodite
goddess of love/beauty

Hephaestus
god of fire

Mortal

Mortal

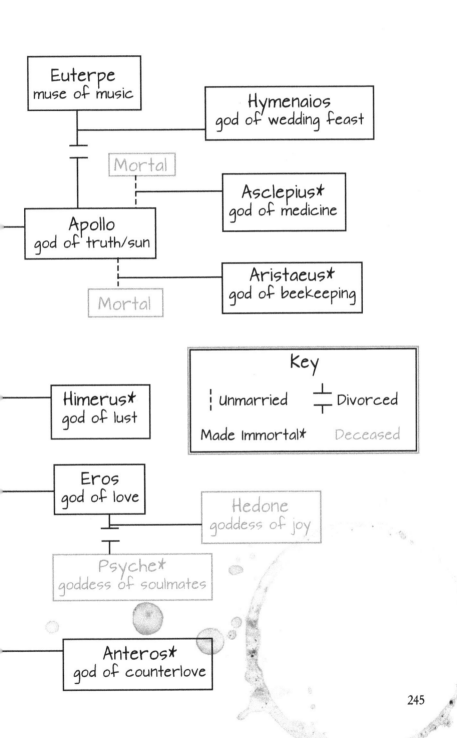

Euterpe
muse of music

Hymenaios
god of wedding feast

Mortal

Asclepius*
god of medicine

Apollo
god of truth/sun

Aristaeus*
god of beekeeping

Mortal

Himerus*
god of lust

Key

| Unmarried   ⊥ Divorced

Made Immortal*   Deceased

Eros
god of love

Hedone
goddess of joy

Psyche*
goddess of soulmates

Anteros*
god of counterlove

245

OLYMPIAN PANTHEON ALIASES

PANTHEON	ALIAS	POWERS
Aglaea	Belle	Beauty, splendor
Anteros	Antony	Unrequited or thwarted love, "magnetism"
Aphrodite	Aroha Ambrose	Love and beauty, swimming
Ares	Chase Gideon	War, strength, and speed
Aristaeus		Beekeeping
Artemis		Moon, hunting, and childbirth
Asclepius		Medicine, healing
Athena		Wisdom, justice, warfare, courage, inventions, arts, and crafts
Atlas		Holding the sky
Demeter		Agriculture, harvest
Dionysus	Uncle D	Wine, madness, and theater
Epimetheus		Afterthought
Eros	Archer Ambrose	Love, "flying"
Euphrosyne	Ada	Mirth, bliss
Euterpe		Music, lyric poetry
Hades		Underworld, scotopia, and invisibility

PANTHEON	ALIAS	POWERS
Hebe		Youth
Hedone		Joy, pleasure, and "flying"
Hephaestus	Heph(ie)	Fire, forging
Hera		Marriage, family, pregnancy
Hermes		Messenger, teleporting, theft
Himerus	Russ	Lust, strength, and speed
Hymenaios	Aios	Marriage ceremony, soul fusing
Hypnos		Sleep
Iris		Rainbow, teleporting
Janus		Duality, passages
Leto		Motherhood
Mnemosyne		Memory
Moirae	The Fates	Birth, destiny, and death
Muses		9 sisters of the arts
Persephone		Spring, plant life, and death
Phoebus Apollo	Lucien Veras	Sun, light, truth, prophecy, music, poetry, medicine, and healing
Poseidon		Sea, earthquakes

PANTHEON	ALIAS	POWERS
Prometheus		Foresight, prophecies
Proteus		Shapeshifting, foresight
Psyche		Soulmates, mindreading, and "flying"
Thalia	Thalia	Delight, charisma
Thanatos		Death, soul bearer
Themis		Justice, law, prophecy
Zelus		Zeal, ice, and "flying"
Zeus		God of gods, lightning, thunder, sky, and omniscience

ACKNOWLEDGMENTS

Usually, I'll acknowledge a lot of people at the end of my book, but this novel has a tricky, long past. *Quiver* was my first finished novel; I'd begun it in 2006 and finished my first full draft by 2008. This was the same time I was in graduate school and job hunting, so it was a miracle I finished at all. It had started as a writing prompt and a desire to write something that wasn't an academic analysis or dissertation. I picked up my Greek mythology book to reread the tales of lovers for inspiration.

Why Greek? My great-grandfather had been from Greece and passed away long before I was born, but the stories my grandmother would tell about him were fascinating. Combined with learning mythology in school, Greek myths always stuck with me. It was that elusive part of my family's history that I couldn't fully grasp. This series is a way of me connecting to those lost roots.

Fast forward to 2006, when I met Katie Grant, who became a great friend. She was an avid reader, so one day when she was around, she insisted on reading my handwritten six-page writing prompt result. From the bat, she loved it, which meant a lot because she's brutally honest. She demanded more, critiqued it, edited it, and typed it up for me. She was essential in pushing me to finish and in finding the confidence to attempt to publish it.

Next came Cameron Scott Wright. I'm privileged to work at a university where I can submit a manuscript to a grad school editing course and have students perform developmental and copy edits. Sometimes this is only mildly helpful, but with Cameron, it went well. He was a returning student, so he already had knowledge about writing, grammar, and publishing. I was expecting a brutal assessment, but his enthusiasm was staggering, and his belief in my novel was genuine. After so many drafts, I forget which suggestions I took that were his, but the one that stands out the most was my change of series's title. It had been called The Amores, and Cameron had suggested a title with "Transcripts" in it. He also had the idea that because I wrote four different first-person points-of-view, I should make a beginning page that introduces it as an actual transcript allowing mortals into their world. These two key elements shifted the story for me. Unfortunately, after he graduated, we lost touch.

I queried with some success in 2012, but the agents who contacted me wanted me to revise so much that I passed on representation rather than completely alter my vision. This shook my faith in my novel, and I listen to too much conflicting advice on how to improve it; I ended up killing my novel, inflating it to a 120,000 word mess. The lack of responses from further queries confirmed this. So *Quiver* sat shelved for years, and I worked on other novels. After I published other novels, I pulled *Quiver* off the shelf and blew off the dust. After rereading the early versions and the newest, I realized Katie and Cameron proved to be my best critics, that my third draft was the best. After one quick revision, I submitted it, and was accepted.

After I told family and friends, someone was missing. I reconnected with Cameron to tell him the news via Facebook. After all these years, he remembered my novel and was overjoyed for me. That was when I found out he was dying of cancer, and although not stated aloud, we both realized he would never get to read the book in print. Cameron passed away the summer of 2019, but he knew that his editing had assisted in the novel being published and of my appreciation. I recognized he cared more about my novel than a simple school assignment. Looking back, I regret not continuing contact with Cameron after he left school. I imagine he would've wanted to help me with every manuscript. That's the type of kind man he was.

As always, Authors 4 Authors Publishing has taken *Quiver* and teased out every little nuance of my writing to make it its best and shined it up pretty through such a collaborative and personal process.

Almost fourteen years after the first words were written, with the help of those whom the book is dedicated to and Authors 4 Authors Publishing, *Quiver* has launched The Immortal Transcripts series. Thank you for reading it.

ABOUT THE AUTHOR

LISA BORNE GRAVES

Lisa Borne Graves is a YA author, English Lecturer, wife, and supermom of one wild child. Originally from the Philadelphia area, she relocated to the Deep South and found her true place of inspiration. Her love for all literature led her to branch out from the academic arena to spin her own tales. Lisa has a voracious appetite for books, British television, and pizza. Her inability to sit still makes her enjoy life to its fullest, and she can be found at the beach, pool, or on some crazy adventure.

Follow her online:

lisabornegraves.com
Twitter: @lisabornegraves
Facebook: @lisabornegravesauthor
Instagram: @lisabornegraves

Also by Lisa Borne Graves

CELESTIAL SPHERES
FYR

At seventeen, Toury arrives in Fyr, where magic is power, a prince's love is deadly, and female autonomy is a dream. Formerly a loner and burden to her adoptive parents, she ruins her chances of a fresh start by offending an ogler who just happens to be the prince.

Alex, the Prince of Fyr, is no novice when it comes to pressure. He has to face his father's ailing health, the expectation to marry soon, and the hidden necromancers trying to take over the realm by exploiting his dark curse. At least there's hope in a cheeky savior, but Earth girls aren't so easy.

Toury and Alex learn that the strongest magic cannot be conjured but must be earned. They must risk their lives, hearts, and futures to save the land from a darkness of apocalyptic proportions. But can they trust each other enough to save Fyr? Or will everything they hold dear turn to ash?

books2read.com/fyr

AUTHORS 4 AUTHORS
PUBLISHING COOPERATIVE

A publishing company for authors, run by authors, blending the best of traditional and independent publishing

We specialize in speculative fiction: science fiction, fantasy, paranormal, and romance. Get lost in another world!

Check out our collection at https://books2read.com/rl/a4a
or visit Authors4AuthorsPublishing.com/books

For updates, scan the QR code or visit our website to join our semi-monthly newsletter!

Want more romantic fantasy? We recommend:

KISS OF TREASON
by Brandi Spencer

Two forbidden lovers share the rare gift to heal others with a kiss—but at a cost. Odelia's life has been a lie. When the queen tries to remove her from the palace, Odelia uncovers the truth. Now she must decide whether to forsake her people or embrace a destiny that would pit her against the current heir to the throne...her best friend. Though her only hope of avoiding a civil war lies in winning his heart, revealing her secrets too soon could cost both their lives. And a kiss might not be strong enough to save them...

books2read.com/kisstreason

CPSIA information can be obtained
at www.ICGtesting.com
Printed in the USA
JSHW010146170123
36305JS00001B/51